Emma Miller lives quietly in her old farmhouse in rural Delaware. Fortunate enough to be born into a family of strong faith, she grew up on a dairy farm surrounded by loving parents, siblings, grandparents, aunts, uncles and cousins. Emma was educated in local schools and once taught in an Amish schoolhouse. When she's not caring for her large family, reading and writing are her favorite pastimes.

Rebecca Kertz was first introduced to the Amish when her husband took a job with an Amish construction crew. She enjoyed watching the Amish foreman's children at play and swapping recipes with his wife. Rebecca resides in Delaware with her husband and dog. She has a strong faith in God and feels blessed to have family nearby. Besides writing, she enjoys reading, doing crafts and visiting Lancaster County.

EMMA MILLER
The Amish Bride

&

REBECCA KERTZ
The Amish Mother

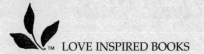

LOVE INSPIRED BOOKS

Recycling programs for this product may not exist in your area.

ISBN-13: 978-0-373-83812-7

The Amish Bride and The Amish Mother

Copyright © 2016 by Harlequin Books S.A.

The publisher acknowledges the copyright holder of the individual works as follows:

The Amish Bride
Copyright © 2015 by Emma Miller

The Amish Mother
Copyright © 2015 by Rebecca Kertz

www.Harlequin.com

Printed in U.S.A.

CONTENTS

The Amish Bride

EMMA MILLER

A friend loves at all times.
—*Proverbs* 17:17

Chapter One

Lancaster County, Pennsylvania

It was half-past nine when Ellen Beachey halted her push scooter at the top of the steep driveway that ran from her parents' white farmhouse down to the public road. Normally, she would be at the craft shop by nine, but this had been one of her mother's bad days when her everyday tasks seemed a lot more difficult. Her *mam* was in her midseventies, so it wasn't surprising to Ellen that she was losing some of her vim and vigor. After milking the cow and feeding the chickens before breakfast, Ellen had remained after they'd eaten to tidy up the kitchen, finish a load of wash and pin the sheets on the line.

She didn't mind. She was devoted to her *mutter*, and it was a gorgeous day to hang laundry. There wasn't a cloud in the sky, the sticky heat of August had eased and there was a breeze, sweet with the aroma of ripening grapes and apples from the orchard. But with her *dat*'s arthritis acting up, and her *mam* not at her best, Ellen felt the full weight of responsibility for the shop and the household. The craft store was her family's main source of income, and it was up to her to see that it made a profit.

This had been a good week at Beachey's Craft Shop. School would soon be starting, and many English families were taking advantage of the last few days of summer vacation to visit Lancaster County. Ellen had seen a steady stream of tourists all week, and the old brass cash register had hardly stopped ringing. It meant good news for Lizzie Fisher, in particular. Her king-size *Center Diamond* quilt, meticulously stitched with red, blue and moss-green cotton, had finally sold for the full asking price. Lizzie had worked on the piece for more than a year, and she could certainly use the money. Ellen couldn't wait to tell her the good news. One of the best things about running the shop was being able to handle so many beautifully handcrafted Amish items every day and to provide a market for the Plain craftspeople who made them.

A flash of brilliant blue caught Ellen's attention, and she glimpsed an indigo bunting flash by before the small bird vanished into the hedgerow that divided her father's farmstead from that of their neighbors', the Shetlers. Seeing the indigo bunting, still in his full summer plumage, made her smile. All her life, she'd been fascinated by birds, and this particular species was much rarer than the blue grosbeak or the common bluebird. Ellen wondered if the indigo bunting had a mate and had built a nest in the hedgerow, or was just passing through in an early migration. She scrutinized the foliage, hoping to see the bird again, but it remained hidden in the leaves of a wild cherry tree. She could hear the bird's distinctive *chrrp*, but it didn't reappear.

And, Ellen reminded herself, the longer she stood there watching for the bird, the later she'd be for work. She needed to be on her way. She shifted her gaze to the steep driveway ahead of her.

Maybe this was the morning to be sensible and act like the adult she was. She could just walk her scooter to the bottom of the lane and then hop on once she reached the road. But the temptation was too great. She scanned the pavement in both directions as far as she could see for traffic. Nothing. Not a vehicle in sight. Taking pleasure in each movement, Ellen stepped onto the scooter, gripped the handles and gave a strong push with her left foot. With a cry of delight, she flew down the hill, laughing with excitement, bonnet strings flying behind her.

Ellen waited until the last possible moment before squeezing the handbrakes and leaning hard to one side, whipping the scooter around the mailbox, onto the public road. A cloud of dust flew up behind her, and pebbles scattered as she hit the pavement. The scooter fishtailed and she continued to brake, bringing it to a stop.

One of these days, Ellen thought. *One of these days, you're going to come down that hill so fast that you can't stop and land smack-dab on top of the bishop's buggy.* But not today.

As she stepped off the scooter, her heart still pounded. Her knees were weak, and her prayer *kapp* was hanging off her head from a single bobby pin. She was definitely too old to be doing this. What would the community say if they saw John Beachey's spinster daughter, a fully baptized member of the church and long past her *rumspringa* years, sailing down her father's driveway on her lime-green push scooter? Although most Plain people were accepting of small eccentricities within the community, it would almost certainly be cause for a scandal. The deacon would be calling on her father out of concern for her mental, spiritual and physical health.

Chuckling at the thought, Ellen pinned up her *kapp* and shook the dust off her apron. She moved to the crown of the road and began to make her way toward the village of Honeysuckle. However, she'd no sooner rounded the first wooded bend when she saw a familiar gray-bearded figure sitting on the side of the road.

"Simeon!" she called, pushing the scooter faster. "*Vas is?* Are you all right?" Simeon Shetler, a widower and a member of her church district, lived next door with his two grown sons and two grandsons. Ellen had known him since she was a child.

"Hallo!" He waved one of his metal crutches. "*Jah*, I am fine." He gestured with the other crutch. "It's Butterscotch who's in trouble."

Ellen glanced at the far side of the road to see Simeon's pony nibbling grass fifty feet away. The pony was hitched to the two-wheeled cart that her one-legged neighbor used for transportation. "What happened?" she asked as she hurried to help Simeon to his feet. "Did you fall out of the cart?"

"*Nay*, I'm not so foolish as that. I may be getting old, but I'm not dotty-headed." They spoke, as most Amish did when they were among their own kind, in *Deitsch*, a dialect that the English called *Pennsylvania Dutch*. "But I will admit, seeing your pretty face coming down the road was a welcome sight."

"Have you been like this long?" she asked, taking no offense at his compliment, which might have seemed out of place coming from most Amish men. Simeon was known as something of a flirt, and he always had a pleasant word for the women, young or old. But he was a kind man, a devout member of the community and would never cross any lines of propriety.

"Long enough, I can tell you. It took me ten minutes to climb back out of that ditch."

As a young man, Simeon had had a leg amputated just below the knee. Although he had a prosthetic leg and had gone to physical therapy to learn how to walk with it, he never wore it. For as long as Ellen could remember, the molded plastic and titanium prosthetic had hung on a peg on his kitchen wall. Usually, Simeon made out fine with his crutches, which extended from his forearms to the ground, but when he fell, he wasn't able to get back on his feet without a steady object like a fence post, or the aid of a friendly hand.

Simeon grinned. "Some fool *Englisher* threw a bag of trash from one of those *food-fast* places into the ditch. I thought I could pick it up if I got down out of the cart. I would have been able to, but I slipped in the grass, fell and slid into the ditch. And then by the time I crawled back out, that beast—" he shook his crutch again at the grazing pony "—trotted away." He chuckled and shrugged. "So, as you can see, I was stuck here until a Good Samaritan came along to rescue me."

"Are you sure you're all right?" she asked, looking him over.

"I'm fine. Catch the pony before he takes off for town," Simeon urged. "Then we need to have a talk, you and me. I think maybe it was God's plan this happened this morning. I have something important to discuss with you."

"With me?" Ellen looked at him quizzically. Simeon

was an elder in their church, but she couldn't think of anything that she'd done wrong that would cause concern. And if she *was* in trouble for some transgression, it should have been the deacon who'd come to speak to her and her parents to remind her of her duties to the faith community.

Unless…

Was it possible that Simeon or one of his sons had recently seen her antics on the push scooter? She didn't think so. She was careful about when and where she gave in to her weakness for thrilling downhill rides. And Bishop Harvey had approved the bright color of her push scooter, once she'd explained that she'd gotten it secondhand as a trade for a wooden baby cradle.

The unusually bright, lime-green push scooter was an expensive one from a respected manufacturer in Intercourse. She could have had it repainted, but that would cost money and time, even if she did it herself. Bishop Harvey was a wise leader and a practical man. He understood that, with Ellen's father owning only one horse, she needed a dependable way to get back and forth to the craft shop without leaving her parents stranded. And if the fluorescent color on the push scooter was brighter than what was customarily acceptable, the safety factor made up for the fancy paint.

"See, there he goes." Simeon pointed as the pony moved forward, taking the cart with him. "Headed for Honeysuckle, trying to make a bigger fool of me than I already am. We'll be lucky if you catch him."

"Oh, I'll catch him, all right." Ellen reached for the lunch box tied securely in her scooter basket on the steering column. She unfastened it, removed a red apple and walked down the road toward the pony. "Look what I have!" she called. "Come here, boy."

Butterscotch raised his head and peered at her from under a thick forelock. His ears went up and then twitched.

Ellen whistled softly. "Nice pony."

He pawed the dirt with one small hoof, took a few steps and the cart rolled forward, away from her.

"Easy," Ellen coaxed. "Look what I have." She held up the apple. "Whoa, easy, now."

The pony wrinkled his nose and snorted, side-stepping in the harness, making the cart shift one way and then the other. Ellen walked around in front of him and took a bite out of the apple before she offered it again. Butterscotch sniffed the air and stared at the apple. "*Goot* boy," she crooned, knowing he was anything but a good boy.

The palomino was a legend in the neighborhood. For all his beauty, he was not the obedient pony a man like Simeon needed. This was not the first time Butterscotch had left his owner stranded. And Butterscotch didn't stay put in his pasture, either. He was a master of escape: opening locked gates, squeezing through gaps in fences and jumping ditches to wander off into someone's orchard or garden to feast on forbidden fruit. He'd been known to nip and kick at other horses, and more than once he'd run away while hitched, overturning the cart. Ellen couldn't imagine why the Shetlers kept him. He certainly wasn't safe for Simeon's grandsons to ride or drive. A clever pony like him was a handful for anyone to manage, let alone a one-legged man in his sixties.

Cautiously, Ellen took a few steps closer to the pony. Butterscotch tossed his head and moved six feet farther down the road. "So that's the way it will be," she

said. The sound of a vehicle alerted her to an approach-
ing car. The driver, coming from the direction of Honeysuckle, slowed. The pony stood and watched as the
sedan passed. He wasn't traffic shy, which was the one
good thing that Ellen could say about him.

When the car had disappeared behind her, Ellen took
another bite of the apple, turned her back on Butterscotch and retraced her steps toward Simeon. She heard
the creak of the harness and the rattle of wheels behind
her, but she kept walking. She kept going until she was
almost even with Simeon, then stopped and waited. It
wasn't long before she felt the nudge of a soft nose on
her arm. Without making eye contact, she held out the
remainder of the apple. Butterscotch sunk his teeth into
the piece of fruit, sending rivulets of juice dripping
down Ellen's arm. Swiftly, she reached back and took
hold of the pony's bridle.

"Gotcha," she murmured in triumph.

Once Simeon was safely on the seat of the cart, reins
in hand, with the cart turned toward Honeysuckle again,
he waved to her scooter. "Why don't you put that in the
back? Ride with me. We can talk on the way."

Curious and a little apprehensive, Ellen lifted her
scooter into the back. He offered his hand. She put a
foot into the iron bracket and stepped up into the cart.
"Have I done something wrong?" she asked.

She couldn't imagine what. She hadn't been roller
skating at the local rink in months, and she took care
to always dress modestly in public, even if she did wear
a safety helmet when she used her scooter in high-
traffic areas.

"Of course not." Simeon shook the reins. "Walk on."
Butterscotch moved forward and the cart rolled along.

"You're an excellent example for our younger girls, Ellen," he said, turning to favor her with a smile. "You're devout and hardworking."

Now he *really* had her attention. The familiar sound of horse's hooves alerted her to a horse and buggy coming up behind them. Ellen glanced over her shoulder; the driver was Joseph Lapp. She and Simeon waved as Joseph swung around, passing the pony cart. He waved back and quickly moved on ahead of them.

"Wonder if we'll start tongues clucking, riding together," Simeon remarked.

Ellen looked at him, hoping he was joking. Simeon wasn't going to ask if he could come courting, was he? It seemed like once a month he was asking *someone* permission to court—a matter that kept the women of the community, from age eighteen to eighty, chuckling. But the twinkle in his faded blue eyes told her that he was teasing, and she relaxed a little.

"I want to discuss with you a problem that's been worrying me in my household." He tugged at his full gray beard thoughtfully. "As you know, ours is a bachelor house—one grandfather, two grown sons and two small boys. And we're sorely in need of a woman's hand. Oh, we cook and clean and try to keep things in order, but everyone knows a good woman is the heart of any home."

Unconsciously, she clasped her hands together and tried to think of what she would say if he asked to walk out with her. A few months ago, he'd asked her twenty-nine-year-old widowed friend, Ruthie.

"You're what, Ellen? Two and thirty?"

"Thirty-three," she said softly.

"*Jah*, thirty-three. Almost three years younger than

my Neziah." He fixed her with a level gaze. "You should have married long ago, girl. You should be a mother with a home of your own."

"My parents…" she mumbled. "They've needed help, and—"

"Your devotion to your mother and father is admirable," he interrupted. "But in time, they'll both be gathered to the Lord, and you'll be left alone. And if you wait too long, you'll have no children to care for you in your old age."

Her mouth went dry. What Simeon was saying was true. A truth she tried not to think about. It wasn't that she hadn't once dreamed of having a husband and children, simply that the time had never been right and the right man had never asked her. She'd had her courting days once, but her father had gotten ill and then there was the fire…and the years had simply gotten away from her. She believed that God had a plan for her, but her life seemed whole and happy as it was. If she never married, would it be such a tragedy?

"I've long prayed over my own sons' dilemma," Simeon confided as he loosened the reins and flicked them over Butterscotch's back to urge him on faster. "Neither one is married now, and both would be the happier if they were. So I've prayed and waited for an answer, and it seems to me that the Lord has made clear to me what must be done."

Ellen turned to him. "He has?"

Simeon turned the full force of his winning smile on her. "You should marry one of them." He didn't wait for her to respond. "It makes perfect sense. My land and your father's are side by side. Most of his is wooded with fine old hardwood, and we make our living by the lumber mill. I've known you since you were a babe in arms, and there's no young woman I'd more willingly welcome into our family."

She, who never was at a loss for words, was almost speechless. "I…" She stopped and started again. She couldn't help but stare at Simeon. "You think I should marry Neziah or Micah?"

"Not only think it, but am certain of it. I already told them both at breakfast this morning." He narrowed his gaze. "Now I expect you to be honest with me, Ellen. Do you have any objection to either of them for reason of character or religious faith?"

She shook her head as the images of handsome, young, blond Micah and serious, dark-haired Neziah rose in her mind's eye. "*Nay*, of course not. They're both men of solid faith, but—"

"*Goot*," he pronounced, "because I don't know which the Lord intends for you. I've told both of my sons that I expect each of them to pay court to you and make a match as soon as may be decently arranged. The choice between them will be yours, Ellen. Steady Neziah and his children or my rascally, young Micah." He gazed out over the pony with a sly smile. "And I care not which one you take."

It was an hour later at the craft store when Ellen was finally able to share her morning adventure with Dinah Plank, the widow who helped in the shop and lived in the apartment upstairs. Dinah, a plump, five-foot-nothing whirlwind of gray-haired energy, was a dear friend, and Ellen valued her opinion.

"So, Simeon came right out and told you that you should marry one of his sons?" Dinah paused in rearranging the display of organic cotton baby clothing and looked at her intently through wire-framed eyeglasses. "Acting as his sons' go-between, is he?"

"So it seems." Ellen stood with an empty cardboard box under each arm. She had two orders to pack for mailing, and she wanted to get them ready for UPS.

"What did you tell him?" The older woman shook out a tiny white infant's cap and carefully brushed the wrinkles out of it. Light poured in through the nine-paned windows, laying patterns of sunlight across the wide-plank floor of the display room and bouncing off the whitewashed plaster walls.

"Nothing, really. I was so surprised, I didn't know what to say." She put the mailing boxes on the counter and reached underneath for a couple of pieces of brown-paper wrapping. "I didn't want to hurt his feelings. They've been such *goot* neighbors, and of course, my *dat* and Simeon are fast friends."

"You think Simeon has already said something to your father?"

"I can't imagine he did." She lined the first cardboard box with two pieces of brown paper. "*Dat* would have certainly said something."

Dinah propped up a cloth Amish doll, sewn in the old-fashioned way, without facial features. The doll was dressed for Sunday services with a black bonnet and cape, long black stockings and conservative leather shoes. "Well, you're not averse to marrying, are you?"

"*Nay.* Of course not." She reached for the stack of patchwork-quilt-style placemats she was shipping. "I'm just waiting for the man God wants for me."

"And you'll know him how?" She rested one hand on her hip. "Will this man knock on your door?"

Ellen frowned and added another layer of brown paper to the box before adding eight cloth napkins.

"My marriage to Mose was arranged by my uncle, and it worked out well for both of us." Dinah tilted her head to one side in a way she had about her when she was trying to convey some meaning that she didn't want to state outright. "We each had a few burrs that needed rubbing off by time and trial and error, but we started with respect and a common need. I wanted a home and marriage with a man of my faith, and Mose needed sons to help on his farm."

Ellen nodded. She'd heard this story more than once, how Dinah and Mose had married after only meeting twice, and how she'd left Ohio to come to Lancaster County with him. The marriage had lasted thirty-four years, and Dinah had given him four sons and three daughters. Most lived nearby, and any of her children would have welcomed Dinah into their home. But she liked her independence and chose to live alone here in the apartment in Honeysuckle, and earn a living helping with the craft shop.

"I was an orphan without land or dowry," Dinah continued, fiddling with the doll's black bonnet. "And few ever called me fair of face. But I was strong, and God had given me health and ambition. I knew that I could learn to love the man I married. Mose was no looker, either, but he owned fifty acres of rich ground and was a respected farrier. Together, with the help of neighbors, we built a house with our own hands and backs."

"And were you happy?"

Dinah smiled, a little sadly. "*Jah*, we *were* very happy together. Mose was an able provider and he worked hard. Respect became friendship and then partnership, and…somewhere along the way, we fell in love." She tapped the shelf with her hand. "So my point of this long story is that Mose didn't come knocking on my door. Our marriage was more or less arranged."

Ellen sighed and smoothed the denim blue napkins. "But it sounds so much like a business transaction—Simeon deciding that his sons need wives and then telling them who they should court. Me living next door, so I'm the nearest solution. If one of them wanted to walk out with me, why didn't he say so, instead of waiting for their father to make the suggestion?"

Ellen sank onto a three-legged wooden stool carved and painted with a pattern of intertwined hearts and vines. She glanced around the room, thinking as she always did, how much she loved this old building. It had started life nearly two hundred years earlier as a private home and had been in turn a tavern, a general store, a bakery and now Beachey's Craft Shop.

"Maybe you should have married when you had the chance."

"I wasn't ready," she said. "And you know there were other reasons, things we couldn't work out."

"With Neziah, you mean?" Dinah passed.

Ellen nodded. She was as shocked by Simeon's idea that she should consider Neziah again, as she was by the whole idea that he should tell her or his boys who they should marry.

"That was years ago, girl. You were hardly out of your teens, and as hardheaded as Neziah. Are you certain you're not looking for someone that you've dreamed up in your head, a make-believe man instead of a flesh-and-blood one?" The sleigh bells over the front door jingled, indicating a visitor.

Ellen rose.

Dinah waved her away. "I'll see to her. You finish up packaging those orders. Then you might put the kettle on. If it's pondering you need, there's nothing like a cup of tea to make the studying on it easier."

"Maybe," Ellen conceded.

Dinah shrugged. "One thing you can be glad of."

"What's that?"

"That old goat Simeon wasn't asking to court you himself." She rolled her eyes. "Thirty-odd years difference between you or not, he wouldn't be the first old man looking for a fine young wife."

"Dinah!" she admonished. "How could you say such a thing?"

Dinah chuckled. "I said it, but you can't tell me you weren't thinking it."

"I suppose Simeon *is* a good catch, though a little too old for me." Ellen glanced up, smiling mischievously. "Maybe *you're* the one who should think about courting one of the Shetler bachelors."

Dinah laughed as she walked away. "Maybe I should."

Chapter Two

T hat afternoon Ellen walked her scooter up the steep driveway to her house. "Start each day as you mean to go," her father always said. And today surely proved that wisdom. She hadn't reached the craft shop until past her usual hour that morning, and now she was late arriving home. She left the scooter in the shed in a place where the chickens wouldn't roost on it, and hurried toward the kitchen door.

Ellen had left chicken potpie for supper. On Tuesdays and Wednesdays, the days that she closed the store at five, she and her parents usually had their main meal together when she got home. It was after six now, though. She hoped they hadn't waited for her.

Ellen had been delayed because of a mix-up with the customer orders that Dinah had packed and mailed a week earlier. The reproduction spinning wheel that had been intended for Mrs. McIver in Maine had gone instead to Mrs. Chou in New Jersey. And the baby quilt in the log cabin pattern and an Amish baby doll Mrs. Chou had been expecting had gone to Mrs. McIver. Mrs. Chou had taken the mistake with good humor when Ellen had called her from the store's phone. Mrs. McIver hadn't been so understanding, but Ellen had been able to calm her by promising to have the spinning wheel shipped overnight as soon as she received it back from Mrs. Chou.

Dinah felt terrible about the mix-up; unfortunately, it wasn't the first time she'd made a mistake shipping an order. Dinah was a lovely woman, but other than her charming way with tourists who came into the shop, her shopkeeper's skills were not the best. After two years behind the counter, she still struggled running credit cards, the cash register continually gave her a fit and Ellen had given up trying to get her to make the bank deposits. But Dinah needed the income, and since the fire, it had been comforting to have someone living in the apartment upstairs. So, in spite of the disadvantages of having Dinah as an employee, Ellen and her father agreed to keep her as long as she was willing to work for them.

As Ellen climbed the back steps to her parents' house, voices drifted through the screen door, alerting her that they had visitors. And since they were speaking in Deitsch, they had to be Amish. *But who would be stopping by at suppertime?*

Ellen walked into the kitchen to find Simeon Shetler, his two sons and his two grandsons seated around the big table. The evening meal was about to be served.

Ellen covered her surprise with a smile. "Simeon. Micah. Neziah. How nice to see you." The table was set for eight, so clearly the Shetlers had been expected. Had her mother invited them for supper and forgotten to mention it? It was entirely possible; there were many things that slipped Mary Beachey's mind these days.

Of course, there was the distinct possibility that plans to have dinner together had been made *after* her conversation with Simeon this morning. Ellen's cheeks grew warm. Surely Micah and Neziah weren't here to—

The brothers got to their feet as Ellen entered the kitchen, and she saw that they were both wearing white shirts and black vests and trousers, their go-to-worship attire—which meant that the visit was a formal one. For them, not their father. Simeon wore his customary blue work shirt and blue denim trousers.

It appeared that the two younger Shetler men had come courting.

She opened her mouth to say something, anything, but nothing clever came to her, so she looked at her father. Surely there had been a misunderstanding or miscommunication with the Shetlers. Surely her father would have wanted to talk in private with Ellen about Simeon's proposition before inviting them all to sit down together to talk about it.

John Beachey met his daughter's gaze and nodded. He knew her all too well. He knew just what she was thinking. "*Jah*, Ellen. We've talked, Simeon and I."

"You have?" she managed.

"We have, and we're in agreement. It's time you were married, and who better than one of the fine sons of our good neighbor. A neighbor, who," he reminded pointedly, "helped us out so much when we had the fire."

The fire, Ellen thought. *That weighty debt: rarely mentioned but always remembered.*

How many years ago had it been now? Seven or eight? The suspicious fire, probably caused by teenaged mischief makers, had started at the back of the store and quickly spread through the old kitchen and up through the ceiling into the second floor. Quick-thinking neighbors had smelled smoke and seen flames, and the valiant efforts of a local fire company had prevented the whole building from being a loss. But smoke and water had destroyed all of the contents of the shop, leaving them with no means of support and no money to rebuild. Simeon had showed up early the next day with a volunteer work force from the community to help. He'd provided cash from his own pocket for expenses, lumber from his mill and his sons' services to provide the skilled carpentry to restore the shop. Over the years, her father had been able to repay Simeon's interest-free loan, but they owed the Shetlers more than words could ever express.

"Sit, please." She waved a hand to the men and boys.

Having Simeon's sons standing there grinning at her was unnerving. Or at least, handsome, blond-haired Micah was grinning at her. Neziah, always the most serious of the three Shetler men, had the expression of one with a painful tooth, about to see the dentist. He nodded and settled solidly in his chair.

The room positively crackled with awkwardness, and Ellen wished she were anywhere but there. She wished she could run outside, jump on her push scooter and escape down the drive. Everyone was looking at her, seeming to be waiting for her to say something.

Neziah's son Joel, age five, came to her rescue. "Can we eat now, *Dat*? I'm hungry."

"*Jah*, I'm hungry, too," the four-year-old, Asa, echoed.

The boys did not look hungry, although boys always were, Ellen supposed. Joel, especially, appeared as if he'd just rolled away from a harvest table. His chubby face was as round as a donut under a mop of unruly butter-yellow hair, hair the same color as his uncle Micah's. Asa, with dark hair and a complexion like his father's, was tall for his age and sturdy. Someone had made an effort to subdue their ragged bowl cuts and scrub their hands and faces, but they retained the look of plump little banty roosters who'd just lost a barnyard squabble and were missing a few feathers. Still, the boys had changed the focus from her and the looming courtship question back to ground she was far steadier on—the evening meal.

"We waited supper for you," Ellen's mother explained. "Come, *Dochter*, sit here across from Micah and Neziah."

Ellen surveyed the table. There would be enough of a main dish for their company because she'd made the two potpies. She also saw that her mother had fried up a platter of crispy brown scrapple and brought out the remnants of a roasted turkey. "Let me open a jar of applesauce and some of those delicious beets you made this summer, *Mam*," she suggested. As she turned toward the cupboard, she took off her good apron, which she wore at the shop, and grabbed a black work apron from a peg on the wall. "I'll only be a moment," she said. "I'm sure the boys like applesauce." Tying the apron on, she retrieved the jar and carried it to the table.

"Do you have pie?" Joel called after her. "*Grossdaddi* promised we would have pie. He said you always got pie."

"And cake," Asa chimed in.

"Boys," Neziah chided. "Mind your manners."

"But *Grossdaddi* said," Joel insisted.

Ellen went to the stove and scooped biscuits from

a baking sheet and dropped them into a wooden bowl
that had been passed down from a great-grandmother.
They were still warm, so they must have just come
from the oven.

Her mother rose to seek out a pint of chow-chow, and
a quart of sweet pickles that they'd put up just a week
ago. In no time, they were all seated, and Ellen's father
bowed his head for the silent prayer.

When Ellen looked up once prayer was over, Micah
met her gaze, grinning. He seemed to be enjoying the
whole uncomfortable situation. But as she started to
pass the platters and bowls of food, she found herself
smiling, as well. Having friends at the table was always a blessing. She might not have expected to find
the Shetlers here this evening, but here they were, and
she'd make the best of it. So what if they were there to
talk about a possible courtship between her and one of
the Shetler men? No one was going to *make* her marry
anyone.

Shared meals were one of the joys of a Plain life, and
it was impossible not to enjoy Simeon's and Micah's
teasing banter. The children concentrated on devouring
their supper, eating far more than Ellen would suppose
small boys could consume. Unlike Micah, Neziah ate
in silence, adding only an occasional *Jah* and a grunt or
nod of agreement to the general conversation. Neziah
had always been the quiet one, even as a child. How he
could have such noisy and mischievous children, Ellen
couldn't imagine.

Simeon launched into a lengthy joke about a lost
English tourist who stopped to ask an Amish farmer for
directions to Lancaster. The story had bounced around
the community for several years, but Simeon had a way

of making each tall tale his own, and Ellen didn't mind. At least when he was talking, she didn't have to think of something to say to either of her would-be *suitors*.

Joel looked up from his plate, waved his fork and asked, "Now can we have pie?"

"Rooich," Micah cautioned, raising a finger to his lips. *Quiet.* He then pointed his finger in warning to keep Asa from chiming in.

Ellen glanced at Neziah to see his reaction to his brother chastising his boys, but Neziah's mouth was full of potpie and he seemed to be paying no mind. It was his third helping. She was glad she'd made two large pies, because the first dish was empty and the second held only a single slice.

Neziah suddenly began to cough and Micah slapped him on the back. Neziah reddened and turned away from the table. His brother handed him a glass of milk, and Neziah downed half of it before clearing his throat and wiping his mouth with a napkin. "Sorry," he gasped, turning back to the table. "Chicken bone."

Ellen blushed with embarrassment. "I'm sorry," she said hastily. She'd been so certain that she'd gotten all the bones out of the chicken before adding it to the other ingredients.

"I may be a dumb country pig farmer," Simeon said, delivering the punch line of his story, "but I'm not the one who's lost." He looked around, waiting for the re-action to his joke and wasn't disappointed.

Her *mam* and *dat* laughed loudly.

"Jah," her mother agreed. "He wasn't, was he? It was the fancy *Englisher* with the big car who was lost."

Simeon slapped both hands on the table and roared

with delight. "Told him, didn't he?" Tears ran down his cheeks. "Lot of truth in that story, isn't there?"

Ellen's father nodded. "Lot of truth. Not many weeks pass that some tourist doesn't stop in the craft shop to ask how to find Lancaster. And I say, you're standing in it."

"Course he means the town," Ellen's *mam* clarified. "Lancaster County's one thing, the town is another."

"Town of Lancaster's got too many traffic lights and shopping centers for me." Simeon wiped his cheeks with his napkin. "But I do love to laugh at them *Englishers*."

Joel wiggled in his chair and whined. "I want my pie. *Grossdaddi*, you promised there'd be pie for dessert."

Ellen eyed the two little boys. Asa and Joel were unusually demanding for Amish children; some might even say they were spoiled. And, to her way of thinking, Joel's father allowed him perhaps too many sweets. He was a nice boy when he wasn't whining, but if he got any chubbier, he'd never be able to keep up with the other kids when they ran and played. If he were her child, he'd eat more apples and fewer sugary treats. But, as her *mam* liked to say, people without kids always had the most opinions on how to raise them.

"Enough, boys!" Neziah said, clearly embarrassed by their behavior. "You'll have to forgive my children. Living rough with us three men, they're lacking in table manners."

Micah chuckled.

Since he was still unmarried, he didn't have a beard. The dimple on his chin made him even more attractive when he laughed. Ellen couldn't imagine what he would want with her when half the girls in Lancaster

County wished he'd ask to drive them home from a Sunday night singing.

"It's more than table manners, I'd say," Micah teased. "These boys are wild as rabbits and just as hard to herd when it comes time for bath or bed."

"Which is why they need a mother's hand," Simeon pronounced. "And why we came to ask for your daughter in marriage, John."

"To one of us," Micah added. "Your choice, Ellen." He chuckled again and punched his brother's shoulder playfully. "Although, if she has her pick, Neziah's starting this race a good furlong behind."

Ellen glanced at Micah. Self-pride wasn't an attribute prized by the Plain folk. Everyone knew that Micah was full of himself, but still, with his likeable manner, he seemed to be able to get away with it.

And to prove it, he winked at her and grinned. "Tell the bishop I said that, and he'll have me on the boards in front of the church asking for forgiveness for my brash talk."

"Micah! What will the John Beacheys think of you with your nonsense?" Simeon asked. "Be serious for once. Your brother is as good a candidate for marriage as you. And Ellen would be a good wife for him, as well." He shrugged. "Either way, we'll have a woman in the house to set it right and put my grandsons' feet on the narrow path."

Ellen frowned, not liking the sound of that. Did the Shetlers want her, or just some woman to wash, cook and look after the children? Maybe it was true that she was getting too old to be picky, but she wouldn't allow herself to be taken advantage of.

She glanced at the plate of food she'd barely touched.

She couldn't believe they were all sitting there seriously talking about her marrying one of the Shetlers.

The kitchen felt unusually warm, even for a late-August evening, and Ellen ran a finger under the neck-line of her dress to ease the tightness against her skin. What could she say? Her parents and the Shetlers were all looking expectantly at her again.

Folding his arms over his chest, Neziah spoke with slow deliberation. "You're telling Ellen that she should choose between us, but I've not heard her say that she'll have either of us. This is your idea, *Vadder*. Maybe it's not to Ellen's liking."

"Not just *my* idea," Simeon corrected. "*Nay*. I say plainly that I believe it's God's plan. And John's in agreement with me. Think about it. I don't know why we didn't see it before. Here I sit with two unwed sons, one with motherless children he struggles to care for and the other sashaying back and forth across the county from one singing to another in a rigged-out buggy with red-and-blue flashing lights." His brow furrowed as he stared hard at Micah. "And don't mention *rumspringa*, because it's time you put that behind you and came into the church."

"Listen to your father." Ellen's *dat* nodded. "He's speaking truth, Micah. He wants what's best for you. He always has."

"*Jah*," Simeon said. "I've held my tongue far too long, waiting for the two of you to stop sitting on the fence and court some young woman. Neziah's mourned the boys' mother long enough, and Micah's near to being thought too flighty for any good family to want him. It's time."

Micah toyed with his fork. "I'm not yet thirty, *Vadder*. It's not as if no girl would have me."

"I'll fetch the coffee and apple pie," Ellen offered. She began clearing away the plates while Simeon wagged a finger at Micah.

"You know I'm but speaking what's true. Deny it if you can. Neither of you have been putting your minds to finding a good wife. And you must marry. It's not decent that you don't. I've talked to you until I'm blue in the face, and I've prayed on it. What came to me was that we didn't have to look far to find the answer to at least one of our problems."

"Jah." Ellen's mother leaned forward on her elbows and pushed back her plate. "And you've worried about your sons no more than I've lost sleep over our girl. She should have been a wife years ago, should have filled our house with grandchildren. She's a good daughter, a blessing to us in our old age. But it's time she found a husband, and none better than one of your boys."

"I agree," Ellen's father said. "I've known Neziah and Micah since they were born. I could ask no more for her than she wed such a good man as either of them." He smiled and nodded his approval. "The pity is, we didn't think of this solution sooner."

"No solution if Ellen's not willing," Neziah pronounced. His serious gaze met hers and held it. "Are you in favor of this plan or are you just afraid to speak up and turn us out the door with our hats in hand?"

Everyone looked at her again, including the two children, and Ellen felt a familiar sinking feeling. What *did* she want? She didn't know. She stood in the center of the kitchen feeling foolish and clutching the pie like a drowning woman with a lifeline. "I… Well…"

"Is the thought of marrying one of us distasteful to you?" Neziah asked when she couldn't answer.

He had none of the showy looks of his brother. Neziah's face was too planed, his brow too pronounced and his mouth too thin to be called handsome. Not that he was ugly; he wasn't that. But there was always something unnerving about his dark, penetrating gaze.

Neziah was only three years older than she was, but he looked closer to ten. Hints of gray were beginning to tint his walnut-brown hair. The sudden loss of his wife and mother in the same accident three years ago had struck him hard. Maybe it was the responsibility of being both father and mother to two young children that stamped him with an air of heaviness.

"We're all friends here," Neziah continued. "No one will think less of you if this isn't something you want to consider."

Micah relaxed in his chair. "I say we've thrown this at her too fast. I wouldn't blame her for balking." He met Ellen's gaze. "Give yourself a few days to think it over, Ellen. What do you say?"

"Jah," Ellen's mother urged, rising to take the pie from her hands. "Say you will think about it, daughter."

"You know your mother and I wouldn't even consider the idea if we thought it was wrong for you." Her father beamed, and Ellen's resistance melted.

What could be wrong with thinking it over? As Simeon and her *dat* had said, either of the Shetler brothers would make a respectable husband. She would be a wife, a woman with her own home to manage, possibly children. She took a deep breath, feeling as if she were about to take a plunge off the edge of a rock quarry into deep water far below. She actually felt a little light-headed. "I will," she said. "I'll think on the whole idea, and I will pray about it. Surely, if it is the Lord's plan for me, He'll ease my mind." She held up her finger. "But my agreement is to *think* on the whole idea. Nothing more."

Simeon smacked his hands together. "*Goot.* It is for the best. You will come to realize this. And whichever one you pick, I will consider you the daughter I never had."

Ellen turned toward Simeon, intent on making it clear to her neighbor that she hadn't agreed to walk out with either of his sons when the little boys kicked up a commotion.

"Me!" Asa and Joel both reached for the pie in the center of the table. "Me!" they cried in unison.

"Me first!" Joel insisted.

"*Nay!* Me!" Asa bellowed.

"I knew you'd see it our way, Ellen," Micah said above the voices of his nephews. He rose from his chair. "I was so sure you'd agree that I brought fishing poles. You always used to like fishing. Maybe you and me could wander down to the creek and see if we could catch a fish or two before dark."

Ellen looked at Micah, then the table of seated guests, flustered. "Go fishing? Now?"

"Oh, go on, Ellen," her father urged. "We can get our own pie and I'll help your mother clean up the dishes." He glanced at Micah. "Smart thinking. Best strike while the iron is hot, boy. Get the jump on Neziah and put your claim in first."

Mischief gleamed in Micah's blue eyes. "It'll get you out of here." He motioned toward the back door.

"Come on, Ellen. You know you want to. I'll even bait the hook for you."

She cut her eyes at him. "As if I need the help. If I remember correctly, it was me who taught you how to tickle trout."

"She did," Micah conceded to the others, then he returned his attention to her. "But I've learned a few things about fishing since then. You don't stand a chance of catching the first fish or the most."

"Don't I?" Ellen retorted. "Talk's cheap but it never put fish on the table." Still bantering with him, she took off her *kapp*, tied on her scarf and followed him out of the house.

Fifteen minutes later, Micah stepped out on a big willow that had fallen into the creek. The leaves had long since withered, but the trunk was strong. Barring a flood, the willow would provide a sturdy seat for fishermen for years. And the eddy in the curve of the bank was the best place to catch fish.

He turned and offered Ellen his hand. "Don't worry," he said, "it's safe enough." He had both fishing poles in his free hand, while Ellen carried the can with the bait.

The rocky stream was wide, the current gentle but steady as the water snaked through a wooded hollow that divided his father's farm from her *dat*'s. When they were children, he, Neziah and Ellen had come here to fish often. Now, he sometimes brought his nephews, Joel and Asa, but Neziah didn't have the time. Sometimes the fishing was good, and sometimes he went home with nothing more than an easy heart, but it didn't matter. Micah thought there was often more of God's peace to be found here in the quiet of wind and water and swaying trees than in the bishop's sermons.

"Thanks for asking me to come fishing, Micah," Ellen said as she followed him cautiously out onto the wide trunk. "I needed to get out of there, and I couldn't think of a way to make a clean getaway without offending anyone."

"Jah," Micah agreed. "I wanted to get away, too. Not from supper. That was great. But my *dat*. When he takes a crazy notion, he's hard to rein in."

"So you think that's what it is? His idea that you and Neziah should both court me, and that I would choose between you? It's a *crazy notion*?"

The hairs on the back of Micah's neck prickled, warning him that he'd almost made a big misstep, and not the kind that would land him in the creek. *"Nay,* I didn't mean it like that. It's a good idea, one I should have come up with a long time ago. Me and you walking out together, I mean, not you picking one of us. I don't know why I didn't think of it. My *vadder* is right that I've been *rumspringa* too long. I didn't want to discuss it back there, but I've been talking to the bishop about getting baptized. I'm ready to settle down, and a good woman is just what I need."

Ellen sat down on the log and dangled her legs over the edge. She was barefooted, and he couldn't help noticing her slender, high-arched feet. "I'm nearly four years older than you," she said.

He grinned at her. "That hasn't mattered since I left school and started doing a man's work. I've always thought you were one of the prettiest girls around, and we've always gotten along." Maybe not the prettiest, he thought, being honest with himself, but Ellen was nearly as tall as he was and very attractive. She'd always been fun to be with, and she was exactly the kind of woman he'd always expected to marry when he settled down. Ellen never made a fellow feel like less than he was, always better. Being with her always made him content…sort of like this creek, he decided.

"And our fathers' lands run together, of course." She took the pole he offered and bent over her line, carefully threading a night crawler onto the hook. "Handy for pasturing livestock."

He studied her to see if she was serious or testing him, but she kept her eyes averted, and he couldn't tell. He decided to play it safe. "We've been friends since we were kids. We share a faith and a community. Maybe that's a good start for a marriage."

"Maybe." She cast her line out, and the current caught her blue-and-white bobber and whisked it merrily along.

"*Dat* says all the best marriages start with friendship," he added.

"And it doesn't bother you that I'm thirty-three and not twenty-three?"

"Would I be here if it did?" Now she did raise her head and meet his gaze, and he smiled at her. "It was my *vadder*'s idea, but I wouldn't have agreed if I didn't think it was something I wanted to do. You're a hard worker. I hope you think the same of me. I've got a good trade, and I own thirty acres of cleared farmland in my own name. And the two of us have a lot in common."

"Such as?"

"I like to eat and you're a good cook." He laughed. She smiled.

"Seriously, Ellen. You get my jokes. We both like to

laugh and have a good time. You know it's true. There's a big difference between me and Neziah."

"He has always been serious in nature."

"And more so since the accident. He doesn't take the joy in life that he should. Bad things happen. I didn't lose a wife, I know, but I lost my mother in that accident. You have to go on living. Otherwise, we waste what the Lord has given us."

She nodded, but she didn't speak, and he remembered that he'd always liked that about her. Ellen was a good listener, someone you could share important thoughts with.

"Sometimes I think my brother's meant to be a preacher, or maybe a deacon. He's way too settled for a man his age. Just look at his driving animal. I always thought you could tell a man's nature by his favorite driving animal."

"Neziah drives a good mule," she suggested.

"Exactly. Steady in traffic. Strong and levelheaded, even docile. An old woman's horse." It was no secret that he was different than Neziah. He liked spirited horses and was given to racing other buggies on the way to Sunday worship, not something that the elders smiled on.

"Don't be so hard on your brother," Ellen defended. "He has his children's safety to think about. You know how some of these *Englishers* drive. They don't think about how dangerous it is to pass our buggies on these narrow roads."

"*Jah*, I know, but I'm careful about when and where I race. I don't mean to criticize Neziah. He's a good man, and I'd not stand to hear anyone criticize him. But he's too staid for you. Remember that time we all went to

Hershey Park? You and me, we liked the fast rides. Neziah, he got sick to his stomach. We're better suited, and if you'll give me a chance, I'll prove it to you."

"I think I—" She sounded excited for a second then sighed. "I had a bite but I think the fish is playing with me." She reeled in her line and checked the bait. Half of her worm was missing. "Look at that. Now I'll have to put on fresh bait."

He steadied himself against a branch and watched her, wondering why it had taken his father's lecture to stir him into action. For years he'd been going to all the young people's frolics, flirting with this girl and that, when all the time he'd hardly noticed Ellen. He had seen her, of course, gone to church with her, worked on community projects with her, eaten at her father's table and welcomed her to his own home. But he hadn't thought of her in the way he suddenly did now, as a special woman whom he might want to make his wife. The thought warmed him and made him smile. "You don't think I'm too young for you, do you?" he asked.

"Nay," she said, taking her time to answer. "I suppose not. But it's a new idea for me, that I marry a friend, rather than someone I was in love with."

Micah felt a rush of pleasure. "How do we know we won't discover love for each other if we don't give ourselves the chance?"

Her dark eyes grew luminous. Her bobber jerked and then dove beneath the surface of the creek, but Ellen didn't seem to notice the tension on her fishing pole. "You think that could happen?"

He grinned. "I think that there's a very good possibility that that's *exactly* what might happen."

Chapter Three

They walked back to her lane just as twilight was falling over the farm fields. "*Danki,* Micah," Ellen said. "The fishing was fun. I'd forgotten how much I liked it."

Her first moments alone with him, when they'd left the house, had been awkward. But then they'd fallen back into the easy rhythm of their younger days with none of the clumsiness of the situation that she'd feared. Being so comfortable with Micah made her wonder if maybe they could be happy together. What if Micah *was* whom God had intended for her all along?

"You should take these," he said, holding a string of three perch.

"You caught two of them. Don't you want to take them home to fry for breakfast?"

He still held them out. "Three measly fish for the five of us? Not worth the trouble of cleaning and cooking them. No, you'd best take them."

"*Danki* for the fish, too, then. *Dat* loves fried fish for breakfast."

"You're welcome. And you *are* going to think about walking out with me," Micah reminded. "Right?" He stood there, fishing poles in hand, smiling at her and completely at ease.

"*Jah*, I will." She smiled at him. "God give you a restful sleep."

"And you, Ellen." He used no courting endearments, but she liked the way he said her name, and she felt a warm glow inside as she savored it. She didn't want to spoil the feeling and was afraid that he might linger, might want to sit with her on the porch or stay on after her parents had gone to bed. Instead, he bestowed a final grin and strode off whistling in the direction of his own home.

Ellen walked slowly up the driveway and through her father's barnyard, inhaling deep of the scent of her mother's climbing roses and the honeysuckle that grew wild along the edge of the hedgerow. She drank in the peace of the coming night. Crickets and frogs called their familiar sounds, and evening shadows draped over the barnyard, easing her feelings of indecision. How wonderful life is, she thought. You expect each day to be like the one before, but the wonder of God's grace was that you never really knew from one hour to another what would come next.

A single propane lamp glowed through the kitchen window, but the house was quiet. Simeon, Neziah and the boys had left. The only sign of movement was a calico cat nursing kittens near the back door. But the light meant that her parents were still up. Her father was too fearful of fire to retire and leave a lamp burning. Ellen stepped inside, the string of fish dangling from her finger. *"Mam?"* she called softly. *"Dat?"*

"Out here." Her father's voice came from the front of the house.

Their home was small as Amish homes went, but comfortable. When her father and his neighbors had built it, he and her mother were already past the age when they expected to be blessed with children. A big kitchen, a pantry, a living room, bath and two bedrooms comprised the entire downstairs. Her room was upstairs in an oversize, cheerful chamber with two dormer windows and a casement window that opened wide to let in fresh breezes from the west. She also had a small bath all to herself, a privacy that few Amish girls had. Growing up, her girlfriends, most from large families, had admired the luxury, but she would have gladly traded the cheerful room with its yellow trim, clean white clawfoot tub, fixtures and tiny shuttered window for a bevy of noisy sisters crowded head to foot in her bedroom.

The double door near the staircase stood open, and her father called again to her from the front porch. "Come, join us. And bring another bowl for beans."

Butter beans, Ellen thought. The family often sat on the porch in the evenings this time of year and shelled butter beans. She and her mother canned bushels of beans for winter. Quarts of the beans already stood in neat rows in the pantry beside those of squash, English peas, string beans, corn, tomatoes and pickles. She wrapped the fish in some parchment paper and put it in the propane-run refrigerator. They'd keep until morning when she or her father would clean them. She washed her hands, found a bowl and carried it out to the porch. Her parents sat side by side in wooden rocking chairs, baskets of lima bean hulls and bowls of shelled beans around them.

"Catch any fish?" her father asked.

"In the fridge. If you clean them, I'll fry them up for

our breakfast." Ellen took the chair on the other side of him. Her chair. Her mother sat still, her chin resting on her chest; she was snoring lightly. Her mother often drifted off to sleep in the afternoon and early evening. She didn't have the vigor that Ellen was used to, and she worried about her. "Has she been asleep long?"

"Just a little while. Company wore her out." He dumped butter beans still in their shells into Ellen's bowl. "Course, you know how she loves to have people come. And she adores children, even those rascals of Neziah's. Nothing makes her happier than stuffing a child with food, unless it's singing in church. Your mother always had the sweetest voice. It was what drew me to her when we were young."

Ellen nodded and smiled. She knew what her father was up to. They were so close that she was familiar with all his tricks. He was deliberately being sentimental about her mother to keep Ellen from talking about what she'd sought him out for. He knew that she was unhappy with the ambush that had happened at supper, and he wanted to avoid the consequences. But she suspected that he'd be disappointed if she let him get away with it, so she went straight to the heart of the pudding.

"You shouldn't have asked the Shetlers here for supper to talk about this courting business without talking to me first," she admonished gently. "I can't believe you didn't wait to see whether I was in favor of this or not."

"*Ach...ach*, I was afraid you'd be vexed with me. I told your mother you would." He gestured with his hand. "But it is such a good solution to Simeon's problem and ours. And how could I refuse him? He came to me at midday, told me what was on his mind and said that he'd already approached you with the idea and you were in favor. Then he invited himself and his sons to supper." He shrugged as if to say, *what could I do?* "He's a good neighbor and an old friend."

"Friends or not, I'm your daughter, and who I will or won't marry is a serious matter. If you knew I wouldn't approve, you shouldn't have done it," she said, unwilling to surrender so easily to being manipulated.

She had the greatest respect for her father's judgment, but he'd always fostered independence in her. Even at a young age, he'd treated her more as another adult in the home than as a child. Maybe it was because her mother had always been an uncomplicated and basic person, content to allow her husband and the elders of the church to make decisions for her, while his was a keener mind that sought in-depth conversation. Or perhaps it was because she'd been the only child and he doted on her.

In any case, the Bible said "Honor thy father and mother," and she hoped she hadn't taken advantage of his leniency. She'd taken care not to be forward in front of others, especially with the more conservative of the community. But here, in their own home, with none but him to hear, how could she do less than protest his high-handedness?

"What was I to say to Simeon?" he went on. "'*Nay*, old friend, you can't come to share bread with us until I see if my daughter wants to marry either one of your boys?'" He found a withered lima bean and cast it to the brown-and-white rat terrier sitting at his feet. Gilly caught the bean in the air and chomped it joyfully.

"It was a shock to see Micah and Neziah all dressed in their best, here at the table." Ellen glanced at her mother, but she snored on, her hands loose in her lap, her bowl of unshelled beans hardly started. "She was good tonight, don't you think?" she said, waffling by talking of something easier. "Her morning started bad, so I worried…"

Her father's face was lost in shadow now, but Ellen knew he was smiling. He had such fondness for her mother, his love seemingly growing stronger with his wife's slow mental decline. "She perked up when I told her that the children were coming. Buzzed around the kitchen like she was forty. Her biscuits were light enough to float, don't you think? And she was sharp as a needle at supper." Her father continued to hull limas, his fingers moving unconsciously without pause. Fat beans dropped by ones, twos and threes into the wide basket in his lap.

"Jah," Ellen agreed. "No lapses in memory." And her mother's biscuits *had* been good tonight. She'd not forgotten the rising or the salt as she did sometimes. And she hadn't let them stay in the oven until the bottoms began to burn. Once, not long ago, Ellen had come in from the garden to find the kitchen full of smoke and her mother standing motionless in the center of the room, staring at the stove and coughing. Ellen had had to get the biscuits out of the oven and shoo her mother outside where she could breathe. It was those lapses in judgment that made Ellen apprehensive about her mother's health.

"So, *Dochter*, did you enjoy yourself on your outing with young Micah?"

"I did have a good time," she admitted. "But you know I would have put the Shetlers off if I'd had the choice. This isn't something that I can decide in a few hours."

"But you *are* open to being courted by Micah or his brother?" When she didn't answer right away, her father pressed on. "You have to marry, Ellen. You know that, don't you? What will you do when your mother and I go to our reward? We're not young, either of us. You're a healthy young woman. You need a family of your own. And it would fill our hearts with joy if you could give us a grandchild before we die."

She swallowed. Her throat felt tight, as if an invisible hand was squeezing it. It was all perfectly logical, of course, but what about her heart? Her parents had married for love, and she had hoped for the same.

"I'm not asking you to marry either of Simeon's boys," he father went on. "I'm only asking that you give them a chance."

Her gaze met his, but she still didn't speak.

"Just…just a month. That's all I ask of you. Give them a month." He smiled the smile he knew she could never resist. "Is that too much for an old man to ask of his daughter?"

He said it so sweetly that she sighed and looked at the lima bean in her hand. "No, I suppose it's not too much to ask, so I will walk out with them," she said softly. "But I'll tell you now—" she pointed with the empty hull at him "—I'll only truly consider Micah, not Neziah."

"Don't be foolish. You cared for Neziah once. You came close to marrying him."

She tightened her mouth. "That was a long time ago," she said. "Marrying Neziah would have been a mistake. We were—*are*—too different. He isn't the husband for me, and I'm certainly not the wife for him." Memories she hadn't stirred up in years came back to her, and she felt her heart trip. Things had been so complicated with Neziah, and she had been so young. "I'd feel trapped in a marriage with him."

"Then you're wise to refuse him." He leaned closer to her. "But you *are* open to being courted by Micah?"

She nodded. "*Jah*. If you think I should do that, I will."

"And you don't think it's being unfair to Neziah to allow him to believe you're considering his suit?"

"Honestly, *Dat*, I think he went along with Simeon's idea just to please his father. I bet he's trying to figure out at this very moment how to get out of this."

"Then we will put this all in God's hands," her father said. "He's never failed to be there when we need Him. It pleases me that you are willing to walk out with the Shetler boys, and I will place my hopes and prayers on the best solution for all of us."

She nodded, her heart suddenly lighter. "I'll put my trust in Him," she agreed. And for the first time in years, she allowed herself to think of a different life than she had thought hers would be...one that included a husband, a baby and new possibilities.

"I'm hungry," Joel said in Deitsch as Neziah lifted him out of the bathtub and wrapped him in an over-size white towel.

"*Jah*, me, too," Asa agreed in Deitsch. "I want milk and cookies. Can we have milk and cookies, *Dat*?"

"English," Neziah reminded them. "Bath time is English. Remember? Soon Joel will go to school, and the other children will speak English. You wouldn't want them to call him a woodenhead, would you?" Asa wriggled out of his grasp and retreated to the far end of the claw-footed porcelain tub. "Come back here, you pollywog." He captured the escapee and stood him beside his brother. It always surprised him how close they were in size, even though Asa was nearly two years younger. Neziah wrapped his younger son in a clean blue towel and sat him on the closed toilet seat.

The bathroom was large and plain with a white tile floor, white fixtures and white walls and window shutters. Neziah wondered if his boys ever realized how lucky they were not to have to use an outhouse as he had for much of his childhood. He hadn't minded the spiders and the occasional mouse or bat as much as he had the cold on winter nights. He smiled. This modern bathroom with its deep sink, corner shower and propane heater was a great improvement. The Amish elders might be slow to change, but they did make some concessions to the twenty-first century, and bathrooms, in his opinion, were at the top of the list.

"My tummy hurts," Joel said in English, sticking out his lower lip. "I have hungry."

"After the big dinner and all the pie you ate at the Beacheys?" Neziah chuckled. "I don't think so. You'll have to wait for breakfast."

Joel's face contorted into a full-blown pout, and Asa chimed in. "Me hungry, too."

"Bed and prayers." Neziah whisked off the towels and tugged cotton nightshirts over two bobbing heads. "Brush your teeth now, and maybe we'll have time for a little *Family Life* before lights out." *Family Life* was one of the few publications that came to the house, and Neziah made a practice of reading short stories or poems that he thought his sons might like at bedtime.

"But we're hungry," Joel whined, retreating to the Deitsch dialect. "My belly hurts a lot."

"Then cookies and milk will only make it worse," Neziah pronounced. He scooped up Asa and draped him laughing over his shoulder and took Joel's hand. "Bed. Now." Joel allowed himself to be tugged along reluctantly to the bedroom and the double bed the boys shared. Neziah deposited Asa between the sheets then reached down for Joel.

"Read," Asa reminded. He pulled the sheet up to his chin and dug his stuffed dog out from under his pillow while Joel wormed his way over his brother and curled up on top of the light cotton blanket and sheet.

A breeze blew through the curtainless windows on the north side of the bedroom. Like the bathroom, this was a sparse chamber: the bed, a bookcase, a table and two chairs. There were no dressers. The boys' clothing was all hung inside the single, small closet. Neziah pulled up a chair, lit the propane lamp and together they shared a short prayer. Then he took the latest copy of *Family Life* magazine from the table. He'd read to Joel and Asa every night since their mother had died. It was something she'd always done with the children, and although he wasn't as much at ease with reading aloud as Betty had been, he felt it was the right thing to do.

Strangely, the practice, which he'd begun out of a sense of duty, had become the highlight of his day. No matter how tired he was, spending a few moments quietly with his sons brought him deep contentment. Asa, in particular, seemed to enjoy the poetry as much as Neziah did. It wasn't something that Neziah would have willingly admitted to anyone, but he found the sounds of the rhyming words pleasing. Joel preferred the stories, the longer the better, but Neziah suspected that it was simply a way of delaying bedtime.

Tonight, Neziah chose a short and funny poem about a squirrel that stored up nuts for winter and when he had finished it he said, "Sleep well," as he bent to rest a hand lightly on each small head. Joel's hair was light and feathery; Asa's thick and curly. "God keep you both," he murmured.

"Dat?"

"Jah, Joel, what is it? No more about cookies tonight."

"Nay, Dat. I was wondering. Is Ellen going to be our new *mutter?"*

Neziah was surprised by the question; he had wondered how much his sons had understood from the conversations he and Micah had had with their father and later at the Beacheys' table. Apparently, they'd caught the gist of it. "I don't know," he answered honestly. He made it a point never to be dishonest with his children, not even for their own good. "Maybe. Would you like that?"

"Grossdaddi said she might marry you," Joel said, avoiding the question.

"Jah, and…and Uncle Micah, too," Asa supplied.

Neziah chuckled. "A woman can only marry one man, and a man only one woman. Ellen might marry me or your uncle Micah, or she might not marry either of us." Neziah slid the chair back under the table and retrieved a crayon from the floor. It was almost too dark to see, and he wouldn't have noticed it if he hadn't stepped on it. "Good night, boys."

"But will she?" Joel persisted.

He stopped in the doorway and turned back to his

boys. "We'll have to wait and see. If she marries your uncle Micah, she'll be your aunt."

Joel wrinkled his little nose. "Is that like a *mutter*?"

A lump rose in Neziah's throat. Joel had been so small when his mother died, and Asa only an infant. Neither of them could remember what it was like to have a mother. Neziah felt a faint wave of guilt. Had he been selfish in waiting so long to remarry? His sons deserved a mother; everyone in Honeysuckle thought so. But would Ellen be right for them? For *him*?

"Ellen makes good pie," Joel said.

Asa yawned. "I like pie."

"Ellen *does* make good pie," Neziah conceded. "Now, no more talking. Time for sleep." Pretending not to hear the muted whispers behind him, Neziah made his way out of the boys' room and down the stairs. He didn't need a light. He knew the way by heart.

He continued on through the house, past the closed door to the parlor, where a thin crack of light told him that his father was still awake reading the Bible or working on correspondence as part of his duties as a church elder. He walked through the kitchen and outside, making his way to the old brick well that stood near the back porch. The windmill and a series of gears, pipes and a holding tank delivered water to the house and bathroom, but the coldest water came from the deep well. Neziah unlatched the hook and slid aside the wooden cover. With some effort, an overhead pulley, a rope and a wooden bucket rewarded him with an icy drink of water scooped out with an aluminum cup that was fastened to the iron frame.

Neziah leaned against the old brick and savored the water. This was another habit of his. Every night, if it wasn't raining, sleeting or snowing, he'd come out to the well and draw up fresh water. He liked the sensation of the liquid, the rough texture of the bricks and the familiar curves of the bucket and cup. He'd always loved the well. It was a good place to think.

He was still standing there, one hand steadying the bucket, when he heard the rhythmic sound of a stone skipping across water. Instantly, he knew what it was. He finished his water, hung the cup back on the hook and walked across the yard, past the grapevines. At the edge of the small pond in the side yard, he spotted the outline of a figure. The figure tossed something just so and again Neziah heard the familiar splash, splash, splash of a rock skipping across water.

"Only three. Can't you do better than that?" he called, walking toward his brother.

"It's not about how many hops. I'm practicing my technique," Micah explained.

"Ah." By the light of the rising moon, Neziah picked up a stone from the water's edge and slid it back and forth over his fingertips, judging its shape and weight. A good rock had to be flat and oval and just the right weight. "Your spin's still not right."

"My spin is fine." Micah picked up another rock, crouched and threw it.

Four skips.

"You should try standing up to start…like this." Neziah lifted his hand above his head, his wrist cocked, and then swung down and out in one smooth movement. The stone hit the water and skipped one, two, three, four, five times before disappearing beneath the surface.

"Okay, that was just practice. Best two out of three tries," Micah challenged, picking up another rock.

Neziah smiled. The two of them had been competitive for as long as he could remember, mostly because of Micah, he liked to think. To Micah, everything was a game. But the truth be told, though, Neziah had a small competitive streak himself. Or maybe it just bugged him that his little brother was so good at everything. Nothing ever came hard to Micah.

"Best score of three," Neziah agreed. He leaned over to find three perfect rocks. "How was fishing with Ellen?"

"Great."

Neziah could just make out Micah's face; he was grinning ear to ear. "And Ellen really is agreeable to marrying one of us?"

Neziah saw Micah shrug in the darkness as he picked up a stone, ran his fingers over it and rejected it. "It makes sense, and she's a sensible woman. Or haven't you noticed that?"

"You're not usually so quick to seize on one of *Vadder*'s ideas." Finding a near-perfect stone, Neziah passed it to his left hand for safekeeping.

"He's right. It's past time I married. I look at you with your two boys and…" Micah turned to Neziah, casually tossing a stone into the air and catching it. "You know what I think of them. Scamps or not, it's time I had a few of my own. And for that I need a wife. Why not Ellen?"

"She's older than you."

Micah laughed. "That's what she said. Wasn't our *mutter* older than our *vadder*?"

"A year, I think, but there's more than that between you and Ellen."

"If it doesn't bother me, it shouldn't bother you,

brother." Micah stared at Neziah for a moment. The grin came again. "Not having second thoughts, are you? Wishing you hadn't called things off when you did?"

"Of course not," Neziah said a little too quickly. "We walked out together, that's true, but there were differences that we couldn't seem to…" He sighed and stood at the edge of the water. "Your turn."

Micah squatted down. "If my courting Ellen is a problem for you, now's the time to speak up. I like her, but I won't let a woman come between us. Not even Ellen." He let go of his first stone. "Yes!" he cheered when it hopped five times.

"*Dat*'s idea is that she choose between us. I agreed to it, same as you." Neziah tossed his stone and it skipped five times. "I just don't want you to hurt her, Micah. Don't make promises you can't keep."

Micah tossed his next stone. Three skips. He didn't cheer. "Sounds like you've made up your mind to step aside."

Neziah skipped his second stone. Five again. "I didn't say that." He didn't like it when people put words in his mouth.

Micah prepared to toss his final stone, taking his time to glance at the water and get himself into position. "So you do still have feelings for her?" He let the stone fly…five skips.

Neziah thought about it for a minute and realized that as much as he would like to deny it, he couldn't. He raised his hand high over his head, the rock just right between his fingers. "We didn't break up because we didn't care for each other. It was because we weren't sure that we were suited to be the best partners. Marriage is for life, and some differences can loom large as years pass." He let the rock go, spinning it just right… six skips. "I win," he declared.

Micah turned to Neziah, his tone teasing. "So what you're saying, brother, is that you're in?"

"I'm in," Neziah admitted.

"And no hard feelings if she picks me?" Micah opened his arms wide. "Because you know I'm hard for the girls to resist."

"Why would there be any hard feelings?" Neziah asked and then glanced away. He loved his brother, always had, but he wondered, as the words came out of his mouth, how he would feel seeing Ellen marry him. "It's her choice."

"*Goot.* Contest on. And may the best Shetler bring home the bride!" Micah snatched up another stone. "Now come on. One more time. Best out of five stones."

Chapter Four

Ellen pushed her scooter into the yard and scanned the road below. Immediately, she caught sight of a horse and buggy coming from the direction of town. It was Micah. He reined in the gelding and waited. Suspecting that she'd been ambushed, Ellen smiled and walked down the hill toward him.

As she approached the buggy, she saw Micah grinning at her. She knew the expression. He hadn't changed much since he was a mischievous boy. He knew that she hadn't been expecting him to be here this morning, and he looked delighted to have surprised her. "You're right on time today," he called.

"Good morning, Micah." She wasn't sure if the tingling she felt in her chest was pleasure or aggravation. She felt as though everyone around her was trying to manage her, and she liked to make her own decisions. Was this how it was going to be—Micah popping up everywhere, grinning?

"Good morning."

"Did you come to see my *dat*?" she asked, pretending innocence, but certain Micah had come to see her, probably to offer to drive her to the shop. "He's in his workshop." She stood there a few yards from the buggy. "We had the fish for breakfast this morning. Delicious. Thanks for letting me keep them."

"Wish I'd been here to have some with you." Blue eyes twinkling, Micah swung down lightly out of the buggy. He wasn't a small man. He was muscular, with broad shoulders and long legs, but Ellen had always thought Micah moved easily, like a fine-blooded horse. Maybe it was because he liked playing ball. He'd always been more athletic than his brother, Neziah.

"Maybe not. I burned the last batch."

"I doubt that," he said, laughing. "I've come to drive you into Honeysuckle."

Unconsciously, she folded her arms, tightening her mouth into a thin line. If only he wasn't so cute, she thought. It was so hard not to be flattered by Micah's attention, but he got his way far too often because he was hard to resist. "No need to put yourself out. I've got my scooter." She offered a half smile. "I'm sure you've got a lot of work to do today at the sawmill."

He spread his hands in an endearing gesture. "No trouble at all. *Dat* needs turnip seeds. He's a mind to put in a fall crop where we tore down the old shed. So I've got to drive right past your shop. It would be foolish for you to take the scooter when you could ride."

She nodded. "I can see your point. But you can't convince me that you'd drive all the way into town for turnip seeds so early on a workday."

Micah chuckled and reached for her scooter. "I'll put this in the back of the buggy so you'll have a way home after work."

She wasn't letting Micah off so easily. "Tell the truth. This is all part of some scheme of yours, isn't it?"

His smile broadened, showing even white teeth. One thing about the Shetler brothers, Ellen thought. They'd been fortunate enough to inherit their mother's beautiful teeth. Neither Neziah nor Micah had ever had a cavity, while she had made regular trips to the dentist. If she did marry one of them, maybe their children would have good teeth. She almost laughed out loud at the thought. Was she really considering marriage prospects based on dentistry?

"Just giving a neighbor a lift into town." Micah tucked her scooter under his arm. "But that brother of mine will be wishing he thought to come this morning. He can be slow at the start, but he likes a good competition as much as I do. He just doesn't like to admit it." Behind him, the black gelding shook his head and shifted impatiently. Like his owner, the spirited horse was happier when in motion.

"I'm not sure I like being part of a *competition*. And I haven't said I'd ride in with you, have I?" she asked.

It was flattering to have Micah show up bright and early this morning, and she'd enjoyed herself on their fishing expedition the previous evening, but her quiet life was suddenly moving way too fast. Simeon had only mentioned this scheme to her the previous morning, and this would be the second time she and Micah had been alone together in less than twenty-four hours. And riding to town in his buggy would set tongues to wagging. This was a close community, and by nightfall people would be wondering if she and Micah were walking out together.

"Come on, won't you ride into Honeysuckle with

me?" Micah asked. "I'm already here. You might as well." And for the first time this morning, behind the teasing, Ellen could see that it was important to him. He'd be hurt if she refused.

"I suppose you're right," she replied. "It's going to be a warm day for September. Better I arrive looking fresh for my customers."

"You look fine to me," he said as he loaded the scooter into the back of the vehicle. "Is that a new dress you're wearing? I like green on you. It makes your eyes green."

"My eyes are just hazel," she said as she climbed onto the front seat. "I wasn't looking for you to give me compliments, but *danki* for saying so."

"Didn't suppose you were." He slid onto the seat beside her and picked up the reins. "It's one of the things I've always admired about you, Ellen. Your eyes aren't always the same color. They change."

"Change how?" She averted her gaze and brushed at the wrinkles in her apron. Was this what it would be like to court Micah, all compliments and blushing? Was this what she wanted, a woman of her age?

"Just, whatever color dress you wear, your eyes look different. It's one of the things I remember about you from school. Thanks to your eyes, I ate Henry Chupp's whoopie pies four days in a row."

Puzzled, she stared at him. "How and why did you eat Henry's dessert?"

"I bet him that he couldn't guess the color of your eyes each day before you arrived and I could." He grinned at her. "Your eyes were always the color of your dress, and you always wore the same color dress on the same day—green on Monday, blue on Tuesday, then the green again and then the blue. On Friday it was supposed to be a lavender dress, but that week you wore brown instead and ruined the whole thing." He shrugged. "I told Henry your eyes were going to turn purple and I lost."

Her eyes widened. Gambling was forbidden by the *Ordnung*, the rules most Amish communities lived by. "That was very wrong of you. We don't bet on things, not horse races or what color a girl's eyes will be."

Micah grimaced. "I know. Neziah found out and threatened to tell *Dat* if I didn't make it up to Henry. I had to give him my Little Debbie cakes for a whole week. My favorites. The ones with the sticky cream inside."

"Served you right."

"I guess. Neziah was tough. I didn't think he would tell *Vadder* because Neziah wasn't a tattletale, but he had ways of making me toe the line. It was enough to make me give up gambling for life." He sighed dramatically. "My mother didn't buy us store cakes often. Usually we had the ones she made. Those Little Debbie cakes were a big deal."

"I suppose children do make mistakes. How old were you?"

"Let me see. Neziah was out of school and working in the sawmill. I must have been eleven. Teacher used to have you give us spelling tests, and you always gave us more than one chance to spell the word correctly."

"You didn't need an extra chance. You were the best speller in your grade." It was strange to think that the rosy-cheeked boy in suspenders and bare feet she'd once known might now become her beau. Micah had always been a handful, never a bad kid, but always full of mischief. She'd always suspected that Micah had been the one who'd put a frog in her lunchbox when she was in the eighth grade.

"But I always liked you, Ellen. Even though the teacher called on you to be her helper, you never took advantage of it. You weren't silly like most of the other girls. You don't play games with people."

She chuckled. "Don't I? And who used to strike you out when we played softball at school?"

"Not those kinds of games," he said as he maneuvered the horse to turn the buggy around. "You know what I mean. You always went out of your way to include the shy girls in your group. You were popular with the teacher and the other kids, but it didn't make you stuck up."

"I hope not."

"*Nay*, you weren't. If you had been, I'd have noticed." He glanced at her. "You didn't have any brothers or sisters. That's unusual. A lot of people expected you to be spoiled, but you weren't. It was something my *vadder* used to talk about, how much he admired your parents for being sensible raising you."

"I was blessed with good parents," she said softly. "And I think you were, too."

"*Jah*, but I wish..." He trailed off and Ellen suspected that he was thinking of his mother, who'd died so tragically in that van accident, the same accident that had claimed the life of Neziah's wife, Betty.

"That you hadn't lost your mother."

"True enough," he said. "*Dat* never says much, but I know he still grieves for her."

"We have to believe that she's safe in the Lord's hands."

"We do," Micah agreed. "I pity those who have no faith to hold them up in hard times. It must be bitter...

not to know that." His brow furrowed. "Easier by far for me, a man grown, to lose a mother than Neziah's two boys. They need a mother's hand, and if you pick one of us, I hope you'll give them what they're lacking."

"I'd do my best," she promised.

"And that's all anyone can do, I suppose. Do your best." He eased his horse to a halt at the end of the driveway. A car approached, and Micah held the lines firmly. "Easy. Good boy." When the car passed, he said, "Walk on." He flicked the leathers over the gelding's back, and the horse started forward, first at a walk and then at a pace.

"You've done well with him," she said as the buggy rolled swiftly along the blacktop. She had to admit to herself that she liked fast horses almost as much as Micah did. And it was plain to her that he'd taken a roughly broken saddle horse and worked with him until the animal showed amazing promise as a driving horse. When Micah had come home from the auction with the three-year-old last fall, his father and her own had expressed doubt that the gelding would ever make a reliable driver.

"He was bred to be a racehorse," Ellen's father had explained more than once. "Lots of standardbreds turn out to make good driving horses, but that animal was left a stallion too long. I wouldn't trust him."

As usual, her mother had echoed her father's warning, but Ellen had kept her opinion to herself. Micah was known for having patience and a soft hand with horses. She'd secretly hoped that the dire predictions would turn out to be groundless. Flashy the black might be, but the horse Micah called Samson had intelligent eyes, and she'd seen no evidence of meanness around other ani-

mals. This was the first time she'd ridden in a buggy behind Samson, and it was too soon to pass judgment, but
she thought the gelding seemed well suited to his owner.

"He has a sweet mouth," Micah said. "Still a little
nervous around motorcycles, but he's young yet. I think
he'll be fine."

"Worth a lot more than you paid for him," she agreed.
"If you wanted to sell him."

"Which I don't. I'm not fickle. When I commit to
something or someone, I stick with it."

Ellen didn't answer. She felt safer when the conversation was confined to the horse or to other ordinary
subjects, but she felt that Micah was straying from the
shore into deeper water. She slid over on the seat a little, widening the distance between them so that she
could brace her hand on the buggy frame. "Thanks for
thinking of driving me in this morning," she said. "It
was kind of you."

He raised his shoulders and let them fall. "I'm giving my good neighbor a ride to town. It isn't as if we're
crying the banns for our wedding."

He was right, and she felt a little foolish for making
so much of his showing up in her lane this morning.
Slowly, she nodded. "It's just that it takes some getting
used to, thinking of you as a…"

"A suitor?" He smiled and clicked to the horse. Samson quickened his pace. "I thought we'd settled that
last night."

"Did we, Micah?"

"I thought so."

She tightened her grip on the edge of the seat. "But it
doesn't bother you that this was all your father's idea?"

"*Dat* said that he thought that it came as an answer

to his prayers. And maybe it did. We can't say for sure how God tells us what He wants us to do, can we?"

She shook her head. "I guess not."

"Maybe it was me who needed the nudge to see what was right in front of my eyes for years. I like you, Ellen. If it's meant to be and we give it a chance, maybe…"

"Jah." She sighed. "Maybe." A bubble of happiness tickled her insides. Maybe Micah was right. Maybe he'd been right in front of her and she'd never really looked at him. The possibilities were intriguing.

"It *is* just a ride to town," he reminded her. "No strings attached…unless you decide you want them."

They exchanged a smile, and she closed her eyes and savored the sensation of the wind on her face. This was certainly cooler than she would have been pushing her scooter along the road. She found herself relaxing and enjoying the ride.

Micah, never at a loss for words, began to tell her about a pig that had escaped from Roland Yoder's wagon. Roland, a butcher, was taking the animal to his brother's place to be fattened for autumn, but as he was crossing the highway near Bird-In-Hand, a dog ran out at the buggy. The barking frightened the pig that then jumped over the rails and landed in the center of the road. Cars braked and horns honked. The pig ran back and forth causing a traffic jam.

Ellen smiled and waited for the punch line. Like his father, Simeon, Micah's stories were usually funny, sometimes hilarious. But Micah abruptly broke off in midsentence and reined in the horse.

"Did you see that turtle?" he asked.

She glanced over her shoulder. "Turtle?"

"*Jah*, a box turtle. Just a little one, smaller than your

fist." He guided Samson onto the shoulder of the road. "Sit tight," he said. "I'll be right back." Micah handed her the reins, climbed down off the seat and hurried back along the road. About thirty feet behind them, Ellen saw him cross to the center of the blacktop and pick up a round object. "Got him!" he proclaimed, holding the creature up for her to see. He carried the turtle to the far side of the road and put him down safely at the edge of the woods.

"That was a small one," she agreed as Micah got back into the buggy. "You don't usually see them on the roads by the first of September." This wasn't the first time Micah had shown compassion for a small animal. She remembered him catching a six-inch black snake in the school cloakroom. Some of the other boys had wanted him to snap its neck against the shed wall, but he'd faced down two sixth graders and marched the snake to a hedgerow where he released it in the brush.

"I always liked box turtles," Micah said. "When we were young, Neziah and I always wanted to keep them as pets and train them to do tricks, but *Dat* wouldn't let us. He always made us put them back exactly where we found them. He said they have their own territory, and if you move them out of it, they won't rest until they get back to where they belong. A lot of them are run over by cars on the roads. I feel sorry for them, so I always take them across when I see one." He arched an eyebrow. "You probably think it's dumb."

"Nay." She shook her head. "I think it's a decent thing to help any of God's creatures." She smiled in approval. "And I think you are a *goot* person, Micah Shetler, one any woman would be proud to have court her."

* * *

The day at the shop was spotty, customer-wise. No one would come in for an hour, and then two or three cars would stop. Once, Ellen was ringing up an English woman, Dinah was showing quilts to another and two more people were waiting in line. At midday, she and Dinah took advantage of a lull in business to take their lunches out onto the porch where they could eat and watch the tourists and her Amish neighbors drive by.

"I'm so excited about the new watercolors that arrived today," Ellen told Dinah as she took another bite of her ham salad sandwich. There were four watercolors of Amish scenes painted by an ex-Amish woman in another area of the state. Each one showed a different season of the year. Her favorite, summer, was a scene of a mother hanging clothes on a line. Two daughters helped while a baby played on a blanket. All of the figures were shown from the back so that none of the faces could be seen, a concept that fit perfectly with the Plain way of living. The artist had signed her work simply as Rachel. Ellen thought the paintings were beautiful. The colors were soft blues and greens, and the frames were handcrafted of cherry. She expected them to sell quickly because Amish art was a favorite with her out-of-state customers.

"They're fine paintings," Dinah agreed, sipping from a pop can. She cocked her head toward the shop. "Did you hear something?"

"I don't think so." Ellen shook her head. "What do you mean?"

"It's nothing." Dinah adjusted her glasses. "Been hearing things all week. Yesterday morning I was sure

I heard someone on the back porch in the middle of the night. Silly."

"Do you think someone was trying to break in?" Ellen asked, immediately concerned. They had a very low crime rate in Honeysuckle, but she wasn't so naive as to think nothing bad could ever happen.

"No, nothing like that," Dinah pshawed. "I should probably have my hearing checked next time I see that doctor." She returned her full attention to Ellen. "What do you think you want to do with the watercolors?"

"I was thinking that we have enough stock to open the other front parlor." Pushing the last corner of bread into her mouth, Ellen carefully folded the waxed paper and tucked it into her lunch box to use again. "I think pottery and the two Windsor chairs would go nicely in there with the paintings and the carvings. Then we'd have more room in the main area for jams and the display of baby clothing."

"Jah," Dinah agreed. Since she lived upstairs in the apartment, the older woman could easily have gone up to have her lunch, but eating on the porch was one of the highlights of their day. "Remember, I'm leaving early today. Right after lunch. I've got to help Naomi get ready for tomorrow night's haystack supper."

"That's fine, we can do it later in the week. I'd like to hang these paintings on the wall by the fireplace." That section of the old house hadn't been damaged in the fire, and the woodwork and floor were lovely in there. "I'll have Carl make another of those oak benches and put it in there for customers to sit on." Ellen removed a peach from her lunch box. It smelled heavenly. She took a bite, and juice ran down her chin. She quickly wiped it with a napkin. "How is the Blauch baby? Do the doctors know when he can come home?" She knew that the widows' group's upcoming supper was to raise money for Mary's little Raymond. The baby had been born several months early and had been rushed to the children's hospital in Philadelphia.

"Nay," Dinah said. "He has to be five pounds. He's gaining, but he still has some other issues that have to be taken care of. It's a blessing that Mary and David didn't lose him, like the last two."

"But the doctors are hopeful?"

"Jah. Little Raymond is a fighter. My daughter says the doctors expect him to be just fine." She shook her head. "But the hospital bills are awful. The widows' group can help, but I think the whole community will have to pitch in."

Ellen nodded. Their faith didn't hold with insurance, but whenever tragedy struck a member of the church, other families were quick to offer help. There had already been a livestock auction for the Blauch baby, and the youth group was planning a pancake and sausage breakfast. The bishop had asked for donations, and she knew her parents had contributed. It was one of the things that made life in Honeysuckle, and in all Amish communities, fulfilling. There were many families, but they came together as one when someone needed help.

As Ellen finished her peach, a tour bus pulled into the restaurant down the street, and dozens of people got out. Some went into the Mennonite restaurant, but others made their way toward the businesses along the street. A group of three women crossed over and came in Ellen's direction.

"Maybe I should stay," Dinah said. "You might need the help."

"*Nay*, you go on. I'll manage," Ellen said. "Naomi and the others need you."

"Are you coming to the supper?"

"I wouldn't miss it. And I'll bring that tray of brownies I promised you. Folks love their desserts."

Dinah took her leave, and Ellen welcomed her potential customers. One of the three purchased an Amish rag doll and complete set of clothing for it. They were just making their way out when two more women entered. By 2:00 p.m., she'd surpassed the previous day's total. Before the afternoon was over, Ellen had made two more substantial sales and several smaller ones. And in the midst of the confusion, two acquaintances arrived to add and remove food from the large freezers on her enclosed back porch.

Since electricity had been approved by the bishop for use in the shop, Ellen had convinced her parents that it would be worthwhile to buy several commercial freezers. Members of the Amish community paid a fee to rent space in the freezers, so there was constant coming and going. Often friends would come in to chat or drop off crafts for her to sell. It added to her enjoyment in managing the shop.

Just before closing, Lizzie Fisher stopped by to pick up her money from the sale of her quilt. Since there were no other customers in the store, Ellen made tea and the two sat and exchanged neighborhood news. Ellen reached over and clasped Lizzie's hand. She was a petite girl of nineteen who appeared much younger. Far too young to be a widow and a mother of so many, Ellen thought. When her husband suddenly died recently, she was left with seven stepchildren, ranging in ages from three to thirteen. "How are you doing?"

"All right." She nodded. "Everyone has been so kind. Selling that quilt was a big help to me." Lizzie sighed. "The kids have taken the loss of their father very hard. Between trying to help them through this and managing the garden and the children, I don't know when I'll find time to return to my quilting. I keep telling myself that I should be working in the evenings after they go to bed, but..." She shrugged. "The days just keep getting shorter." She finished her tea. "I better run. The kids are with family, but I don't want to be gone too long."

"I understand." Ellen couldn't imagine how full Lizzie's day must be. "If there's anything I can do to help, please let me know."

Lizzie tucked a loose strand of dark auburn hair under her *kapp*. "Are you coming to the haystack supper tomorrow night?"

"Absolutely. My *vadder* and *mutter*, too. They're looking forward to it."

"The kids are, too." She offered a slight smile.

Ellen walked to the door with her. Lizzie limped slightly due to a birth defect, but it had never slowed her down. "You're in my prayers, Lizzie. Please remember that."

"*Jah*, I do. I think prayer is what will get us through this bad time. See you tomorrow night at the supper."

Ellen was clearing away the teacups, the sugar and the milk when the sleigh bells on the front door jingled. To her surprise, it was Neziah who walked into the store, his wide shoulders filling the open doorway.

"Neziah." She laughed, flustered, not sure why.

His two boys peeked around him into the shop.

"Stay where you are," he warned them.

"It's all right. They can come in." Ellen walked toward them, drying her hands on her apron.

"Not unless you want half the things in your shop broken. A store is no place for them. Where they go, trouble follows."

Ellen wasn't sure how to respond; his observation was accurate. Instead, she just smiled.

"You close early on Wednesdays," he said.

"*Jah.* I do."

"And it's past closing time. I was wondering—"

"Ice cream!" Asa blurted.

"We're going for ice cream cones, and Asa and Joel and I thought maybe you'd like to come along," Neziah explained. "Have one with us. I'd like to talk with you."

Ellen knew immediately what he wanted to talk about. He wanted to talk about the fact that he wasn't interested in courting her. He probably just wanted to discuss how they would handle their parents. To her surprise, she was disappointed. Just a little, though why, she had no idea. "Ice cream?"

"Don't you like ice cream?" Asa demanded. "*Dat* said you did."

Ellen smiled at Asa. "*Jah,* I do. Very much." She couldn't believe that he remembered she loved ice cream.

"I think they have strawberry," Neziah said. "I'm buying."

And he remembered her favorite flavor. She sighed to herself. If this conversation had to take place, she thought this was as good a way as any. With the boys with them, it wouldn't get too personal. Ellen's smile widened at the boys. "How could I say no to strawberry ice cream?"

Chapter Five

Neziah and the children waited on the front porch while Ellen went through her routine to close the shop for the day. She locked the side door that Dinah would use when she returned, and the inner back doors. She left the outer doors leading to the enclosed porch unlocked for those who might want access to the freezers. She counted out the cash drawer and locked the contents in an old safe that had come with the property. Then she turned off the lights. As she went out the front door she reversed the wooden sign in a window that read Open to reveal the other side, which declared: Closed, Please Come Again.

"Almost ready," Ellen said as she joined them on the front porch. "My push scooter is around back."

"We can pick it up after we have our ice cream." Neziah lifted his gaze to meet hers for just a second. "We thought maybe you'd ride home with us in the buggy."

"Danki," she replied softly, following him down the steps. She was apprehensive about having this talk with Neziah, but she admired him for coming to her. Maybe he would have some idea about how to deal with their

parents concerning the matter. Of course, she would have to make it clear to Neziah that just because they wouldn't consider each other, that didn't mean she was just going to agree to court Micah. Agreeing to court a man, at her age, was a serious matter. It meant she was considering marrying the man, barring any serious issues. Issues like the ones she and Neziah had encountered when they were courting.

Ellen smiled down at Asa as he trudged down the sidewalk, holding his father's hand, and peering back at her with curiosity on his face. The boy spoke well for a four-year-old, although most of what he said was an echo of his brother. He was an attractive child, but like his father, appeared to be serious in nature.

Several cars passed as the four of them walked along the street, but Honeysuckle was only a small village, so traffic was light. The historic village, consisting of old stone-and-frame buildings, a few stores and a tiny post office in what used to be a bank, had been there since the early nineteenth century. Large trees shaded the homes and sidewalks, their gnarled roots pushing up through the concrete to make the path uneven, but the residents had long grown accustomed to the irregularities. Porches were lined with rocking chairs, window boxes of flowers and friendly neighbors who smiled and waved as Ellen, Neziah and the children passed.

"Afternoon, Ellen." A gray-haired man looked up from his flower bed and raised a garden trowel in greeting. "Nice weather today."

"Not too humid. Fall's in the air," she replied. "Your roses are wonderful."

George beamed. He was a retired high-school principal and an avid gardener who had, several years ago, rescued a neglected Queen Anne–style house on Main Street and restored it.

Although most of the residents of the actual town of Honeysuckle were English, no one stared rudely or pointed fingers at the Amish in their quaint dress. Those *Englishers* who lived and worked there had long come to accept their Amish neighbors and were often on a first-name basis with them. It was a friendly village, a place where Ellen always felt at ease, unlike busy Lancaster or the larger towns that were overwhelmingly worldly.

McCann's Grocery occupied the site of a 1920s schoolhouse, and the parking lot had once been the play yard. Several pickup trucks, a few cars and two gray Amish buggies stood outside the brick store. Baskets of fresh vegetables were displayed on wide tables on either side of the peaked entranceway. Jason, a teenage stock boy, stopped stacking watermelons to greet them.

"Hey, Ellen."

"Hi, Jason," Ellen said. "We've come for ice cream. What's the flavor of the day?"

Jason, a freckle-faced redhead with a flattop buzz, grinned. "Peach. And it's great!"

"I want a double dip!" Joel cried. "*Dat*, can I have a double dip?"

Ellen chuckled, looking down at the boy. "I think a single dip is plenty of ice cream, even for a big man like your *vadder*. You couldn't eat a double if you tried."

"I could!" Joel protested.

"*Jah.*" Asa nodded vigorously. "I could."

Neziah pushed open the door, and the boys rushed past him, dodged around the two checkout lanes and ran toward the ice cream counter, where another Amish family was waiting for their order.

Neziah held the door for Ellen. Their gazes met, and she felt her cheeks grow warm. "*Ach*, sorry," she said quickly. "I didn't mean to interfere." Why couldn't she control her tongue? What Neziah did with his sons was none of her affair.

To her surprise, his expression was more relieved than defensive. He offered a lopsided grin that was similar to his brother's. "You weren't interfering. I agree with you. The servings of ice cream here are huge. One dip should be enough, but..." He shrugged. "It's not easy knowing how strict to be with Asa and Joel when it comes to food." He followed her in. "My *vadder* says that Joel is just healthy, a boy with a *goot* appetite and that his weight will even out over time. But Joel doesn't run around like other boys his age. He always seems out of breath. I think he eats too much, but how do you refuse your child food when he tells you he's hungry?"

"It must be hard for you, being both mother and father." She reached into the pocket of her apron for her change purse, but Neziah stopped her with a wave of his hand.

"I told you this is my treat. I invited you."

"*Danki.*"

The expression in his eyes warmed. "You know how it is, living with parents," he said quietly. "My *vadder* is a wise man, and he has raised children to adults, and it's not my wish to argue with him in his home, but..." He lifted a broad shoulder and let it fall.

"Sometimes it's difficult for our parents to see us as grown-ups," she offered. They reached the ice cream counter where Joel was bouncing eagerly.

"Two scoops," Joel begged.

Neziah laid a hand on his shoulder. "Four cones," he told the teenaged Amish girl behind the counter. "One dip each." He glanced at her. "Strawberry?" She nodded, and he went on. "Two chocolate, one strawberry and a butter pecan."

When they had all gotten their ice cream and Neziah had paid, Ellen took napkins from a dispenser and pointed out the window. "Would you like to go out back to the picnic area? The boys can play on the playground. It's shady and we can eat without worrying about dripping ice cream all over the store."

"*Goot* idea," Neziah agreed. "I just need to remember to come back in and pick up a loaf of bread, and some ginger cookies for my *dat*. He likes a sweet after supper."

"We want whoopie pies," Joel said. He had ice cream on his chin. "The chocolate ones."

Asa was busy licking his ice cream, and for once didn't repeat what his brother had just said.

Neziah glanced at Ellen and then at his son as he led the way to a side door. "No whoopie pies today."

McCann's sold a large assortment of wooden sheds, lawn furniture, children's play equipment, picnic tables and small, portable chicken houses for backyard flocks, all of which were enclosed by a tidy split-rail fence. Store customers were welcome to lunch or snack in the picnic area, and children were free to play on the sturdy swings, climbing walls and slides.

Ellen and Neziah sat down at a picnic table while the two boys ran to explore the play area. For a few minutes they just sat and ate their ice cream and watched the boys. This was something she'd always found admirable in Neziah. He didn't always feel as though he had to keep a conversation going. It was one of the things she remembered fondly from the days when they had courted. The two of them would often go for long stretches of time without speaking. But he had asked her there to talk. She wondered if she should start the conversation.

Neziah pointed out a brown thrasher in the grass on the far side of the enclosed yard. "Bold, isn't he?" He pointed to the little bird. "To be more concerned with what he can scratch out of the dirt than frightened of those two." He indicated Asa and Joel, who'd devoured their ice cream cones and were now attempting to cross a narrow swinging bridge that led to a barn-red tree house at the top of the structure.

"We have a pair of brown thrashers nesting in our orchard," she answered. "I think they raised little ones this summer." She'd always favored the rusty-brown birds with their long tails and bright eyes. Thrashers were in the mockingbird family and usually got along well with other species of backyard birds, unlike the grackles and cowbirds.

Asa had successfully crossed the swaying bridge and was scampering ahead of Joel up the ladder to the small structure on stilts. Joel plopped down on the bridge and dangled his legs over the side of the wooden walkway. "Come on!" Asa yelled in *Deitsch.* Joel shouted back, but Ellen couldn't make out what he'd said.

Neziah finished his last bite of cone and wiped his hands on a napkin. "I'm glad you came for ice cream, Ellen. I wanted to talk to you. Alone."

"*Dat! Dat!* Look at me!" Asa cried from the top of a sliding board.

"I see you!" Neziah waved and looked back at Ellen. "Well, not *exactly* alone," he said wryly. "I'm never alone."

Ellen popped the last bit of cone into her mouth.

He slid a napkin to her. "I wanted to talk to you about this whole courting business. First, I want to apologize for my *vadder*'s—" He shook his head. "I don't even know what to call it."

"You don't have to apologize, Neziah." She wiped her mouth and then her fingers, beginning to relax a little. He was being so kind. She didn't know why she'd been nervous about talking with him about this. They weren't kids anymore. They both knew what they wanted, and neither of them was going to be controlled by their parents. "My *vadder* was a part of it, too," she told him. "I know our parents mean well, but sometimes it might be better if they didn't get so…*involved*."

He smiled and looked down at his hands. "My father, and my brother for that matter, can sometimes border on being meddlesome, but this time I think our fathers might have a point."

Ellen had been watching Asa as he exited the tree house, sliding down a pole. She turned to look at Neziah, thinking she must have misheard him. "You think…" She just stared at him for a moment in confusion. Was he saying she *should* consider both him and Micah for a husband? That couldn't have been what he meant. She could feel herself frowning. "You mean you think our fathers have a point in saying it's time we each thought about getting married?"

He met her gaze. He was the same Neziah she had once thought she was in love with, the same warm, dark eyes, but there was something different now. A confidence she hadn't recalled seeing on his plain face.

"Yes. And I think our fathers are right in saying that you and I, Ellen—" he covered her hand with his "—should consider courting again."

Ellen was so shocked, it was a wonder she didn't fall off the picnic table bench. Again, all she could do was stare at him. This was the last thing on earth she expected to hear from him. The warmth of his hand on hers made her shiver...and not unpleasantly. She pulled her hand away. "I..." She was rarely speechless. And had never been so with him, but she was so taken aback that she didn't know what to say. "Neziah, I..."

"The past is the past," he said when she couldn't finish her thought. "I think it would be fair to say that we were both young then, emotionally if not in years. But we're older. Wiser. Neither of us is the same headstrong, stubborn young person we once were. I know I'm not." He kept looking at her, his gaze searching hers. "Ellen, I was in love with you once and I think—" he glanced at his boys "—I think I'm still in love with you." He looked back at her. "I *know* I am."

She glanced away. The boys were seesawing. The birds were chattering in the trees. She could hear a young woman speaking *Deitsch* through an open window in the store. The world around her seemed normal, but hearing a man—an Amish man—speak of his feelings was not something she normally encountered. Even her father, who had always been a sensitive man, avoided talk of his emotions when he could help it. "I...I don't know what to say, Neziah," she said finally.

"Then don't say anything. Just think about it. Pray about it. It's important to your parents that they see you married. I don't mean this unkindly, but they're aging. As a parent, I understand the desire to see your children happy and cared for." He leaned back, crossing his arms over his chest. "As for me, enough time has passed since Betty died. My boys need a mother and I need a wife. Everything my father said is true." He shrugged. "We live next door to each other. It would be a good match. We would be able to take care of your parents and my father when the time comes that they can't care for themselves. And I would be a good provider. The lumber mill is doing well, and you've sold two pieces of my furniture in your store in the last two weeks."

Ellen studied his face for a moment, so confused, so overwhelmed that she couldn't think straight. Neziah was still in love with her? That made no sense. They had ended their courtship mutually, agreeing they were unsuited as husband and wife. Neziah had never spoken of love before or after the courtship had ended. He had married another woman, had children. He couldn't possibly have been carrying a flame for her for the last ten years. And yet…he sounded sincere.

Could she really consider courting Neziah? Would she actually consider marrying him?

Neziah would be a good catch for any woman. He was hardworking, intelligent and a faithful member of the church community in the prime of his life. While he might not be as strikingly handsome as his younger brother, Neziah's appearance was pleasant. As a widower, Neziah had kept his beard, but it was close-cropped, and Ellen thought that the few flecks of gray scattered amid his dark whiskers gave him a distinguished appearance.

It was a good face, serious but honest, with strong

features and striking eyes. She'd always liked Neziah's dark eyes with their varying shades of brown. When Neziah's gaze locked with hers, she had always known he was giving her his entire attention, that he would listen and give serious thought to what she was telling him. Listen, but not be moved from his own position, she reminded herself.

"Neziah, I...I wasn't expecting you to... This isn't what I was expecting at all." She gave a little laugh. "I thought you wanted to tell me you weren't interested in our fathers' proposal."

"I'm not."

She blinked. She was beginning to feel like she was going too fast on a merry-go-round at the state fair. "I'm confused."

"I'm *not* interested in our fathers' proposal. I've thought this over. I think you and I should begin courting and you should tell my brother to look elsewhere for a wife. The two of you wouldn't be suited for marriage. I've been praying a long time over this and I think *Gott* has answered my prayers. You're the wife for me, Ellen."

She drew back a bit. She didn't like being told what she should do and certainly not by Neziah. "I can't tell Micah I won't see him, Neziah. He was at my house first thing this morning to give me a ride to work. He's very interested in courting me. I told my father... I told Micah I'd consider you both."

He stared at her for a moment, then the smallest hint of a smile appeared. "So you're saying you *would* consider marrying me? You still care for me, don't you?"

This was more like the old Neziah she had always known, trying to force his opinions, his way on her. And yet, not the same. The man she had known, the man she had almost married, had not been one to talk about feelings. Anyone's. "I'll admit no such thing." She felt heat rising in her cheeks, and she got up from the bench.

"Of course you won't. Not yet at least." Another smile. Then he stood. "Joel! Asa! Time to go." He turned to Ellen. "I'm going to go inside and grab the things we need. Meet you out front with the boys?"

She nodded. Once he had gone into the store, she gathered the two little boys and then walked out to the sidewalk. Neziah joined them, carrying a paper grocery sack. The four of them walked the short distance back to the craft shop in silence.

"I'll get your scooter," Neziah said when they reached his wagon. He dropped the groceries into the back. "Is it on the porch?" He didn't sound upset with her. In fact, he sounded pleased with himself.

Walking back to the craft store, Ellen had considered turning down Neziah's offer of a ride home. Right now all she wanted was to be alone and think about what he had said. Neziah was in love with her? Still in love with her, according to him. Was that possible? And how did she feel about him? The truth was, she didn't know. She definitely needed some time by herself, but refusing his ride home seemed childish. "I can get my scooter," she said. "I want to make certain the inner door is locked, anyway." She hurried up onto the back porch landing and then inside.

The freezers were to the right, and she always parked her push scooter against the wall across from them. As she reached down to grab the handlebars of her scooter, her foot struck something and set it spinning away, making a loud clattering sound. It was a soda can. Apparently, someone who'd come to access the freezer space had forgotten it. Ellen tossed the can into the recycle container, went back for her scooter and pushed it out the back door.

Neziah was just coming up the back steps. "I'll take that."

He stowed the scooter in the back of the wagon and then helped her up onto the wagon seat.

The boys were unusually well behaved on the way home. Neziah didn't have much to say, which was fine with Ellen because she'd had quite enough honest talk with him for one day. Her mind was flying in so many directions that she had to take a breath and try to relax and enjoy the summer evening ride, listening to the familiar sounds of the mule's hooves striking the blacktop.

When they arrived safely at her door, she thanked him for the ice cream and the ride home. She said her goodbyes to Asa and Joel and was about to walk away when Neziah called after her, "Will I see you at the widows' supper tomorrow night?" he asked.

She turned back to him. "*Jah*, I'll be helping out."

Normally, she would work late on Thursday evening, but the English high-schooler she'd just hired would work until closing.

"*Goot. Goot,*" Neziah repeated. "See you there, then."

She watched him climb into the wagon; as he headed down the driveway, he touched the brim of his hat and offered the warmest smile. It wasn't big and full of joy like Micah's; it was… Ellen couldn't think how to describe it.

"Ellen?"

Her mother's voice startled her, and she turned to see her standing on the front porch.

"Did Neziah bring you home from the store?"

"*Jah*, he did. I went for ice cream with him and the boys."

Her mother flapped her apron at a stray chicken. "Shoo! Shoo! Get away from my flowers!" She descended the wooden steps and chased the black-and-white hen away from the porch. "Pesky birds. Why your father wants to keep chickens I don't know. All the time they scratch, scratch, scratch at my flowers."

Ellen pushed the scooter toward the shed. "Maybe it would be better to keep them in the pen, *Mam*." The poultry was her mother's and had always been her mother's. In the fall, her mother had always raised extra ducks to sell to other Amish families for the holiday meals. Ellen knew it would be a waste of time to remind her mother that her *dat* didn't let the hens out of the chicken coop, she did. And it was her father who had often said that the chickens were too much work for her *mam*. But her *mam* loved her chickens and could not be persuaded to part with any of them, other than the old hens that went into the stewing pot or the young roosters that ended their lives as Sunday dinner.

By the time she'd put the scooter away, her mother had returned to the porch and was sitting on the steps with her feet in a pan of soapy water. It was another of her mother's odd habits; in spite of having two perfectly good bathrooms in the house, she liked to wash her feet outside at the end of the day. It was fine in summer, but one day in March, Ellen had come home to find her mam soaking her feet on the porch. The afternoon had been a bitter one, but her mother hadn't seemed to notice that it was too cold for bare feet, let alone washing them outside.

Ellen sat down on the steps next to her. "Tomorrow night is the widows' haystack supper. We'll be eating there, so you won't have to cook anything for supper tomorrow."

Her mother smiled and nodded. "I won't forget. They're raising money for that baby, the one in the hospital in Philadelphia. Poor little *bubbel*. We should all remember him in our prayers. You were always a healthy child, *Gott* be thanked. We were not so fortunate with the others, but you came plump as a partridge, screaming to bring the roof down." Her *mam* patted her hand. "A *goot* girl always. Never a trouble to your parents." She chuckled. "Other than to be so choosy about picking a husband. Happy we are to see you courting Neziah."

Ellen glanced at her mother. "I'm not courting Neziah," she corrected gently. "Or his brother, Micah."

Her mother's eyes widened in distress. "But…" she stammered. "They came to supper. Simeon said… Your father said…" Her eyes narrowed and her jaw firmed. "I'm sure you agreed to marry—" she thought for a minute "—one of them," she finished. She looked at her daughter, obviously confused. "Here's Neziah bringing you home. Taking you for ice cream. What are we supposed to think?"

Ellen slipped an arm around her mother. "You're supposed to think I had ice cream with a neighbor and his boys. And before anyone else tells you, Micah drove me to Honeysuckle this morning in his buggy."

Her mother's mouth gaped open and she clasped her hands. "You're courting *both* of them? *Nay. Nay.*" She shook her head. "That will not do. You must remember what is decent for a respectable young woman. Decide between them. One or the other, but not both Shetler boys. What will the bishop say?"

"What will the bishop say about what?" Her father stepped out on the porch.

"*Mam* thinks I'm walking out with both Micah and Neziah." Ellen rose off the step. "I told her that Micah drove me to the shop, and Neziah brought me home."

Her father raised an eyebrow. "Neziah did, did he?"

Ellen threw her father a look of warning. "But I've not agreed to court either of them yet," she said firmly. "I just said I'd…" She searched for the right phrase. "I said I'd get to know them and *consider* courting one of them."

"One of them, now, is it?" her father asked. "I thought you said you wouldn't consider Neziah."

"You must speak to her, John," her mother fussed as she removed her feet from the basin. "You must tell her that people will talk if she runs up and down the roads with two beaus at the same time."

He took her mother's arm. Ellen picked up a towel from a chair and handed it to him.

"Not to worry, Mary. Our Ellen will do the right thing. She always does."

Her mother sat down on the chair, took the towel and began to dry her feet. Ellen dumped the water from the basin into the flower bed. "I'm not worrying," her mother fussed. "It's an easy choice. Such a *goot*-looking young man, that Micah. Such nice hair. If I were her age and still single, I tell you, John, I would not be thinking too long. Some other girl will snatch him up, and she'll have to take the older one."

Her *dat* winked. "So you think our Ellen should marry Micah because of his nice hair?" he teased.

"*Jah*, yellow hair like Joel's. It's like spring butter. So sweet you just want to pinch his cheeks."

"Joel's or Micah's?" her father asked innocently.

Her mother gasped and her hands flew to her cheeks. "*Vadder!* To say such a thing. The little boy. You know what I meant. Little Joel." She sputtered. "All the time, you make jokes, but this is serious. Our daughter must marry, and she has a nice young man who wants to court her and she has to be difficult."

"When she could have a suitor with butter-yellow hair?" Ellen's father asked. Then he chuckled. "Let her be, *Mutter*. She's a sensible girl. She will do nothing to shame us or herself."

Ellen made eye contact with her father, deciding to simply not address his question about Neziah. "I'm promising nothing," she reminded him. "Just thinking on the matter."

"It's all we ask," he replied. "Nothing would make us happier than to see you make a good marriage and nothing would make us sadder than to see you enter a bad one." He held open the door for her mother. "Now, can we go in and have supper before my lima beans and dumplings are cold as last winter's turnips?"

Chapter Six

Ordinarily, suppers and other fund-raisers in the community were held in an Amish home, the same as worship services. Naomi Beiler, leader of the widows' group, often hosted the widows' benefit affairs, but due to the large number of people expected, she and the other members had decided to serve the meal at one of Honeysuckle's Amish schools. That evening was a haystack supper, a community favorite that provided sustenance and fun for everyone.

"Naomi thinks that we may have a lot of outsiders at the supper," Saloma Hochstetler said to Ellen as the two set plates, glasses and utensils on the first of the long tables set up under the trees. "And an Amish family from Delaware is here visiting relatives. They've been in Ohio with their family, and are on their way home to Kent County. Have you met them? Charley and Miriam Byler? She's about my age. They have the sweetest little boy. And Miriam is so friendly. You'll like her."

"I heard they were coming, but I haven't met them yet," Ellen answered, setting down another fork. "I'll be certain to look for them. We want to make them welcome."

Visiting between Amish communities and friends and families was one of the joys of Plain life. Often people would travel hundreds, even thousands of miles to spend time together. It was always wonderful to exchange news with those who shared the Amish faith from other communities in other states.

"It's not too hot tonight. There's a breeze, so there'll be no mosquitoes. Perfect, don't you think?" Saloma moved along her side of the table, keeping pace with Ellen and continued prattling on.

Ellen smiled. It was difficult to keep her mind on what her friend was saying when all she could think of was the possibility of her looming courtship and marriage, or, she corrected herself, her *possible* courtship and marriage. A flash of heat under her skin made her swallow hard.

Micah or Neziah? She was so certain she and Neziah weren't well suited, but after having ice cream with him the previous day, she wasn't as sure. There was something about him that had stayed with her long after they parted.

She was dying to say something to Saloma about the Shetler boys and the agreement she had made with her father concerning them. It would have been a relief to share her confusion—to tell Saloma about the frank conversation she and Micah had had when fishing. About how Neziah had declared that he loved her over ice cream in broad daylight, but she couldn't bring herself to talk about anything so intimate, not even to a dear friend.

Saloma could be trusted not to gossip, but how could

Ellen confide in her when she didn't know her own feelings? She'd already told Micah she would consider courting him. She'd made up her mind that she would not consider Neziah. But then, being with Neziah had stirred up emotions and memories that she'd thought she'd put behind her. She'd barely been able to sleep a wink.

Love. Neziah had said he loved her. He'd sounded sincere, and she'd have given anything to hear that from his lips years ago when they were courting...when they'd almost agreed to have the banns called. How was it possible that he felt this way about her after so long and after all that had happened since: Neziah's marriage, having children, losing his wife in that terrible accident? It didn't seem possible.

"Lizzie told me—" Saloma rolled her eyes, pulling Ellen back into the moment. "Are you listening to a word I'm saying?"

"*Jah*, I am," Ellen said hastily. "Sorry."

"I was saying that the widows put up signs advertising the supper at the restaurant and the general store and the post office. One of the newspapers ran a story on the Blauch baby and how he's in the hospital, so that should bring in more of our neighbors from Lancaster County, English and Mennonite. You know, the regulars who always support our suppers and breakfasts."

"*Jah*. And maybe some tourists will come, as well." Ellen folded a snowy-white cloth napkin beside each place setting. One of Dinah's granddaughters was coming behind them, putting ice in the glasses. Children raced around the tables in spite of their mothers' warnings to not get in the way, and a girl of eleven or twelve years of age sat on the grass urging a chubby toddler to take his first steps. Inside the schoolhouse kitchen, Anne Stoltzfus was frying ground meat with sloppy joe seasoning, and wonderful smells drifted through the open window. "The widows should have a *goot* turnout."

Saloma grimaced. "I suppose, but you know sometimes those strangers don't respect Amish privacy. My *Endie* Rhody had two *Englisher* tourist women walk into her house last week and start taking photographs with one of those telephones that's a camera. Can you believe it?"

Ellen shifted the basket of silverware from one arm to the other. "Your aunt? Really? Which Aunt Rhody?" Saloma had two aunts named Rhody, one who lived in the next church district over and another near Bird-In-Hand.

"Menno's Rhody, the one with bushy eyebrows and the seven boys. Anyway, my *endie* was gathering eggs in her henhouse. She heard a car pull up. You know Uncle Menno sells those funny yard spinners that look like horses and buggies. The wheels and the horses' feet move when the wind blows. Anyway, the English buy them all the time. Nineteen dollars for a little one. Well, before my *Endie* Rhody could get to the house, she heard the kitchen screen door slam."

Ellen hadn't heard about the incident, but she knew of others that were similar. Still, it never ceased to amaze her how insensitive some people could be when they were away from home. "Your aunt found them actually *inside* her house? What did she say to them?"

"I don't know exactly, but she shooed them out and sent them on their way. They— Oh, look who's coming! It's Micah Shetler. *Nay*, don't let him know you're looking!" Saloma grabbed Ellen's arm and cut her eyes in the direction of the road. "I knew he'd be here," she whispered excitedly, still holding on to Ellen. "Isn't he just the cutest thing?"

Ellen glanced at the horse and buggy turning into the schoolyard. That was definitely the Shetlers' family buggy and Samson was pulling it. *"Jah,"* she agreed. "That's Micah."

"Isn't that horse of his beautiful?" Saloma demanded. "If he asked to drive me home, I wouldn't know what to say." She let go of Ellen. "I wish he would. Agnes went out with him a few times, with other couples, not a *date* date. And she said Micah's sweet, not wild, like some people say. But my *mam* would have a hen if I started walking out with Micah. She thinks he's not Plain enough. You know, because he's almost thirty and not baptized yet. My mother thinks that's a disgrace."

Ellen wished she had said something to her friend about her predicament with the Shetler brothers earlier. Saloma finding out later that Micah had driven her to Honeysuckle and that Neziah had driven her home the previous day would be even more awkward to explain now. And Saloma would learn about it. Nothing got by her for long. She would find out, and she would ask why Ellen had kept it a secret. But Saloma babbled on without seeming to notice that Ellen hadn't said anything.

"But you know Micah really well," Saloma continued. She'd paused in setting the table, resting one hand on her hip. As much as Ellen loved Saloma, sometimes her constant chattering and abundant gestures were a bit much. "You're neighbors, and you and Neziah used to walk out together. You know the Shetlers. What do you think? Should I set my *kapp* for Micah?" She chuckled. "Would he make a good husband for me, do you think?" She fluttered her lashes dramatically, making Ellen giggle, too.

Micah drove his horse to the open shed and got out of the buggy. As he was tying Samson to the rail, Bishop Andy approached him with a smiling stranger that Ellen thought might be the visitor, Charley Byler. The three began a conversation.

Ellen moved on to the next table. She hoped Micah would keep his distance at the supper. At least, she *thought* she did. As much as she hated to admit it, a tiny part of her was pleased with Micah's attention. But she didn't want it to cause hard feelings with Saloma.

Only in her midtwenties, Saloma was far from being an old maid, but she worried constantly that no one would ever ask to court her. Apparently, her old community in upper New York State had a shortage of available young men, and Saloma was one of five girls, all but one of marriageable age. Since their arrival in Honeysuckle two years ago, an older sister had married and another, two years younger, had just had her banns cried for a November wedding.

Saloma was a nice-enough-looking girl with blue eyes, rosy cheeks and a dimple in her chin. Her curly hair was tucked into an untidy bun that seemed ready to come down at any moment, and her silver, wire-rim glasses usually perched precariously on her nose. Other than Saloma's habit of talking nonstop, Ellen could see no reason why she didn't have more beaus. She was hardworking, good-natured and vivacious, though she did, sometimes, appear too eager to like others of the opposite sex and be liked in return. Ellen's *mam* thought that Saloma bordered on being fast, but Ellen knew better. Saloma's flirting was harmless, and she would have been shocked and hurt if she suspected anyone thought otherwise.

More buggies were arriving, as well as families on foot. The night's fare was a haystack supper, which meant that food tables would be set buffet-style with huge bowls of seasoned ground meat, shredded cheese, cooked rice, shredded lettuce, onions, tomatoes, peas, raw shredded carrots, chopped celery, green peppers, sliced pineapple, crumbled potato chips, Ritz crackers and corn chips and sunflower seeds. Guests could choose any combination they wanted and top it with melted cheese, salad dressing or sour cream.

Serving at a haystack meal was easy because each person took his or her own plate, helped themselves and returned to the table, where pitchers of iced tea, lemonade and ice water were readily available, as well as yeast rolls, butter and homemade jams and jellies. Part of the fun of the evening's meal was that, unlike Sunday communal dinners, there was no hierarchy in seating arrangements. Tonight the only rule was that everyone ate together, and people sat male, female, male, female. It didn't matter if you were married or single; the point was to interact with friends, guests and relatives in a relaxed atmosphere and make everyone feel welcome. Ellen hoped to keep busy in the kitchen or refilling the bowls of haystack filling. Thus, she reasoned, she could tactfully avoid being seated next to either of the Shetler brothers. Unfortunately, her wish wasn't to be.

No sooner had Ellen and Saloma helped to carry out the last bowl of cheese sauce than Dinah appeared behind them, thanked them for their help and waved them toward a half-empty table of younger people. "You girls go on and enjoy yourselves," she urged. "It was kind of you to help out, but it's time you had some fun."

"But you may need someone to go for refills," Ellen offered.

Dinah chuckled. "I believe Lizzie, Naomi and I can handle that, dear. You two go along now. Find some nice young man and sit by him."

"You heard her," Saloma whispered when Dinah bustled away to seat an English family who'd just arrived. "Maybe I can find an empty seat next to Micah or that sweet Abram Peachy. He was dating someone from one of the other church districts, but I heard she's going with a stone mason from Bird-In-Hand now."

"You'd better hurry," Ellen said. "If Abram's available again, he won't be for long. Look, there he is." She smiled at Saloma and moved away.

There was quite a crowd gathering for the fundraiser. Ellen spotted Neziah's Joel seated between two girls; she didn't see Neziah, Micah or little Asa. She drifted toward the place where the elders were seated, noting that her mother and father, Bishop Andy and a local Mennonite couple had settled at a table. Simeon was there, as well, Asa on his knee. Dr. Gruwell, a popular pediatrician who made house calls to the Amish, was laughing at something Ellen's *mam* had just said, and his wife was deep in conversation with Neziah and Micah's *Grossmutter* Lydia.

Where to sit? Ellen's gaze drifted beyond the schoolhouse to an orchard. When she was small and troubled, she would retreat to a big black cherry tree at the edge of the woods line. She would climb high into the branches, find her favorite fork in the trunk and sit there looking out at the valley until she figured out a solution. She'd loved the solitude, the peaceful sound of the birds and the stirring of green leaves around her. What she needed was an hour or two in a treetop to think.

So many decisions to make…

First, did she want to be married to one of the Shetler boys? Second, which one would she prefer, Micah or Neziah? Marriage to Micah would never be dull. They had so much in common, and their household would always be merry. Or, should she try to reclaim what she'd once felt for Neziah? She sighed. Round and round like a snapping turtle in a barrel. Her thoughts kept coming back to memories that she'd tried so hard to erase.

"Ellen! Come here a moment." Dinah motioned from the end of the food table. "I want you to meet this couple from Delaware." When Ellen joined them, Dinah introduced her to Charley and Miriam Byler.

"It's good to have you here with us," Ellen said. As Saloma had told her, both Charley and Miriam were friendly. Ellen liked them at once. "Don't you have a little boy?"

"We do." Miriam laughed, taking a chair beside her husband. "But he's making the rounds with his cousins, Ava and Zoey King, and I can't seem to get him back. I wish I could scoop the twins up and take them back to Seven Poplars with me. He's a handful, and they're wonderful with him."

"Wayne King and Charley are cousins," Dinah explained. "The Bylers are staying with the Kings."

"Would you like to sit with us?" Miriam asked. Ellen nodded, and she, Miriam and Charley proceeded to take their plates to the buffet tables. Miriam chatted on, telling about their extended vacation, first to Ohio to see an aging aunt, and then to Honeysuckle. "Believe me,

Charley will be busy when we get home. My brothers-in-law and my stepfather have filled in for him on the farm. But my sister Anna will be having a baby next month, and I'd like to give her a hand with canning. Still—" she sighed "—it's been fun seeing all the family and all the sights."

They returned to the table, and Ellen took an empty seat between Charley and Wesley King, the eighteen-year-old brother of the King twins. Charley pulled out his chair then backed away. Ellen's eyes widened in surprise as Micah slid into the seat, taking Charley's place. Laughing, Charley circled the table and sat across from his wife. As he sat down, he and Micah exchanged looks and both grinned. Ellen was sure that it had been a setup.

"Nice supper." Micah's eyes twinkled with mischief.

"Jah," Ellen said. "And excellent company." She couldn't help smiling back at him. She'd been had, but now that he was here, seated close enough for his trouser legs to brush her skirt, it wasn't so bad. In fact, she decided, not unpleasant at all. When had being with Micah not been entertaining? Between him and Charley, they soon had the whole end of the table laughing at their jokes and stories.

Charley was relating an amusing incident about a neighbor's goats when Micah leaned close to her. "Would you ride home with me, Ellen? After the supper?"

"I have to be up early in the morning," she hedged. She wasn't ready to agree to a long buggy ride that might end with Micah wanting to come in and stay until midnight.

"Straight home," he promised. She noticed that

Micah was dressed in his good church pants, a crisp
white shirt and a vest, not in the clean working clothes
that most of the men were wearing. He was wearing
his courting clothes.

She felt a flush of excitement. "I rode with my parents."

Micah poured water into her half-empty glass. "Your
dat won't mind. I'll tell him that you're with me, so he
won't worry."

"All right," she agreed. It had been years since she'd
ridden home from a frolic or a supper with a young man,
and she couldn't resist.

Micah raised his glass of iced tea and clinked it
against a grinning Charley's lifted one. "I told you she
would."

"Would what?"

There was no mistaking that deep voice. Ellen turned
to where Wayne King had been seated a moment ago,
and there was Neziah, slipping into his place. The King
boy was nowhere in sight. Ellen shook her head in disbelief.

"Evening, Ellen," Neziah said.

"Hello, Neziah." She smiled at him, surprised by his
boldness. "Have you met Miriam and Charley Byler?"

Charley stood and offered his hand across the table
to Neziah, and by the time introductions were complete,
the three men were talking, and Ellen was able to eat
her supper. The food was good, but the dessert would
be even better, and she hadn't taken a large portion of
the main course because she wanted to leave room for
peach cobbler and hand-cranked ice cream.

Neziah didn't speak directly to her until she and Miriam rose to start clearing away the empty plates. He laid

a big hand on her wrist. "The boys and I were wondering if you'd like to ride home with us?"

Ellen felt her face grow warm. "I can't. I promised Micah—"

"Too late, big brother," Micah interrupted, leaning forward. "You're going to have to be faster than that. I'm taking Ellen home."

Ellen stepped away from the table and glanced at Neziah. "I'm sorry," she said. "He asked me first."

"Sure," Neziah said.

Micah leaned over again and this time slapped his brother on the back. "Cheer up. Tomorrow's another day."

Gathering a stack of plates, Ellen started toward the schoolhouse. Miriam kept pace with her. "I hope Charley didn't do anything wrong, giving up his chair to Micah. I think he just assumed that you and Micah were walking out together."

Ellen looked at Miriam. She liked her, but she didn't really know her, and it would be difficult to explain the situation to a stranger. "It's complicated," she admitted. "Micah *has* asked me to walk out with him, but…" She took a deep breath. "But so has his brother, Neziah."

"Ah, his *brother*," Miriam said. It was growing dark, but Ellen could make out the young woman's thoughtful expression. "And how do you feel about that?"

"I don't know." Ellen grimaced. "I've known them both all my life, and they're both good men. Either one would make a good husband."

Miriam made a sympathetic sound. "I understand completely. Before Charley and I started seriously courting, there was someone else, a man I had great respect, even affection for. I spent a lot of time worrying over my choosing between them. Both had good qualities to be a husband, but they were different in many ways."

"How did you decide?" Ellen asked, moving closer to her new friend.

"It wasn't easy. I spent a lot of time praying. I knew that God had a plan for me."

Ellen nodded. "I know He does for all of us. But sometimes it's difficult to know what God is saying to us, and what's our own will."

"Jah," Miriam agreed. "What's important is that you take your time, and not be influenced by what others—even your own family—want for you. You have to think carefully, consider what each of you has in common." She smiled warmly. "And you have to follow your heart."

Other women approached, arms filled with dishes and silverware. "We best get these dirty things into the dishpans," Ellen said. "They'll be putting out dessert."

"Can I help with the washing up?" Miriam offered.

"Nay. The boys' youth group has volunteered for cleanup tonight."

Miriam followed her inside. The school kitchen had no electricity and no dishwashing machines, but it did have two double sinks, two large gas ranges, a propane-powered refrigerator and lots of counter space for preparing food. A long table with a butcher-block top ran down the center of the spacious room. Tubs of vanilla ice cream, pies, cakes, cookies and cobblers stood there ready to be dished up and carried outside.

Saloma came in with a huge smile on her face. "Abram sat with me," she whispered to Ellen. "And he asked to take me home." She elbowed her teasingly.

"I saw you sitting between Neziah and Micah. Which one do you like?"

Ellen shrugged. "Maybe neither of them."

"But it's a *goot* start, isn't it, Miriam?" Saloma said. "First you talk, and then you see if you are attracted to each other. Ellen lives next door to the Shetlers. Pretty convenient, if you ask me." She giggled, reached for a tray and began to arrange paper plates on it.

Ellen cut slices from a coconut cake and slid them onto plates. "How are you serving the ice cream?" she asked Dinah.

"Some of the men have brought tubs of ice. We'll put the ice cream in those and dip it out as people come through the line," Dinah answered. "If you would just carry those trays of pie and cake, it would be a big help."

Ellen and Miriam were caught up in the serving and didn't get another chance to continue their conversation. Instead, with Saloma's help, they carried trays of desserts to some of the elders. Ellen found her father and told him that she had a ride home with Micah.

He beamed and patted her arm. "Take your time," he said. "No need to hurry home. A nice night for a buggy ride."

"We're coming *straight* home," she said.

Simeon joined them, Asa trailing him. "Micah tells me that he's taking you home," he said cheerfully. "Glad to hear it."

"I want ice cream," Asa said.

Simeon laughed. "All right, if your brother hasn't eaten it all. Joel already had two slices of cake with ice cream."

"Boys are always hungry," Ellen's mother said. "I love to see a boy with a *goot* appetite."

Ellen was just going when Charley came up with his sleeping son. "I think we'd better get this one home to bed," he said.

Miriam said her goodbyes and hugged Ellen. "We're going home in the morning," she said. "I wish we'd had more time to spend together. You must come and visit us in Delaware. My *mam* has a big house, and there's always room for visitors. Bring your parents, too."

"I'd like that," Ellen said, "but the shop keeps me pretty busy."

"You should take time off once in a while," Miriam insisted. "Come whenever you like. The invitation is always open." She took her little boy from Charley. "As much as I want to get home to my family, it's hard leaving so many new friends." She and Charley walked away.

Soon everyone was leaving. The teenagers were folding chairs and benches, and the last of the guests were finishing their desserts. The evening had been a success, and Ellen expected that the widows' group had raised a record amount of money for the Blauch child. Pulling together was one of the greatest strengths of an Amish community, and Ellen couldn't imagine living anywhere else. Not everyone in Honeysuckle was well-off financially, but they were all rich in friends, a shared faith that never failed them, the warmth of family and a true sense of belonging.

"Ellen?" Micah stood behind her in the gathering darkness. "Are you ready to leave?"

She glanced around. There seemed to be nothing more that she was needed to do. *"Jah,"* she said softly. There was something solid in Micah that she admired.

For all his teasing and lightheartedness, she felt that he really cared for her.

"You're not angry with me for trading seats with Charley?"

"Nay." She shook her head. "I don't mind."

"Good. We'd better be off. Samson's getting restless." He led the way to his buggy.

Ellen's heart beat a little faster. She felt a small shiver of excitement as Micah helped her up into the buggy. She sat up straight on the bench seat and smoothed out her skirt as Micah unhitched the horse and came around to get in on his side. He gathered up the reins and clicked to Samson. "Walk on."

Micah guided the horse into a line of other buggies that were exiting the schoolhouse lane. "You look awfully pretty tonight, Ellen," he said.

"Jah," came Neziah's agreement from the back of the carriage. "Very pretty."

"Neziah?" Ellen and Micah both exclaimed together.

"What are you doing here?" Micah demanded over his shoulder.

"Just riding home, same as you." Neziah leaned forward so he was almost between Micah and Ellen. "You don't mind, do you, Ellen? *Dat* took the boys with him, and I thought I'd just keep you and my little brother company."

Ellen couldn't help but laugh, and soon both brothers were laughing with her. And the ride home that she'd been both anticipating and dreading at the same time turned out to be more fun than she'd expected.

Chapter Seven

"What did you say?" Ellen raised her voice, hoping Saloma could hear her amid the hubbub around them. It was midmorning on Saturday, and they were standing in a line of eager visitors waiting for seats on Storm Runner, a popular roller coaster at Hershey Park. To be heard above the crowd, they had to compete with the metallic reverberations of the rides and the excited conversations of the multitude of visitors who'd come, as they had, to enjoy a day at the amusement park.

"I said, we should go eat after the ride." Saloma moved closer to Ellen. "I'm starving." She took a sip of her oversize soda pop and passed it to her sister Irene.

Two of Saloma's single sisters had come with them, making five girls, including herself and newlywed Susan Brenneman. Susan's husband, Ivan, Saloma's date, Abram, and Micah made up the rest of their party. As a married couple, Susan and Ivan were considered proper chaperones for a Saturday's outing to the amusement park, even though they were younger than Ellen and Micah.

Micah touched Ellen's elbow. "Move up," he urged her. "We'll be next." Being Micah, he'd been the one to arrange the trip. Usually everyone in the party would chip in to hire a van and driver, but today it was Micah and Abram's treat. They'd left home early, and because Hershey Park was less than an hour away from Honeysuckle, the group had arrived just as the gates opened.

The amusement park was the last place Ellen had expected to spend her Saturday, and she'd been uncertain if it was responsible to take off work and accept Micah's last-minute invitation. Saloma had mentioned at the haystack supper that she, Verna and Irene were going today with some friends to celebrate Verna's upcoming birthday. She hadn't said anything about Abram or Micah being part of the group.

Micah had surprised Ellen with an invitation Friday when he stopped by her shop. Since Micah was as persuasive as his father, it was difficult to refuse him, once he'd seized on a plan. The truth was, she had a secret passion for Hershey Park, and she loved the rides, the faster and more thrilling, the better.

"You'd never get Neziah on this," Micah said when the smiling attendant waved them forward. "He gets nauseated on roller coasters."

Ellen shrugged as she allowed Micah to help her into the car. What Micah said was true, but she didn't want to be critical of his brother. Neziah had brought her to Hershey Park when they were walking out together because she'd wanted to come. Because Neziah didn't like the wild rides, though, Ellen had spent most of the day with his little brother, Micah. "Not everyone likes extreme rides," she said. "Nothing wrong with that."

He grinned at her. "It's something we have in common, loving the thrill. And when it comes to roller coasters, you're crazier than I am. You must have nerves of steel."

Ellen chuckled. "Maybe it's just a lack of good sense."

The attendant ushered Verna and Irene and the Brennemans into the seats behind them, but Saloma and Abram had to wait for the next ride. Ellen gripped the over-the-shoulder restraint as the coaster slid away from the boarding station and came to a stop on the track. She'd taken the precaution of knotting her bonnet strings tightly to keep her head covering from blowing off.

She heard the recorded sound of a heartbeat, then a voice from the loudspeaker said, "Get ready, here we go!"

The coaster rocketed forward, and Ellen felt a rush of excitement. Verna and Irene screamed. Their screams mingled with those of other riders, but Ellen only laughed with delight and prepared herself for the first inversion. The ride looped and dipped, flying faster than she'd ever gone on wheels, and was so exhilarating that she wished it would go on forever.

All too soon the coaster finished the last twist and plunge, and the ride was over. The group from Honeysuckle climbed out of the cars, ignoring several tourists who stared at them. "Must be from the city," Micah commented. He tugged his straw hat on and followed Ellen down the walk to wait for Saloma and Abram, whose car had just launched.

"I think Ellen and I will go on by ourselves for a while. Unless you girls want to dare the Skyrush?" Micah offered.

Ellen glanced at him. Leaving the group wasn't exactly following the unwritten rules of a date, but they were in a public place so she didn't see the harm.

Irene giggled. "That was enough for me. When Saloma gets off, we want some cotton candy."

"How about if we meet up for lunch at that place that has the good pizza?" Ivan pulled a small black cell phone from his pants pocket. "Call if you need us. Have fun."

"Call?" Ellen looked at Micah. "You have a cell phone?"

"Just a little one," Micah admitted sheepishly as he tapped his pocket.

"Oh, look!" Irene pointed. The roller coaster had just made its first inverted loop and a man's straw hat went spinning off to sail through the air and finally land in the grass at the base of one of the *Storm Runner*'s massive supports.

Micah laughed. "That looks like Abram's hat."

"How can you tell?" Irene joked and shaded her eyes with a hand to peer at the Amish hat, a small tan object against the green of the close-cropped lawn.

Micah laughed and turned to the group. "Sure none of you want to come with us?" There were no takers, so he and Ellen walked away in the direction of the Skyrush.

"There's a dolphin show," Ellen said, keeping pace beside him. "Would you like to see what time the performances are? After we ride Skyrush?"

"If you want," he said without much enthusiasm. "Thirsty?" He stopped and pointed to a refreshment stand. "They have good lemonade."

"Jah, danki." Micah bought the drinks, and the two found a shady spot to sit and watch the passersby. "It was nice of you to ask me here today," she said.

The last-minute invitation had caused her to suspect that Micah might have had another girl in mind when he made the plans for the excursion, but she wouldn't men-

tion that. She supposed that Simeon's plan had surprised
Micah as much as it had her. Sunday past, her life had
been set in a pattern, and now… Ellen sighed with pleasure. She didn't like to be pushed or pulled into anything,
but now that she'd had a chance to get used to the idea, she
could see all sorts of exciting possibilities. Maybe Simeon
was right. Maybe God had spoken to him, and maybe
this was exactly what He had planned for her all along.

Micah favored her with a broad smile, and she felt
her stomach knot.

"So you're having a good time?" he asked.

She nodded. "I am. I love Hershey Park. It's such a
nice family place."

He removed his hat, brushed his hair back out of
his eyes and rested the hat on his knee. "Did you mind
coming away from the others?"

"Nay," she answered. "I wouldn't have come if I did."

"I suppose you wouldn't." He spun the hat slowly in
a circle, and Ellen suspected that he was trying to sum-
mon the nerve to tell her something.

As she waited, she thought to herself how handsome
Micah looked, with his blond hair and brilliant blue
eyes. His short-sleeve shirt was lavender, his trousers
blue denim and suspenders black leather. She noticed
other women looking at him, and it pleased her that she
wasn't the only one to find him attractive. *I could be
his wife*, she thought. *I have only to say* jah, *and in a
few months the deacon will cry banns for us.* But was
it what she wanted? Maybe it was exactly what she'd
been waiting for. Maybe Micah Shetler was the man
she'd been waiting for all her life.

"Ellen…" He hesitated, and his Adam's apple moved
beneath the skin of his tanned throat. "I started the

classes…with Bishop Andy. For baptism." He glanced up and smiled sheepishly. "He said it was high time."

"And you feel right with your decision?"

Baptism in the Amish faith was a huge step, not to be taken lightly or irreverently. Giving your word before God and the church community meant that you were accepting the Amish lifestyle for the rest of your life. Like marriage, such a decision was final. It was a great responsibility. She had wanted to be baptized since she was fifteen, but her parents had urged her to wait until she was twenty and certain. In the years since she'd pledged her faith, she'd never wavered. Accepting God's word and trying to live as He instructed had been and was her greatest joy. She couldn't imagine any other path but this narrow and steep one.

"It feels right," Micah said soberly. "Like coming home after a hard day's work, or watching the sun come up after a stormy night."

"I'm happy for you," she said and meant it.

"I want you to know that I'm serious about settling down," he went on with continued sincerity. "I want you for my wife. We'll be happy together, I promise you." He glanced around, his sweeping gesture taking in the whole amusement park. "If you accept my proposal, I'll buy us season tickets and bring you to Hershey whenever you like."

She laughed. "But it wouldn't be so special, if we came all the time. Part of the fun is *thinking* about coming. And when we're married, *if* we're married," she corrected, "we'll be too busy to take many days off. We'll have to be responsible members of the church community and set a good example for the younger folk."

"I thought we were doing that already, or, at least,

you were." His twinkling eyes grew serious. "So let's be done with this. Will you marry me, Ellen?"

"We're not even courting yet," she admonished teasingly. When he didn't laugh, she went on. "I'm considering it, Micah. I am," she told him, "but this has all been so sudden. It's a lot to consider. The whole idea only came up a few days ago."

"It's not been just days. You've known me for a lifetime. It might be too soon if we'd just been introduced, but you already know all my faults and my good qualities."

She smiled at him. "And you know mine, as well— the faults, anyway."

He nodded, as if considering. "Bossy, outspoken, stubborn."

She knew he was teasing, trying to get a rise out of her. "You must be pretty desperate to think of marrying such a terrible woman."

He stroked his clean-shaven chin. "How do you think I'll look with a beard?"

"We were discussing my faults."

"Were we? How could that be when you don't have any? You're smart, pretty, hardworking and my father approves of you. What more could I ask for?" He made a wry face. "And you didn't answer my question. I'll be even better-looking when I let my beard grow in, won't I?"

She chuckled. "I don't know. I suppose it will be all right if it doesn't come in sparse like Marvin's." Marvin Smucker, a young man who worked in Simeon's sawmill, was so fair that his hair looked white, and when he'd married, his beard had grown in sparse and stringy.

Micah groaned. "Don't wish that on me. My brother

has a fine growth on his face. Why wouldn't my beard be equally fine?"

"Because Neziah has had to shave every day since he was sixteen, and you…" She tried not to laugh. "Not so much."

He put his hat on and pushed it back at a rakish angle. "How would you know when I started shaving?"

"Well, didn't you just say we've known each other all our lives?" She raised her cup to finish her lemonade. "Shall we tackle that Skyrush line?"

"Absolutely." Micah took the empty cups and deposited them in a trash container. "And then I suppose I'll have to go with you and watch those fish do tricks."

"They aren't fish," she said, "they're dolphins, and watching them perform would be very educational."

"If you say so. But to me, they're just big fish."

They rode Skyrush twice before meeting the others for lunch. Ellen had checked the time for the next dolphin show, and they all went together. The performance was a big hit, so much so that even Micah had to admit that for fish, the dolphins were pretty clever. They rode the Ferris wheel, and then another roller coaster called Fahrenheit. It was thrilling, but Ellen had to agree with Micah that the newer Skyrush was the best one. At his insistence, they rode Skyrush one last time before leaving the park around five, and then stopped at a family-style restaurant for supper before heading home.

The van stopped at the end of her lane, Ellen said her goodbyes to her friends and thanked the driver.

Micah got out with her. "Mind if I come up a while and sit on the porch with you?" He asked.

She smiled at him. "I'd like that." She waited while

he spoke to the driver and paid him from his wallet. Then he joined her again.

He reached for her hand, and she let him enfold it in his. His fingers tightened around hers. Together they walked up the lane. It was the soft time between dusk and dark, and the air was filled with the chirp of crickets and the croaking of frogs. The chickens had gone to roost, and the horse was settled in his stall for the night.

"I had a really good time today," she murmured. "Thank you for asking me." She felt a little breathless, and wondered if the sensation was from the walk up the steep driveway, or from the warmth of Micah's hand.

"Ellen!" Her mother called to her from her rocker on the porch. "*Vadder. Vadder!* Our girl is back from… back from the singing. Did you youngsters have a good time?"

Ellen's father came out the door. He went to her mother's chair and placed an affectionate hand on her shoulder. "The amusement park, *Mutter*. Ellen went to Hershey today with—"

"Neziah!" her mother supplied. "I knew that. Just the wrong words popped in my head. Come sit with us. Did you bring the boys? I do love little boys."

"Mam," Ellen said gently. "Micah took me. Simeon's other son. Not Neziah. Micah. This is Micah."

"Little Micah. Are you the blond one or the dark-haired, chubby one?" Ellen's mother clapped her hands together. "Come and sit down and I'll see if I can find you some raisin cookies and milk."

Ellen swallowed hard. She looked at Micah, a lump rising in her throat. *"Nay, Mam*, he can't stay. He has to go home now." She gave Micah's hand a squeeze and pulled away, hoping that he would understand.

"Jah," he agreed quickly. "But thank you. And thank you for going with me, Ellen. I'll see you at church tomorrow."

"Not far to go this week," she answered. Church was being held at their neighbor's, two farms down. "I'll see you there."

"Thank you for seeing our girl home," her father called from the porch. "Good night."

Ellen walked up the steps, bent and kissed her mother's cheek.

"Did you enjoy yourself, dear?"

"Jah, I did," Ellen said. And she had, but the excitement of her day faded fast. Her mother's remarks worried her. She wanted her father to make a joke of it, to say that they'd put their heads together and decided to play a joke, but he didn't say anything. He just sat in his rocker and sighed. She could feel his distress without him speaking a word.

Ellen rested her hand on the back of her mother's chair. "Are you tired, *Mam?"* she asked.

"She did a lot of baking today," her father explained. "I think it's just that she's tired. Cooking for tomorrow's church dinner. I told her she didn't need to make so many muffins and cookies. We always have plenty."

Ellen felt a wave of guilt for not being there to help her mother. She'd planned to bake tomato and cheese pies tonight. No cooking could be done on a church Sabbath, and not much on a visiting Sunday, every other week. The Sabbath was supposed to be a day of prayer and rest so Saturdays were usually busy ones for the women, preparing food that could be served cold at the break in worship service.

And, she thought, even more guiltily, *if I marry*

Micah—if I marry anyone and leave home, who would be here to help Dat? Her mother was not getting any better. The occasional memory losses and confusion were becoming more common. Trying to brush off the incidences as normal with age was no longer possible. Her mother had some failing of the mind...and it would only get worse with time. How could she think of leaving the household when her parents needed her more than ever?

A misty rain was falling the following morning when Ellen rose to prepare a light Sunday breakfast of muffins, cold cereal, juice and hard-boiled eggs. Her father would have to hitch up the horse and buggy, and the Petershwims would have to host the dinner inside, buffet-style, rather than outside on tables under the trees. It would make for more work for the women and probably more confusion, but the rain would be good for the late crops. Most of their neighbors were farmers, and farmers always welcomed rain in late summer. Ellen didn't mind. She loved the feeling of gathering for worship with her friends and neighbors with rain or snow pattering on the roof and against the windows. It always made her feel safe and content, even if the ride home was somewhat less than comfortable.

She threw a light raincoat on and went out to feed the horse and chickens. She'd heard her parents moving around in their bedroom, and she wanted to have everything ready when they came out to breakfast. Back inside, she washed her hands, put the coffeepot on and poured the tomato juice. She'd dressed for church earlier. All she had to do was trade her work apron for her Sunday apron, cape and bonnet. She'd been up late the night before finishing food preparation, so she had

missed a few hours of sleep, but she felt good this morning. The promise of a day of peace and worship always
lifted her spirits. The problems that had seemed so overwhelming last night had receded. She would find her
answers in prayer, and whatever the outcome was, God
would be her rock, as He always had been.

She had just gotten the butter and jam from the refrigerator when she heard a knock at the door. *Who
would be coming so early on a church Sunday? Pray
God it wasn't an emergency.* Wiping her already dry
hands on her work apron, she hurried to open the door.
To her surprise, Neziah was standing there, wet black
wool hat in hand. "Neziah."

"Ellen." He shifted from one foot to another. "I
thought I'd come over and drive you and your parents
to church this morning. That way, you won't need to
take your horse out in the rain."

"It's early yet," she said, and then felt foolish. Would
he think she was ungrateful? "Please, come in. We're
just sitting down to breakfast."

He smiled and ducked his head as he came into the
kitchen. It was a low sill, and if a man as tall as Neziah
didn't duck, he'd get a rude awakening. "I thought you
might be eating, but I wanted to get here before your
father hitched up the buggy. Save him the trouble."

"It's thoughtful of you."

He glanced at the stove. "And hoping maybe I could
have a cup of that coffee I smell brewing." He grimaced.
"*Dat* heated up last night's coffee. Says making it fresh
is work, and work is against the rules on the Sabbath."

She couldn't resist an amused expression. "If I remember, you once told me that yourself. Didn't you?"

Neziah hung his hat on a hook by the door and went

to the cupboard for a large white mug. "I probably did," he admitted sheepishly. "I admit I was pretty strict the year or two after I was baptized." He offered her another hopeful look. "But I've mellowed since then. I can't see where making a decent pot of coffee to get a man's blood moving in the morning goes against the Lord's law."

She rested her hands on her hips. "Neziah Shetler. You do astonish me sometimes."

"Do I? Good. Because no matter how many amusement parks and frolics my brother takes you to, in the end, you'll come to see that you and I are the best match."

"You think so, do you?"

"I do." His dark eyes grew serious. "I changed in more ways than my choice of Sunday coffee, Ellen. I'm not a foolish boy any longer." He hesitated. "But I am still the man I think you loved."

She tried to think of what to say to that, but found herself speechless. The Neziah she'd known had been unmoving on such things as whether his wife could work outside the house in a public place. It had been one of the chinks in their relationship that had led to their breakup. And what was this with his talk of love? Did he mean love in the same way she did? "I don't…" she began. "I mean—" She spied her father coming through the door. *"Dat."*

Neziah turned to greet her father as he entered the kitchen. "John, a blessed Sabbath to you. I've come to drive you and your family to services."

Her father smiled and offered Neziah his hand. "Have you now? Isn't that thoughtful of him, Ellen?

Well, don't just stand there with your coffee cup. Sit and have breakfast with us. I insist."

"I guess the boys didn't want to come with you?" Ellen asked.

"Oh, Joel wanted to come but I told them to stay put." Neziah pulled out a chair and folded his long body into it. "My boys will ride to services with Micah and my *vadder*. Asa was still abed when I left the house. You don't want to wake him too early or you've got a cranky child on your hands all day. Let him wake easy and he gives no trouble."

"Sounds wise to me," her father said. He took his normal place at the table. "Your mother will be right out. She's good this morning. Real good."

"I'm glad to hear it," Ellen said.

Neziah eyed the muffins hungrily, but she knew he wouldn't touch one until after the silent grace. "Did you make these muffins?" he asked Ellen.

She shook her head. "*Nay, Mam* did."

"Well, I won't complain. She always was a fine cook."

Was, Ellen thought. She hadn't tasted these and hoped that her mother hadn't confused the salt with the sugar again, as she was wont to do. "Don't say you won't complain until you've tasted them," she warned.

Neziah's gaze met hers. "I'll not complain," he repeated. "I'd give your mother no reason to be embarrassed no matter what she fed me. Or you, either." His smile widened. "I told you, I'm a changed man."

"We'll see about that," Ellen teased, and the two men joined her in laughter.

Chapter Eight

It was a short distance from John Beachey's place to Uriah and Nellie Petershwims's big stone farmhouse down the road, but Neziah drove cautiously, as always. His mule Jasper ignored the rain and the loud motor vehicles that occasionally passed the slow-moving gray buggy. Neziah was uncommonly fond of Jasper. He was a steady beast of burden, sure-footed and streetwise. Neziah could brush off his brother's and his friends' jests about mule speed and long-eared transportation for the knowledge that those he cared most about were safer with the big Missouri mule between the shafts. Micah's fancy horse might be showy for the girls, but the animal was too high-spirited for Neziah to want him for a driving horse, especially where the safety of his sons was concerned.

His mother and his late wife had died in a traffic accident when the van they'd been riding in had been struck by a tractor trailer, and Neziah had seen several fatal buggy accidents. He didn't like the idea of taking his chances with flighty horses who might not be steady enough to remain calm when a motorcycle or a wailing fire truck approached. Micah accused him of worrying like a *grossmutter*, and maybe he did, but he was never one to take unnecessary chances. He placed his faith in the Lord but felt that a man had to do his share by showing common sense.

"Looks like we're one of the first to arrive this morning," Ellen's father commented as he climbed down out of the buggy and brushed lint off his black wool coat. Her father was wearing identical clothing to Neziah's—his best go-to-meeting garments, which included the formal *mutze*—a long coat with split tails normally worn only to worship.

Neziah gave the order to Jasper to stand and got out to help Ellen and her mother with the baskets of food they'd brought for the midday meal. Ellen favored him with a warm smile, which went a long way toward easing the discomfort of what had become a downpour. "I'd be glad to carry these to the house," he offered, indicating the containers of muffins and the tomato pies. Even in the rain, she shone like the first star of evening. Most women would be fussing about getting wet, but Ellen took the day in stride with good humor.

"No need," Ellen said. "We can manage." Her father took a tray with the pies, and two of the Pettershwim girls came out with umbrellas to cover them in their run to the house.

"*Will komm*, Neziah," the one in the brown dress said. "Your brother's coming today, isn't he?" She gave him a toothy smile.

"We made schnitz pies yesterday," squeaked the one in lavender. "I know how he loves them."

He returned the greeting politely, trying to recall which of Uriah's daughters they were. There were four girls still at home with their parents, though they were all of marrying age. They always looked alike to him: average height, plain, freckled faces, reddish-blond hair, faded blue eyes that peered out at the world through thick, wire-rim glasses. The Pettershwim daughters all had small hands and feet, squeaky voices and not a single one had eyes that danced like Ellen's.

The girls' father was a man of substance in the community, owning five hundred and twenty acres of prime Lancaster County farmland, a dairy and a harness shop. He had approached Neziah on the subject of his available daughters on more than one occasion. Uriah had pointed out that he was well able to provide good dowries for his daughters. Neziah knew the size of the jointure down to the dollar because not two months ago, Uriah had offered him his choice of any of his girls and the harness shop.

He hadn't been interested. Uriah's daughters were pleasant enough and they were devout members of the church. Any of the four would probably be kind stepmothers to his sons, but he wasn't willing to go into another marriage for practical reasons. He'd set his hopes on Ellen now, and if he couldn't have her, he might not marry at all.

As he guided the mule away from the house, Neziah scanned the long, open shed for his brother's horse and their other family buggy. He'd warned Micah to hitch up the driving mare, a steadier horse than Samson. He hoped Asa and Joel hadn't been too much trouble this morning. Sometimes, getting them fed, dressed and tidy for church seemed harder than a nine-hour day at the sawmill. They needed a mother to see to their needs, that was certain, but not just any woman. They deserved someone who would accept them as her own, love them and take them in hand. It was a great responsibility, and he wasn't certain he could convince Ellen to take on the task.

Keeping an eye out for his boys, Neziah led Jasper into the stone shed, removed his bridle and snapped his halter rope to a round iron ring in the old wall. He unharnessed the mule and pushed the buggy back far enough so as not to make Jasper feel confined. Some men wouldn't bother to unhitch their animals, but there would be a three-to-four-hour service this morning, the break for the midday meal and then at least another hour of final services. Neziah wouldn't see any animal of his standing so long in discomfort, especially with the inclement weather. Jasper was a social creature, and he was content with whatever horse or pony was tied beside him in the shed. Lastly, Neziah took a section of burlap, wiped the wet from Jasper's back and fed him an apple from his pocket. The boys would see that he and the other horses and mules were watered and given hay.

Other families were arriving, and friends and neighbors soon joined Neziah. He waited in the shelter of the shed until his brother and father came in and was pleased to see that Micah had heeded his advice and had hitched up the mare instead of his Samson. He chatted with them all for a few moments before dashing with his sons through a lull in the rain to the huge stone barn where the men were gathering. Asa and Joel ran to play with other boys, and Neziah joined the men. It was always pleasant, the visiting with other men before church: discussing crops and weather, congratulating new fathers, inquiring after the health of older folk in the community and listening to the latest jokes.

They all waited in the barn until the bishop and the two preachers entered the house. When the last elder had taken a seat inside, the married men and widowers filed into the rambling farmhouse followed by younger men and finally the male children. Earlier, teenage boys had removed furniture and carried the rows of benches into the keeping room and two parlors. The big stone house was spacious, giving ample space for an aisle down the middle of the largest room, separating the women's section from the men's.

Neziah settled Asa on his knee; Micah took charge of Joel. The boys couldn't be still for the entire service, but they would wander with other children their age in and out of the kitchen, have a snack and return, hopefully without causing a commotion. Normally, Asa, because of his young age, would have remained with his mother on the women's side. Since Betty's death, Neziah had tried to keep his sons with him during church, even though the women always offered to take them. It just seemed like the right thing to do.

Once the men were seated, the married women entered in much the same order, with the older or infirm given comfortable chairs near the front. Next came the unwed women, followed by the teenaged and younger girls. The widows sat with their own age group, or near friends or family. Many of the women carried babies or small children.

Neziah had eyes only for Ellen. She was tall and graceful, her posture erect, her hair neatly twisted into a bun, her modest *kapp*, apron and dress without a wrinkle. Neziah's throat tightened as he watched her. He admonished himself. It was the Sabbath; his thoughts should have been on the opening hymn, but all he could think of was Ellen and how it would be to drive her to service every worship Sunday and to have her seated beside him.

An elderly man, the song leader, known as the *vorsinger*, rose shakily to his feet, opened the *Ausbund* and began the first hymn of the morning a cappella. There was no accompanying organ or piano, as musical instruments were considered worldly. As every voice joined in the sixteenth-century Anabaptist hymn, the bishop and the two preachers retired to another room to plan the morning's service. Once, an English acquaintance had remarked to Neziah that Old Order Amish worship hymns sung in the high *Deitsch* dialect sounded like medieval chanting. To Neziah, it was natural and right, and the combined voices of his community filled him with peace. Both he and his brother had been blessed with their father's singing voice, and Neziah took more pleasure than he should have from adding his resounding bass to the cherished hymn.

The song had many verses, and it was nearly a quarter of an hour later that it ended and the *vorsinger* led them into "Das Loblied," the traditional second hymn of the service. It was then that Asa wiggled free from his grasp, crawled under the bench ahead of them and darted down the center aisle to where his grandfather was sitting. He climbed up on the bench beside Simeon and began to dig in his grandfather's pocket for the peppermints he usually carried there. Neziah was mortified. His first instinct was to go after the boy, but doing so would only disturb the service more as he'd have to climb over four other men to reach the aisle.

His father bent and whispered to Asa, but instead of heeding Simeon, Asa persisted in digging in first one pocket and then the other. More people were noticing. Then Asa found a wrapped peppermint, laughed and carried his prize back to the aisle. Neziah knew that he had to act, but as he was rising, Ellen suddenly appeared in the aisle, scooped up a protesting Asa and carried him out of the room. With a sigh of relief, Neziah returned to his place and took up the hymn again.

Hours later, when the community stopped for the midday meal, Neziah approached Ellen as she carried a platter of sandwiches from the pantry to the kitchen counters. Due to the weather, the dinner would be inside, but with so many people and not enough tables, there was a lot of commotion. "Thanks for seeing to Asa," he said. "Where is the scamp? When I get my hands on him—"

"He's with Micah." She deposited the sandwiches, wiped her hands on a towel and motioned for him to follow her back into the pantry.

"He's only four," she said. The long, narrow room lined with shelves was in semidarkness, lit only by a single window high on the wall. Jars of canned peaches, green beans and tomatoes rose head high, and cured hams and slabs of bacon hung from the ceiling along with strings of onions and bunches of dried herbs and flowers. Ellen walked to a table loaded with trays of sandwiches. "It was a naughty thing to do during worship, but he's little more than a baby."

"He knows better," he answered. "It's my fault. I let go of his hand to turn the pages of the *Ausbund*."

"But there was no harm done."

She was so close that he could smell the clean scent of her starched apron and *kapp*, and something more. Honeysuckle? He took a step closer. "Ellen…" he began.

She turned to pick up one of the trays. "It was nothing, Neziah. I was on the end of a row. It was easy for me to get to him without bothering anyone. Little boys will be boys."

He raised an eyebrow. "Of course, if the boys had a mother, like you, they wouldn't be into mischief all the time."

She looked at him and pursed her lips. "Don't think you can guilt me into this, Neziah. I'm not the kind of woman who needs or wants to be controlled."

Now she had her dander up, which hadn't been his intention at all. "I was joking." He felt foolish. He didn't want to argue with her. Not ever again. "I didn't mean—"

"Ellen!" a woman called from beyond the sliding door. "Have you got more sandwiches?"

"I have to go," she murmured, holding the tray between them.

"I can carry that," he offered.

She gave him a quick smile that seemed more polite than anything else. "You best not. Excuse me."

He stood there for a minute chastising himself. It had been silly to make that remark. He hadn't meant to guilt her into anything; he really *had* been just teasing. *Attempting* to tease her. Why had he spoken before thinking, before realizing how it might sound to her? When they'd been courting, there had been arguments over what she had seen as controlling behavior in him. And in all fairness, she'd probably been right. But he wasn't that man anymore. Why didn't she see that? It was his own fault for trying to make a joke. Micah was the jokester in the family, not him.

He debated if he should go find Ellen and apologize

or just let it go. Maybe he could bring it up when he took her home. But would it matter what he said? Was he kidding himself to think Ellen would ever choose him over Micah? If he were her, who would he choose?

He emerged from the pantry into the kitchen to find it empty. Or so he thought. As he crossed the kitchen, just out of the corner of his eye, he registered movement on the dessert table. As he turned, he saw a pie sliding across the white tablecloth…with the assistance of a small hand. Then a second hand appeared. The child's fingers closed around the rim of the pie pan and the lemon meringue pie vanished.

It would have been funny, had Neziah not known to whom the hands belonged. He strode across the room and lifted the hem of the spotless white tablecloth.

Two pairs of guilty eyes widened in shock. The pie rested on the floor between them, ruined by little fingers. Joel burst into tears and covered his round face with quivering hands covered in meringue. Asa's mouth gaped, revealing partially chewed pie.

"What do you think you're doing?" Neziah demanded, reaching for the nearest boy, who happened to be Asa.

Asa was too quick for him. He scooted out from under the table and fled past a sturdy woman carrying a tray of bread, cheese and jam.

"Vas is?" Nellie Pettershwim exclaimed. The bishop's wife, coming just behind her, gasped. A third woman, behind her, laughed behind her hand.

"Joel. Come out here," Neziah said in an attempt to regain his composure.

Joel wailed louder, started to crawl out and managed to put a knee in the pie.

Neziah pulled him out gently, stood him on his feet and took a firm hold of his hand. "I'm sorry. Leave the mess, Nellie. I'll clean it up, after I scrub this one off." Joel had so much meringue on his face that he looked as though he was wearing a beard. Lemon custard trailed down his shirt and soiled his pants and shoes. A large gob of lemon clung to one knee.

Neziah looked from the boy to the circle of amused faces that had gathered around him and wished he were anywhere but there. And then, he couldn't help himself. He began to laugh, not simply an embarrassed chuckle that anyone could understand, but a deep, rolling belly laugh.

Which was how Ellen found him when she came back in the room, exposing himself for what he was: an indulgent father who allowed his sons to misbehave at church and then didn't even have the decency to discipline them as they so soundly deserved.

"I don't see that what they did was so terrible," Ellen's father said the next morning at breakfast. They had been talking about Neziah's boys and their exploit with the pie. He held out his cup and she refilled it with steaming hot coffee. "Better to laugh than to have the opposite reaction," he added. "If it had been your grandfather, it would have been off to the woodshed for me. I'd not have been able to sit for a week."

"*Grossvadder* Beachey was strict?" Ellen asked. She had never known him, other than by reputation, because he'd died before she was born. She walked to the stove to bring over the scrambled eggs and scrapple. Toast, stewed prunes and tomato juice were already on the table.

"Very strict," her father said. "He used to quote from the Bible all the time, 'Spare the rod and spoil the child.'"

"So it says. Thankfully, you were of a different opinion. For if anyone was a gentle father, you were, *Vadder*." Her mother smiled at her husband. "Let us give thanks."

This was one of her *mam*'s good days, and Ellen was grateful for that. Her mother had even insisted on cooking most of the meal, and the eggs were fluffy and the scrapple crispy on the outside and perfectly done. Ellen looked around the table and felt a surge of love for her parents. They had raised her with gentleness and patience, and she'd never doubted how much they both treasured her. She slid into her chair and clasped her mother's soft hand. All three closed their eyes and lowered their heads for the blessing.

"And what little boys *wouldn't* want a whole lemon meringue pie to themselves, if they could get away with it?" her mother asked when grace was finished. She laughed. "I might have done the same thing if no one had been looking!"

Ellen's father laughed and added milk to his wife's coffee.

The theft of the pie hadn't surprised Ellen as much as Neziah's reaction. She would have thought that he would have insisted on punishing the children. The old Neziah certainly had been more rigid. It was to his credit that he'd carted the boys off, cleaned them up and seen that they had at least the appearance of a good dinner before the final service. And he'd made not the slightest reference to the incident when he'd driven them home after church. *Maybe he has changed*, she thought.

But the reasons they'd broken up were still lodged firmly in her memory. Many times in the past ten years she'd reminded herself that she'd been wise to call off their courtship when she did...or they did. She had believed that Neziah would be happier with someone whose inclination was more biddable than her own, someone like Betty, the wife he had later chosen. He and Betty had been happy, as far as she could see, and probably would be happy still if she hadn't lost her life at such a young age.

"You remember that I wanted to go into the shop this morning?" Ellen said when there was a lull in the conversation. She had bills to pay and bookkeeping to do. The craft shop was always closed on Sundays and Mondays, but she liked to go in for a few hours on Monday because she could get so much done with no customers to tend to.

"*Jah*, you go on, dear," her mother said. "I'll clean up the dishes. If you go now, you can be home in time for dinner. I'm making succotash with tomatoes and onions. It's a Delaware recipe my sister Sara sent me in her last letter. She lives in Kent County now, you know. Moved there from Wisconsin."

"Your sister?" her father asked. "You talking about Sara Yoder? Isn't she a second or third cousin?"

"*Jah*, *Vadder*, didn't I just say so?" She waved toward the door. "Go on, go on, Ellen. I'll *rett* up this kitchen faster than a horse can trot."

Ellen glanced at her father, and he nodded. "You heard your mother," he said. "We'll be fine. If she needs help, I'm here."

Ellen arrived in Honeysuckle early enough that it was still pleasantly cool. Early September could be overly warm, but it was still cloudy after the previous day's heavy rain, and she suspected there might be another shower before dark. She waved to one of the neighbors walking his dog and pushed the scooter around behind her store. All was quiet. No horses tied at the hitching rail and no hummingbirds at the feeder. The glass feeder with its faux red flowers was almost empty. She'd have to boil up a fresh batch of sugar and water for the hummingbirds this morning. She and Dinah loved to watch the tiny birds hovering in the air and zooming past the windows of the shop.

Ellen pushed the scooter up to the enclosed back porch and opened the wooden door. It was dim inside, and she paused to allow her eyes to adjust to the semidarkness. When she could see again, she wheeled the scooter past the first of the big freezers.

She sensed, rather than saw, the dark lump along the far wall. Alarmed, she stopped short, peering at the object, a blanket or— Suddenly, Ellen's heart began to beat faster. There was a low murmur, and then a figure leapt up out of what appeared to be a sleeping bag.

Uttering a startled cry of alarm, the intruder scrambled past her. "I'm sorry! So sorry!" She rushed through the open doorway and into the backyard. Ellen dropped the scooter, which fell to the floor with a crash. She hurried to the door in time to see the girl with a ponytail, wearing English clothing, fleeing across the backyard toward the line of trees that separated the store property from the house behind them.

"Wait!" Ellen called after her. "Come back!" She picked up a worn pink sneaker the girl had dropped. "You won't get far without your shoe!"

Chapter Nine

The trespasser stopped and turned around. "I'm sorry," she repeated. "I didn't steal anything. I promise."

Ellen came down the back steps still holding the young woman's shoe. "I didn't accuse you of taking anything." Now that she had a better look at her, Ellen was certain she'd seen her before, but not in jeans and a Philadelphia Eagles T-shirt. "You'll need your sneaker." Ellen held it. The footwear had clearly seen better days. The canvas material was worn thin; the lace had broken and was held together with knots.

Ellen heard the scrape of a window raising on the second floor of the house. *"Vas is?"* Dinah called down. "What's all the shouting? Is everything all right down there?"

"Everything's fine." Ellen smiled and waved up at her. "Everything's fine."

Dinah looked down at the girl suspiciously, then at Ellen and slowly closed the window.

Ellen returned her attention to the girl, who was definitely older than she seemed at first glance, probably late teens or early twenties. It was difficult for Ellen to guess the age of *Englishers* because of their dress, hairstyles and makeup. But this girl wasn't wearing makeup, not even lipstick.

She was small and rail-thin with a heart-shaped face and large brown eyes that were shiny with tears she was obviously trying to hold back. Ellen suddenly remembered where she'd seen her before; the jeans and T-shirt had thrown her off. Last time she saw the girl, she'd been wearing a below-the-knee, blue gingham dress with a white apron and scarf—the uniform that all the waitresses wore at the Mennonite restaurant down the street. "Please, take your shoe." Ellen's heart rate had returned to somewhere near normal, and she tried to keep her voice soft as she moved nearer. "I'm not angry. You just startled me."

"Please don't call the police." The young woman was trembling from head to foot. "I'm not a thief." She moistened her lips nervously with the tip of a small pink tongue. "Please don't have me arrested."

There was something so vulnerable in her eyes that Ellen felt her stomach knot. She didn't look like a dishonest person or a dangerous one, but she *did* look desperate...and possibly hungry. "I'm not going to call the police," Ellen said. "Please, come inside. I'll put on a pot of tea, and we can talk about it."

The girl shook her head as she reached for her shoe. "If I could just have my sleeping bag, I promise I won't ever bother you again."

"You work for Margaret, don't you?" Ellen rested her hand on her hip. "At the restaurant? I've seen you waiting on tables, but we haven't met. What's your name?"

The girl stood on one foot while she hastily tugged her shoe over her bare foot. "I shouldn't have sneaked into your house, but…" She wiped her hand on her jeans and extended her hand. "I'm Gail…Bond."

Ellen studied her. There was a definite *Deitsch* accent, enough that she suspected the girl's last name might be something less English. "Well, Gail Bond, you'd best come inside with me before Dinah gets even more curious. There's no need for us to alarm the neighbors, is there?"

Gail shook her head.

"Come on." Ellen waved her toward the door. "Troubles always seem lighter over tea." She led the way back to the house, half expecting the girl to cut and run. Inside the enclosed porch, Ellen removed a ring of keys from her pocket and unlocked the door that led to the back rooms of the shop. Picking up the basket of food her mother had sent for Dinah, she stepped into the back hall.

Gail followed hesitantly as Ellen led her through a storeroom and into the large, old-fashioned kitchen with its rose-patterned linoleum floor, vintage Hoosier's cupboard and round oak table. "The whole building used to be a single-family home once," Ellen explained as she switched on an electric light.

The kitchen of the original house remained, altered over so many years and changes of owners, and rebuilt after the fire destroyed the floor and built-in cabinets. Nothing was fancy, but the twenty-year-old stove and aging refrigerator worked well enough, and there was hot and cold running water.

"You're Amish." Gail glanced up at the overhead light fixture. "You're not supposed to use electricity."

"*Nay*, I'm not supposed to use electricity," Ellen agreed. She filled the teakettle with water and put it on the stove to heat. "But because this is a business, we have to have a telephone, electricity, even a computer. Our Bishop Andy is understanding. He allows modern conveniences for commercial establishments, within reason. Please, sit down." She waved toward the table.

"I really shouldn't," Gail protested, hovering in the doorway. "It was wrong of me to sleep here. The only reason I did," she added hesitantly, "was because it rained yesterday, and I didn't have anywhere else to go."

Ellen thought about the sounds Dinah thought she had heard, and the empty soda can she herself had found. "But this isn't the first time you slept on my porch, is it?"

Gail shook her head slowly.

"Thank you for being honest." Ellen pointed to a closed door. "That hallway leads to the bathroom. It's private. There's no one here but the two of us. Why don't you take a few minutes to freshen up while I make our tea?" Ellen lifted the lid of her basket and removed a container of deviled eggs, several biscuits, a quart jar of canned peaches and a generous helping of sausage.

Gail eyed the food. "I couldn't. You've been kind enough. I should go. I can't be late for work."

"What time do you have to be at the restaurant?"

"Eleven. For the noon shift. I'm not full-time, not yet, but—"

"It's early yet. You have plenty of time. I won't take no for an answer," Ellen said. "You know Margaret wants her staff to be spotless. Why don't you take a shower and wash your hair. There are towels under the sink. We'll have tea and a bite to eat when you're done."

Gail eyed her warily. "Why would you be so nice to me after what I did?"

Ellen thought for a minute. "Because you'd do the same for me."

"I hope so." A shy smile brightened her thin face. "No, I would. I know I would," she answered. "But promise you won't call the police?"

Ellen responded in *Deitsch*. "Nonsense. Of course I won't. And if I'd spent the night on a dusty floor, I'd want to wash up. There's shampoo, soap in there, too. Please, make yourself at home." She smiled at her. "My guess is that you've had a rough time."

Gail didn't have to answer. The look on her face was proof enough.

"How old are you?" Ellen switched back to English.

The girl stared down at small hands, nails bitten to the quick. "Nineteen."

"Really?" She could be younger, and Ellen didn't want to encourage an underage runaway.

"Nineteen years and two months." The certainty in Gail's answer made Ellen believe that she was being truthful. Gail hovered by the table, hands trembling, clearly wanting to stay, clearly needing a friend.

"And you're Amish, like me."

"*Was* Amish. I was raised in the faith." Gail swallowed and looked down at the floor. "I ran away…" She raised her head and met Ellen's gaze. "You must think that I'm a terrible person."

Ellen chuckled. "I'll think you're a foolish person if you don't go in there and have a shower."

Gail was in and out of the shower in less than ten minutes, face scrubbed shiny clean, hair pulled back tight into a finger-combed ponytail, looking all of fourteen. She came back into the room shyly, glancing around as if she expected to see Pennsylvania State

Troopers ready to snap handcuffs on her. "How did you know I was *Deitsch*?" she asked when she decided the coast was clear. "Is it the way I talk?"

Ellen chuckled and waved her to the table. Actually, Gail looked enough like some of her younger cousins to be part of the family. It was hard to miss the fair German complexion and the ruddy cheeks. But more than that, it was the *look* that most young Amish women had, an appearance of unworldliness that you didn't see in the English. "Tea first and then talk," she suggested.

It took some coaxing, but eventually Ellen got Gail to eat two deviled eggs, a biscuit with sausage and a dish of peaches. Ellen was certain that the girl hadn't had breakfast, and she suspected that there had been no supper the previous night.

"When did you last eat?"

"After work Saturday. Margaret lets us have anything from the buffet on Saturday night. They don't serve any of the leftovers on Monday. Someone picks it up for animal feed."

Ellen sipped her tea. "If you've been working, why are you homeless?"

Gail grimaced. "I was renting a trailer with two other girls out on Fox Hole Road. I paid my share every week, but I came home from work one night to find everything gone, even my clothes. All I had left was what I had on me and twelve dollars. The next day the landlord padlocked the doors. I guess Jackie kept my money and never paid the rent." She shrugged. "I thought I could trust her."

"And this Jackie used to work at the restaurant?"

"For almost a year. She was a cashier."

Ellen had heard from Margaret that she'd had to let

a girl go because her register never balanced out correctly at the end of the day. "How long ago was this? That you lost the trailer?"

"About a month ago."

"Where have you stayed since then?"

"Here and there. Once, I slept in a barn. It wasn't bad, but it was smelly, and I didn't want to go to work smelling like sheep. But then I saw people going in and out of your back porch, so I knew it wasn't locked." Gail looked down at her hands, clearly embarrassed. "Usually, I'm out by six-thirty, but your store isn't open on Mondays, so I slept later." She wrinkled her nose and rose to take her plate and teacup to the sink. "Too late, I guess."

"Aren't you scared?" Ellen asked. "Living on the street?"

"Sometimes, maybe a little, but people in Honeysuckle are nice," Gail admitted. She turned from the sink. "Please don't tell Margaret. If she fires me, I don't know what I'll do. It's hard getting a job without papers, and my father wouldn't give them to me."

Ellen understood. Some Amish parents refused to hand over birth certificates and social security cards in an attempt to force their kids to come back home. Amish teens often had only an eighth- or ninth-grade education. Boys who wanted to leave the Plain life had carpenter skills. They could get construction jobs, but most girls knew nothing but homemaking and childcare. The English world could be a dangerous place for a young woman without skills and life experience, especially one who trusted strangers too easily.

Gail washed her cup and plate and set it in the drying rack on the counter. "I should go. This was really nice of you to let me shower. And to share your breakfast with me."

"I'm glad I had something to share."

"I'm going to go." Gail walked to the doorway and picked up her crumpled sleeping bag and big backpack. "Thanks again. I mean it."

"Where will you go tonight?" Ellen asked, carrying her teacup to the sink.

"Don't worry about me. I'll be all right."

Ellen walked toward Gail. "Have you thought about going home?"

"Every day." She hung her head, then slowly lifted it to look at Ellen. "But I'm not going to." She exhaled. "My father is not a 'spare the rod' sort." She looked down at her feet and then back up at Ellen again. "I'll save up, rent a room somewhere and maybe buy a car. Then I might want to go to school, get a high-school diploma." She straightened to her full height. "I can't thank you enough for being so nice to me."

Ellen walked her out through the back and watched her cut across the grass toward the street. Ellen was just walking down the hall toward the front of the shop when Dinah came down the stairs. "Who was that?"

"Um…Gail. You might know her from the diner? She's a waitress."

Dinah made a sound of disapproval but didn't respond. She hustled into the main shop, carrying a broom. "After I've dusted and swept I have some visiting to do. I'll be back late in the afternoon to unpack the boxes that came Friday."

"It's your day off, Dinah. You know I don't expect you to work on your day off," Ellen said, walking around the counter to grab her accounts notebook. She tried to do her accounting on the computer the way her accountant had showed her, but she liked to keep tallies on paper, as well.

There was a knock at the door and both women glanced in that direction. The Closed sign hung in the window.

Ellen bent to see who was at the door. "It's Simeon," she said with surprise. "Let him in."

Dinah went to the door, turned the dead bolt and opened it.

"You're closed today," Simeon said, smiling at them both. "And here the two of you are, hard at work as usual."

"Not so hard," Dinah said, latching the door behind him. "Just sweeping up a bit of dust."

He gave Dinah an appraising look. "I don't know why you want to live in Honeysuckle, away from the community. An attractive woman like you." He winked at her. "Don't you think it's time you remarried?"

"I like my independence," Dinah proclaimed as she resumed sweeping. "You giving advice on getting married is the pot calling the kettle black, Simeon Shetler." She rapped one of his crutches with the bristle end of the broom to make him move. "Even as troublesome, longwinded and free with sweet talk as you are, I imagine someone would have you."

Ellen grinned and went back to looking for her notebook in the bin under the counter. If she didn't know better, she'd think the two of them were sweet on each other.

"You may not believe me, Dinah, but I'm only speaking the truth." Simeon leaned against a set of shelves his boys had made for the store the previous year. They were pine and meant to be utilitarian, but they were beautiful just the same. "You look ten years younger than you are," he went on. "And you can outcook and outsew any young woman in Lancaster County."

"Go on with you," Dinah fussed. "I wasn't born in a celery patch. Everyone knows you can charm the crows off the fence posts with your blather." But Ellen knew by the flush of Dinah's cheeks that she was pleased.

Simeon grinned and glanced at Ellen. "Neziah and I brought that painted hope chest he's been working on. He walked over to your house this morning to tell you it was done, and your mother said you were here. I was going to the mill for feed, so we just brought the chest along."

"Does Neziah need help carrying it in?" she asked.

"*Nay*, we brought Abram with us."

Neziah was a fine craftsman. He built his chests, stools and small tables out of white pine and then painted old Pennsylvania Dutch patterns on them in primitive reds, blues and yellows. His stylistic doves and flowers were particularly popular with the English tourists.

"I can hold the door open, at least." Ellen went out the front door and from the front porch saw the two men unloading the pretty piece of furniture from the back of the wagon.

"Morning, Ellen," Neziah said. "The finish on this is dry, so I thought you wouldn't mind if we delivered it today." He smiled up at her. She returned his greeting and exchanged a few words with Abram.

"Where are your boys?" she asked as the two men carried the chest up onto the front porch and into the store. "Here, let me get the door for you."

"Micah took them fishing," Neziah answered. "The last time we took them to the feed mill, we almost lost one in the millpond and the other in the machinery. Didn't want the same thing to happen today. I try to watch them, but they're unruly."

Abram laughed. "You can say that again. Joel put two worms in my lunchbox last week."

She smiled, remembering Sunday's pie episode. "I hope you didn't get in trouble with the bishop about yesterday."

"Nay," Neziah said. "Bishop Andy came by the sawmill early this morning. Wanted to order oak posts for his new stable. I asked him if he'd heard about my pie snatchers, and he said he'd spent a lot of church services as a boy trying to figure out how to do exactly the same trick and not get caught."

"We're fortunate to have such a wise spiritual leader," Ellen commented as she showed them where to put the chest.

"Jah, but don't forget," Simeon reminded them. "Bishop Andy was God's choice. He doesn't make mistakes in those he leads to head up the faith." He walked slowly with the aid of his crutches to admire the chest. "I think the blue and yellow ones are the best. This should sell quick, don't you think?"

"I believe it will," Dinah said. "I had a customer earlier this month who asked about a hope chest. I didn't even know that English girls collected linens and such for their weddings anymore."

"If you have anyone show interest, you can tell them that Neziah can carve the names of the bride and groom on the front," Simeon said.

Neziah nodded. "Or make something special to order."

"Come back to the office with me, and I'll give you a receipt," Ellen said.

"No need for that, is there?" But he followed her, leaving his father, Abram and Dinah to continue talking about the items that sold best to the tourists.

"It's a beautiful piece," Ellen said, turning on the light in her office. "I don't know where you find the time. You keep pretty long hours at the sawmill."

"Not as much as I'd like," he said. "The mill is our livelihood. I took up the job of sawyer because it was my father's craft, but the woodworking, that I do for pleasure. It calms me—sanding, fitting together the joints. I like taking a length of wood and turning it into something useful."

"And beautiful," she reminded him as she entered his bridal chest in her ledger.

"*Jah*, if you say so. That, too."

He moved closer to her desk, and she looked up at him. He'd put on a clean blue shirt and dark trousers to come to town, but the scents of fresh sawdust, leather and evergreen boughs hovered around him. She knew that scent, and with it came a wave of memories, memories she thought she'd forgotten.

"Ellen, I wanted…*we* wanted to invite you and your parents to supper tonight. It won't be fancy. None of us are great cooks, but it would make me happy if you would join us."

She nodded, wishing he wasn't standing so near. "Will Micah be there, too?"

"*Jah*, he will. Just our family, though. My father, Asa and Joel, my brother and me."

She took a deep breath and let it out slowly. She'd thought to have this evening to herself. But the days were fast coming one after another. One month, she'd promised her father. She'd said she'd give this seeing both Shetler boys a month. But she knew very well that her father, that all the men in her life, including the Shetlers, would expect to hear her opinion after that time. And while no one had suggested she need to choose one of the brothers by October, she knew that's what everyone expected of her. Which left her with what? Three more weeks? Of course, she could choose to stop seeing both Micah and Neziah, but that was seeming more unlikely as time passed. She was becoming accustomed to thinking of herself as someone who would marry in the immediate future…a woman who could look forward to being a mother and managing her own home.

"Thank you for asking me," she said softly. "I would like to come, but…" She hesitated.

"But what?" He leaned over her, making the room seem suddenly small.

"But…" She smiled up at him. "I think it would be best if I came alone this evening, if you don't mind. It might be easier for all of us if we didn't feel that my mother and father were watching every move, listening to every word."

He smiled in response to her smile and nodded. "A good idea. A very good idea." He rested a hand on her desk. "They *do* seem in favor of you marrying a Shetler. I just hope it isn't Micah they're rooting for, because I would make you happiest."

She got to her feet. "I think I'm the one to decide that. It is my future, after all."

"Not just yours, but mine and my sons'. And Micah's, too."

He reached out and brushed her cheek tenderly with a callused thumb, a touch as gentle as the one she'd used when she'd caught a Luna moth trapped inside the screen porch and set it free. Ellen's mouth went suddenly dry at his familiarity.

"You need to think this through carefully," he said quietly. "Because whatever you decide, nothing will ever be the same for any of us again."

Chapter Ten

At six o'clock that evening, after she'd finished the milking and seen that her parents were sitting down to a light supper, Ellen started down a lane that led from her father's property to the Shetlers'. It was an old logging road: narrow, dirt and wooded on both sides. She'd taken care to use mosquito repellent liberally before she began the walk. She carried a wicker basket with cinnamon-raisin sticky buns and her birding binoculars.

Evening was the best time to sight unusual species. She'd heard warblers in the orchard, but the little birds had been fluttering from one heavily leafed branch to another, making it difficult to identify them. She'd seen a magnolia warbler on Saturday and wanted to log it before they took on autumn coloring and became what birders referred to as *confusing fall warblers*, because they looked so much alike. Like many other birds, warblers migrated from north to south, and birds that had spent the summer in Pennsylvania would soon be leaving for warmer climates. Lancaster County was a good place for birding, but not as good as the coastal areas farther east. Someday, Ellen hoped to be able to travel to Chincoteague, Virginia, or the Delaware Bay during fall or springtime migrations.

As she walked, Ellen thought about the girl who had been sleeping on her porch. It pained Ellen to think that the girl might spend another night in a barn. Should she have done more for her than just given her a meal and let her take a shower? Had she failed in charity by merely giving her food and a place to bathe and then sending her off with nothing more than a prayer? Where was the line between helping a stranger in need and putting one's self and family in danger?

Ellen had never hesitated when it had come time for her to join the church, but for Amish young adults, it was a personal decision. Naturally, families wanted their children to accept baptism in the faith, but no one could make that decision for them. In the Honeysuckle community many families had a child who'd chosen the English world, and so long as they hadn't joined the church when they left, they were usually welcomed home with open arms. If she knew Gail better, there wouldn't be a question about helping her—unless Gail had accepted the faith and *then* run away. Then Gail would have been under a ban. No one in the community would be able to eat with her. They weren't even supposed to speak to her. It wasn't meant as punishment but as a way to bring the lost sheep back to the fold; anyone who returned to the faith was welcomed with open arms. Gail hadn't said if she had been baptized or not, and Ellen hadn't asked. Should she have?

Perhaps, after a year or two away, Gail would decide to return to the faith. Staying away was difficult because church was the heart of Old Order Amish lives. Or maybe family was the heart of the church. Ellen couldn't imagine living without the quiet beauty of community worship or living apart from those she loved.

That was one reason Simeon's suggestion was gaining so much favor with her. Amish wives accepted that they would go wherever their husbands chose to live. Some families who'd lived in Lancaster County for generations were pulling up roots and moving out west, where there was cheap land to be had. She'd read that their county had some of the richest farmland in the world, and very little was ever sold. And the majority of that farmland was already in Amish hands, land never to be sold, but passed down to sons and grandsons.

The sound of hooves and the creak of wheels pulled Ellen from her reverie. As she glanced up, Butterscotch came trotting around the bend ahead. Simeon waved from the two-wheeled cart. Joel smiled at her but kept both hands tightly on the reins.

"Guder owed," she called. *Good evening.* She'd half expected either Micah or Neziah to walk out to meet her, but she was surprised to see Simeon and Joel. Simeon waved and returned her greeting. "I'm driving!" Joel shouted. His grandfather slipped an arm around the boy's shoulders and aided him in gently reining the little palomino to a walk and finally a halt. "I drove all the way here," the little boy boasted. "Did you see me? *Grossdaddi* hardly helped at all!"

"Wonderbor," Ellen said, brushing the golden mane out of the pony's eyes and stroking his face and velvety nose. "Your *dat* will be pleased with you."

"We thought you might like a ride up to the house," Simeon explained. "Mosquitoes are pretty fierce out here in the evenings."

"Haven't been bitten," she replied, coming around to climb up into the cart beside Joel. "Mosquito spray."

"Micah always tells me to put it on," Simeon said. "But I hate the smell of the stuff. And it always feels greasy on my skin." He took the leather reins from Joel, gave the pony the command to walk on and turned the cart at the first wide place in the lane. "The boys are putting supper together," he explained. "I have to warn you, I'm not sure what they'll come up with. Neziah wanted to make a chicken stew, and Micah argued for spaghetti."

"*Onkel* Micah burned the biscuits," Joel volunteered. "Asa had to throw them to the chickens."

"Whatever we have, I'm sure it will be fine," Ellen said.

"Neziah and Micah are both trying their best to impress you," Simeon confided. He made a clicking sound, and Butterscotch broke into a trot. "Either one would be a good match for you. Neziah inherits the house, but Micah won't come to a wife empty-handed." He stole a glance in her direction. "You know I've made provision for his future. There's land for him here, and he'll always have a job with Neziah. He's a hard worker, and you'd never do without."

She turned her head to face him. "I'm making no promises, Simeon. I haven't said I'd be willing to marry either of your sons."

"*Nay*, you haven't said, but you and I know you will. Come on, you can tell me." He ran his fingers through his beard thoughtfully as he studied her. "Which one is your favorite?"

"My *mam* likes Micah for me, but I think *Dat* favors

Neziah," she replied. "Although he hasn't come right out and said so."

"But you," Simeon persisted. "Which one do *you* like best?"

"It's not a matter of which I like best, is it? If I choose, I have to choose who would make the best husband for me. Who God has chosen for me."

"*Onkel* says you like him best," Joel put in. "Because if you marry our *dat*, you get stuck with Asa and me." He made a face. "*Grossdaddi* says we are not *goot* boys."

Ellen wasn't sure how to reply to that. Joel was young, but he took delight in being mischievous in order to get attention. So if she agreed with him, she would only add to the problem. "I think that when you go to school and see how the bigger boys behave, you will do better," she pronounced. "Especially since you are the older brother, and Asa watches you to see how he should act."

Joel seemed to consider that for a moment then nodded.

"Would you like to have a new mother?" Ellen asked him thoughtfully. "Or do you like having your *dat* all to yourself?"

"Just me and Asa and *Dat*," he said loudly. "*Onkel* says that a *mutter* will make us wash behind our ears and eat cauliflower and Brussels sprouts every day." He screwed up his face. "I don't like them. Yuck."

She met Simeon's gaze and they both laughed. "It doesn't sound like Micah's playing fairly," she pointed out.

"It sounds like he wants you for his wife," Simeon countered.

Ellen returned her attention to Joel. "I don't have Brussels sprouts with me, but do you like raisin-cinnamon buns and *kuchen*?" she asked. When he nodded, she lifted the cloth on top of the basket, letting Joel get a whiff of the sticky buns her mother had sent. "So, if a *mutter* cooks healthy vegetables," she told him, "she can also bake delicious goodies that small boys enjoy."

Simeon chuckled. "She has you there, Joel. This boy can eat his weight in raisin buns."

"With sugar icing!" Joel exclaimed, and his round little face creased in a grin. "Can I have one now?"

Ellen shook her head. "After supper, and only when your *vadder* or *Grossdaddi* says you may."

Joel frowned and his lower lip came out, but when neither of the adults paid attention, he reached for the pony's reins again. "I want to drive," he insisted. "Let me drive, *Grossdaddi*!"

"*Nay,* enough for tonight." Simeon held on to the reins. "Maybe tomorrow if you get into no trouble tonight." He glanced at Ellen. "You have a *goot* way with *die kinner.* You will make a fine mother, and I know my Irma would be pleased whichever of my sons you choose to marry."

The pony cart jounced into a rut in the dirt road, and Ellen took hold of the seat to keep her balance. "*If* I choose either," Ellen reminded him. But from the satisfied expression on Simeon's face, she knew that he took her agreement to wed either Neziah or Micah as something she had already accepted.

Ellen remembered the Shetler household back when Neziah and Micah were small and their mother, Irma, was in full control of the house. It had been a tidy, pleasant place, smelling of newly baked bread and polished floors. Lines of laundry had stretched outside on Mondays, which was always wash day, and she'd often seen the brothers on hands and knees scrubbing the porch or washing the windows. But this evening, she was clearly in a home managed by three men and occupied by active children.

Wash hung on the line still, although it was past the time to bring it in. And had her mother seen the manner in which the clean clothes had been hung, she would have thrown her apron over her head and wailed in disapproval. Most things had merely been thrown over the line, rather than pinned neatly. There was no order. Towels dragged on the ground, and men's trousers were interspersed with boys' nightshirts, washcloths, undergarments and scrub cloths. Sheets had been tossed over shrubs, and one had slid off and lay in a damp pile on the ground. Worse, blackbirds sat on the clothesline, soiling clean, or what should have been clean, garments and linens.

Inside the house, an effort had clearly been made to sweep the floor and put the kitchen in order. Someone had scrubbed the floor; the bucket full of dirty water and the mop remained in a doorway. The windows needed cleaning, and cobwebs hung from the ceiling. Thanks be, there were no food scraps or unpleasant smells in the kitchen, but in order to reach the table, Ellen had to step over or dodge a whirl-a-gig, a child's toy wagon missing one wheel and turned upside down, and a collection of wooden toy animals. The wagon was attached to Asa, or Asa to the wagon, by a rope looped around his waist, and he was demanding that someone replace the missing wheel.

Neziah stood at the stove stirring a huge kettle of what, Ellen wasn't certain, but he welcomed her in and waved her to a seat at the table. Micah came in right behind them, scooped up Asa and the wagon and carried them both down the hall. "Evening, Ellen," he called over his shoulder. "Glad you could come have supper with me."

There was a loud squawk and Asa squealed with laughter. Joel rushed through the kitchen into the front room and immediately joined the fun. Something heavy fell or was pushed over, and Micah came out with a brown hen tucked firmly under his arm. "Asa let Rosy in again," he explained, stray feathers trailing behind him. Asa, protesting loudly, was right behind him. Micah carried the chicken to the back door and deposited her on the porch. "Rosy cannot come into the house, Asa. Chickens belong outside."

"I want Rosy!" Asa cried.

"You heard your uncle," Neziah threw over his shoulder from the stove. "No chickens in the house. Now, wash your hands for supper. You, too, Joel."

"Something smells good. What are we having? Stew or spaghetti?"

"Neither," Neziah said. "Vegetable soup." He smiled at Ellen as he carried a loaf of store-bought white bread and a cracked saucer containing a stick of butter to the table. "I hope you like vegetable soup. Have a seat."

She glanced at the bread as she sat and wished she'd brought a loaf of her homemade honey-wheat bread with her. She'd almost tucked it into her basket, then thought better of it, not wanting the Shetlers to think she thought they couldn't set a meal to a table.

Micah commanded the seat next to hers. "It's sort

of a spaghetti, stew, steak and vegetable soup," he explained. "What would you like to drink? We have milk, coffee or water. Or..." He winked at her. "Water, coffee or milk."

"Water, please." She noticed gratefully that the faded tablecloth was clean and the mismatched dishes and bowls spotless. The place settings were haphazard. Her spoon had a bent handle, the fork was missing a prong and her knife was tarnished silverplate.

Simeon took a seat at the head of the table. "Crackers? Are there crackers for my soup?" he asked.

"I'll get them." Micah jumped up and went to the cupboard. He rummaged through several tin cans and then another cupboard before producing an unopened box of saltines. He returned with a triumphant grin, and the boys cheering him. But before he reached the table, Neziah pulled out the chair his brother had just vacated and sat beside Ellen.

"Tricked by my own father," Micah declared dramatically. "You're on his side, aren't you, *Dat*? You like him best."

"He does," Joel said. "Jah, *Grossdaddi* likes our *dat* bestest." He giggled. "But I love you, *Onkel*."

Asa pounded his spoon on the table. "Me, too! *Onkel! Onkel!*"

Ellen looked from Micah to Neziah, saw that they were all in on a family joke and laughed with them. Then Simeon motioned for grace, and everyone, even Asa, grew quiet and closed their eyes. When the silent prayer time was over, both Neziah and Micah rose to serve the heavy pottery bowls of thick vegetable soup.

"We like to talk about our day when we finally all get together for supper," Micah said as he placed Ellen's nearly overflowing bowl in front of her. "Did you see anything interesting today?"

"Or bad?" Joel giggled. "We have to tell if we did something bad, too."

"Bad, too," Joel's echo, Asa, added.

Ellen's first thought was to tell them about the stranger sleeping on her porch, but she wasn't certain that was a proper supper topic. Instead, she told them about the magnolia warbler.

"There was a flock of yellow throats here earlier in the week," Neziah said. "And I think I saw one myrtle warbler with them."

"Today," Simeon reminded him. "You're supposed to tell about today."

"What did you see today, *Grossdaddi*?" Joel asked.

"Hmm." Simeon stroked his beard again. "What did I see? I know. I saw a small boy driving a pony cart. A *goot* job he did of it, too."

"*Grossdaddi!* I wanted to tell that," Joel exclaimed. "I did, *Dat*. I drove Butterscotch by myself."

"Did you?" Neziah asked, wide-eyed. "Bet you did a fine job."

"So what else did you do today?" Simeon asked the boy. "See any blue cows?" Both children giggled. "*Nay?* No blue ones? What about flying cows?"

The game went on around the table with much laughter and teasing. Ellen found herself more relaxed than she'd thought possible. She'd been afraid that coming for the evening meal would be uncomfortable, but it was the opposite. She was pleasantly surprised to discover that she felt at home in this house, at ease with these three men, as she had been when she was a child. Even Asa and Joel seemed endearing. They were scamps, certainly, but if their upbringing the past few years had been lenient, it was plain for anyone to see that they were loved and loved back in return.

I could be really happy here, Ellen thought. *I could be an aunt or a mother to these boys and a daughter-in-law to Simeon.* He was a good man and he'd raised decent sons who were devout and faithful to the community.

But which son? she fretted. Which man was the one the Lord wanted her to marry? Because she *would* take one of them. It wasn't an abstract question anymore. Simeon had been right in the pony cart when he'd driven her through the woods. The question was no longer *if* she would choose one of his sons. It was: *which one* would she choose?

"Let me help with the dishes," she offered when they had finished off the last of the cinnamon sticky buns.

"Not tonight," Simeon said, rising from the table. "Come with me, boys. We'll see if I have any peppermints left in my candy can." He glanced at Micah. "You two can do the cleaning up. Ellen is our guest. Plenty of time for her to tend the kitchen when she marries one of you," he called as he left the kitchen, boys trailing behind him.

"I don't mind," she said.

"You heard *Vadder.*" Neziah rose and began gathering up the plates. "Tonight you're our guest."

"You wash, I'll dry," Micah told his brother. "After I walk Ellen home."

Neziah gave him a stern look. "I invited her. I'm walking her home. But not yet. First we visit, talk, like people do."

"And then I walk her home," Micah said.

Neziah's voice grew louder. "You do *not* walk her home. I do."

Ellen stood there in the middle of the kitchen not sure what to say or do. Micah and Neziah sounded a little like Joel and Asa fussing.

"Are you two arguing again?" Simeon called from the parlor. "Micah, stop giving your brother a hard time. Neziah will walk Ellen home. When *you* invite her, you can walk her home."

"Fine," Micah said.

Neziah picked up a damp towel off the sink and tossed it at Micah. *"Jah*, Micah. Stop interfering between me and Ellen."

"I could say the same about you," Micah replied with a grin.

"Boys!" Simeon bellowed.

Eventually, amid much horseplay and teasing between the brothers, the dishes did get washed, dried and put away. Neziah made fresh coffee and they joined Simeon on the porch, where they watched twilight settle around them. The children, tired after a long day, curled up in the nearest male lap until Neziah announced that it was time for baths and bed.

"I can handle that chore," Micah offered. "If you're to have Ellen home before dark, you'd best start out now." Asa and Joel protested, begging to go with their father, but Micah picked up one under each arm and carried them off amid much giggling and pleading for a bedtime story.

Neziah and Ellen ended up talking with Simeon a while longer and they didn't set off down the woods' lane until an hour later. She offered the use of her flashlight, as it was completely dark, with only a partial moon and a few stars illuminating the sky.

"Nay," Neziah said, waving away the flashlight. "I know every bend in the path. Unless you prefer we use it."

"I trust you."

Micah groaned from the dark, somewhere behind them. "Your first mistake, Ellen. Never trust him," he called. "He's sneaky." And when neither answered him, he said, "I could come along and protect you, if you need me."

Neziah shook his head and chuckled at his brother's antics, but then his thoughts became more serious. It had seemed in the beginning as if Micah had seen this as just another contest, but he was beginning to think his little brother really did care for Ellen. That worried him. What if she fell in love with him? And in all fairness, what wasn't there to love about Micah?

"Ignore him," Neziah told Ellen.

"I'd make a *goot* chaperone!" Micah persisted, following them a few yards into the woods.

"We don't need one," Neziah called back.

"You'll be sorry!" Micah shouted. "Remember, I warned you, Ellen."

Ellen laughed and looked up at Neziah. "Maybe he's right." She turned on her flashlight, shining the yellow beam on the rutted track ahead of her. "Maybe we should invite him to come along."

"He's not right," Neziah argued good-naturedly. "This is my time with you, and I'm not going to share."

They walked for a while in easy silence. The sounds around them were familiar and comforting to Neziah… the chirp of crickets, frogs croaking and the rustling of small animals in the leaves and undergrowth. He and Ellen had often walked together in silence during their earlier courtship. Because they both enjoyed bird-watching, it came naturally to them. Talking frightened away some of the species they were attempting to identify. Of course, they'd not see many birds at night, but the dark was nice.

When Neziah was certain they were alone, he said, "It wasn't so bad, was it?" he asked. "Tonight?"

"I had a really nice time," she answered.

He took her hand. It felt small and warm, familiar but strangely exciting at the same time. "There's a fallen log, here, just ahead on the left. Will you sit with me for a few moments?"

He felt her hesitation, but something more…

"Maybe we *should* have taken Micah up on his offer as chaperone," she said teasingly. But he knew she was serious.

"*Nay*, I'd never do anything to threaten your honor. I love you, Ellen. I think I've always loved you."

"I loved you, too, Neziah, but…"

"But?" He led her to the log and they sat, only a few inches of space between them. He was afraid that she was going to say that she loved him like a brother. And that wasn't what he wanted.

"I don't know, Neziah," she admitted. "We're talking about love. Love we had for each other a long time ago. You've been married since then. You were a married man."

"And that bothers you?" he asked quietly. He had known they would have to talk about Betty at some point; he just hadn't be eager to do so. It was a strange place for a man to be. A widower with the possibility of a second marriage with the first woman he ever loved.

"I… It doesn't bother me," Ellen said. "It's just… I…" She exhaled.

"You want to know about Betty. About Betty and me."

"No. No, of course not." She sounded flustered. "That wasn't what I meant. I only…" Again she didn't finish her thought.

Neziah brought her hand to his lips and gently kissed her knuckles. "I don't mind talking about Betty. I think you're right. We do need to talk about her."

He smiled in the darkness, liking the feel of her hand in his. He'd held her hand quite a bit in their courting days, but he didn't remember it feeling this way. So simple. So good. So right. "If you accept my proposal, I'd not have any secrets between us, Ellen." Reluctantly, he let go of her hand.

"All right." Her voice sounded small.

He tightened his hands into fists, then relaxed them and leaned forward and rested them on his knees. "The accident was such a shock. Losing her that way. I've grieved for her over the past three years."

"I understand. It must have been terrible, losing Betty and your mother in that accident, being left with no mother for the children." She let out a long breath. "I didn't know her that well, but she seemed patient and cheerful, hardworking."

"She was," he continued, torn between sharing what was in his heart and being disloyal to Betty. "Ours was a solid marriage. I had great respect for her, and I felt deep affection, as well. It's important that you know that."

Ellen didn't reply, so he went on.

"I will always keep a special place in my heart for her. Every night I pray with my boys, and I try to keep the memory of their mother alive for them."

"As you should."

His throat constricted with emotion. "But it really is time we moved on. Joel has forgotten her, and Asa never really knew her. There's only me, and sometimes… sometimes I have trouble remembering her face."

"Neziah, you don't have to tell me these things. You're embarrassing me."

He rose to his feet, unable to remain seated. "That's not my intention. But I think I need to explain my relationship with my wife if I have any hope that you'll agree to marry me."

She was quiet, sitting in the darkness. He went on. "Betty was nothing like you. She was a gentle girl who accepted without question the traditional role of wife. It was what I believed I wanted when I asked her to marry me. She was brought up in a strict community in Missouri. She had been taught to turn to me as head of the house to make all decisions, even domestic ones that my mother would make without going to my father. Betty and I never argued. Whatever I wanted, she was content."

Insect song chirped and peeped all around them.

"But over time, I learned that it wasn't what I wanted at all," he said. "I would have honored her and our marriage so long as I lived. But…" He stopped and started again. "The love between us was different from the way I feel about you. I've felt guilty sometimes, thinking I should have been a better husband to Betty. Thinking that I don't deserve a second chance to be with you."

Neziah stood in front of her, listening to the sounds of the woods. "I wanted to come to you after my year of mourning had passed, but I didn't know how. I didn't know what to say to you. And the more time that passed, the more impossible it seemed. For me to come to you. Then, a few weeks ago, I went to my father and confided my shortcomings to him."

"Oh, Neziah." She sighed.

The way she said his name made his heart thump in his chest. He had to make himself go on. With every word he spoke, he was afraid he would turn her away from him, but he knew he had to say these things. "You know what he told me?"

"What?" she murmured.

"He said it was time I put aside my mourning for Betty. 'Life is a gift from God,' he said. 'You were faithful to your vows while your wife was with us. You take nothing away from that by seeking happiness in marriage again. My son, if you had been the one lost in that wreck, I would give the same advice to Betty. None of us knows what the Lord has planned for us, but we must strive to accept and make the most of whatever that may be. To do less is to squander the precious gift of life.'"

They were both quiet for a moment. "And he was right," she said.

Neziah sat back down on the log and stared into the dark. "You think so?"

"I do. And I think that, no matter what happens between you and me, Neziah, I think you should take his words to heart and find the wife who's meant for you."

"Does that mean you prefer Micah over me?"

"I didn't say that."

He felt his heart swell with…hope. "So I'm still in the running?"

She turned to him and in the darkness he could feel her more than he could see her. "Now you sound like Micah. This is not a contest." She rose. "I should get home."

He jumped up. "I guess we need to talk about what happened with us. When we ended our courtship. Do you want to talk about that, Ellen?"

To his surprise, she gave a laugh. "I think we've had enough serious discussion for one night, don't you?"

He smiled and fell in step beside her. "Can I hold your hand?" he whispered.

She laughed again and gave him a little push. And then he felt her small, warm hand slip into his, and he grinned all the way to her farmhouse steps.

Chapter Eleven

By seven-thirty Tuesday morning, Ellen was halfway to Honeysuckle on her push scooter. So far, no motor vehicles had passed her, and she'd seen none of her Plain neighbors walking or driving. It was one of the things she liked about leaving early for the shop. She spent so much time in the company of others that she treasured time alone with her own thoughts.

It hadn't been a particularly restful night, and she'd had a lot on her mind this morning when she left her barnyard. She'd enjoyed her visit at the Shetlers, and the walk home had been exciting, but also unsettling. She believed Neziah now when he said he still loved her. The question was, did she still love him or had that period in her life passed? What if her future was with his brother?

The problem was that both Shetler brothers were good men, and she cared for each of them. Being with Micah felt so exciting and new. But she found a certain comfort in being with Neziah, a comfort that came from having a past with a person. She was so confused. How could she tell if her affection for Micah was budding love? Or what if what she felt for Neziah wasn't real, but simply a longing for what they once shared?

And the Shetlers hadn't been the only thing that had troubled her night's rest. She hadn't been able to stop worrying about the homeless girl she'd found on her porch the previous morning. She kept wondering if she had shown Gail due charity or if she'd taken the easy way out, simply giving her a meal and saying a prayer to ease her own conscience. Should she have done more for Gail than offer a few platitudes?

In the middle of the night, Ellen had risen from her bed and gone to the window to stare out at the moonlit barnyard. Standing there, she had wondered where Gail was. Had she taken shelter in someone's stable again, or had a friend offered a spare bed? Did she even have any friends in Honeysuckle? Had Gail eaten or had she gone to sleep on an empty stomach? What if something awful had happened to her in the night and Ellen could have prevented it?

Ellen balanced both feet on her scooter and rolled down a hill, enjoying the feel of the wind in her face. She felt so strange, as if her life had lost its balance, though not in a bad way. Still, it was unnerving. So much was happening so fast. It was only the previous Tuesday that Simeon had made his proposition and changed the entire direction of her life. She felt as though she were caught up in the swirl of wind and tumbling leaves that came before a thunderstorm. One minute, she had been resolved to remain unwed and care for her aging parents, and now she was being courted by not one, but two suitors. Two *serious* suitors.

It was hard to believe that when November came, the traditional time of weddings, she might be one of those happy brides celebrating her marriage with her family and community. It was a dream come true and one that filled her with excitement. The truth was, all the time she'd been assuring herself that it wasn't God's plan for her to wed, she'd been secretly studying each eligible male visitor to Honeysuckle. She'd watched the faces and listened to the voices of strangers for years, but never thought to look next door.

The sound of a horse and buggy coming up fast behind her caught her attention. She laughed aloud, guessing that it was either Micah or Neziah, but she refused to look back over her shoulder to see which one. Whoever it was must have gone up to her house only to find her gone.

Of course, she could be wrong and then she would feel silly. It might be some other member of the Honeysuckle community, but she didn't think so. She supposed that she should feel guilty that she was keeping either Neziah or Micah from starting his workday on time, but instead she felt deliciously giddy.

In her teens, Ellen had read a few forbidden English romance novels where couples walked together through clouds of apple blossoms. Sometimes, sweethearts parted over some misunderstanding and then when all seemed lost, he came galloping back on horseback to fall on his knees and propose marriage. In other stories, the handsome young man and the girl met when he rescued her from danger. They had been chaste stories, nothing like the revealing covers she saw on book racks in Lancaster, but daring enough to make her heart race.

For herself, Ellen had long since given up on romance. She had thought that if she did ever marry, because of her age, it would be to an older widower, someone with grown children or a man who needed a younger wife to nurse him in his later years. Suddenly, everything was different, and she was being swept up in a whirlwind romantic courtship with not one but two men, both of whom professed to love her. She had to admit that she was enjoying every moment of it.

The rhythm of hooves on the pavement grew louder, and seconds later, Micah's showy driving horse drew up beside her. "Morning!" Micah called from the buggy.

"Morning." Ellen pushed harder, and the scooter kept pace with the buggy.

Micah removed his straw hat and waved it at her. "I've come to drive you to town!" How handsome and dashing he looked, with his yellow-blond hair and square, clean-shaven chin.

Breathlessly, she slowed and the horse and buggy pulled slightly ahead. Micah reined in the horse to remain alongside her. "Move over! You're blocking the road," she shouted above the sound of Samson's hooves striking the blacktop.

"I know." He grinned. "It will be all over Honeysuckle if anyone sees us. You better get in."

She wanted to say something clever in reply but she was quickly becoming winded. Surrendering gracefully, she stopped pushing, let the push scooter roll to a stop and got off to walk. Micah reined Samson to a walk and then a halt.

"Does this mean you need a ride?" he asked innocently.

She laughed. Minutes later, her scooter was in the back, and she was sitting on the front seat of the buggy beside him. He shook the reins and gave Samson the signal to walk on. "I thought you'd wait for me this morning because you were feeling so guilty about letting Neziah walk you home last night," Micah teased.

Ellen straightened her *kapp*. It had slipped down, and she'd nearly lost it when she was racing along the road to keep up with the buggy. Why was it that Micah always brought out her reckless nature? She smiled to herself. Life with him for a husband would never be humdrum or boring. He was exciting, and Ellen liked excitement. Didn't that mean they would be a good match? "Why aren't you at the sawmill?" she asked, choosing to ignore his question.

"I had to see you this morning. Wanted to ask you if you'd go bowling with me tomorrow night."

She looked straight ahead. A van full of tourists stared at them through the open windows of a minivan as they passed. Micah grinned and waved. Ellen saw several phones pressed against the windows. Pictures, she supposed. Someone was always trying to take pictures of them, as if they were exotic animals at the zoo. She'd often thought of buying a camera and snapping photos of the tourists, but she supposed that it wouldn't be good for business. You never knew when a tourist might become a customer at the shop, and she was attempting to be a successful businesswoman.

"So, will you?" Micah asked. "Bowling? Pizza after?"

"Just the two of us?"

He shook his head. "Abram's going. And Nat. They're bringing dates. I don't know who, but there will be other girls, so you don't have to worry about me trying to steal a kiss or anything."

She should have chastised him for his inappropriate joke, but when she looked at him he was grinning.

She couldn't help smiling back. "All right. You know I love to bowl."

His grin grew broader, if that were possible.

"I warn you, though," she said. "I might be better than you."

He chuckled and urged Samson into a trot. "That was pretty easy. Neziah thought you wouldn't agree to go with me so easily."

"And if I didn't?" she teased.

"I'd just keep pestering until you agreed." His blue eyes twinkled with mischief. "My brother should know by now that I'm impossible to resist."

Micah left her at the back of the shop with the promise to pick her up the next evening at six-thirty. That would give her time to close up, go home and make certain her parents had their supper before she left to go bowling. In spite of her boasting to Micah, Ellen hoped that she wouldn't be too rusty at the game. She loved bowling, but she hadn't been in more than a year.

As Ellen pushed her scooter up onto the back porch, she couldn't help wondering if Gail would be there again. But everything was as Ellen had left it the previous day. There were no empty soda cans, no sleeping bag and no evidence that anyone had been there since she'd left. She unlocked the inner door and went into the shop. All was quiet; Dinah hadn't come down yet. She put coffee on to brew for Dinah, then went into the office to turn on the computer. There, her gaze fell on a box of baby clothes that she hadn't had time to price and put on display yet. Drawn to the contents, Ellen opened the box. Inside were infant sleepers, dresses, sacques and caps, hand sewn of the softest cotton in green, yellow, lavender and cream. The sewing was exquisite, the style of the clothes simple and traditional.

She lifted a newborn-size sacque and pressed it to her cheek. Longing to have a baby of her own blossomed in her chest, and she found her eyes welling up with tears. If she married, God willing, she could have a child of her own, one that she could dress in such tiny garments.

The sound of a door opening and footsteps made Ellen dash away the moisture from her eyes and quickly return the baby clothes to the box. "Morning, Dinah," she called, feeling silly by the intense emotion that had bubbled up inside her. "I'm in the office."

"Wee gayts," Dinah answered. "A good day to you, too." Her cheerful face appeared in the open doorway. Dinah was wearing her work apron and carrying a bucket and cleaning cloths. "I thought I'd wash those windows in the front room before we open. They looked smudgy yesterday. I can't abide dirty windows." She set her bucket on the floor. "Coffee smells *goot*. Will you have a cup with me before I start?"

Ellen murmured assent. There was little chance of any dirt collecting when Dinah was around. Although she'd been thinking of having a cup of tea, she joined Dinah, accepting a mug of the strong coffee. Dinah liked hers black. "My husband liked it that way," she explained, "and in time I came to think that was the only way to drink it. He'd say, 'If a spoon won't stand straight up in the cup, the coffee's not strong enough.'"

"I guess we didn't have any visitors last night," Ellen commented.

"Quiet as a graveyard. Just the way I like it."

They talked about what Dinah had cooked herself for supper the previous evening and then discussed the best way to can peaches. Three-quarters of the way through her coffee, Dinah leaned forward, elbows on the table. "How was last night's supper at the Shetlers'?"

"Fine." Ellen studied the mug between her hands. "It was nice. They're a nice family."

Dinah pushed her glasses back up her nose. "So which one are you planning on? The serious, older one or the young, sassy one?"

"I don't know, Dinah." She glanced up at her friend. "And that's the truth."

"My advice is to use your head as well as your heart. Marriage is nothing to go into lightly. You get out what you put in. It's past time you had a husband and a family of your own, and either of those boys will do, so long as you can pick one and never question your choice. Trouble comes when a woman weds one and yearns after another." She rose from her chair, went to the sink and rinsed out her cup. "Best I get to those windows." She patted Ellen's shoulder as she went by. "Pay no heed to my nosing into your business. Just an old woman who lives by herself and talks too much when she has someone to listen."

"I value your advice, Dinah. You're one of my best friends, and you're a wise woman."

Dinah gathered her cleaning supplies and removed a bottle of ammonia from the cabinet. "I walked down to the restaurant last night," she said. "Asked Margaret right out about that girl."

"What did she say?"

"Wasn't disposed to say much. If the girl doesn't have her papers, she shouldn't be working there. The government has rules. If you ask me, Margaret suspects Gail's Amish and is giving her some rope."

Ellen stood. "She must like her or she wouldn't be bending the rules for her."

"Oh, she likes her, I could tell that. Says Gail has never been late for work and never missed a day. Honest as a bishop. Apparently, a customer left her purse on the counter in the restroom. She had a lot of cash in it. Gail found it and turned it in. She offered the girl a reward, but Gail turned it down."

Ellen brushed her forehead with her fingertips. "I couldn't sleep last night for worrying about her," she admitted.

Dinah frowned. "Best you let it go, Ellen. You've enough on your shoulders without taking on more. And…" She glanced around as if she thought they might be overheard. "What if her people shunned her?" She shook her head. "No *goot* can come of poking into some stranger's troubles." She picked up her bucket and carried it into the front showroom.

Ellen returned to her office work, but she couldn't concentrate. Restless, she shut the computer down, priced the beautiful baby clothes and put them on display. She was headed for the office again when someone knocked at the front door. She hoped it wasn't a customer because they weren't open until nine. "Dinah?" she called.

"It's just Simeon," Dinah said. "He told me he'd be bringing some more of his boxes in today. We sold the last of what we had."

Simeon made small boxes out of cedar and pine and inlaid them with designs in cherry. Suitable to hold jewelry or trinkets, they were attractive and reasonably priced and sold as quickly as he crafted them.

"I can let him in," Ellen said, turning in the doorway.

"I can handle this." Dinah set down her mop. "No need for you to bother."

Ellen hesitated, thinking about what Dinah had said about Gail. "Okay. I think I'll take an order to the post office. I'll be back in a few minutes." The post office wasn't her primary destination, but she did need to mail off some aprons that had been ordered. As she left the office, she glanced into the front room and saw Simeon and Dinah deep in conversation. On the back porch, she put the carefully wrapped package into the scooter's basket and made her way to the small post office a block away.

After collecting the mail and mailing her package, Ellen continued on to the Mennonite family restaurant. She just wanted to say hi to Gail if she was there. Check on her. She propped the scooter against the porch and started up the steps. As she reached the door, it swung open, and Gail nearly collided with her.

"*Ach!* I'm so sorry," Gail said. Her cheeks reddened. She wasn't in her waitress uniform and was wearing the same clothing she'd had on when Ellen had surprised her on her back porch.

"Good morning," Ellen said. "Are you off today?"

"*Nay.* No," Gail corrected. "They don't need me until later."

"Have you found a place to stay yet?"

Gail shook her head. "Not yet, but I know I will soon." She glanced back at the restaurant. "You aren't going to say anything to Margaret about me sleeping on your porch, are you?"

Ellen shook her head. "I hope you don't mind me asking, but...where *did* you stay last night?"

"With a friend," Gail said quickly. But she averted her eyes, and Ellen wasn't sure she believed her.

"You know, you might talk to Margaret. Her church helps people sometimes."

Gail shook her head and backed away. "I don't want charity. Don't worry about me. I'll be fine." She forced a half smile. "I know you mean well, but really, I'm *goot*. I can take care of myself." She turned away and waved. "Have a good day."

"You, too," Ellen called. And then, under her breath, she murmured a prayer for Gail and all the vulnerable young women like her.

Chapter Twelve

Friday evening, Micah arrived to pick Ellen up, said all the right things to her father and had her mother laughing and blushing like a fourteen-year-old before they drove out of the yard. Ellen had looked forward to the bowling expedition from the moment Micah had invited her. Bowling dates for twentysomething young people were not exactly encouraged but were allowed by the church elders so long as they were group activities. Mennonite parents in the neighborhood regularly took their children to bowling alleys for birthdays and other special occasions, but it was rare that Amish families participated. Ellen's father had been an exception, and she'd gained some proficiency and a love for the sport by going with him when she was a teenager.

"You look pretty tonight," Micah said as he guided Samson out onto the blacktop at the end of Ellen's lane.

She murmured a thank-you and sat up tall on the leather seat, pleased that she'd worn one of her newest dresses, a modest, pine-green dress and a matching green headscarf. She wasn't trying to look English, but knew that she'd attract less attention from strangers than she would if she wore her prayer *kapp*. She'd brought twenty dollars in a plain black purse, a precaution she'd taken after Neziah had once forgotten his wallet and they'd had to convince the English manager of a pizza restaurant that he would return the following day with enough money to pay the bill for their refreshments. That had been more than ten years ago, but the memory of Neziah's and her own embarrassment remained vivid in her mind.

A mile from the house, Micah reached under the front seat, pulled out a battery-operated radio and tuned in to a Christian rock station. Ellen knew she should have scolded him. She was a baptized member of the church, and listening to the radio, no matter what station was playing, was definitely forbidden by the community. Music, other than hymns and *praise songs* sung without accompaniment, was forbidden as being too worldly. But Micah wasn't baptized yet, so officially, he was still in his *running around* stage.

Rumspringa was the time in a young person's life when they were permitted to experience some of the English lifestyle. A few kids—mainly boys—took it too far, getting driver's licenses and buying motor vehicles, even moving away to sample a reckless lifestyle among the English. Micah hadn't done that, and he was studying for baptism, so chastising him for the radio might make her appear too strict.

Those were the excuses that rose in Ellen's mind, and she almost convinced herself that they were good ones. But she'd never been one to be less than honest with herself, and the truth was, the beat was really catchy, and she enjoyed the guitar, drums and whatever other instruments were accompanying the male singers.

"Great song, isn't it?" Micah asked as the final notes rang out from under the seat. Before she could answer, a young woman's voice began another song, every bit as enthusiastic and exciting as the first one. "That's Myra Grace. She's terrific, isn't she?"

This music was a long way from the spirituals sung at youth singing frolics, and further still from the *Deitsch* hymns that played such an important part of the Sabbath worship services. But she couldn't deny that this Christian rock thrilled her and filled her with emotion. *"Wonderbor,"* she said, and meant it.

"So you like it? For real?" Micah asked. He patted the seat next to him. "You could sit a little closer, you know. I don't bite."

She shook her head and laughed. "I'm fine where I am."

Micah guided his horse to the shoulder of the road as an oversize truck carrying farm machinery approached. "We're picking up Abram and Linny," he said. "Do you mind?"

"Nay." She didn't know Linny well. She was much younger and belonged to another church district, but she'd seemed pleasant enough when Ellen had met her at a farm auction recently. "So, Abram is walking out with Linny now?" she asked him. "I thought he and Saloma—"

"Oh, Saloma's coming, but with Marvin Yordy and another couple from Marvin's church district. Abram likes Saloma well enough, but he's still dating different girls. Abram's a long way from settling down yet. He's a few years younger than me."

"Are you certain you're ready?" she asked. He glanced at her with a slow, heartfelt smile and nodded.

"Even if it means giving up your radio and cell phone?" she reminded him.

One blond eyebrow shot up. He pushed his hat back and asked, "How did you know I had a cell phone?"

Ellen laughed, folding her arms and replying, "Hershey Park. You told me."

Micah grimaced. "Right." Then he shrugged and grinned.

He was trying to charm her and Ellen knew it, but he was hard to resist. Life with Micah would always be full of laughter and fun. She could almost picture a small boy or girl with Micah's dimple and bright, inquisitive eyes. He was a good uncle to Neziah's sons, and he would make an excellent father, if a bit indulgent. Micah was slow to anger and quick to forgive. She'd have to be a fool not to let herself love him.

The clatter of hooves alerted Ellen to the approach of another horse-drawn vehicle coming up behind them. When she glanced in a side mirror, she saw an open courting buggy pulled by a gray horse. After a moment or two, the topless buggy's sole occupant reined his horse to the left lane, drew alongside and passed them, his showy gray stepping high. Ellen recognized the driver as one of Solomon Schwartz's sons, maybe Jonah. It was difficult to tell which one it was at a brief glance. There were several brothers of running-around age, all about the same height and all with longish bowl haircuts. The Schwartz boys took turns using the open buggy and driving the fine gray mare. Everyone knew that she was fast, and the Schwartzes were fond of saying that she had been a winning pacer before being sold at an auction when she grew past racing age.

Micah frowned as the open buggy passed them. "Show-off," he muttered.

As horse and driver pulled back in line ahead, the Schwartz boy turned, grinned and waved at Micah before turning on a string of blue-and-red lights that flashed on the back frame.

It was definitely Jonah, Ellen decided. She rolled her eyes. "Juvenile." She looked over at Micah. "Seriously," she continued. "Joining the church will make a lot of changes in your life. Are you sure you're prepared for it?"

"I'll be sure the day you agree to marry me." Micah's eyes narrowed, and he urged Samson to move a little faster. They quickly closed the distance to the rear of the buggy ahead of them.

"Micah," she warned. "Don't get too close."

He caught her hand and squeezed it, but he didn't take his gaze off the flashing lights and rolling buggy just ahead. "You mean everything to me, Ellen. It's what I want. You as my wife, baptism, a life that has meaning."

She gauged the distance between Samson's nose and the string of blinking lights. Micah's horse wasn't happy, because his ears were back and he was leaning forward in the harness. "Don't do anything foolish," she murmured. "This is a busy road."

"Don't worry," he assured her. "I'd never take chances with you in the buggy." He was saying all the right things, but his expression was exactly the same as it had been the day one of the sixth-grade boys had dared him to walk the ridgepole of the bishop's barn, two stories up.

"And you think we can be happy together, live according to our faith, make our families content?"

"I do," Micah answered. "If I didn't, I'd never have agreed to my father's proposition. I've been waiting for a woman like you, a wife, children, responsibilities. We're a lot alike, you and me. And you're steady. We'll make a *goot* match." He hesitated. "I know that you and Neziah...you know." He shrugged and glanced at her. "Anyway, he's probably a better man than I am, but he's too serious for you. Being Amish, living Plain, doesn't mean we can't still enjoy ourselves, does it?"

"Nay," she agreed. "It doesn't."

"Goot!" With a triumphant grin, he slapped the reins over Samson's back and reined the horse left, surprising Jonah and quickly gaining on the open buggy ahead of them.

"Micah!" Ellen braced herself against the front dashboard as one of their wheels hit a pothole, and the buggy jolted hard enough to make her fly an inch off the seat.

"Get up!" Micah shouted, and Samson's head went up and his stride lengthened. "Hold on tight!" In barely a minute, Micah's horse inched up and then drew nose to nose with the gray mare.

Jonah's eyes widened in surprise as he saw them passing him. Grabbing his long buggy whip, he snapped it through the air over the mare's withers. The gray leaped ahead, and the race was on.

Ellen knew she should be protesting, insisting that Micah stop this nonsense, but she found the race thrilling. Seemingly evenly matched, the two horses stretched out, hooves pounding the pavement. First one buggy edged ahead, and then the gap narrowed between them before the other took the lead. "Faster! Faster!"

Ellen cried, her heart pounding with excitement. "Go, Samson!"

Wheels spinning, buggies rocking from side to side, they pounded through an intersection. Two Amish teenage boys, waiting at the stop sign on the left side of the crossroad, waved and whooped excitedly at the horse race. Jonah, on Ellen's right, stood in the two-wheel open carriage, reins in both hands, yelling encouragement to his gray mare.

Fifty yards, a hundred, and finally Jonah's horse seemed to be tiring. Inches, and then by a head, and finally a length, Samson pulled ahead. Far down the road, Ellen caught sight of a blue garbage truck. "Micah, rein in. There's a truck coming!"

Jonah saw the truck at almost the same time. He pulled back on the leathers, slowing the gray so that Micah could safely pull into line ahead of him. Micah eased Samson's pace to a slower one, and by the time the English vehicle passed them, the two buggies were proceeding at a steady pace.

Ellen sank back on the seat, exhilarated. "You won! Your Samson is faster than his gray."

Micah looked at her and grinned as he turned to wave triumphantly at Jonah, who whooped and waved back good-humoredly. "Ellen Beachey! Listen to you," Micah admonished. "And you're supposed to be an example for other young women?" He glanced down at the toggle switch on the buggy dashboard. Mischief danced behind his intense blue eyes. "I dare you," he challenged.

Ellen didn't hesitate. Before she lost her nerve, she threw the switch that powered Micah's string of battery-operated, flashing red-and-blue lights. She leaned far out and waved at Jonah. "Slowpoke! Dust-eater!"

Micah roared with laughter and she couldn't help joining in, laughing until tears ran down her cheeks. *Maybe he's right,* she thought. *Maybe Micah is the one I belong with.*

Hours later, Micah guided Samson up Ellen's steep driveway. The house was quiet, lights out, with no sign of either of her parents. He reined in the horse in the deeper shadows of the oak trees at the edge of the yard and slid closer to her on the buggy bench. "Did you have a *goot* time tonight?" he asked her.

"I did."

It was strangely intimate, just the two of them sitting so close in the buggy. The moon was up, and a blanket of stars glittered in the navy blue sky. "I did, too," he said.

"You don't mind that my score was higher than yours?"

"*Nay.* I'm proud of you."

"The preachers tell us that pride is a bad thing."

"Pride in one's self, not for someone else's accomplishments. Besides, we beat everyone, didn't we? We left them in the dust."

She laughed. "Like Jonah and his gray mare."

"Exactly." He chuckled and slid an arm around her waist. Ellen leaned close, so close that he thought he smelled the scent of her shampoo. Peaches. Happiness surged up in his chest, seeping through him from the crown of his head down to his toes. Samson shook his head, and the harness jingled. Micah could imagine that this was *their* home and they were coming home together after a frolic or visiting friends. Being with Ellen made him content, made him eager to join the church community and join in marriage.

He caught her chin between his thumb and forefinger, turning her face toward his, and bending to kiss her.

"Nay." She pressed two fingers to his lips. "It's not seemly that we behave this way."

He let out a slow breath. "You want to kiss me, don't you?"

"Jah, I do, and that's all the more reason we should show restraint." She gently took his hand and lowered it.

"You're not a girl, Ellen," he said. "We're old enough to know our own minds. I'd never do anything that would shame you."

She sighed. "But *I* might. I care for you a great deal, Micah, but some things are best kept for marriage."

Her voice was soft and sweet, no longer the teasing Ellen or the one so quick with a crisp comeback. The sound of it made him go all shivery inside. And maybe she was right. If he allowed himself to pull her into his arms, if he kissed her with all the pent-up emotion he felt, would he be able to remember what was proper for a courting couple and what went beyond what was decent?

"It's all right," he said, and his words came out deep and scratchy. "I like the idea of marrying a chaste woman, one who can teach our children by example the right way to live." He chuckled. "But then again, maybe it would be better to share at least *one* kiss before we take our wedding vows. What if I'm a terrible kisser?"

She laughed. "I doubt that, and I doubt that you think so."

"Would it be so dangerous? One good-night kiss between friends?"

She got down out of the buggy. He scrambled after her and found her hand again.

"Between friends might be harmless," she told him, "but with a man I'm considering marrying, maybe more than I want to dare."

"Other girls don't consider a few harmless kisses so dangerous."

"I'm not other girls."

He nodded, knowing when she had the best of him. "I know you aren't, Ellen. You're special. And if you'll marry me, I promise I'll try to be the man you deserve."

She squeezed his hand and pulled free. "Thank you for tonight," she said.

"Will you come with me again? Soon?"

"Maybe." Her face was in the shadows, but he sensed that she was smiling at him.

"Can I walk you up to the house?"

"If you like."

A funny hollow feeling settled in his stomach. A minute ago, he'd felt sure of her...sure of his chances, but now he wasn't so certain. Was she teasing him? "*Nay*, Ellen, only if you want me to."

It wasn't that far to her back porch. He wished it were a mile. Neither spoke until she stopped at the bottom step.

She turned to him in the darkness. "Have you kissed a lot of girls?"

Her question surprised him. "*Nay*, only two. But nothing serious. Not something I should be ashamed of." He straightened. "And don't ask me who, because I'll give no names. All I can say is it was nothing I, or they, took seriously."

"You're sweet, Micah." She raised up on her toes and kissed his cheek. "Good night."

He touched his fingertips to where her mouth had just been on his cheek. "Night."

In seconds, the door closed behind her, and he stood there wondering if things had changed between them. Inside, he felt like they had. Something important had happened this evening, but whether it was for good or bad, he couldn't tell. As he made his way back to Samson and the buggy, he tried to think what was different in their relationship.

He was still puzzling over Ellen's responses when he reached his father's stable. As he approached the barn, he saw a tall figure leaning against the double doors. "Neziah?"

"Jah. You're late getting home. Everything all right?"

"Right as rain," Micah said.

"You went bowling with Ellen?"

"Jah." He got down and led Samson through the double doors into the barn. Neziah followed him, and Micah began to worry that maybe something was wrong. It wasn't like his brother to be waiting for him this way. *"Dat* all right? Kids?"

Neziah took down a lantern from inside the barn door. Micah heard the scratch of a match, and then a circle of yellow light glowed from the kerosene lamp. Neziah hung it back on the wooden peg. "Everything is *goot* here." Neziah began to unharness Samson. "Okay to give him water now?" He stroked the horse's neck. "He feels a little warm. You weren't driving him hard on the way home, were you?"

"Walked him from Ellen's. Water's fine." He backed

the buggy into an empty space near the stalls and waited while Neziah hung up the harness.

"Much traffic on the road tonight?"

"Not much." He found a curry brush and began brushing Samson's neck and chest in long, sweeping strokes. Neziah went out of the barn and returned with a bucket of fresh water from the well. He carried it to Samson's head and offered it to the horse. Samson drank until he was satisfied, then blew a spray of wet slobber over Micah's trousers. *"Danki,"* he said. "Fool horse." But he grinned as he said it and took care as he brushed along Samson's back. "You know that gray that Jonah Schwartz drives, the one that used to race on the tracks in Delaware and New Jersey?"

"Strong legs, that mare."

Micah drew the brush along Samson's rump. "She's not as fast as they say."

"Who isn't?" Neziah asked.

"Jonah's horse." He threw the brush into the open aisle outside the stall and turned to Neziah. "Are you jealous? Because I took Ellen bowling?"

"Took a long time at her house. After you got her home, I mean."

"How do you know when I got her home?" Micah asked. Feeling out of sorts, he found the brush and put it back on the wall where it belonged. Their *vadder* liked things in place. If he found it on the barn floor tomorrow, he'd ask questions.

"Saw your lights coming down the road," Neziah said. "Quite some time ago."

"Not that long. We were talking." He made a sound of exasperation. "You *are* jealous. We went bowling.

Two other couples went with us. Then we had pizza and sodas. Then we came home. End of story."

"That's all?"

"I didn't kiss her, if that's what you want to know."

"But you tried, didn't you?"

Trying to tamp down his irritation, Micah led Samson to the back door that led to the fenced-in compound and turned him out. It was a warm night, and he would be more comfortable outside than in his stall. "What Ellen and I do on our date is none of your business, big brother."

"It is my business," Neziah insisted. "Because Ellen's going to be my wife."

"And that would bother you? If she ever kissed me?"

"It would."

Micah closed the half door and locked it so neither Samson nor any of the other animals could get back into the main area of the barn and raid the feed barrels or the haystack in the night. "I didn't kiss her, Neziah, but it's not something you should be asking. You might *not* be marrying her. She could well choose me, instead of you."

"No need for me to worry about that, little brother. It's me she'll marry, and you'd best get used to the idea."

"We'll see about that." Micah walked off into the dark, making the decision it was time to pin Ellen down and set their wedding date.

Chapter Thirteen

On Saturdays, merchants in Honeysuckle hosted a farmer's market and auction at the northern end of town. It was one of Ellen's favorite aspects of the village, and she rarely missed a market day. Vendors came from all over to rent outside space for tables, selling everything from household items to vintage furniture to seasonal food. That day, the tables were a feast of colors with red-and-gold mums, and baskets of early apples. There was also an area where farm equipment, both horse-drawn and motorized, was auctioned off. And there were always tables of odds and ends. Ellen liked to look for old handmade items: wooden butter churns, oil lamps and small antiques, things that customers who visited her shop were eager to buy.

The real draw for tourists and the Amish community alike were the food stalls inside, offering choice cuts of beef and pork, cold cuts, locally made cheese, baked goods, ice cream and homemade moon pies and funnel cakes. A pizza truck and other mobile snack stands sold scrapple and sausage sandwiches, hand-cut fries and non-alcoholic drinks. Picnic tables stood inside and outside under the trees, so that shoppers had a place to sit and talk or enjoy a simple meal. Like most Saturdays, Dinah had come early to the market to meet friends from her widows' club for breakfast, and she was happy to keep an eye on the store and their new *Englisher* employee while Ellen took a break.

As Ellen was walking between tables, she came upon Saloma and her sister Joanie sitting at one of the tables in the shade. Ellen saw from the outline of Joanie's dress that she was expecting a child, and Ellen couldn't help the smallest wince of envy. Joanie was younger than she was by at least five years, but she'd found a husband she adored and was already starting a family. One by one, most of Ellen and Saloma's friends had married. With God's help, Ellen prayed, she would make the right choice and become one of those wives before the first snowfall.

"Sit down, sit down," Saloma urged. "Joanie was telling me about a new job that her husband has just gotten. He won the contract to build a big barn for an English family that bought the old Peterson farm. He'll have to hire more people to help him, but the work will keep them busy for three or four months."

"I'm so happy for you, Joanie." Ellen set her cup of lemonade on the table and slid onto the bench across from the two sisters. She didn't say anything about the coming baby. Pregnancy was a subject not spoken about outside the family until the last few weeks.

"Ellen's walking out with the Shetler brothers," Saloma said as she finished off her scrapple sandwich and wiped her mouth with a napkin. "Both of them." Joanie looked dubious, but Saloma laughed. "It's true. Tell her, Ellen."

Ellen smiled and shrugged. "I don't know that we're walking out, but I have been seeing a lot of both Micah and Neziah," she admitted. "My parents would like to see me marry one of them."

Joanie narrowed her gaze. "And you? Is it what you want? I can understand you considering Neziah's suit, but Micah…" She spread her hands, palms up, in a gesture that said a lot about her opinion of Micah without putting her criticism into words.

"Well, I hope she *doesn't* pick Micah," Saloma said eagerly. "Then maybe I'd have a chance. He's so cute."

"*Jah*, he is." Joanie glanced at her sister. "But cute doesn't put groceries on the table. Micah has a reputation for being flighty. And he hasn't joined the church yet." She turned her attention to Ellen. "Are you sure he's ready for the responsibility of baptism and marriage?"

"We've been talking about that and I think he is," she answered.

"I know you and Neziah courted once before," Joanie said. She opened a Ziploc bag of homemade potato chips and offered some to Ellen. "Maybe that's where your heart will lead you. He seems to be the steadier of the two."

Ellen selected a potato chip and ate it slowly. They were salt and vinegar, her favorite. "I do know Neziah better, but…" She shook her head. "I'm not sure. They are both solid men, and Micah…he's so easy to be with. So much fun, you know?"

"Pray on it," Joanie suggested. "When I accepted my husband's proposal, there was someone else who'd written to me to ask me to be his wife. He seemed like a better choice. He was well set up, with a big farm."

"And an interfering mother," Saloma put in. "A widowed mother who would have tried to run their marriage."

"*Nay*, sister," Joanie admonished. "Caring for elders is a privilege, not a duty. That he had responsibilities that I would have shared wasn't something that would have kept me from accepting his offer." She smiled and touched the place over her heart. "It was a feeling in here, and the sense that the man I chose is who God wanted for me. Sometimes important decisions can seem overwhelming, but remember, if you hold with our faith, you are never alone. Listen with your head and your heart, and you'll know who is right for you."

"*Goot* advice." Ellen nodded as she munched on another potato chip.

Talk then turned to less personal subjects as they finished their snacks, and she was just about to go inside to purchase goat cheese for her father when she saw a familiar figure strolling between two vendor stalls. Certain that the young woman in the blue dress was Gail, Ellen said her goodbyes to Joanie and Saloma and strolled nonchalantly across the market to intercept her.

"Oh, hey," Gail said when she nearly bumped into Ellen. She stopped short, a mixed expression of eagerness and embarrassment on her face.

The girl looked tired. Dark circles beneath her eyes smudged her fair complexion, and she was scratching several large mosquito bites on her arm.

"Gail. It's good to see you." Ellen noticed that Gail had a stuffed backpack over her left shoulder and was carrying the rolled-up sleeping bag under her other arm. It was everything she owned, probably. "How are you doing?" Ellen asked. "Are you on your way to work?"

"Not until four." Gail shifted her feet nervously and

lowered the backpack to the ground. "I...I like to see what people have for sale."

"Me, too." Ellen smiled at her, hesitated, then spoke her mind. "Would you think me rude if I ask where you slept last night?"

Gail flushed and averted her eyes. "Not on your porch. Honest."

"But where?" Ellen pressed. She couldn't shake the feeling that this meeting hadn't been by chance. Sometime in the night, she'd awakened in a cold sweat. She'd suspected that she'd had a bad dream but couldn't remember any of the details. Gail had certainly been at the heart of her concern. All the way to the shop this morning, she'd wrestled with her conscience. Dinah's advice about not being too trusting of strangers was wise, but... Could it be that they'd both been too cautious?

"I can take care of myself," Gail said, edging away. "You don't have to..."

"Wait." Ellen laid a gentle hand on Gail's forearm and gazed directly into the girl's eyes. It was obvious that Gail was struggling to keep from crying.

Gail swallowed hard. "A sheep barn," she admitted, looking down at her feet. "Without permission."

"Well, that won't do," Ellen said. "It's going to get cold soon and I want to help. Will you come back to the shop with me?"

Gail looked uncertain.

"Please. I have a proposition to make," Ellen said in a rush. "If you don't mind a little work."

Gail shook her head vigorously. "I'm not afraid of work. If I could earn a little extra, it would help me save up for the security deposit to rent a room. They come up sometimes, you know, in the paper."

"I think I can do better than that," Ellen told her with a smile. "Come on."

Gail stood there for a moment and then, with what could only have been a leap of faith, she fell into step beside Ellen.

"There used to be an apartment up on the third floor of my shop," Ellen explained as they walked. "It's not much, but it's yours if you think it will suit you."

"Really?" Gail's eyes widened. "You'd let me stay in your shop?"

"I couldn't ask any rent for it. It's a bit of a mess. We've been using it for storage." She glanced at Gail, whose face now seemed bright. "Maybe in exchange for the room you could help by sweeping the sidewalk of leaves, scrubbing the porch, little chores that I hate to ask Dinah to do."

Gail beamed. "I'd be glad to help in any way I can."

It was only a short walk back to the shop and once they'd reached it, Ellen led the way around to the side of the building to the foot of an exterior staircase. "The rooms will need a *goot* cleaning and airing out, but there's a cot in the storeroom. You're welcome to stay here as long as you need to, until you find something permanent. I'll warn you, though, the place hasn't been dusted in over a year. It's probably full of cobwebs."

"Spiders I can deal with," Gail declared, gazing up the metal staircase that somewhat resembled a fire escape. "They don't bleat at night like sheep."

She laughed, and Ellen laughed with her. Then Gail grew serious. "How can I thank you enough?" Tears suddenly glistened in her eyes. "This is the nicest thing anyone has ever done for me. *Ever.*"

"I'm glad that I can help. I just feel bad that I didn't

think of this sooner," Ellen told her. "I'll have to tell my father and Dinah that you're staying here, of course, but I'd appreciate it if you didn't say anything to anyone else about it. Let's just keep it a secret between us."

"Because you'd get into trouble with your church...for helping someone who left their community." Gail nodded. "I understand." She offered a trembling smile, and her cheek grew pink. "I guess you already figured it out, but my name isn't Bond. It's Bontrager. Abigail Bontrager."

Ellen returned the smile. "I'm pleased to meet you, Abigail Bontrager."

She shrugged. "Everyone will know soon enough that I fibbed, anyway. My brother found my birth certificate and my social security card and sent them to me, so Margaret won't get in trouble for letting me work there."

"So your family knows where you are?" Ellen asked.

Gail shook her head. "Just my brother, and he won't tell. He's leaving home, too, as soon as he turns eighteen. One of my mother's uncles is going to hire him to work on his dairy farm. He's going, but he's not turning English."

"And you are?"

"Maybe, I'm not sure. It's something I have to think about." Again, she stared at her canvas sneakers. "I'm just, you know...trying it out."

"Your community would take you back," Ellen said thoughtfully. She crossed her arms over her chest. "You can always go home, if it's what you want."

Gail sighed. "*Nay.* I can't. I won't."

"But surely your mother and father—"

"You don't know my father." Gail shook her head. "He would never forgive me, no matter what the bishop or the elders said." She glanced up at Ellen, making eye contact. "Not all fathers are kind ones."

There was something in Gail's tone that made Ellen think there was more to her story. She was suddenly grateful for the man who was her father. She had always known how blessed she was, but sometimes it took a reminder, such as this girl in the faded dress, to remind her that she should give thanks every day for the family God placed her with.

Gail glanced up the stairs, clearly eager to investigate her new quarters.

Ellen reached into her apron pocket, plucked out a ring of keys, sorted through them and removed the key that would unlock the door at the top of the steps. "You go on up and look around," Ellen said, handing the key over. "I'll see about that cot and some bedding and cleaning supplies. I need to let Dinah know you'll be staying here."

After looking in on the high-school girl behind the counter, Ellen climbed the stairs to Dinah's apartment on the second floor. Dinah was busy making oatmeal-raisin cookies to take to a friend and invited Ellen to have a cookie just out of the oven that was as big as the palm of Ellen's hand. They were one of Dinah's specialties that always went over well at potlucks and schoolhouse auctions.

Ellen accepted the sweet, warm cookie, spiced with cinnamon and told Dinah about inviting Gail to stay in the third-floor apartment. Her decision didn't go over as easily as she had hoped. Ellen tried to convey Gail's plight sympathetically, but Dinah's brow furrowed and her eyes narrowed behind her glasses. If she'd been a hen, Ellen could picture her feathers ruffling.

"You can't be serious," Dinah exclaimed. "I don't believe you handed a total stranger the keys to your shop and told her to make herself at home. You're too trusting, Ellen."

"She's Amish, the age of your own granddaughter. She's just a young girl who needs a friend. And having her up there on the third floor is no danger to us or the business." Ellen shrugged. "I didn't give her the keys to the shop, just to those unused rooms in the attic. The inside door from the third story to the hall is locked. What harm could she do?"

Dinah pursed her lips and again Ellen imagined an angry chicken, beak poised to peck. "It isn't as if we haven't had prowlers before. Have you forgotten the fire that nearly ruined your father? I warrant that was no accident."

Ellen waved away her older friend's objection. "That was years ago. Gail would have been only a child. Surely you don't think she started the fire."

Dinah shook an accusing finger. "You're a softy for a sad story."

Ellen took a big bite of her cookie. "Doesn't the Bible teach us to offer kindness to strangers?"

"What will your father say?"

"He'll respect my decision." *As should you,* Ellen thought, though she didn't dare say it for fear of hurting Dinah's feelings.

"I don't know that he'll agree with you. It sets a bad example, harboring a girl who's run away from her people."

"It will be all right. I promise." She got up from the

table to hug Dinah. "You're not fooling me. You aren't as prickly as you'd like to pretend. You've a generous heart."

Dinah squeezed her back and pushed her gently away. "I hope I do," she murmured, "but when you've lived as long as I have and seen people behave in ways they shouldn't, maybe you won't be so trusting."

The following day was the Sabbath, but not a day of community worship. It was a visiting Sunday, one where friends and relatives would call on each other and spend time together, resting from the week's labor. Sometimes Ellen and her parents spent a quiet day together on visiting Sunday, but this week it was far from quiet at their home. Dinah's friends from the widows' group had gathered there to plan their next benefit and to give thanks for little Raymond Blauch's continuing recovery at the hospital. Ellen had invited Dinah to welcome the widows to her house rather than the apartment over the store because Dinah's space was small, and negotiating the stairs was difficult for some of the older women.

It was a beautiful September day with a breeze that carried the sweet smell of ripening apples from the orchard and ruffled the hair of the laughing youngsters who chased each other around the yard. Some of the widows had brought children and grandchildren, and several other families who were not members of the widows' club had stopped by. The older women tended to gather in the kitchen and front room, while the teenagers and younger women congregated on the porch or in the yard, where they could see and be seen by the younger men, who stood and talked in the shade of the barn and windmill.

"Anne will stop by later if its another false alarm," Naomi Byler informed Ellen, speaking of the local midwife. Naomi, widow of the former bishop, was the unofficial leader of the women's group. She'd settled into a comfortable rocker in the kitchen where she could observe the comings and goings and make certain that no one was behaving in a manner improper for a Sunday. "This is Dora Stoltzfus's first child. She's not due until the first of October, but her husband's gone to fetch Naomi three times this week. Twice it was the middle of the night."

"Poor Anne," Dinah remarked as she made room on the counter for a bowl of applesauce. "I don't know what's worse, anxious young mothers or worried first-time fathers."

"The fathers for certain," Ellen's mother said. "My John made such a fuss when Ellen was born that the midwife said he was in more danger than I was." Her friends laughed and were quick to share stories of their own childbirths, some funny, others harrowing. Ellen's mother wasn't a widow, but she'd known most of the women, including Dinah, for a lifetime, and they were all dear friends.

To Ellen's amusement, what had begun as a typical Sunday with a few guests dropping by had grown to a large gathering. Ellen's parents had neglected to tell her that they'd invited the five Shetlers, and with the promise of a fine dinner, nothing short of a flood or snowstorm could keep Simeon and his sons and grandsons away.

It was a matter of fact that the widows' group included some of the finest cooks in Lancaster County, and it was a point of honor that every woman brought the results of her best recipe for their potluck dinners. Casseroles, trays of sandwiches, baskets of yeast bread, platters of cold ham and chicken, jars of pickled beets, salads and plates of stuffed eggs covered the counters and spilled over onto the kitchen table. Ellen's *mam*'s prize hand-carved buffet was lined with pies, cakes, puddings and apple tarts.

"More food here than a wedding supper," Ellen's father had teased as the largess continued to arrive. But there were no complaints from him. Ellen knew that he was looking forward to the delicious meal and the leftovers that would remain behind when the widows went home. He'd always enjoyed company, and playing host to his friends and neighbors pleased him greatly. If the female chatter became overpowering, the weather was nice enough that he and his comrades could always retreat to the barn or to the fields for peace and quiet.

Ellen had just found another folding chair on the porch for an elderly latecomer when she caught sight of Micah standing near the grape arbor. She paused to wave and smile at him, and he motioned for her to join him. She carried the chair inside and then went back out.

As she approached Micah, he stooped to pick up a soccer ball that had bounced off a tree and tossed it back to Joel, who gave a whoop and dashed off with three other boys in his wake. Micah moved back into the arbor and gestured for her to sit beside him on the high-backed swing. There, shielded from the house and yard by the still-green grape vines, they could have a measure of privacy without breaking the rules of propriety.

"It's crazy in the house," she said and gratefully took a seat. "Dinah says that it's rare that nearly everyone can make a meeting." The grass was cool under her bare feet, and she was all too aware of Micah's commanding presence. A few bees buzzed and flew overhead, but the Concord grapes had ripened and vanished for the year. Only bare stems and a few dried remnants of the fruit that had hung so heavily on the vines remained. She'd always loved the grape arbor. As a child, it had been her favorite place to read. Now she found another reason for it to give her sweet memories.

"I wanted to talk to you about something," Micah said. He folded his arms and regarded her seriously. "I heard that you're letting some runaway sleep in your shop."

Ellen grimaced. "That didn't take long. I expected the news to make the rounds by church Sunday, but…" She shrugged. "Who told you?"

"*Vadder*. What are you thinking, Ellen? You don't know this girl, and you don't know if she's under a ban from her church."

She was so surprised by the tone he was taking with her that it took a moment for her to respond. "You haven't even met Gail. She's a *goot* person in bad circumstances. She had a place to live but her roommate didn't pay her share of the rent and they were both evicted."

"I have to admit I'm surprised. You're usually so sensible, Ellen." He frowned. "And I don't know what's gotten into your father that he'd allow—"

"Micah!" She stared at him, more than a little annoyed that he'd speak to her as if she were one of his naughty nephews.

Just then, Neziah appeared at the entrance to the grape arbor. "Melvin's here," he told his brother, "and he's looking for you. Something about a horse race?"

Micah glanced at Ellen as he rose from the swing.

"We'll talk about this later," he said. "I think you need to give it serious thought."

Speechless and now more than a little irritated, she watched Micah walk away. Neziah took his seat on the swing next to her. "I was looking for you."

She turned toward him and held up a hand. "If you've come to talk to me about Gail, I'm not in the mood to discuss it."

He looked at her oddly. "Are you talking about the Bontrager girl?"

"Is there anything that anyone in the community doesn't know about my personal business? Yes, I did offer to let Gail sleep at the shop, and I'm standing by my decision. I'm not a child, Neziah. I've thought about this for days. I've prayed about it, and God showed me His way. Gail's a sweet young woman, and she's going through a bad time. What's wrong in extending a hand of—"

"Ellen, Ellen." He raised his hand again, this time in a calming motion. "I didn't come to criticize you."

"Micah certainly did. I'm thirty-three years old!" She took a breath and started again. "Old enough to make my own decisions. Was I supposed to let Gail sleep in a barn? What if something terrible happened to her? The world outside our community isn't a safe one for a young woman alone. Aren't we supposed to show charity?"

He smiled down at her. "Can I say something, or do I just get to listen?"

She sighed loudly. "Go ahead. Get it off your chest. Tell me why I've made a foolish decision and why I'll live to regret it."

His smile became laughter.

"I'm glad you think my actions were—"

"Admirable? Brave? I came looking for you, Ellen, because I heard about Gail Bontrager, and I wanted to tell you how proud of you I am. It's easy for people to talk about extending a helping hand, but actually going out on a limb for a stranger? You don't see that often. Not even in our community, where it should be taken for granted. It's where the Mennonites put us to shame, don't you think? They go out into the English world and help those who need it most."

"Wait!" She seized his hand. "You're saying you don't think what I did was wrong?"

He raised her hand to his lips and kissed it. He looked at her with his cinnamon eyes. "*Jah*, Ellen. I agree with what you did. I think it was right and *goot*. I would hope that, put in the same position, I'd make the same choice you did."

She stared at him, suddenly feeling light-headed. "Neziah, I never expected *you*…" She stopped and started again. "When we walked out together, you admonished me for attending those Bible classes where we were free to talk about interpretation. You didn't want me to speak out against tradition. You told me that you'd never allow your wife to work outside your home…to associate with the English." She looked down and then up at him again. "You've changed," she murmured.

"I hope I've gained a *little* wisdom in ten years." He stroked the back of her hand. "What can I say? I was wrong about you working in the craft shop. I was wrong about the Bible class. I was wrong not to give you the respect you deserved. I'll make no excuses for myself except to say that I was young and foolish."

She pulled back her hand, unable to think clearly while he was holding her hand so intimately, as small tingles of excitement were running up her arm. "You disagree with what our bishop teaches?"

"Nay." Neziah shook his head. "I didn't say that. But I sometimes *do* question our interpretation of it. I think sometimes I've thought too much about the rules and have forgotten the message that the Lord came to deliver to us. What does Jesus say is the greatest of the laws? 'Love one another'?" He steepled his hands, as if searching for the right words. "I was born Amish. My blood and bones are those of the martyrs who came before us and died for our faith. I could never live outside our church. But I would be less than what I believe God wants if I refused to question or to think for myself."

She felt as if a weight pressed on her chest. Was what she had believed all this time about Neziah's rigid mindset wrong? She scrambled for clarity. "Do you still believe that a husband should be the head of the family?"

"Jah," he said. "I do. I believe that it is God's plan for us. I think the man should be the head of the household, but I believe just as strongly that the woman should be the heart. Can a head live without a heart?" He smiled at her and extended his hand. "Ellen, I know it hasn't been long since—"

A child's scream brought them both to their feet. Neziah dashed out of the arbor, and Ellen hurried after him.

"Neziah!" Simeon shouted. "Come quick! It's Joel! He's hurt bad!"

Chapter Fourteen

Neziah ran toward his father. *"Vas is?"* he shouted. "Where?"

His brother came around the stable holding Joel in his arms. Blood poured from the boy's mouth and nose, running down his chin and dripping onto the ground.

Asa, shrieking at the top of his lungs, darted after them. "He's dead! Joel's dead!"

Neziah raced across the yard toward his injured child. *So much blood.* What could the boy have done to hurt himself so badly? Other men crowded around, forming a barrier between him and Joel, but he shoved his way through and held out his arms to Micah. "What happened?" he repeated. "Is he breathing?"

At that instant, Joel began to kick and scream at the top of his lungs.

Neziah gathered his son against his chest. *Not dead. Not dead.* Despite Asa's continued wailing that Joel was dead, it was evident that the howling child in his arms was very much alive. *But how badly was he hurt?* Neziah looked at Micah expectantly.

"He fell off the chicken house roof. He may have struck his face on a cultivator before he hit the ground."

A cultivator? His son had fallen on a cultivator? Neziah's blood ran cold. *They would need an ambulance. A doctor. Had his head struck the metal prongs?* The front of Joel's shirt was bloody. Did he have broken ribs? A fractured skull? Everyone was talking at once. His father was bellowing orders. Asa was still wailing. A woman shouted questions from the porch.

Neziah had always considered himself levelheaded. When one of their hired hands had severely cut his arm at the sawmill, he'd been the one to apply a tourniquet, bandage the wound and drive the man in a wagon to the nearest phone where he could call 911. He knew how to react to an emergency. Or so he'd thought. But now, with his child, Neziah felt as though he were wading through waist-deep mud. He couldn't get his mind and hands to coordinate. He knew he needed to examine his son's wounds, but it was difficult to see for the tears welling up in his eyes.

"Let me see him." Ellen appeared in front of Neziah. How she'd gotten through the press of men and the frightened children, he didn't know, but she was suddenly there, calm and soft-spoken. "Stand him up," she said. "He's choking because you're holding his head on an angle."

"But if he has serious injuries, won't that make it worse?" he said.

"Look at him, Neziah. Listen to him. No child on his deathbed has that much lung power." She waved her hand at the onlookers. "Please. Give us room to get a *goot* look at what's wrong."

Given a definite task, his father, Simeon, was all too

ready to take charge. "You heard Ellen. Back up, everyone. Give the boy room to breathe."

Joel was sobbing now. His mouth and nose were still seeping blood, but when Neziah stood him on his feet, nothing seemed to be broken. Joel clung to his father's leg and tried to talk, but fell prey to a bout of hiccups and clamped a hand over his mouth.

"You're all right," Ellen soothed, stroking Joel's bare head. "Let me see."

"But…but Asa said…" Joel's garbled attempt at speech was muddled by a combination sob and hiccup. Joel glanced down, saw all the blood on his shirt and started screaming again.

"Can someone bring me water and a clean towel?" Ellen squatted down. She rubbed Joel's back in slow circles. "Shh, shh, it will be all right."

Lizzie Fisher, a veteran of mending scrapes and spills because of her seven young stepchildren, had already guessed what they would need for an injured child. The small but capable woman slipped between the men and shyly offered a basin of water and several towels.

"Shh, shh," Ellen murmured. She dipped the corner of a towel in the water and began to dab it on Joel's face.

"Matthew…said…said I'm *dead*," Joel sobbed. His upper lip was swelling fast, and his words came out barely coherent.

Matthew Fisher was eight and one of Lizzie's brood. In Joel's mind, whatever the older boy said must be true, despite the fact that Matthew was known for his vivid imagination. "You aren't dead," Neziah said. He ruffled his son's hair. He wanted to keep holding him, to kiss his tear-streaked, bloody face, but Amish men didn't publicly show affection. Alone, he would have followed his instinct and embraced Joel as he did every night when he tucked him into bed. With his father and the other men and women watching, it didn't seem right. "You're going to be fine," he said gruffly.

"I don't want…want to go to the hospital!" Joel protested. "*Nay* shots." His sobs were coming slower now. The hiccups continued, but the bleeding from his nose and mouth had clearly slowed.

Ellen dabbed gently at Joel's face with a wet cloth. "You're going to be fine, Joel," she said, glancing up at Neziah. "He's fine. He just knocked out his two front teeth when he fell."

"I don't know. They said he fell on a cultivator," Neziah said. He didn't want to overreact. They didn't run to doctors and the hospital the way *Englishers* did because they didn't believe in insurance, but Joel's well-being was more important than medical bills. "Maybe he should go to the hospital."

"I think he looks worse than he is." Ellen's tone was reassuring. "If he'd fallen on the cultivator, he'd be hurt a lot worse. Look at him," she said. "Legs whole, arms intact." She mopped at Joel's upper lip. "Nose took a bump. Probably had the wind knocked out of him, but he's not acting like he lost consciousness. The total damage seems to be a nosebleed and two baby teeth dislodged before their time."

"His front teeth?" Neziah asked woodenly. "He knocked out his front teeth? That's all?" He took a deep breath, willing his heart to slow. How was it that Ellen could make everything okay in the space of a few moments? And then he felt shame that he hadn't given thanks to God. Surely, it was the Lord who'd prevented far worse from happening. *Praise be,* he thought. *For Your mercy.*

"Shouldn't we try to find the teeth?" Micah asked. "Take him to the dentist and see if she can...do something."

"Put them back in," Neziah finished. "Thomas told me that his brother's child knocked a tooth out, and a dentist put it back in. It didn't even turn black."

"Try to put Joel's teeth back in after they've been laying in the chicken yard?" Ellen shook her head. "They're baby teeth. He would have lost them by next year, anyway."

Joel's lower lip quivered. His nosebleed had slowed to a thin trickle. "My teeth?" It came out more like *m'teef.* He blinked back tears. "I fell," he said.

"Apparently fell off the roof," Micah repeated. "Matthew said that the soccer ball got stuck there. Joel climbed up to get it, but then he was walking on the edge to show how brave he was. He must have gotten too close to the edge."

Asa, who'd squeezed between his uncle Micah's legs nodded. "Joel climbed on the roof."

"No serious harm done," Simeon announced to his neighbors. "Nothing to worry about. Boy just knocked out a tooth." The group began to disperse—the single women gathered to whisper to each other and the young men to relate similar incidents from their own childhood.

"*Two* teeth," Neziah corrected quietly. He didn't want to show disrespect to his father, but neither did he want the incident dismissed as nothing.

"Luckily not his second teeth," Lizzie added. She held the basin of water for Ellen, waited until she'd dried Joel's face and then carried the basin and towels back to the house.

"Thank you, Lizzie," Neziah called after her. "I appreciate it." Joel's fall must have brought back terrifying memories. Lizzie's husband had died in a fall out of his hayloft.

Micah knelt beside Joel and gave his nephew a playful nudge on the shoulder. "You gave us quite a scare."

Joel tried to smile, revealing the hole where his top teeth had been.

"We were on our way to throw a few lines in the water when the kids started yelling that Joel had fallen off the roof," Micah said to Ellen as he got to his feet. He pointed to Abram, who'd come up into the yard driving a farm wagon heaped with loose straw. Nat, holding several fishing poles, was sitting on the board seat beside him. On the back of the wagon, Saloma's younger sister and two other unmarried girls were sitting with their bare feet dangling over the edge. "Dinah said we won't be eating until after they finish their meeting, so we're going down to the creek for an hour. Want to come along?"

"Come on!" Saloma's sister called to Ellen, with a wave. "It will be fun."

Ellen glanced down at Joel and shook her head. "*Danki*, but I'll stay here and keep an eye on him."

"Are you sure?" Micah asked. He seemed disappointed.

She brushed at a small bloodstain on her apron. "*Nay*, you go. I think Joel could use something cold on that lip."

Micah's brow furrowed as he glanced from Ellen to

Neziah. "You can take it from here, can't you, brother? You don't want her to miss out on the fun, do you?"

It was exactly what Neziah wanted. He wanted Ellen to skip the fishing and stay here with him and Joel, and he was ashamed of himself for thinking it. He averted his eyes. "You should go." He rested a hand on his son's shoulder. "I can handle this from here."

"I want to go fishing, Uncle Micah," Joel declared. "I wanna go!"

"No children this time," Neziah murmured to his son. "Just adults. Maybe next time."

Ellen waved to Micah as he walked away. "Have a good time."

Neziah watched Ellen as his brother joined the young folks in the wagon. "You sure you don't want to join them? Joel can't be too hurt if he's begging to go fishing." He picked up his son. "Let's see if we can talk the women out of some ice for that lip."

Ellen followed him to the house, but Neziah noticed that she was watching the wagon full of young people as it bounced across the field toward the creek. The thought that she was missing out on the fun to care for his boy didn't sit well with him. Marriage to him would mean the heavy responsibility of motherhood from day one. There'd be no honeymoon as most newly married couples had; there would be no trip out of state to visit relatives and spend time getting to know each other as man and wife. Ellen would immediately be a mother of two, with less time for leisure and the lightheartedness that often went with being a newlywed. He knew Ellen would never complain, but he wondered if he was asking too much of her. He loved her and wanted her to be his wife, but was he being selfish? Was he thinking of his own happiness at her expense?

The following week was so busy that Ellen wasn't sure where the days went. Business at the shop had increased measurably, and she and her mother were trying to preserve the abundant harvest from the garden before any went to waste. She found herself rising before dawn to begin regular household chores and breakfast, and returning from the store to can vegetables or to prepare them for drying, late into the evening.

All week, either Neziah or Micah drove her to work, and when she left the shop at the end of the day, one of them was waiting to drive her home. Usually it was Micah, but Neziah came once. The intention was nice and it was fun waiting to see who would be there to greet her, but a part of her missed her quiet times, scooting along on her push scooter. When she rode with Micah, she didn't have to talk. He always had plenty to say, and it was always entertaining. Her rides with Neziah and the children were very different; Asa and Joel chattered on like a pair of bluejays, and she and Neziah shared bits of their day, with Neziah often consulting her on some issue with his boys. Still, she found herself comfortable around both brothers, making her looming decision even more difficult.

With the resilience of childhood, Joel's injuries healed quickly. He'd started school, and—according to Micah—his accident and his missing front teeth made him quite popular among the other first-graders. Neziah had explained that he'd considered keeping his oldest son home another year, but since he had an October birthday, the teacher had convinced the family that school would be good for Joel. Secretly, Ellen agreed. He was a bright child, and keeping him occupied and facing new challenges every weekday would prevent him from coaxing too many sweet treats out of his grandfather.

One of the things that Ellen and Neziah and the children had done together that week was to go to the general store and pick up healthy snacks and fruit to go in Joel's lunch. Not to be left out, Asa had asked for his own lunchbox. Apparently, packing lunch for both boys for the following day had become part of bedtime routine at the Shetler house. And Ellen was pleased to learn from Micah that individual bags of potato chips and packaged whoopie pies had been replaced with apples, cut-up carrots and raisins. Most Amish children walked to school, but since Joel's school was located on a narrow, twisting road more than a mile away, Simeon drove Joel, in the pony cart, to and from the one-room schoolhouse daily.

Neither her mother nor her father had said anything to her about her promise to decide if she would court Neziah or Micah before the month was up, but one of them had drawn a circle in red marker on the calendar that hung in the kitchen. She suspected the culprit was her *mam* because the circle had a small tail at the bottom like a capital *Q*, her mother's trademark. Of course, her father was known for his practical jokes, and when Ellen was a child, he'd sometimes play tricks on her. He'd never own up to his teasing, but always blamed her *mam*. Her *mam* would shake her head and say, "You'll never know, I suppose." Her mother was always loyal, even when it meant taking the blame for mischief she hadn't created.

In any case, the circled date was always the first thing she saw when she came downstairs in the morning, and the last thing she saw before going up to bed. "Nothing like a little pressure," she had muttered under her breath the first time she had spotted it. But she didn't really blame them. They were, as always, thinking of her best interests. She hoped she'd be as good a parent as they had been, and she never failed to thank God for them in her evening prayers.

Saturday found Ellen with both families, her own and the Shetlers, at a community apple-cider gathering. That year, a few varieties of apples had come ripe early, so the work frolic was being held nearly a month earlier than usual. The husband of one of Dinah's daughters owned a large apple orchard, and it was their custom to host a community gathering every fall.

The older men and women, aided by teenagers and younger women with babies, watched over the children, providing pony rides, apple bobbing and taffy pulls. There were sack races, tug-of-war contests and games, all intended to keep the little ones entertained while their mothers made huge kettles of apple butter over open fires. The younger men were equally busy. They were in charge of making enough apple cider to share with the entire Amish community. It was a much-awaited day of work and play, visiting and plenty of food to offset the business of cider-and-apple-butter making.

With so many hands to help, even the tasks of stirring the bubbling apple butter and sorting and grinding bushels and bushels of ripe apples were enjoyable. Ellen and Micah had arrived early and contributed their share of labor before noon so that they could take part in the corn-toss games, the wood-chopping contest, the egg and spoon races and the corn-husking and shelling competitions. Ellen had come in first in the blindfolded egg-and-spoon race, and Micah had won the wood-chopping contest. The prize was a new ax, a gift that brought a lot of laughter from the onlookers.

"If you run out of wood to cut, you can come over to my woodshed this afternoon," Bishop Andy called. "Or the schoolhouse. They're always looking for firewood."

Micah rubbed the blisters on his hands and groaned. "I think I've had enough chopping for one day." That brought more laughter from the crowd.

"If I'd known he could cut wood that fast with an ax," Simeon shouted, "I wouldn't have bought that new saw."

Micah's friend Abram came over to slap Micah's back and congratulate him. "Don't forget there's a singing at the Rupps' tonight," he reminded. "You two are coming, aren't you?"

Micah looked at Ellen and grinned. "What do you say?"

"I don't know," she hedged. "Tomorrow's church."

"I promise I'll get you home early." Micah reached for the cup of cider she was drinking, and she laughed and held it out of his reach. In turn, he scooped up a handful of woodchips from the grass and threw them at her.

Ellen giggled as woodchips fell into her cup. "Now you can have it," she said.

"See how she treats me?" Micah grimaced, putting on an aggrieved expression for his friend. "What will she do once we're married?"

"*If* we're married," she answered saucily. "I haven't made up my mind about you yet." She picked the wood-chips out of the cup and tossed them back at him. Several struck his shirt and rolled off, leaving apple-cider stains.

He reached for her hand. "Come to the singing with me," he said.

"I'll think about it." She was tempted. She loved the singings but if she didn't get enough sleep tonight, she'd be yawning through the next morning's sermons. And that definitely wouldn't set a good example for the younger girls.

"Cutting wood is thirsty work." Micah indicated the barn where the men were still making cider. "Shall we walk over there and get some more before I collapse and die of thirst?"

They walked down the lane through the apple trees. On either side, young people were climbing ladders to reach the ripe fruit. Girls were holding out their aprons to catch apples tossed from boys in the trees and children ran under the branches snatching up fallen apples and taking bites. It was a wonderful day, a day of laughter and fun and combined work that would provide delicious cider and apple butter in the snowy days of winter.

As they walked, Micah's hand closed around hers. "Have you had as much fun today as I have?" he asked. "I hope so. Because any time I'm with you is the best time."

She tried to pull her hand free, but he held it tightly. "We shouldn't—" she began and then broke off when she spotted Neziah standing a few yards away, watching them. Surprised, Micah released her, and she tucked her hand behind her back like a guilty child caught with her fingers in cake icing.

There was something in Neziah's eyes that worried Ellen. Was he upset that she and Micah had been holding hands? She met Neziah's gaze. No, she sensed it was something else.

"I need to tell you both something," Neziah said as he walked toward them. His features were solemn, his eyes dark with swirling emotion.

Ellen and Micah exchanged glances as they approached his brother.

Neziah cleared his throat when they were standing in front of him. "I've been watching the two of you together and…" His voice was deep and raspy. "I see how happy the two of you are together. And I realized that…" He looked away and then back at them, making eye contact with first Micah, then Ellen. "I realized you belong together."

Micah frowned. "Brother—"

Neziah held up his hand. "Let me speak my piece while I have the nerve for it. I've been thinking on this all week. Praying on it. What I'm trying to say is that I'm stepping out of the…whatever this is we've been doing." He motioned to all three of them. "Micah, you and Ellen belong together. And I wish you…happiness." He straightened to his full height, and his lips thinned as he swallowed. "There's no need for you to wait. Ask Bishop Andy to cry your banns."

"You're sure?" Micah asked. "You're all right with this? Giving Ellen up?"

Neziah shook his head and smiled faintly. "Do you not know her any better than that? Ellen isn't mine to give." A look of resignation passed over his face. "Congratulations, brother. Ellen, I wish you all the best."

She stared at Neziah, feeling as if the wind had been knocked out of her. She was shocked by his words and if she admitted it to herself, a little angry with him.

"You've changed your mind? Now you don't want to marry me?" She exhaled. "After everything you said about—"

"It's best this way," Neziah interrupted. "As you said a long time ago, we're too different." He grasped Micah's hand and shook it. "You and Ellen have more in common. You'll make the best match."

Micah broke into a grin. "You're serious, aren't you?"

"*Jah.* Make her happy, Micah. I know you can. Just don't ever give me reason to think I made the wrong decision."

"I won't," Micah assured him, pumping his hand.

Ellen suddenly felt as though all the strength had gone out of her legs. She had the strangest desire to sink down on the grass and lean against the trunk of an apple tree. She couldn't think of what to say to Neziah and so she said nothing as he strode away. Then it occurred to her that she should be relieved. Her decision had been made for her. Now she didn't have to choose between the brothers. She would marry Micah. He would accept baptism, and they would wed with the full approval of their families and the church. Micah would be the father of her children, and they would live as best they could in their faith and grow old together.

"You heard him!" Micah caught her by the waist and swung her in a circle. "You're mine! Let's go to Bishop Andy right now! Neziah's right. There's no need to wait another day! We can start planning our wedding! Isn't it wonderful?" He lowered her to the ground. "We can be married in November," he went on. "I'll ask to join the church immediately and get them to cry the banns as soon—"

"*Nay,*" Ellen managed, pressing her hand to her forehead. She felt dizzy, from Micah spinning her around, no doubt. "Not yet."

"What do you mean, *not yet*?" He looked at her, his eyes crinkling at the corners. "You heard Neziah. He's taking back his offer of marriage. I've won you. You're mine, Ellen. Finally, really mine." He laughed and clapped his hands together. "This is the best day of my life. Of course, I know you'd have picked me in the end, but having Neziah's blessing makes it easier, doesn't it?"

Ellen pressed her lips together, only half hearing what Micah was saying. "We'll not make the announcement yet. Our agreement was for a month. To announce sooner would be inappropriate."

He scowled and opened his arms. "There's nothing inappropriate. We've known each other our whole lives. Neither of us is a kid. No one will think poorly of you for such a fast engagement."

It wasn't herself she was thinking about. It was Neziah. She didn't want to hurt him, not for anything. And it would hurt him, wouldn't it? For her to announce the engagement so quickly. Or was that what he wanted? To be done with her. To be over with it. "My father gave me a month," she said stubbornly. "We'll wait until the full month has passed. Then we'll tell everyone. Until then…" She nodded. "Until then, it will be our secret."

Chapter Fifteen

On Wednesday morning Gail stopped by the craft shop. She came in by the front door and waited, looking at the merchandise until Ellen rang up purchases for two customers and they left the store. "Good morning," Ellen said.

Gail smiled shyly. "Good morning." She looked as if she wanted to say something, but she just stood there.

"Is everything okay upstairs?" Ellen asked finally. "Bathroom working? You have enough hot water? The hot water heater is getting finicky."

Gail smiled again. "It's all wonderful. I love it up there. Did you know that through the west window you can see all the way to the farms on the far side of Lincoln Road?"

Ellen could hear Dinah rattling around in the kitchen, making an early lunch. Ellen had to take over the customers at two, while Dinah did her weekly grocery shopping. Dinah's sister always shopped on Wednesdays, too, and the two would enjoy coffee and a visit afterward.

When Gail didn't say anything, Ellen smiled at her. "Is there something I can help you with?"

"*Nay*, it's you I wanted to…" Gail caught the hem of her T-shirt between her fingers and twisted it nervously. "I was wondering if you'd like to come to lunch with me today. My treat," she added quickly. "I wanted to thank you."

"Gail," Ellen began. "That's not necessary. I'm glad you're staying here. It's company for Dinah, just knowing someone else is in the building at night. You don't need to spend your money on me."

"Please. Please come," Gail said all in a rush. "And it isn't costing me a penny. Except for the tip," she added. "Margaret allots us so many meals, and I saved one for you. We can have anything, so long as our bill doesn't go over ten dollars each. I know you always take off early for lunch on Wednesday, and it would make me happy if you'd have lunch with me."

"All right," Ellen agreed. It was clear that it meant a lot to Gail, and wasn't she always telling her mother that she had to learn to accept help from other people? What had she said to her just this morning? "You have to learn to be a gracious receiver as well as a giver." And besides, she would welcome the opportunity to get to know Gail better. Even if they'd gotten off to a poor start, Ellen felt that Gail was someone that she'd like to have as a friend.

Half an hour later Dinah was behind the counter at the store, and Gail and Ellen were seated in a quiet corner at the Mennonite Family Restaurant. To Ellen's delight, she was enjoying her time with her new tenant. There on neutral ground, Gail was more relaxed, even friendly. She didn't talk a lot, but what she said was sensible and interesting.

"Today's one of my days off," Gail explained after they'd ordered. She spooned sugar into a tall glass of iced tea. "Wednesday is meatloaf and mac and cheese day. It's one of their lunch specials, but you can have whatever you like. The meatloaf is so good that I asked the cook for the recipe."

"Did she give it to you?" Ellen asked.

Gail shook her head. "Not yet, but she will. She likes me. She even asked me to come to one of their church services."

"Do you think you'll go? To Mennonite worship?"

Gail stirred her tea. "I don't know. Not yet, but maybe one day. It's all sort of confusing. I've always gone…" She sighed and glanced up at Ellen. "I've never gone to any other church service but Amish. It's hard to think of worshipping with another faith."

"The Lord is still with you, Gail, wherever you are."

She nodded. "I pray. A lot. But there's a lot of stuff that I haven't figured out yet."

"Can I ask if you were baptized?" Ellen kept her voice low. "It's none of my business, but—"

"You think I've been shunned?" Gail shook her head. "No. I wasn't baptized so I wasn't shunned by the church. Probably by my family, though. My father would…" She broke off and looked away.

Ellen waited and was rewarded when Gail went on.

"My father doesn't forgive easily. I love him, but I can't live with him. Not ever again." She met Ellen's gaze. "He's not a bad man, but I think he's troubled… in his head." She sighed again. "When he was a child, he went into the barn and found his father dead by his own hand. *Mutter* says it preys on his mind. He was only seven years old. Too young to see such a thing."

"I'm sorry," Ellen said, seeing that Gail was near to tears. "I shouldn't have asked."

"Nay." Gail gave her a half smile. "I should have told you that I hadn't been shunned. I would never do anything to get you or anyone in trouble." She took a sip of her iced tea. "I guess you could say that I'm *rum-springa*. I never joined the church. *Vadder* wanted me to. Said I shamed him by not being baptized with my younger sister. That's why I left when I did. It has to be my decision to accept the Plain life, doesn't it?"

"It does," Ellen agreed. "Let's talk about something else. I'm sorry if I've upset you."

"Jah." Gail forced a smile. "It is your treat and my pleasure to have you. At home, I had friends. And my sisters and brothers. I was close to them. It hurts to think I might not see them again."

"Because you don't think you can go home?"

"Jah."

"Life changes, Gail. It may not be as bad as you think. As they grow up, they can choose to visit you if they like."

"I suppose, the ones that *Vadder* hasn't convinced that I'm *schlecht*." Wicked.

"I don't think you're bad," Ellen assured her. "I think you're a kindhearted person."

Gail lowered her hands to her lap. "I try to be. But sometimes I have resentful thoughts about my father. It is a failing of mine, to always question and not accept my father's rule. Honor your mother and father, the Bible tells us. *Mutter* said I should just obey him, and everything would be all right. That was her way, but not mine."

Ellen listened without saying anything.

"Usually I honor *Vadder* with my actions, but not always in my thoughts." She crumbled her napkin and laid it beside her plate. "Here I am still talking about my troubles when I should be congratulating you. I hear that you and Micah Shetler are going to marry. That's wonderful." Her eyes took on a sparkle. "I've seen your Micah. He's very tall and very handsome."

"*Jah*, he is, isn't he?" Ellen agreed. "We've been talking, spending time together for the last few weeks, trying to decide if we want to walk out together. It's a big decision, who you will marry. Someday, you'll have to choose a husband. Is there anyone you left behind? In your community?"

"Me?" Gail chuckled. "*Nay*. There is no one special." She glanced around to see if anyone was close enough to hear and said, "I've seen you with the other one, too. Micah's brother?"

"My *vadder* and his *vadder* wanted me to marry one of them," Ellen admitted. "I just didn't know which one."

"The older one looks nice, too, but very serious. And he has *kinner*. How many?"

"Two boys. One is four and one almost six. The oldest just started school."

"Ah, the chunky one. He's cute. They are both cute children. Well behaved."

"Not always. They need a mother. It was one of the things that I considered—if it was God's plan for me that I should nurture these motherless children."

Gail nodded. "But you're happy with your choice of Micah?"

"Very happy. We're perfectly matched." Ellen paused as the waitress brought their lunches, thanked her and then continued after she left the table. "The last few weeks have been so busy I haven't had time to sew a single piece for my trousseau. Micah took me to Hershey Park, bowling and to the apple butter frolic on Saturday."

Gail bowed her head, and Ellen clasped her hand and did the same. Steam rose from Ellen's soup as she offered a silent grace. And when she opened her eyes, Gail was studying her intently.

"What? What is it?" Ellen asked.

"Nothing." Gail poured catsup on her meatloaf. "I just wondered…" She shook her head. "It's nothing."

"It must be something," Ellen said.

"Forgive me. I speak when I should hold my tongue. It's another of my faults."

"What?" Ellen looked at her across the table. "Tell me."

Gail sighed. "You say you're happy, but your eyes are sad, and there's no shine to you. Usually, you bustle about and everyone can feel the joy shining out of you. But when you speak of the man you will marry, you don't look happy."

"Nonsense," Ellen protested. "Of course I'm happy. Micah and I are perfect for each other. We're so much alike. He likes to laugh and have a good time and so do I."

"Pay no heed to me." Gail gave a wave. "I talk when I shouldn't. You know your own affairs best. I wish you

happiness in your marriage." She flushed pink. "And…
and I hope you will invite me to the wedding."

Although she'd thoroughly enjoyed her lunch with
Gail, something about their conversation troubled Ellen,
and she kept going over and over it in her head as Micah
drove her home that evening. Gail's statement about her
not *looking happy* lingered in her mind all evening. The
next morning, as she was cleaning away the breakfast
dishes, she couldn't resist mentioning her uneasiness
to her mother. Her *dat* had already gone outside, and
Ellen and her mother were alone. Her mother seemed
fine this morning, cheerful and energetic, and it eased
Ellen's heart to see her old self.

"*Mam*, are you pleased that I've decided to marry
Micah?" she asked as she carried the milk and butter
back to the refrigerator. Her mother was standing at
the big farm sink, scrubbing away at the already spotless surface.

Her mother turned and smiled at her. "Of course I
am. He is a *goot* boy. With Micah you will always have
laughter at your table. And you always were one who
loved to laugh. Like your *dat*." She dried her hands
on her apron, went to the cupboard and retrieved the
sugar bowl that she'd just put away. Removing the lid,
she sprinkled sugar liberally into the sink and started
scrubbing again.

Ellen suddenly felt uneasy. "*Mam?* Did you just pour
sugar in the sink?"

"*Jah*. I'm cleaning. I always use *tzooker*. Didn't I
teach you that? And to clean out the drains, mix it with
vinegar. Better than the stuff in the can from the store
it is."

"Drains? *Ach*, you mean baking soda, don't you? Not sugar, baking soda."

"*Nay*, you have the wrong of it, girl. *Tzooker*. Would you teach a hen to lay eggs? Who taught you all you know about cleaning and cooking?"

Ellen nodded. Once her mother got a thing in her head, it was best not to argue with her. And what harm would it do, to wash the sink with sugar? Other than to attract a few ants? And empty the sugar bowl.

"So," her mother went on. "It worries you. That you chose Micah over the other one. What's his name?"

"Neziah." Surely her mother hadn't forgotten Neziah's name. "Neziah is the oldest. But I didn't say I was worried."

"The one with the two sweet children. So sweet, those *kinner*. Like little *fett fastnachts*. You ask the Shetlers to supper tomorrow night. I will make gingerbread for them. Your Micah, he likes gingerbread, too. When he was a boy, he used to steal it off my windowsill when it was cooling." She laughed. "He didn't know I left it for him on purpose."

"Micah stole gingerbread?"

"*Jah*. His mother, you remember her." She wouldn't mention Irma's name if she could help it. It was a habit of the older generation. Dead was dead. In heaven. In a better place. And best not to linger and grieve too long. At least not in theory. Or in public. "A *goot* woman, she was. A kind heart. But a terrible cook. I tasted her gingerbread once." Mam grimaced. "Fit for *hink el fress a*." Chicken feed. She emptied the remaining sugar into the sink. "So you think maybe you have made a mistake?"

"I didn't say I made a mistake." Ellen crossed the kitchen to stand within an arm's length. Her mother turned from the sink, dried her hands on her apron and hugged her. It was such an unusual gesture that Ellen's throat constricted. Her arms tightened around her mother and for long seconds they stood there, content in their embrace.

"You will be a bride," her mother said softly. "You should be happy. It's one thing to be nervous, but you should be thinking about Micah all the time. His face is the last one that should come to you before you fall asleep and the first when you open your eyes in the morning." A rosy flush tinted her cheeks. "I was like that with your *vadder*. That I do not forget. Some things I do. I know that. But the time before we married…" Her smile lit up her eyes. "Just seeing him walk down the road toward me was as sweet as molasses candy. And if Micah doesn't make you feel that way…" She shrugged and gestured with her hands. "Then maybe you should think some more."

"But…but you like Micah best. You said—"

"Pfff." Her mother shook her head. "What I like is nothing. What's not to like about a pleasant young man from a *goot* family with a face like his?" She raised a warning finger. "Always you were the logical one. Even as a child. Thinking. Sensible. But maybe for this picking of a husband, you are too sensible."

"I don't understand," Ellen protested. "You always said that marriage was a great responsibility, that a woman had to choose carefully because it would dictate the rest of her life."

"*Jah.* True, true," her mother agreed. "But it is not that simple. For me…well, you know that I came from a family…" She struggled for the words. "Not rich, but comfortable. Very comfortable, with rich land and big barns full of fat cattle. So many horses to work the land we had to have a separate stable for them. There was another young man who came courting me, and my *mutter* and *vadder* liked him best because his family had even more land than we did. He was a preacher's son with his own dairy farm, while your *vadder* was poor, without a cow to his name. No disrespect to your *vadder*. They wanted only that I, their daughter, should be well cared for."

"But you loved *Dat* and so you chose him."

"*Jah*. Sometimes a woman must follow her heart. Logic said marry the man with the farm, but your *vadder* warmed my heart."

"And you never doubted your choice?"

"*Nay*, never once. We have been happy together. Our greatest trouble was that I could not give him a houseful of sons and daughters. But he never blamed me. And he does not blame me now that my tongue says the wrong word and that I forget—"

A loud knock at the door interrupted her *mam*. "Ellen!"

"Coming, Micah," she answered. Ellen leaned close and kissed her mother's cheek. "Thank you," she murmured.

"Is that Micah?" her *mutter* asked. "Is he looking for gingerbread? Tell him I'll bake gingerbread tomorrow."

"He's taking me to work. To the shop."

"Is your *vadder* going to the shop?"

Ellen shook her head. "He's staying here with you. I'll be late this evening."

"Micah's taking you?"

"*Jah*." Ellen removed her work apron and donned the starched one she wore at the store. "Just a second,

Micah." She hurried out onto the porch. "Just let me get my scooter."

"Don't bother," Micah said. "I'm coming back for you."

"But…we always take my scooter."

"No need for it," he said firmly. "I'm looking out for you now."

As Micah guided Samson out of Ellen's lane and onto the blacktop, she looked back toward the house. Micah was right. He was picking her up after work; she didn't need her scooter. But not having it made her uneasy. They always took the scooter in the back of the buggy so that she'd have it if she wanted it. It wasn't about needing the scooter so much as knowing it was there if she did need it. Or want it. It was silly of her, but the farther she got from home, the more the absence of the green scooter became like a thorn in her heel that she couldn't pluck out. It was a dull ache she couldn't dismiss.

If she was unusually quiet on the ride to Honeysuckle, Micah didn't seem to notice. He was as entertaining as always, relating a story about an Amish farmer he'd met at the sawmill. There was no traffic on the road, and Samson was moving along at a good clip when raindrops began splattering on the horse's back.

"See, it's starting to rain." Micah gestured toward the sky. "Wouldn't you have been a fine sight riding home after dark in the rain on that scooter of yours?"

Ellen squirmed on the seat. Her distress was making her more uncomfortable by the moment. She didn't want to be warm and dry and safe in the buggy with Micah; she wanted to be on her scooter. It made no sense. She didn't know why she felt she'd been wronged when all Micah was doing was trying to take care of her, but that was exactly how she felt.

She'd heard other girls talk about wedding jitters. This must be what they meant. It was probably just the excitement of their pending announcement that was making her feel like she didn't fit in her own skin. She hadn't been herself since Saturday. She nibbled at her bottom lip, thinking about how excited she had been that morning, how eager she'd been to go to the apple frolic. She'd had a wonderful time, and the day had ended with the problem of her husband solved.

She should be relieved, she told herself. She should be elated that Neziah had made the decision of which brother to choose for her.

But then she thought about what her mother had said to her in the kitchen. Her words reverberated in Ellen's head. *If Micah doesn't make you feel that way, then maybe you'd better think some more.*

Did Micah make her feel *that way*? Was his face the last thing that came to mind before she fell asleep and the first thing she imagined when she opened her eyes in the morning?

She squeezed her eyes shut, not caring if she looked silly.

She loved Micah. She *did.*

But did she love him as a husband or a friend? And was part of the excitement having handsome, popular Micah court her? Had she been influenced by what everyone else thought? She loved him, but was she *in love* with him? Would she ever be?

The thought of her scooter sitting in the shed came to mind again and she opened her eyes. Suddenly, she realized it wasn't the scooter she cared about, it was the fact that Micah didn't understand how important her scooter was to her. How important her independence was to her. "Stop," she said abruptly. "Micah, stop the buggy."

"What?" He looked down the road and then glanced in the mirror. "What's wrong? Did I miss something?"

"Please, Micah." She bunched her skirt in both her hands and stared straight ahead at the wet pavement. This was crazy, but she couldn't help herself. She couldn't ride another moment in the buggy. "Stop the horse. I have to get out."

"What do you mean you have to get out? In the rain?"

She gripped the dashboard and got to her feet, even though the buggy was still rolling. "I mean it, Micah. Stop the horse or I'm jumping out."

Micah reined in Samson and turned to her, his face flushed. "What's wrong? Did I say something to upset you? Did I do something?"

"*Nay*, Micah, you didn't. This isn't your fault. Please know that. It's mine. It's me." She reached out and gripped his upper arm and made herself meet his gaze. "I'm sorry, Micah, but I need to think. I have to be alone."

"Is this about your scooter?" He was upset now. She could tell that he was fighting to control his annoyance. "If you want the scooter that bad, I'll go back and—"

"It's not the scooter. Not really." Suddenly, her heart was pounding. "Oh, Micah, I think I've made a terrible mistake," she murmured as much to herself as to him.

"What do you mean, a *mistake*?" His shocked blue gaze locked with hers. "About what?" he asked suspiciously.

He knew.

"I can't marry you, Micah," she blurted, tears filling her eyes. She didn't want to hurt him, but to marry him would hurt him more someday. "I love you, but we're not right for each other. I'm just so sorry I didn't see it sooner."

"What…what do you mean you can't marry me? We're perfect for each other."

"*Nay*, we're not."

He looked away. "But I've told everyone we're going to be married. I'll look like a fool. What will I say to them?"

"That's what matters to you? What others will say?" she asked him.

He looked at her. Blinked. "What?"

She shook her head. Now she was even surer of herself than she had been a minute before. "You can tell people the truth. Tell them that we decided that we were better friends than husband and wife." She climbed down out of the buggy.

"Ellen, you can't be serious," he called down to her. "You can't break up with me."

"I'm sorry," she said once more. Then, straightening her shoulders, she started walking the way they had come. Raindrops wet her face and cheeks and arms, but she didn't stop. And she didn't look back.

Chapter Sixteen

By the time Ellen reached the end of her parents' lane, the spits of rain had turned to full-fledged raindrops, but if she squinted she was certain that it looked brighter to the west. The way the clouds were scudding overhead and the way the air smelled, it seemed to her that serious rain might miss them and the sun might come out. Either way, she'd made up her mind to go to the shop. If it cleared, she'd take her scooter. If it was going to rain, maybe she'd just take the buggy.

It was funny how it was Micah's insistence that she leave her scooter behind that had brought her to the realization that she couldn't marry Micah. She felt bad about the way she had broken the news to him; she knew she'd hurt him. But better to endure short-term pain than one that would stretch through years of marriage. Now Micah would be free to marry the woman God truly intended for him.

As she walked up her driveway she was surprised that thoughts of Neziah drifted through her head. She loved him. And not the way she had loved him as a young girl. She loved him for who he was now: a mature man, a father, a son, a brother.

Ellen fought back tears. What had she done? She'd made a mess of things, that was what. How could she have been so blind not to see it? She'd never stopped loving him and wondering how their courtship had gone wrong. It was Neziah whose plain face rose in her dreams... Neziah, whose fathomless, dark eyes touched a chord in her heart. But loving someone didn't mean that you couldn't live without him. Marriage had to be the coming together of *two* hearts and *two* minds.

But Neziah had been the one to reject her, she reminded herself. *Neziah* had decided she wasn't the one for him.

So now she would have neither of the Shetlers. Maybe God's plan for her had always been to remain unwed. This way, she could devote her life to caring for her parents. She wasn't unhappy. It was a life full of joy. She had friends, her faith, her family and a job that she looked forward to going to. If she didn't marry, she wouldn't have children of her own, but that wouldn't keep her from caring for other children. She could still help raise his little boys; she could volunteer to help other young mothers in her church. She could be content with the many blessings the Lord had bestowed on her.

Ellen continued trudging up the steep driveway, feeling older than thirty-three, wishing she'd been wiser, kinder. Micah hadn't deserved the way she'd sprung her decision on him. She hoped he would forgive her and that they would continue to remain friends. She hoped Simeon wouldn't be too disappointed with her. She didn't know how she would explain things to her parents. But somehow, she would make them understand that she just couldn't do it. It would be unfair to become Micah's wife if her heart longed for Neziah. Of course, she couldn't admit that to anyone, not even to her mother and father. That was too personal. They'd just have to accept her explanation that she'd decided not to marry. And they would accept it. They loved her unconditionally. No matter how they might wish she'd make another choice, they would support her decision.

What she'd done to Micah was awful, but going through with the courtship and wedding would have been worse. Marriage was forever. "God forgive me," she murmured. She only hoped that whatever gossip their parting caused in the community, it would be directed at her and not him. Micah had done nothing wrong. And neither had Neziah, honestly. He had the right to say she wasn't the wife for him, the same way she had the right to say Micah wasn't for her.

As Ellen walked into the yard, headed for the shed where she kept her scooter, her mother came bustling toward her. "What are you doing?" She'd thrown an old apron over her head to protect against the rain and peered out from beneath it at Ellen.

"*Mam*, it's raining. You shouldn't be out in the rain," Ellen admonished.

"Nonsense. Do you think I'll melt? I'm not a sugar cake." Her mother pulled the apron off her head and tugged her blue scarf in place over her gray hair. As always, her bun was secure and not a pin was out of place, a skill Ellen had never learned. "Didn't I see you ride away in Micah's buggy? I thought he was driving you to church service."

"*Nay*," Ellen replied gently. "It's not the Sabbath. Micah came to drive me to the craft shop."

Her mother's eyes narrowed suspiciously. "So why are you here? What's wrong? Did you and Micah quarrel?"

Ellen shook her head. "We didn't quarrel. But I've broken off with him. I can't marry him, *Mam*." She let her hands fall to her sides. "I'm sorry. I just can't."

"And what's wrong with Micah, I ask? Such a *goot*-looking boy. Such a hard worker. But naughty to make you late for church. Shame on him."

"It isn't Sunday, *Mam*," she repeated. "And, it's not Micah's fault that I refused him. Nothing like that. It's me. I don't love him—not in that way. In the way you talked about this morning." Rain ran off the shed's tin roof, dripping down the back of her dress. "Can we talk about this later? I need to get my scooter and go to work."

"On a Sunday? *Nay*. You'll not go to work on the Sabbath." Her mother pushed her firmly back into the shed and followed, stepping around the scooter that blocked part of the door. "Best you tell me all of it," her mother said.

Ellen felt like she had the time she was fourteen and had played hooky from school to spend the afternoon fishing with friends. Her mother had found out, and she'd been more concerned that Ellen didn't consider the gravity of her offense than angry. But the intensity of that concern had stung more than harsh words. Ellen hadn't repeated the mischief. And after that, she'd applied herself to her studies. Mam had never told her father, saying that it would disappoint him too much. That kindness had endeared her to Ellen and strengthened the bond between them.

"There's nothing to tell," Ellen hedged. "I made

a mistake. I thought that I could marry Micah, that those feelings would come with marriage, that being his friend was enough. But it isn't."

Her mother folded her arms. "So? You feel the same about Neziah? You turned him down, too?"

"Neziah turned *me* down. He doesn't want to marry me." She'd told her mother that when it had happened, told both her parents when she'd announced that she'd be courting Micah only. Ellen didn't want to remind her that they'd already gone over this, especially since her mother had seemed so lucid earlier that morning. She'd given her good advice, advice that might have caused a problem today but would prove to be wise in the years to come.

"Neziah decided that I wasn't the right woman for him, remember?" Ellen explained softly. "Isn't that what courtship is for, so that both parties will have the opportunity to get to know each other?"

"*Jah*, that is true," her mother agreed. She tilted her head to one side and tapped the side of her nose in the way she did when she was thinking hard. "But why did Neziah decide not to marry you? Was he thinking of his happiness or yours?"

"His," Ellen replied quickly. "I'm sure…at least…" She hesitated. "I think…"

To her surprise, her mother did an unusual thing. She put her arms around Ellen and whispered, "You are sure you know Neziah's mind, or you *think* you know his mind?" She peered into Ellen's eyes. "There's a difference."

Ellen's throat constricted. "I… I'm sure," she answered. She returned her mother's embrace, amazed that she'd showed so much emotion twice in the same day. Ellen was almost overcome with love for her. She'd never doubted it, but their relationship had been reversed for so long. Oftentimes she felt like the mother instead of the daughter. But at this instant, everything was as it should be. She hugged her mother tightly.

"Doesn't sound like you're sure to me. Best find out. You must go to him," her mother said firmly as she let go of her. "To Neziah."

"To Neziah? I can't do that. What would I say to him?"

Her mother released her and stepped away. "You must go to him and tell him that you've broken off with his brother. That you made a mistake and that he's the one you should have chosen."

Ellen stared at her mother. "I didn't...didn't say that."

Her *mam* smiled. "I'm old, and sometimes I'm confused, but I'm not blind. Go to him, daughter. Tell Neziah the truth."

"And then what? What good will it do?" Ellen asked. "It's too late."

"Nay." Her mother chuckled. "When you're in the grave, only then is it too late to right wrongs. I'm not saying you telling him how you feel will change anything. It probably won't, but you'll have done the right thing. You'll say your prayers tonight with a clear conscience. Now, gather your courage and go to him. Now."

"Now?" Ellen's eyes widened. "I...I can't go now. I have to open the shop. Customers may—"

"Horse feathers. Dinah is there."

She shook her head. "No, she has a doctor's appointment this morning."

"Then your father can hitch up the horse and we can go to the store ourselves. All day he putters around the house spying on me, fussing like a broody hen. You go and make right what you have made wrong with your Neziah." She stepped back to the open shed door and called. "*Vadder!* Where are you?"

Ellen tried in vain to think of a reason not to do as her mother ordered.

Her mother glanced back at her and made a shooing motion. "What are you standing there for? It's stopped raining. Take your silly green scooter and go find Neziah."

Ellen was halfway up the Shetler lane when she realized that there was no reason to believe that Neziah would be at the house at that time of the morning. He would be at the sawmill. She hadn't heard the grinding of the big saw, but if Neziah wasn't there, he could be away from the farm buying or surveying uncut timber. Joel would be at school, and Asa would be with Simeon. Ellen hoped she wouldn't meet Simeon before she found Neziah; she was unprepared to explain her decision not to marry Micah.

It hadn't stopped raining as her mother had said, but it was more of a drizzle than a downpour. Much of the lane passed under trees, and they dripped an unending series of drops on her head and clothing. The dirt road was hard-packed and not so steep as her own driveway, but the rain had made the surface slick. When she reached the fork that led to the sawmill, it became easier to walk than to use her scooter. She propped it up against a fence post and hurried on toward the mill.

A movement at the wood line caught her attention. Just coming out of the trees was a team of oxen pulling a massive log. Two men walked beside the animals, one tall, and the other shorter and stockier. It was too far to be certain, but from the way he carried himself, Ellen guessed that the taller man was Neziah and the other, one of his employees. She waved and shouted.

On her second attempt, Neziah saw her and waved back. He left the plodding team and cut across the field toward her. Ellen's heart sank as warm needles of rain pattered against her face and arms. Wet grass under her shoes squished with every step she took, and tendrils of her wet hair clung to her face. She wished she hadn't come. What was she thinking? Now, not only would she embarrass herself in front of Neziah, but they'd have a witness.

"Ellen!" Neziah called. "What are you doing out in this rain?" He tugged off his rawhide gloves and banged them against his trousers to knock off the mud. "Is everything all right?"

She walked toward him. His shirt was soaked through, and it clung to his broad chest and shoulders. His boots were muddy and the bottom of his trousers caked with bits of leaves and dirt. His straw hat was dark with moisture and bore bits of twigs.

Ellen swallowed hard as they met halfway. She wondered how she could have ever thought his features plain. A flush of heat washed over her throat and crept up to scald her cheeks. Looking at Neziah here in the fields, his callused hands scarred and blistered from the heavy work of cutting timber and handling logs, his stride so confident and graceful. He didn't need the beard to identify him as a mature man. That was evident in his gaze and in his bearing. Next to him, she realized, handsome Micah was still a boy.

"I need to talk to you," she said, her voice sounding oddly vulnerable to her ears. "I've broken off the betrothal with Micah."

He stared down at her. His features revealed nothing of what he was thinking. "This is no place to talk. You'll catch your death of cold." He motioned toward the sawmill's main building. "Let's get inside, out of the rain."

Numbly, she followed him. This was worse than she'd thought it would be. Why had she let her mother convince her to talk to Neziah today, while she was still reeling from the implications of what she'd done? As they walked quickly toward shelter, it began to rain harder, and she started to shiver.

When they reached the overhang that ran around the side of the building Neziah said, "Let me find you something to put on. Wait here." Seconds later he was back with an old denim jacket. She stood stock-still as he draped it around her shoulders.

It smelled like sawdust, the forest and Neziah. She huddled inside the coat, wishing she could disappear. "I...I told your brother I can't marry him," she said.

"And why would you do that?" He was standing very close. His dark gaze held hers.

She sucked in a breath. "Because...because I don't love him."

"But you had told him that you *would* marry him?" Neziah's tone was matter-of-fact, not accusing. Calm.

"I did, but it was a mistake, a terrible mistake."

"I see."

She sneezed, and to her shame, her nose was beginning to run. Neziah pulled a clean handkerchief from his back pocket and handed it to her. Gratefully, she took it.

"And now you've come to tell me."

She nodded.

"In the rain. You rode your scooter here in the rain to tell me?" He offered her the hint of a smile.

"I don't love Micah," she repeated. "I can't marry him." She wiped her nose with his handkerchief again.

He clasped the leather gloves in his hands, twisting them as he spoke, his eyes watching her. "And you won't change your mind about Micah?"

Ellen shook her head. "*Nay.* I won't."

"Is there someone else?" he asked.

She averted her gaze. Why was he making this so hard for her? "I shouldn't have come here," she said. "I just… I didn't want you to think…" She trailed off. Why *had* she come? "I'm sorry. I guess I just wanted to tell you."

"But there is someone else?" he pressed. "Another man you'd rather have?"

She nodded dumbly. "But it's impossible. He doesn't feel that way about me."

"He doesn't?"

"*Nay.*"

"And you're certain of that?" He took a step toward her.

Her shivering had become shaking. She wanted to run. "He told me so." She lifted her gaze to meet his, afraid she would burst into tears at any moment. "You… you told me in the orchard."

"I told you that I didn't want to marry you?" He smiled. "*Nay*, Ellen, I didn't say that. I said that I thought you and Micah would be happier together. It was *your* happiness that I was thinking of. But if you don't want him, then there's no reason why I can't marry you. Is there?"

She stood there for a moment, staring up at him, him staring down at her. "You *do* want to marry me? After the way I've behaved? The trouble I've caused your family?"

"You can be trouble," he agreed. "But then, I think most things worth having can be." He hesitated and then went on. "Don't you see? I've never stopped loving you, Ellen." His smile widened. "So if you've behaved unwisely, you are no worse than me." He chuckled. "Of course, if we are to consider marriage, I have conditions."

She didn't know if she wanted to laugh or cry. Neziah wanted to marry her! He wanted to marry her. "What conditions?" she asked suspiciously.

"I've had some time to think this over, and I'll warn you, it's take it or leave it."

She waited, unconsciously holding her breath.

"First, I don't believe I would be comfortable having you and Micah under the same roof. It would make things too awkward when he starts courting again and later brings home a wife. And my boys are mischief enough without my father adding salt to our butter, so we'll have to live with your parents." He grinned at her. "Until I can build you your own house, of course. Or a *grossdaddi* house for them, whichever you'd prefer."

She nodded. "*Jah*, I would like that. I would like to be close to my mother and father, so I can look after them. And my mother would love to have Asa and Joel at her table."

"*Goot.* That's settled." He reached for her hand. "And two, building a house costs money, so I think it would be best if you kept working at the shop. At least as long as you want to."

Tears clouded her eyes. "You mean it? You don't care if I work?"

"So long as I can hire a girl to help with the housework and tend to the boys. You can hardly be in two places at one time, can you?"

She shook her head.

"And one more thing."

"*Jah*, Neziah?" Her eyes were so clouded with tears that she could hardly make out his sweet, strong face, but she could feel the warmth of his coat around her.

"I think it would be a *goot* idea for you to continue to ride your scooter to work in the morning so you have a few minutes to yourself each day. The boys and I will pick you up in the afternoon. Does that sound right?"

"It sounds exactly right," she said.

"So you agree to my terms?"

She smiled at him through her tears. "I agree, Neziah. But…I have one requirement of my own."

"Do you?"

She nodded. "November is the traditional time for weddings, and I'd like ours to be the first in the community this fall. We've wasted too much time already."

"Agreed." He pulled her into his arms and looked down into her face. He was so close that she could feel his warm breath. Her heart was pounding so hard she was certain that he must feel it through the thickness of the denim jacket and their clothing. "So, will you do me the honor of becoming my wife and the mother of my children?"

"I will, Neziah. With all my heart."

Smiling, he bent and kissed her, and the kiss was every bit as wonderful as she had always imagined it would be. And in that instant, the tenderness of that caress washed away all her doubts. Her mind and her heart filled with joy. In spite of all her missteps and stumbles and the twists and turns of her journey, this was the path the Lord had laid out for her. And she intended to walk every step of the way with her hand in Neziah's.

Epilogue

*Chincoteague National Wildlife Refuge, Virginia
September, one year later*

"There. Just as they told us at the Visitor's Center. We can see the whole Snow Goose Pool from the observation platform." Neziah propped his black push scooter against a post at the end of the walkway, and Ellen did the same with her green one.

They climbed the steps to the viewing platform, and Ellen raised her binoculars to scan the large, brackish pond. There were so many geese, ducks and waterbirds swimming and diving over the surface of the blue-green water that she didn't know where to aim her binoculars. It was early morning, and few visitors were out yet. This was fall migration for a multitude of bird species, but the only other birders they could see were far away. The closest, a man in fatigues wearing a cowboy hat, was sighting in a large telescope near the shore, several hundred yards away.

"Look, black-tipped skimmers." Neziah pointed out a line of gangly, black-and-white waterbirds with distinctive black-tipped red beaks swooping over the surface of the pond.

Ellen turned in the direction he indicated and watched the skimmers scooping up small fish until they swooped in perfect formation and soared out of sight along the edge of the marsh. "Be sure and write them down," she reminded him. Neziah was keeping a tally of species and numbers of each kind of bird that they sighted each day.

Their vacation, actually a belated honeymoon, was to be a week long, and this was their third day at the refuge. Neziah had asked her where she wanted to go, and she'd chosen Chincoteague for bird-watching during the fall migration. They'd saved all year so that they could hire a driver to take them to and from Virginia, stay in a motel, eat in restaurants and have enough money for admission to the refuge.

Although they had taken accommodations on Chincoteague, the refuge was actually on Assateague Island, across the channel. There were over fourteen thousand acres of beach, marsh, dunes and maritime forest teeming with birds and other wildlife, including sitka deer, wild ponies and the elusive fox squirrels.

For Ellen, this was a dream come true. Neziah shared her fascination with bird-watching, and the trip was a welcome escape from their everyday life at home. If the sight of two Old Order Amish pushing their scooters along the Wildlife Loop or parking them outside the Tom's Cover Visitor Center did attract a little attention from the tourists, Ellen didn't care. She'd seen her first oystercatcher that morning, and the day before they'd sighted a merlin, a flock of piping plovers and six brown pelicans.

Neziah pointed to a broad-winged bird circling high

over the pool. "Eagle," he said. "Must be a young one. Has the white tail but not much white on the head yet." He studied the bird through the binoculars she'd given him for his birthday, identical to the ones he'd presented her with as a wedding gift the previous November.

Ellen sighed with pleasure. This trip was everything she'd imagined it might be when they'd spent hours going over the maps and brochures describing the refuge and the restaurants and lodging available on Chincoteague. Neziah had wanted to bring her in May for the spring migration, but her mother had fallen and broken her wrist. Ellen hadn't felt able to leave her at that time. The six of them were still living in her parents' home, but the *grossdaddi* house would be ready for her mother and father to move into by the end of the month. When her father had opted for downsizing to a smaller space, Neziah had started planning for the cottage addition to the house. It had a separate entrance and another off the parlor so that there would be easy access for any of them to move back and forth between the two homes.

The children had settled into their new home easily. Asa continued to spend much of his day with Simeon while Joel was in school. Sometimes, Ellen took Asa to the shop with her, and other days he accompanied his father to the woods or his uncle Micah to the sawmill. Micah was courting a sweet girl from the next town over and seemed to have completely gotten over Ellen, with no hard feelings. Slowly Joel and Asa had come to think of Ellen as their mother, and she had come to love them both. She was still concerned about Joel's tendency to fill up on sweets when he was with Simeon, but she was gradually bringing order into both boys' lives. As she'd expected, her mother had gathered them into her arms and heart. Joel was surprisingly protective of his new *grossmama* and gave little trouble to Maddie, the girl they had hired to keep an eye on both of them. Her father, likewise, adored Asa and Joel, often spending hours making them wooden toys and teaching them how to care for the chickens and how to coax the largest and sweetest tomatoes from the garden.

Neziah stepped back from the railing and slipped an arm around Ellen's shoulders. She smiled up at him, and her heart leaped as she remembered the sweetness of their time together in the hotel room, with its private balcony and view of the water and marshland. The previous night had been a full moon, and the shadowy outline of the Assateague Lighthouse had loomed over the treetops.

"We should do this every year," he said. "Get away for a few days, just the two of us. I like having you all to myself."

She smiled up at him. She was content with life at home in Lancaster County. Her friends, her family, her community, their church and their children were there. Married life suited her, fitting as easily as a worn leather glove that was soft and warm and protective. She'd loved Neziah on the day they'd made their marriage vows, but that feeling had grown with each day that passed. They did not always agree, and some problems required patience and wisdom to solve, but they solved them together, cementing their bonds with love and respect and caring. Like his driving animal, Neziah had substance. There was no doubt in her mind that she had picked exactly the right man. Or perhaps… She smiled. Perhaps he had been chosen for her.

"We should come next May," Neziah suggested, pulling her back into the moment. "For the spring migration."

"Maybe," she answered. "That's a long way off to make definite plans." She had her own reason for thinking next May might not be possible, but she wasn't ready to share that hope with him yet. They had been praying for a child and though it was early yet, she suspected that that prayer had been answered.

"Hungry?" he asked.

She laughed. "Starving." They'd had coffee and a donut before they'd come out to the refuge, but he'd promised her a full breakfast with eggs and pancakes and sausage. There was a good restaurant with reasonable prices on the main street of town. It was a real treat to eat meals that she didn't have to cook or wash up after. In fact, she was ravenous. She was hungry enough to eat one of those snow geese if it came close enough. That was another reason she suspected that she might be with child. No morning sickness for her. She slept like a rock and woke wanting to eat everything in sight.

"A good thing you made me buy that scooter," Neziah said. "Otherwise, we'd have a long walk back across the bridge and into Chincoteague. And we need to have a good breakfast. We have that boat tour at two this afternoon." Neziah had reserved places for them weeks ago.

"Maybe I'll have the fisherman's breakfast," she told him, her mouth practically watering at the thought. "The one with two eggs, sausage, fried potatoes and bacon."

"Keep on like this and you'll get as plump as Maddie."

"Would you mind?" she teased. "If I did?"

"More to squeeze." Playfully he encircled her with both arms and backed her against the railing. "Have I told you this morning how beautiful you are?"

"Only once," she replied. She stood on tiptoe and

brushed his lips with hers, as bold as any English girl kissing her husband in full view of the world. "But I liked it very much."

"And I like you very much," he answered, looking full into her eyes. "There's just one thing I'd like to get straight between us. A small pebble in my shoe that keeps rubbing."

"With me?" She tried to think what she might have done lately that might not have met his approval.

"It's your scooter," he said, straight-faced, his eyes serious.

"My scooter? What's wrong with my scooter?" She folded her arms, ready to make a stand. "You said that you wanted me to keep my scooter. To ride it to work. And now you've bought one of your own. And you just said how useful it is."

Neziah grimaced. "It's the color."

"It's green. It's always been green."

He nodded. "It is. As green as a lime popsicle. A very bright green. I was thinking, maybe we could buy a can of spray paint. And paint both scooters a nice shade of forest-green. So as not to scare the birds."

She could hardly hold back a chuckle. "Not to scare the birds," she repeated.

"Jah." He grinned. "To blend in with the trees so we could sneak up on the warblers."

"Maybe," she said. "It would be more Plain. Not so worldly."

Neziah chuckled, and she laughed with him. He clasped her hand and they walked back together toward their scooters and all the years of peace and happiness that stretched out ahead of them.

* * * * *

The Amish Mother

REBECCA KERTZ

For Maggie, Ellie and Ainsley with love

In my distress I cried unto the Lord, and He heard me.
—*Psalms* 120:1

Chapter One

Lancaster County, Pennsylvania

The apple trees were thick with bright, red juicy fruit waiting to be picked. Elizabeth King Fisher stepped out of the house into the sunshine and headed toward the twin apple trees in the backyard.

"You sit here," she instructed her three youngest children, who'd accompanied her. She spread a blanket on the grass for them. "I'll pick and give them to you to put in the basket. *Ja?*"

"Ja, Mam," little Anne said as she sat down first and gestured for her brothers to join her.

Lizzie smiled. "You boys help your sister?" Jonas and Ezekiel nodded vigorously. *"Goot* boys!" she praised, and they beamed at her.

"What do you think we should make with these?" she said as she handed three apples to Jonas. "An apple pie? Apple crisp?"

"Candy apples!" Ezekiel exclaimed. He was three years old and the baby of the family, and he had learned recently about candy apples, having tasted one when they'd gone into town earlier this week.

Lizzie grinned as she bent to ruffle his hair. Ezekiel had taken off his small black-banded straw hat and set it on the blanket next to him. "Candy apples," she said. "I can make those."

The older children were nowhere in sight. Elizabeth's husband, Abraham, had fallen from the barn loft to his death just over two months ago, and the family was still grieving. Lizzie had tears in her eyes as she reached up to pull a branch closer to pick the fruit. *If only I hadn't urged him to get the kittens down from the loft...*

Tomorrow would have been their second wedding anniversary. She had married Abraham shortly after the children's mother had passed, encouraged strongly by her mother to do so. She'd been seventeen years old at the time, but she'd been crippled her entire life.

"Abraham Fisher is a *goot* man, Lizzie," she remembered her mother saying. "He needs a mother for his children and someone to care for his home. You should take his offer of marriage, for in your condition you may not get another one."

My condition, Lizzie thought. She suffered from developmental hip dysplasia, and she walked with a noticeable limp that worsened after standing for long periods of time. But she was a hard worker and could carry the weight of her chores as well as the rest of the women in her Amish community.

Limping Lizzie, the children had called her when she was a child. There had been other names, including Duckie because of her duck-like gait, which was caused by a hip socket too shallow to keep in the femoral head, the ball at the top of her long leg bone. Most of the children didn't mean to be cruel, but the names hurt just the same.

Lizzie had spent her young life proving that it didn't matter that one leg was longer than the other; yet her mother had implied otherwise when she'd urged Lizzie to marry Abraham, a grieving widower with children.

Abraham had still been grieving for his first wife when he'd married her, but she'd accepted his grief along with the rest of the family's. His children missed their mother. The oldest two girls, Mary Ruth and Hannah, resented Lizzie. The younger children had welcomed her, as they needed someone to hug and love them and be their mother. And they were too young to understand.

Mary Ruth, Abraham's eldest, had been eleven at the time of her mother's death, her sister Hannah almost ten. Both girls were angry with their mother for dying and angrier still at Lizzie for filling the void.

Lizzie picked several more apples, handing the children a number of them so that they would feel important as they placed them carefully in the basket.

"Can we eat one?" Anne asked.

"With your midday meal," Lizzie said. She glanced up at the sky and noted the position of the sun, which was directly overhead. "Are you hungry?" All three youngsters nodded vigorously. She reached to pick up the basket, which was full and heavy. She didn't let on that her leg ached as she straightened with the basket in hand. "Let's get you something to eat, then."

The children followed her into the large white farmhouse. When she entered through the back doorway, she saw the kitchen sink was filled with dirty dishes. She sighed as she set the basket on one end of the counter near the stove.

"Mary Ruth!" she called. "Hannah!" When there was no response, she called for them again. Matthew, who was eight, entered the kitchen from the front section of the house. "Have you seen your older sisters?" Lizzie asked him.

He shrugged. "Upstairs. Not sure what they're doing."

"Matt, are you hungry?" When the boy nodded, Lizzie said, "If you'll go up and tell your sisters to come down, I'll make you all something to eat."

Jonas grabbed his older brother's arm as Matt started to leave. "*Mam*'s going to make candy apples," he said.

Matthew opened his mouth as if to say something, but then he glanced toward the basket of apples instead and smiled. "Sounds *goot*. I like candy apples." Little Jonas grinned at him.

Matt left and then returned moments later, followed by his older sisters, Mary Ruth, Hannah and Rebecca, who had been upstairs in their room.

"You didn't do the dishes," Lizzie said to Mary Ruth.

The girl regarded her with a sullen expression. "I didn't know it was my turn."

"I'll do them," Rebecca said.

"That's a nice offer, Rebecca," Lizzie told her, "but 'tis Mary Ruth's turn, so I think she should do it." She smiled at the younger girl. "But you can help me make the candy apples later this afternoon after I hang the laundry." She met Hannah's gaze. "Did you strip the beds?"

Hannah nodded. "I put the linens near the washing machine."

Lizzie smiled. "*Danki*, Hannah." She heard Mary

Ruth grumble beneath her breath. "Did you say something you'd like to share?" she asked softly.

"Nay," Mary Ruth replied.

"I thought not." She went to the refrigerator. "What would you like to eat?" Their main meal was usually at midday, but their schedule had differed occasionally since Abraham's death because of the increase in her workload. Still, she had tried to keep life the same as much as possible.

"I can make them a meal," Mary Ruth challenged. Lizzie turned, saw her defiant expression and then nodded. The girl was hurting. If Mary Ruth wanted to cook for her siblings, then why not let her? She had taught her to be careful when using the stove.

"That would be nice, Mary Ruth," she said. "I'll hang the clothes while you feed your *brooders* and sisters." And she headed toward the back room where their gas-powered washing machine was kept, sensing that the young girl was startled. Lizzie retrieved a basket of wet garments and headed toward the clothesline outside.

The basket was only moderately heavy as she carried it to a spot directly below the rope. She felt comfortable leaving the children in the kitchen, for she could see inside through the screen door.

A soft autumn breeze stirred the air and felt good against her face. Lizzie bent, chose a wet shirt and pinned it on the line. She worked quickly and efficiently, her actions on the task but her gaze continually checking inside to see the children seated at the kitchen table.

"Elizabeth Fisher?" a man's voice said, startling her.

Lizzie gasped and spun around. She hadn't heard his approach from behind her. She'd known before turning that he was Amish as he had spoken in *Deitsch,* the language spoken within her community. Her eyes widened as she stared at him. The man wore a black-banded, wide-brimmed straw hat, a blue shirt and black pants held up by black suspenders. He looked like her deceased husband, Abraham, only younger and more handsome.

"You're Zachariah," she said breathlessly. Her heart picked up its beat as she watched him frown. "I'm Lizzie Fisher."

Zachariah stared at the woman before him in stunned silence. She was his late brother's widow? He'd been shocked to receive news of Abraham's death, even more startled to learn the news from Elizabeth Fisher, who had identified herself in her letter as his late brother's wife.

It had been years since he'd last visited Honeysuckle. He hadn't known that Ruth had passed or that Abe had remarried. *Why didn't Abraham write and let us know?*

"What happened to Ruth?" he demanded.

The woman's lovely bright green eyes widened. "Your *brooder* didn't write and tell you?" she said quietly. "Ruth passed away—over two years ago. A year after Ezekiel was born, she came down with the flu and…" She blinked. "She didn't make it. Your *brooder* asked me to marry him shortly afterward."

Zack narrowed his gaze as he examined her carefully. Dark auburn hair in slight disarray under her white head covering…eyes the color of the lawn after a summer rainstorm…pink lips that trembled as she gazed up at him. "You can't be more than seventeen," he accused.

The young woman lifted her chin. "Nineteen," she

stated stiffly. "I've been married to your *brooder* for two years." She paused, looked away as if to hide tears. "It would have been two years tomorrow had he lived."

Two years! Zack thought. The last time he'd received a letter from Abraham was when Abe had written the news of Ezekiel's birth. His brother had never written again.

The contents of Lizzie's letter when it had finally caught up to the family had shocked and upset them. Zack had made the immediate decision to come home to Honeysuckle to gauge the situation with the children and the property—and this new wife the family knew nothing about. His mother and sisters had agreed that he should go. With both Ruth and Abraham deceased, Zack thought that the time had come to reclaim what was rightfully his—the family farm.

He stood silently, watching as she pulled a garment from the wicker basket at her feet and tossed it over the line. He had trouble picturing Abraham married to this girl, although he could see why Abraham might have been attracted to her. But why would Lizzie choose to marry Abraham? He saw the difficulty her trembling fingers had securing the garment onto the clothesline properly. He fought back unwanted sympathy for her and won.

"You're living here with the children," he said. *"Alone?"*

"This is our home." Lizzie faced him, a petite girl whose auburn hair suddenly appeared as if streaked with various shades of reds under the autumn sun. Her vivid green eyes and young innocent face made her seem vulnerable, but she must be a strong woman if she could manage all seven of his nieces and nephews— and stand defiantly before him as she was now without backing down. He felt a glimmer of admiration for her that quickly vanished with his next thought.

This woman and his brother were married almost two years. Did Lizzie and Abraham have a child together? He scowled as he glanced about the yard, then toward the house. He didn't see or hear a baby, but then, the child could be napping inside. How did one ask a woman if she'd given birth without sounding offensive or rude? *My* brooder *should have told me about her. Then I would know.*

"I'm nearly done," she said, averting her attention back to her laundry while he continued to watch her. She hung up the last item, a pillowcase. "*Koom.* We're about to have our midday meal. Join us. You must have come a long way." She bit her lip as she briefly met his gaze. "Where did you come from? I wasn't sure where to send the letter. I didn't know if you were still in Walnut Creek or Millersburg or if you'd moved again. I sent it to Millersburg because it was the last address I found among your *brooder*'s things."

"We moved back to Walnut Creek two years ago—" He stopped. He wasn't about to tell her about his mother's illness or that he and his sister Esther had moved with *Mam* from Walnut Creek to Millersburg to be closer to the doctors treating their mother's cancer. *Mam* was fine now, thank the Lord, and she would continue to do well as long as she took care of herself. Once his mother's health had improved, they had picked up and moved back to Walnut Creek, where his two older sisters lived with their husbands and their families.

Zack had no idea how Lizzie's letter had reached him. Their forwarding address had expired over a year ago, but someone who'd known them in Millersburg must have sent it on. He still couldn't believe that Abraham was dead. His older brother had been only thirty-five years old. "What happened to my *brooder*?" She never mentioned in her letter how he'd died.

Lizzie went pale. "He fell," she said in a choked voice, "from the barn loft." He saw her hands clutch rhythmically at the hem of her apron. "He broke his neck and died instantly."

Zack felt shaken by the mental image. He could see that she was sincerely distraught. "I'm sorry. I know it's hard." He, too, felt the loss. It hurt to realize that he'd never see Abraham again. He thought of all the times when he was a child that he'd trailed after his older brother.

His death must have been quick and painless, he thought, trying to find some small measure of comfort. He studied the young woman who looked too young to be married or to raise Abe's children.

"He was a *goot* man." She didn't look at him when she bent to pick up her basket then straightened. "Are you coming in?" she asked as she finally met his gaze.

He nodded and then followed her as she started toward the house. He was surprised to see her uneven gait as she walked ahead of him, as if she'd injured her leg and limped because of the pain. "Lizzie, are *ya* hurt?" he asked compassionately.

She halted, then faced him with her chin tilted high, her eyes less than warm. "I'm not hurt," she said crisply. "I'm a cripple." And with that, she turned away and continued toward the house, leaving him to follow her.

Zack studied her back with mixed feelings as he lagged behind. Concern. Worry. Uneasiness. He frowned as he watched her shift the laundry basket to one arm and struggle to open the door with the other. He stopped himself from helping, sensing that she wouldn't be pleased. He frowned at her back. Could a crippled, young nineteen-year-old woman raise a passel of *kinner* alone?

Lizzie was aware of her husband's brother behind her as she entered the house with the laundry basket. She flashed a glance toward the kitchen sink and was pleased to note that Mary Ruth had washed the dishes and left them to drain on a rack over a tea towel.

"Mary Ruth, would you set another plate?" she said. "We have a visitor." She was relieved to note that her daughter had set a place for her.

Mary Ruth frowned but rose to obey. Lizzie stepped aside and the child caught sight of the man behind her. She paled as she stared at him, most probably noting the uncanny resemblance of Zachariah to her dead father.

"Dat?" she whispered. The girl shook her head, then drew a sharp breath. *"Onkel* Zachariah."

Watching the exchange, Lizzie saw him smile. "Mary Ruth, you've grown over a foot since I last saw you," he said.

Mary Ruth blinked back tears and looked as if she wanted to approach him but dared not. The Amish normally weren't affectionate in public, but they were at home, and Lizzie knew that the child hadn't seen her uncle in a long time.

To his credit, Zachariah extended his arms, and Mary Ruth ran into his embrace. Eyes closed, the man hugged his niece tightly, and Lizzie felt the emotion flowing from him in huge waves.

"Zachariah is your *dat*'s brother," she explained to the younger children.

Chairs scraped over the wooden floor as they rose from their seats and eyed him curiously. Zachariah had released Mary Ruth and studied her with a smile. "You look like your *mudder.*"

"Why didn't you come sooner?" Mary Ruth asked. She appeared pleased by the comparison to her mother.

"I didn't get Lizzie's letter until yesterday," he admitted. "After reading it, I quickly made arrangements to come."

Mary Ruth nodded as if she understood. "Sit down," she told the children in a grown-up voice. "*Onkel* is going to eat with us. You'll have time to talk with him at the dinner table."

The kitchen was filled with the delicious scent of pot roast with potatoes, onions and carrots. Mary Ruth had heated the leftovers from the previous day in the oven, and she'd warmed the blueberry muffins that Lizzie had baked earlier this morning.

Her eldest daughter set a plate before Zachariah and then asked what he wanted to drink. Standing there, Lizzie saw a different child than the one she'd known since Lizzie had married Abe and moved into the household. It was a glimpse of how life could be, and Lizzie took hope from it.

After stowing the empty laundry basket in the back room, Lizzie joined everyone at the table. The platter of pot roast was passed to Zachariah, who took a helping before he extended it toward Lizzie. Thanking him with a nod, she took some meat and vegetables from the plate before asking the children if they wanted more.

Conversation flowed easily between the children and their uncle, and Lizzie listened quietly as she forked up a piece of beef and brought it to her mouth.

"Are *ya* truly my *vadder*'s *brooder*?" Rebecca asked.

"Look at him, Rebecca," Hannah said. "Don't *ya* see the family resemblance?"

Lizzie looked over in time to see Rebecca blush. She addressed her husband's brother. "You haven't visited Honeysuckle in a long time."

Zachariah focused his dark eyes on her and she felt a jolt. "*Ja.* Not in years. My *mudder* moved my sisters and me to Ohio after *Dat* died. I was eleven." He grabbed a warm muffin and broke it easily in half. "I came back for a visit once when Hannah was a toddler." He smiled at Hannah as he spread butter on each muffin half. "It's hard to believe how much you've grown. I remember you as this big." He held his hand out to show her how tall.

Hannah smiled. "You knew my *mam*."

He had taken a bite of muffin and he nodded as he chewed and swallowed it.

"How come we haven't met you before?" Matthew asked with the spunk of a young boy. "You didn't come for *Mam*'s funeral."

"I didn't know about your *mudder*'s passing," Zachariah said softly. "I still wouldn't have known if not for Lizzie. I wanted to come to see you and your family before now, but I couldn't get away." He glanced around the table. "Seven children," he said with wonder. "I'm happy to see that your *mudder* and *vadder* were blessed with all of you." He smiled and gazed at each child in turn. "How old are you?" he asked Ezekiel.

Ezekiel held up three fingers. "Such a big boy. You are the youngest?" He seemed to wait with bated breath for Zeke's reply, and he smiled when his answer was the boy's vigorous nod. He then guessed Anne's and then Jonas's ages and was off by just one year for Jonas, who was four.

"How long are you going to stay, *Onkel* Zachariah?" Rebecca asked.

"Zack," he invited. He leaned forward and whispered, "Zachariah is too much of a mouthful with *Onkel, ja*?" Then he shot Lizzie a quick glance before answering his niece's question. "I thought I'd stay for a while." He took a second muffin. "The *dawdi haus*—is it empty?" he asked.

"Ja," Mary Ruth said while Lizzie felt stunned as she anticipated where the conversation was headed. "'Tis always empty except when we have guests, which we haven't had in a long time…"

"Goot," he said. "Then you won't mind if I move in—"

Lizzie gasped audibly. "But that wouldn't be proper…" The thought of having him on the farm was disturbing.

She became unsettled when Zack put her in the center focus of his dark gaze. "I'll send for my *mudder*— and my sister Esther," he said easily. "The three of us can stay there comfortably."

Dread washed over Lizzie. "But—"

"Not to worry, Lizzie Fisher." He flashed her a friendly smile as he buttered the muffin. "I'll head home and then accompany them back to Honeysuckle. I won't be moving in without a chaperone."

But that wasn't all that concerned Lizzie. She couldn't help but wonder how long he—they—would be staying. Why did he want to stay? She'd never met her mother-in-law or any of Abraham's siblings. What if they didn't like her? What if they judged her incapable of managing the farm and decided that she was no longer needed? Could she bear to be parted from her children? Because, in her heart, they were *her* children although she hadn't given birth to them.

She had enjoyed a good life with Abraham. She'd worked hard to make the farmhouse a home for a grieving man and his children. *And Abraham appreciated my efforts*, she thought. Right before his death, she'd felt as if he'd begun to truly care for her.

"You don't have to worry about us," Lizzie said quietly as she watched him enjoy his food. "We are doing fine." Her hands began to shake, and she placed them on her lap under the table so that he wouldn't see. "There is no need to return. I know your life is in Ohio now."

Zack waved her concerns aside. "You'll be needing help at harvest time. It can't be easy managing the farm and caring for Abraham's children alone."

Lizzie felt her stomach twist. Zack, like everyone else, thought her incapable of making it on her own, and he'd referred to the children as Abraham's. She experienced a jolt of anger. Abraham's children were her children, had been for two years now.

Then a new thought struck her with terror. Zack was the youngest Fisher son. Wouldn't that make him the rightful heir to his family farm? If so, had he come to stake his claim?

Lizzie settled her hand against her belly as the burning there intensified and she felt nauseous. Was she going to lose her home and her family—the children she loved as her own?

She closed her eyes and silently prayed. *Please, dear Lord, help me prove to Zack that I am worthy of being the children's* mudder. When she opened them again, she felt the impact of Zack's regard. She was afraid what having him on the farm would do to her life, her peace of mind and her family.

Chapter Two

Zack had departed for Ohio the same day he'd arrived after making known his shocking intention of staying on the farm. After sharing their midday meal, he'd gone as quickly as he'd come with the promise to return, ready to move in with his mother and sister. Lizzie had no idea when he'd be back, but she and the children immediately went to work readying the *dawdi haus* the day after his departure. She would not have him feeling unwelcome.

"Did you hang up the sheets?" she asked Mary Ruth as the girl briefly entered the bedroom where Lizzie swept the wooden floor. She and Hannah had stayed home from school to help her get ready for Zachariah's return.

"Ja," her daughter said. "I did the quilts and blankets, too."

Lizzie smiled. "That's *goot*. We want to be ready for your uncle, *ja*?"

To her surprise, Mary Ruth grinned back at her. *"Ja. It will be wonderful to have family here."*

Lizzie nodded in agreement with Mary Ruth, but as

her daughter left for the other bedroom with dust cloth and homemade polish in hand, she wondered what the Fishers' stay at the farm would mean for her and her future.

The cottage had two bedrooms, a bathroom, a combination great room and kitchen, and a pantry. A covered porch with two rocking chairs and a swing ran along the front outer wall of the *dawdi haus*. Lizzie had always liked the little house and the comfort it offered guests and the *grosseldre*, or grandparents, for whom it must have been built.

Hannah and Rebecca entered the largest bedroom, where Lizzie continued to clean and prepare for their expected guests. "I wiped inside the kitchen cabinets and the countertops, Lizzie," Hannah said.

"And what about the pantry?"

"I helped Hannah carry all the jars you said to bring," Rebecca said. "Want to see?" There was an air of excitement among the sisters.

Lizzie studied the two happy girls and smiled. "*Ja*, show me." She followed Hannah and Rebecca through the great area to the kitchen nook on the other side.

"*Mam*," young Anne said. "Look how nice they are!"

The jars of tomatoes, sweet-and-sour chow-chow, peaches and jam appeared colorful on the clean pantry shelves. "You girls have been working hard." Lizzie smiled. "*Danki.*" She looked about and didn't see the two youngest. "Where are Jonas and Ezekiel?" she asked with concern.

"Outside with Matt," Mary Ruth said as she approached from the other bedroom across the hall from where Lizzie had been working.

Anne nodded. "They are pulling out weeds and dead things from the flower garden."

No doubt the boys were working, as per her instructions, to clear out the dried rudbeckia blossoms and stems. The flowers also known as black-eyed Susans created a beautiful display of bright color from late spring to mid- or late summer, but in the fall, seeds from the dead centers had to be spread across the soil to ensure next year's glorious display of gold and black.

"You have all worked hard on these today. I appreciate it. I couldn't have prepared the cottage without you." Lizzie noted with pleasure the smile on Mary Ruth's face.

"Is there anything else we need to do?" the girl asked.

"We'll go shopping tomorrow for supplies," Lizzie said. "And we can bake bread, put some in the pantry and freeze a few loaves for them. They are welcome to eat at the farmhouse anytime, but they may want to take some of their meals here in the *dawdi haus*."

"Ja," Hannah said. "It's a nice *haus*. It will be *goot* to see someone living in it."

Lizzie hoped so. "It's been a long morning without a break to eat. Are any of you hungry?"

"Ja!" the girls cried.

Matt entered the house with his younger brothers. *"Ja,"* he said, apparently hearing the last of Lizzie's words. "We're hungry. What's to eat?"

Lizzie thought for a moment. "What would you like? Hard work deserves a special meal."

"Pizza!" the youngest ones cried.

"Pizza," Lizzie said with surprise and a little dismay. Money was tight, but she could make a crust from scratch, and she did have jars of tomato sauce she'd canned earlier in the summer. She could make her own pizza sauce and top it with whatever cheese she had in the refrigerator, fresh green peppers and onions. She could make a second pizza with just the cheese for the youngsters who wanted their pizza plain. "Pizza it is," she said with a smile. "And then afterward, why don't I make those candy apples I promised yesterday." The children wholeheartedly agreed to the plan.

As she and the children left the *dawdi haus* and headed toward the farmhouse, Lizzie felt as if they were a family for the first time since the tragic loss of her husband—their father. She experienced a lightening of spirit and hope for the family's future.

Later that night after the children were in bed, Lizzie went up to her bedroom, the room she'd shared with Abraham, and stared at the bed. Sleep hadn't come easy to her since Abraham's passing. Last night the worry over her late husband's family moving into the *dawdi haus* had caused her to fret into the early morning until, exhausted, she'd finally fallen into a fitful sleep not long before she had to get up to begin her day again.

She had a mental image of Zack as she'd first seen him. He looked like a young Abraham, only with dark hair and more handsome features. Not that her husband hadn't been good-looking. He had been, but she hadn't noticed that at first. She had married him at a time that had been difficult for everyone, a time of mourning for him and the children, a time of concern that she might have made a mistake in agreeing to the marriage.

But we found our way, Lizzie thought as she moved across the room. Time had healed Abraham's grief and his gaze had lost the sadness. Then he had begun to appreciate everything that she had done for the family—taking care of the house, doing the wash, loving his children.

They had married as strangers—he'd needed someone to care for his children after his wife had died, and she'd needed a life of her own.

During the first months of her marriage to Abraham, she had slept in the sewing room after quilting long into the night. She had produced some beautiful quilts by their first anniversary, when Abraham had invited her to sleep in the master bedroom. Afterward she had worked on her quilts in the evening instead, with Abraham seated nearby in his favorite chair while the children had played cards or read stories.

Since Abraham's death, she had gone back to quilting through most of the night until she'd fall into bed exhausted and sleep only to awaken early to begin her chore-filled days. She enjoyed quilting and everyone complimented her on her handiwork. She had recently sold one of her quilts at Beachey's Craft Shop, the money coming in at a time when they needed it. Ellen Beachey, the shopkeeper, had been gracious in taking her quilts and craft items so that she could earn much-needed cash.

She crossed to the sewing room off the bedroom and picked up one of her colorful quilt squares. Her mind reeled with emotion as she went to work. As she began to make tiny, even stitches in the fabric, she thought of Abraham and the children and how difficult their father's death had been for them, how hard it had been to lose their mother two years earlier. They were wonderful children, and she loved them.

Would having Zack and his family here help her relationship with the children or hinder it?

She paused, closed her eyes and prayed. *Please, Lord, help us to become a family. Don't let me lose everything I gained when I married Abraham.* A family. A home. Children who needed her.

Mary Ruth's and Hannah's sweet behavior would have made her feel at peace, if not for the knowledge that Zack would return soon and disturb the life she'd made for herself with the children.

Ah, Abraham, I'm sorry. 'Twas my fault that you're no longer with us.

Tears filled her eyes as she plied needle to cloth in tiny, even stitches. She recalled her husband's face and his eyes, which had eventually looked at her with more than kindness, with caring that had turned into love. In the months before he died, Abraham had begun to see her as a wife rather than a housekeeper and helpmate.

She sniffed as she set down her sewing and rose. She was tired. She undressed by candlelight, carefully removing the straight pins securing her dress, and got ready for bed. She brushed her hair, recalling with a smile when she'd brushed out her youngest daughter's hair earlier.

Her hip ached and she reached for the menthol and camphor salve to rub on the sore and swollen joint. The scent was strong, but she was used to it, welcomed it because any little pain relief was worth it. She could take aspirin or ibuprofen, but she'd used so much of it recently, she decided it was best to save it for when the pain became unbearable without it.

She moved toward the bed, pulled back the quilt and

climbed onto the mattress. She heard a gentle knock on her bedroom door. *"Ja?"*

"Mam?" The door swung open, and her youngest daughter, Anne, peeked inside, holding a flashlight.

"Annie," Lizzie murmured. She waved her in. "What's wrong?"

Her daughter approached the bed. *"Mam,* do you think our *grossmama* will like us?"

Lizzie smiled reassuringly. "She will love you," she said, believing it to be true. "You are her granddaughter. All of you children are her grandchildren. Why wouldn't she love you? Love all of her *kins kinner?"*

Annie tilted her head as she regarded her with unusually grown-up eyes. "Will she love you, too?"

Lizzie smiled, unable to assure her when she didn't know. "You are worrying too much, Anne. They will come and all will be well."

The child smiled. "I am glad. I want us all to be happy together. It is time for us—you—to be happy."

Lizzie reached for the girl's hand, pulled her close. "I am happy," she said sincerely. "You and your sisters and *brooders* make me very happy."

"Even though Mary Ruth can be sharp to you?"

She nodded. *"Ja,* no matter what. I am happy with you all, and I love you."

Anne grinned and leaned over to hug her. "I love you, *Mam.*"

Lizzie closed her eyes as she held on to her daughter. "I love you. You all are everything a *mudder* could ask for and more." She released her child to pat her cheek. "Now run off to bed. We've a busy day tomorrow."

Annie nodded vigorously and spun to race out of

the room, pausing on the threshold to glance back at Lizzie. *"Danki."*

Lizzie raised her eyebrows in question.

"For being my *mam*," Anne explained before she hurried on and shut the door behind her.

Lizzie blinked against happy tears as she leaned to blow out the candle. As the room plunged into darkness, she relaxed and lay back against her pillow. She felt sleepy and hopeful for the first time in a long while.

The next morning she was up and ready to begin her day. Now that the *dawdi haus* was prepared for guests, she needed to clean the farmhouse. She made breakfast first, and soon the children joined her in the kitchen, ready to eat. Lizzie beamed at them as they sat down.

"Hungry?" she asked. "I made pancakes, bacon, sausage and eggs."

"It looks *goot*," Hannah said.

"It tastes *goot*." Matt had grabbed a piece of bacon and popped it into his mouth.

"Matthew, mind your manners and put some on your plate."

"*Ja*, Lizzie." Matt nodded, looking solemn, and then he grinned.

Lizzie laughed; she couldn't help it. The boy was looking at her with such delight that the pure joy of the moment deeply touched her. It was nice to hear laughter in the house again.

Her older children helped the younger ones get their food. Lizzie watched with fondness as Rebecca cut up little Jonas's pancakes for him.

This is what family is about, she thought. Had she ever felt so lighthearted when she was a girl? She couldn't recall laughing at the dinner table. Her mother had treated her differently than her siblings because of her disability. It was as if she'd been unable to accept that her daughter wasn't perfect.

"Anne, be careful with your milk," Lizzie warned without anger.

Anne set her glass down and smiled at her with milk-mustached lips. "When do *ya* think *Onkel* will be here?" she asked.

"*Onkel* Zack," Hannah corrected.

Lizzie sat down and filled her plate. "I don't know. Surely by next week."

"What else must we do to be ready for him?" Hannah asked.

Lizzie looked at her fondly. "I thought we should clean our *haus* next. We wouldn't want *Onkel* Zack, *Grossmama* and *Endie* Esther to see a dirty *haus*, would we?"

"Nay!" the children chorused. The family teased each other as they ate breakfast, and when they were done, Lizzie and her daughters rose and tackled the kitchen first before moving on to clean the rest of the house. She sent the boys outside to make sure that there were no sticks in the yard and the porch was free of any balls and play items. She'd asked Matt to check the honeysuckle bush near her vegetable garden to see if it needed to be pruned back.

Later that afternoon when the children were at the kitchen table enjoying a snack, Lizzie heard a car in the barnyard. She hurried toward the door in time to see Zachariah Fisher climb out of the front passenger side of the vehicle and then reach to open the back door. A woman alighted as Zack went to the trunk and waited while the driver met him. The Englisher lifted out two suitcases and set them on the ground.

She saw Zack exchange words with the driver. Then he and the woman approached the house. Lizzie stepped out onto the porch to meet them. She heard the children behind her, chatting happily after seeing who had returned.

Lizzie was startled to see him. She hadn't expected him back so soon. His gaze locked with hers as he drew closer. Her heart started to pound hard.

Chapter Three

He inclined his head. "Lizzie."

She swallowed against a suddenly dry throat. "Zack."

He drew the woman forward. Lizzie saw that she was older than Zachariah but not enough to be his mother. "This is—"

"Esther," Lizzie said with a smile. "Your *schwe-schter*." She was pleased to note Zack's surprise when she'd addressed his sister by name. "We're glad you could come and stay with us."

Esther's gaze warmed. "And you're Lizzie."

Lizzie nodded. "Are you hungry? May I offer you a snack to hold you until supper? There are cookies and apple crisp. The cottage is ready for you. I believe you'll be comfortable there."

"We all helped to fix it up for you," Rebecca said as she joined Lizzie on the front porch.

Mary Ruth and the rest of the children stepped out of the house and gathered behind Lizzie and Rebecca. Anne and Matt stood behind them, inside the door.

Esther smiled. "*Hallo.* So you are Abraham's children. My nieces and nephews."

Rebecca stepped forward. "Would you like to come in? Matt can put your luggage in the *dawdi haus* for you," she told her aunt. She glanced at her brother and, understanding, Matt came out of the house and approached.

"*Danki.* I wouldn't mind coming in for a bit," Esther agreed.

Zack captured Lizzie's gaze as he handed Matt a suitcase and picked up the other one. Her heart gave a little jump before it started to beat normally again. "I'll go with Matt," he said. "We'll be right back."

Esther nodded before she followed Lizzie and the children into the farmhouse. Once inside, she paused to study her surroundings. "Everything is the same, but different," she said.

Lizzie understood. She hadn't given much thought to the fact that Esther, Abraham and the rest of their siblings had lived here with their parents before their father's passing. As they continued through the house and into the kitchen, Zack's sister smiled appreciatively. "It smells wonderful in here."

Hannah smiled. "We baked today. Would you like some apple crisp?"

Esther shook her head. "We stopped to eat on the way."

"Tea?"

At Lizzie's invitation, Esther sat down at the kitchen table. "*Ja*, that sounds *goot*."

Lizzie studied her sister-in-law. Esther Fisher was a tall, attractive woman with warmth in her brown gaze and soft pretty laugh lines at the corners of her eyes and near her mouth. She wore a black traveling bonnet and a blue dress with black cape and apron. Her features were kind and full of character, and Lizzie immediately felt comfortable in her presence. She thought that she and Esther might become good friends once they got to know each other.

Memories assailed Zack as he entered the *dawdi haus*. His grandparents had lived here when he was a young child. They had passed on when he was seven in a terrible accident. A drunk driver had slammed his car head-on into their small open buggy as his grandfather drove *Grossmudder* and himself to Sunday service. That he and his family were in the buggy several yards in front of his *grosseldre*'s vehicle saved their lives, but Zack had gotten a good view of the awful scene. It had been a traumatic experience for everyone but most especially Zack.

As he followed his nephew through the house and into a bedroom, he noted slight changes to the cottage. There was no sign that his *grosseldre* had lived there. He sighed silently with relief as he set his suitcase in the closest bedroom and then followed Matt into the next room, where his sister would stay.

"Lizzie and the girls made up the beds and put stuff in the kitchen for you," Matthew told him. "They stocked the pantry and the freezer, but Lizzie said that you are *willkomm* to eat with us. She wanted you to have food in case you got hungry or didn't feel like coming over."

Zack studied the boy and nodded. "That is kind of her." He examined Esther's room, pleased how clean and comfortable it appeared. A lingering scent of lemon oil intermingled with the fresh air gently billowing the white window curtains. A quilt in soft blues, greens and cream covered the double bed.

"Lizzie made the quilt," Matthew said after apparently noting the direction of Zack's gaze. "She quilts a lot and makes wonderful things. She sells her quilts at Beachey's Craft Shop."

Zack couldn't help but admire the bedcover. The pattern and colors were striking, but plain enough to be used within their Amish community. He walked to the bed and ran a hand over the soft cotton in solid colors. "Beachey," he murmured. "Ellen Beachey's family?"

When his nephew nodded, Zack smiled. "They've owned the shop since Ellen was a child." He felt a softening inside at the memory of Ellen Beachey, remembering her as a young feisty girl. She was older than him by about ten years, pretty, but she'd been a handful to her parents, although she'd been respectful to the church and the folks within Honeysuckle. He remembered that she and Neziah Shetler had been sweethearts, but by the time he'd returned home for a visit, the couple had broken up. He wondered whom she finally married.

"Do you know she has a bright lime-green push scooter?" Matt said. "She rides it down the hill from her house to the main road and uses it to ride to the craft store."

Zack chuckled. "That sounds like Ellen." He envisioned her flying down the hill, her prayer *kapp* barely held on by bobby pins, her eyes bright with excitement. Following his nephew into the kitchen, he listened as the boy showed him the contents of the food pantry. "Ellen still works at the store, then," he murmured after he'd nodded approvingly at his food stock.

"Ja." Matt closed the pantry door and faced him.

"We're glad you're here," the boy said. His expression became solemn. "We miss *Dat*."

Zack understood. "I haven't seen your *vadder* in a long time. I regret that I won't have the chance to see or talk with him again." He felt a keen sense of loss, but somehow, for his nephew's sake, he managed to smile. "But he is with *Gott*, and so is your *mudder*."

"You knew my *mam*?" The boy seemed eager to hear more about his parents.

"*Ja*. Ruth and your *dat* were married before my *vadder*—your *grossdaddi*—passed and we moved away." Zack recalled how difficult it had been for them, especially his mother, who'd loved her husband deeply and felt the terrible loss. When his father had died, his mother hadn't wanted to stay on the farm. She had moved with her younger children to Ohio to live near his eldest married sister, Miriam, who lived with her husband and children in Walnut Creek. His older brother, Abraham, had remained behind to run the family farm and build a life with his new wife, Ruth.

"We miss *Mam*, too," Matt said as they walked together out of the house and across the yard.

"She and your *dat* loved each other." Zack noted the boy's features so like his brother's. "You favor your *vadder*."

"I do?" Matt appeared pleased by the thought.

"*Ja*. You've got his eyes, yet you have a bit of your *mam*, too."

Matt blinked. "I— *Danki*." The whispered word held a wealth of meaning and gratitude.

"Let's go back to the *haus*. Lizzie and your *endie* Esther will be wondering why it's taken us so long."

Matt picked up his pace, and Zack followed, glad he

had decided to return to Honeysuckle, if only to get to know his brother's children.

Zack pulled the screen door open and waited for Matt to enter first. He noted the difference in the gathering room as he headed toward the kitchen and the sound of laughter coming from the rear of the house. As he entered, he saw his oldest niece, Mary Ruth, chuckling at her little brother Ezekiel, who was grinning from ear to ear as the three-year-old put forkfuls of apple crisp into his mouth. "Ezekiel, slow down," his sister Hannah warned, "or it will choke you."

The boy stopped for a moment and blinked up at her. "But it tastes *goot*, and I'm hungry."

"Zeke," Zack heard Lizzie say quietly, "your sister is right. If you aren't careful, you will choke and hurt yourself. If you take your time, you will enjoy it more."

Zack watched with surprise as the little boy nodded and grinned in Lizzie's direction. *"Ja, Mam,"* he said, and then he began to eat more slowly, chewing his food thoroughly before swallowing. His brother's widow smiled at the child with affection, clearly pleased by his obedience.

Lizzie looked up then as if sensing a presence, saw him in the doorway and stood. "Zack," she said, her expression becoming shuttered. "May I get you something to eat? Some apple crisp—"

"It's *goot*, *Onkel* Zack!" little Ezekiel told him with a mouthful of the treat and a grin.

Zack shook his head. "We ate ourselves full on the way here."

"'Tis delicious." Mary Ruth smiled as she held up the plate as if enticing him to try it.

He had the sudden urge to grin. "Hmm. May we take two pieces to eat later?"

"*Ja*. I'll wrap them up for you." Lizzie cut two slices of the apple treat, set them on a plate and covered it with plastic wrap. She placed the dish within his easy reach. "Is everything in the cottage all right?" she asked almost shyly, referring to the *dawdi haus*. She sat down and cradled her teacup with her hands.

"*Ja*. It looks *goot*. We'll be most comfortable there." He saw that she looked satisfied. As he sat and waited for his sister to finish her tea, Zack studied his late brother's wife. Dressed in a light blue dress with a full-length black apron, Lizzie was stunning. Her dark red hair had been rolled in the Amish way and tucked beneath her white head covering without a single strand out of place. Her green eyes appeared large in her pretty feminine face; her nose was well shaped and small, her lips pink and full. Despite her young age and obvious handicap, he could see why his brother had chosen to make her his bride. He looked away, startled by the direction of his thoughts.

"We should get settled in," he said.

Esther agreed. "*Ja*. The tea was *goot*." She stood and picked up the plate of apple crisp. "We will eat this later."

Zack rose and nodded his thanks. "We will see you tomorrow," he said. "It's been a long day."

Lizzie stood. "Don't hesitate to tell us if you need anything."

He followed Esther through the back door of the farmhouse and sensed Lizzie's presence as he stepped outside. He turned to see her standing in the open doorway. She locked gazes with him. He felt a tightening in his chest before she broke eye contact. The children pushed by her and stood in the yard watching as he continued to the *dawdi haus* behind his sister.

"*Onkel* Zack!" a young voice cried. Zack turned to face his young nephew Jonas. "Do you know how to play baseball?" the boy asked.

Zack smiled. "*Ja*, I used to play." But it had been years ago, when all of his family had been alive and living in the farmhouse.

"Will you play with us sometime?" Jonas asked with hope in his eyes. "Next visiting Sunday?"

"Jonas," he heard Lizzie say softly. "Don't be pestering your *onkel*."

He didn't know why, but the woman's words bothered him. "I'll play ball with you," he said, his gaze rising to Lizzie's face, "come next visiting Sunday." His tone and words were letting her know that he had no plans to leave the farm anytime soon. When he saw her blanch, he realized that she'd gotten his message, and he suddenly regretted it.

His attention went to the young boy whose eyes glistened with excitement. Jonas wore a big smile on his face. Zack flashed him a grin. He heard a little catch in someone's breath and turned to discover that it had been Lizzie.

He'd come to the farm to see how his brother's widow and children were managing and to claim his inheritance. If Abraham had been alive, he would have stayed in Ohio, knowing that the farm was in his brother's capable hands. He would have forgotten that his father had intended him to have the farm. But after learning that Ruth and Abraham were dead, Zack had decided the time had come to step in and take back what was rightfully his. Lizzie Fisher, his brother's widow, was a stranger to him and no blood relation to his nieces and nephews. He'd decided that he couldn't allow her to keep his brother's children or the farm.

But now, after meeting her and seeing the way Lizzie interacted with the children, he was beginning to re-think the situation. He didn't know what he was going to do, but he'd figure out something. The children loved Lizzie, he realized as he crossed the yard toward the *dawdi haus*. Somehow he must consider what was in the best interests of the children as well as the farm property.

Zack sighed as he reached the cottage and held the door open for Esther. He would pray to the Lord that he would choose right for everyone. *Complications*, he thought. He hadn't expected this many of them.

Chapter Four

Lizzie woke up feeling ill. *I overdid it this week,* she realized. All the hard work she'd accomplished on the farm these past few days had aggravated her hip, and the resulting pain made her nauseous.

She'd been sick a lot since Abraham had passed on and she'd felt the stress of managing everything alone. Ever since Zack's first visit, she'd been afraid. Her fears had intensified after his departure. Now that he was back, she wondered if he was silently making decisions that would impact her life with the children. If he chose to claim the farm, what would happen to them? Could she somehow stop him? Would the fact that he hadn't come forward before now work in her favor?

Lizzie frowned. The children were Zack's family and had the right to live on the farm with him. It was she who had no blood ties. She'd married Abraham, it was true, but for most of their married life, she hadn't been a real wife…until the night before Abraham's fatal accident, when they finally had consummated their marriage. Lizzie had been so happy that night because she'd realized then that her husband had begun to care for her as a wife instead of just a housekeeper and babysitter. *If Abraham had lived,* she thought, *we might have had children together.*

Children. Lizzie gasped. *I've missed one month.* She'd missed a month before. Her woman's flow was often irregular. She wasn't sure why, but skipping a period happened to her on occasion. Since Abraham's death, she'd been so busy caring for the children and the farm that she hadn't noticed until now.

She rose from bed. It was early; the children were asleep, but it wouldn't be long before they stirred, ready for breakfast.

A baby. She would love nothing more than to give birth to Abraham's child, to have his baby son or daughter. The child would be a legitimate and accepted member of the Fisher family. *My child would cement the bond between the Fishers and me.*

Her Amish church community accepted her right to the farm as the children's stepmother and Abraham's widow. But did Zack agree?

Lizzie settled a hand on her abdomen. *A baby.* She silently counted the days since Abraham's death. Within the next day or so, she would know for certain. Somehow she just knew she was carrying her late husband's son or daughter. But she would not tell anyone yet. She would save the news for the right moment. She couldn't allow herself to become too excited at the prospect until she was sure. But how could she not be hopeful? She would love to give the children a new baby brother or sister to love, the child of their deceased father. Perhaps Mary Ruth and Hannah would finally accept her.

A door squeaked as if it was being closed carefully. Then she heard the sound of someone moving about in the hall. Lizzie grabbed the flashlight from her bed table and turned it on. She then hurriedly donned a robe over her nightgown before, with light in hand, she peeked into the hall.

"Anne," she whispered as the light fell on the child outside her bedroom door. "Are your sisters up?"

Anne shook her head. The five-year-old wore her nightgown and carried her clothes as if she intended to dress downstairs.

Lizzie waved her into the room. "*Koom.* I'll help you get dressed and do your hair."

Annie smiled and hurried into the room that had once belonged to Lizzie and Abraham.

Lizzie lit an oil lamp, turned off the flashlight and then helped Anne out of her nightgown and into her day clothes. Then she reached for a brush and comb. First, she brushed her daughter's long golden locks. Then she combed, rolled and pinned the roll against Annie's head in the Amish way. Lizzie smiled as she worked. She enjoyed fixing the girl's hair; the simple action of brushing her daughter's hair soothed her.

"Why are you up so early?" she asked softly. There was barely a hint of dawn in the eastern sky.

"I woke up and couldn't go back to sleep."

Finished, Lizzie stepped back and turned Anne to face her. "Is something upsetting you?"

Annie was quiet for a moment. "*Mam*, will *Onkel* Zack marry you and stay with us forever?"

Lizzie froze in shock. "I— *Nay, dochter.* I don't know your *onkel* that well and he doesn't know me."

"But you can get to know and love each other." Annie gazed at her as Lizzie placed a prayer *kapp* on the child's head. "It is possible."

Lizzie worded her reply carefully. "I suppose it's possible, Anne," she said, pausing before continuing, "but unlikely."

"You miss *Dat*."

Lizzie nodded. "Your *vadder* was a *goot* man and a wonderful husband."

"You didn't know him well when you married him."

Lizzie swallowed before answering. "What gave you that idea?"

Annie reached up to lovingly pat Lizzie's cheek. "I heard Mary Ruth and Hannah talking."

Lizzie felt dismayed. She could only imagine what the two girls had said. "I was happy to marry your *vadder* because then his seven children—all of you—became mine. I love you all as if I had given birth to you."

"I remember when Ezekiel was born." Annie shifted to sit beside Lizzie on her bed. "*Mam* didn't feel well, and I heard her crying and screaming. I was afraid."

"I'm sure it seemed worse than it was, Anne. Giving birth is a natural thing. *Ja*, it hurts a *mudder* as it happens, but then the birth is a joyous thing, and she forgets all about the pain."

"*Mam* didn't," Annie said, startling Lizzie with her words. "She wasn't happy after Ezekiel was born. She cried a lot and *Dat* tried to make her feel better, but she didn't listen." Annie looked at Lizzie with confusion. "Why didn't *Mam* love us anymore?"

"*What?*" Lizzie said, taken aback by the child's revelation. "I'm sure that your *mam* must have loved you very much."

Annie blinked back tears.

"*Nay. Mam* didn't want us anymore. I heard her telling *Dat*."

"She was probably tired and upset. I doubt she meant it." Lizzie placed an arm around her daughter's shoulders. "I'm sure your *mam* loved you just as your *dat* did." Annie had overheard things that her mother never should have said. It upset Lizzie to realize that Annie was still hurt by the memory. Some women suffered depression after giving birth. They couldn't enjoy life or their babies. Was that the way it had been with Abraham's first wife?

"I miss *Dat*."

Lizzie nodded. "I know you do," she whispered. "So do I."

"*Onkel* Zack looks like *Dat*, only his hair is dark and he is younger."

Lizzie had noticed and told her so. It hurt her to know that Anne had suffered. She hugged her, put on a happy face and said, "Now, we should go downstairs to fix breakfast. Would you like to help make waffles?"

Annie nodded enthusiastically. "*Ja*, I like helping in the kitchen."

"I'll get dressed and then we'll go downstairs. I need to feed the animals first. Will you set the table while I'm outside?"

Annie agreed, and soon Lizzie and Annie went silently down the stairs to the kitchen. Lizzie took out the plates, napkins and utensils and gave them to Anne. Then she left the house and crossed the yard. She reached the barn as Zack was leaving it.

"Zack!" she gasped, startled.

"Lizzie."

"Is there something I can help you with? I've come to feed the animals and do the milking," she said.

"The animals have been fed." Zack studied her intently. "And your cows have been milked." He held up the bucket of milk she hadn't noticed previously.

"You did my chores?" she said politely, but she was silently outraged.

"I thought I'd help with the chores while I am here," he said. "You have enough to do caring for the children."

"I've been doing just fine since your *brooder* died," she told him. "And I've been managing well."

"Ja." His voice was quiet as he narrowed his gaze on her. "But it's time someone helps you with the burden."

Lizzie stiffened. "I don't consider the children or this farm a burden."

He nodded, looking thoughtful. "I don't suppose you do. But I'd like to work as long as I am staying here. Is that a problem? What would you have me do all day, if not help with the farm chores?"

Lizzie opened her mouth to respond and then promptly shut it. She sighed. She understood how he felt. "Fine. You may help."

His lips twitched. *"Goot."*

"'Tis not because I can't do it," she pointed out quickly.

Amusement gleamed in his dark eyes. "I never said it was."

Lizzie felt satisfied. She would try not to feel threatened just because he needed something to do.

"Will you and Esther come for breakfast? The children should be awake soon. Please join us."

He seemed to think for a minute as his gaze went toward the *dawdi haus*. "I don't believe Esther has eaten yet."

"I'll set places for you." And she left, her composure shaken by her confrontation with Zack.

Lizzie headed toward the house, her thoughts spinning in her head. Having the Fisher siblings on the property disturbed her peace of mind and threatened her place within this family. She shouldn't be alarmed if her brother-in-law wanted to do farm chores. Zack hadn't come out and said that he was here to take over the farm. Perhaps she should confront him and learn the truth? *But what if in the asking, I give him the idea he never had? Do I really want to know? Or must I first convince him that I can manage without help before he'll stop worrying and return to Ohio?*

Lizzie entered the house to find that Annie had set the table, and Mary Ruth, Hannah and Rebecca had come downstairs to help with breakfast. The girls looked over as she entered the room with a smile.

"I'll be making waffles this morning," she told Mary Ruth. "Would you like some?" Mary Ruth was slow to answer, and Lizzie added, "Your *onkel* and *endie* will be eating with us."

Her eldest daughter looked pleased. "I'll get the butter and syrup."

"I'll help with batter," Hannah said.

Lizzie shot her a look of apology. "I promised Anne that she could help."

Hannah looked at Anne, who appeared as if she would cry if someone took away her job of batter making. She appeared to understand. "Can we have muffins, too? *Onkel* Zack likes your muffins. I can open a new jar of your strawberry jam."

"That's a wonderful idea, Hannah," Lizzie said.

Soon, each of the girls had a special job to do to help in preparing breakfast for their aunt and uncle. Matthew and the two young boys, Jonas and Ezekiel, entered the kitchen minutes later. "It smells *goot* in here," Matt said.

Lizzie, who was showing Anne how to stir the batter, glanced over her shoulder. "Zack and Esther are joining us."

Looking pleased, Matt asked what he could do to help.

As the kitchen filled with activity of her and the children working together, Lizzie felt grateful. If nothing else, Zack's visit had brought the family together to work without sadness, sulking or anger.

Zack and Esther arrived for breakfast, and everyone sat at the large kitchen trestle table. Lizzie, with Esther's help, set out the waffles and other breakfast items.

"Waffles!" Zack exclaimed with pleasure as Lizzie handed him a plateful.

"You like waffles, *Onkel* Zack?" Annie asked.

Zack grinned at her. *"Ja."* He took a bite. "These waffles taste especially *goot*."

Lizzie watched her daughter beam and felt grateful to Zack for making Anne happy. He looked over and winked at her, and she couldn't help grinning back at him. He had known that Anne had helped with the batter, and he'd wanted her to feel special.

Zack Fisher is charming. If she weren't worried about his motives, it would be very easy to fall under his charm. She wondered how it would have been if they'd met at another time and under different circumstances. She frowned. She had to stop thinking of such things. Having such thoughts was disloyal to Abraham and to herself.

The children were excited to eat with their aunt and uncle. They chattered nonstop, especially Matt, Hannah and Rebecca, who debated the merits of waffles with maple syrup versus waffles with warm, sautéed apples.

"I like warm cinnamon apples best," Hannah declared.

"*Nay*, there is nothing like *goot* maple syrup," Matt insisted. "Don't ya think, *Onkel* Zack?"

Zack laughed. "Don't ask me. I like them both ways. I'm not partial to either one. I like mine with honey, too."

A discussion ensued then on the merits of honey versus maple syrup.

Mary Ruth was quiet, Lizzie noticed, but when she caught her eldest daughter's gaze, the girl smiled at her warmly and Lizzie realized that Mary Ruth was simply content to happily observe her brothers and sisters with their aunt and uncle. The atmosphere was one of a big happy family, and it was at times such as this that she felt glad that Zack and Esther had returned to Honeysuckle.

When they had finished their breakfast, the older girls left to do their assigned chores. Soon they would return to the kitchen to help prepare food for the next day. The youngest boys scampered outside with Lizzie's permission to enjoy a few moments in the sun under Matthew's watchful eye. Zack excused himself to check on something in the barn. Lizzie watched him go, wondering what needed his attention.

"Tomorrow is church Sunday," Esther said after she and Lizzie had enjoyed a few quiet moments at the table. She began to gather up the empty breakfast dishes.

"*Ja*," Lizzie said as she rose to help. "'Tis to be held at the Thomas Stoltzfus farm." She gathered tea and coffee cups along with the children's milk glasses. "Do you know them? Thomas and Marybeth Stoltzfus?"

Esther thought a moment. "Their names are familiar but I can't place faces on them."

"You'll have a chance to visit with them after church tomorrow." Lizzie filled up a basin with sudsy water and began washing the dishes. Esther joined her at the sink with a dish towel and began to dry.

Zack peeked his head back into the kitchen, startling both women. "Isn't it church Sunday tomorrow?" he asked.

"Ja," his sister said. "We were just discussing this. Lizzie said it's to be held at the Thomas Stoltzfuses'. Do you remember them?"

Zack shook his head. "But it's been years. Seeing them may jog my memory."

"Do you need anything?" Lizzie asked, wondering again what he'd been doing in the barn and now why he'd returned.

"Nay, I just came to check on tomorrow. I'll have the buggy ready in the morning," he said.

As he left again, Lizzie stifled a frown and went back to work. It wouldn't do to give her thoughts away to Esther...that she was beginning to feel as if he were taking over the farm without telling her. She had to talk with her brother-in-law soon. The uncertainty, the fear, was eating her alive, and besides, she had something on her side now...the tiny baby growing inside her.

The morning dawned bright and clear as Lizzie made sure all the children were ready in time for Sunday service. She gathered up the desserts she'd made for the shared meal afterward and went outside to set them in the buggy. Zack and Esther were already outside waiting for her and the children near the vehicle. When he smiled at her, Lizzie felt a funny feeling in her chest.

"*Goot* morning." Matt ran ahead and grinned at Zack, whose lips curved upward in response.

Lizzie inclined her head in greeting as she approached, carrying two pie plates. Zack surprised her when he reached for her plates and stowed them on the floor in the front seat. The children climbed into the back of the buggy that had been built specifically for Abraham's growing family after Jonas was born. Dressed in their Sunday best, the girls wore black full-length aprons over royal blue dresses, with black head coverings. The three boys sported white shirts, black vests and black pants, with black shoes and black-felt brimmed hats. Seeing her sons looking so like their uncle gave Lizzie a flash of memory of their family life when her husband had been alive. Sadness overwhelmed her and she closed her eyes, fighting the urge to cry.

Soon they were on their way to church services at the Thomas Stoltzfus farm. Lizzie found herself in the front, seated next to Zack after Esther chose to sit in the back. As Zack drove, Lizzie was overly conscious of him beside her. She experienced an odd sensation in her midsection. *The baby?* It wasn't her unborn child that made her feel this way, she realized. It was Zack sitting closely beside her. She watched his strong hands handle the reins with confidence. He was relaxed as he steered the buggy along the paved road toward their destination.

She wondered how the congregation would react when they saw her and the children with Zack and Esther. Abraham had been well liked and respected, and they'd known that he'd needed to marry quickly for the sake of his children. But Lizzie had always wondered what they'd thought about Abraham's choice of a crippled seventeen-year-old bride.

Months into her marriage to Abe, the community women had begun to stop by the farm to visit with her, often seeking her company during church and visiting Sundays. Apparently after seeing how hard she'd worked and the love she had for her new family, the community must have decided that Abraham had chosen well.

When her childhood friend Rachel Miller had married Peter Zook, who lived down the road, Lizzie had been happy and excited. She, Abraham and the children had been invited to the wedding, and Lizzie had been overjoyed to see her dear friend happy and in love.

Zack steered the horse into the Stoltzfuses' barnyard and parked at the end of a long row of family buggies. He got out and assisted Esther. The children scrambled out quickly in a hurry to see their friends. Because of her hip, Lizzie slid out more carefully and was relieved to be standing steady and on firm ground, before Zack had a chance to reach her side of the vehicle. She retrieved the pies from the buggy floor and nearly bumped into Zack as she straightened. She gasped, instantly aware of his clean masculine scent—a mixture of her homemade soap, fresh air and a manly smell that belonged only to Zack.

Silently, he reached to take the desserts from her. She passed him the cherry pie while refusing to relinquish the apple. Lizzie firmed her lips. She was more than capable of carrying pies! He must have read her expression, for he captured her gaze, his lips curving with amusement, before he turned his attention to his sister, who joined them with the dish of brownies she'd baked yesterday afternoon.

How dare Zack laugh at her expense! She felt her throat tighten. She had handled the farm and the children since Abraham's death. The children continued to be clothed, fed and cared for. And she'd done it on her own, hadn't she?

She brightened when she caught sight of Rachel, who looked over and waved. Lizzie grinned and raised a hand in greeting, watching Rachel's gaze shift to Zack beside her as they approached. Her friend raised her eyebrows in question, and Lizzie could feel herself blush as she reached the front porch steps and handed Rachel her pie before she reached toward Zack for the other one. She sighed when Rachel looked to her for an introduction.

"Zack, this is a dear friend, Rachel Zook. Rachel, meet Zack Fisher, my late husband's *brooder*."

Zack gave Rachel a nod. "Rachel," he greeted warmly.

Lizzie encountered his gaze and suddenly felt flustered. "Rachel and I grew up together. She recently married Peter Zook, who lives just down the road from us."

"I'm sure you're happy to have her close."

Lizzie gave her friend a genuine smile. *"Ja,"* she and Rachel said at the same time. Lizzie laughed, warmed again by Rachel's friendship. Rachel was the only person who accepted Lizzie limp and all. If not for Rachel's presence during her childhood, Lizzie would have been unable to endure the other children's ridicule.

She saw Rachel's expression change as her friend studied Zack. Confused, Lizzie shot Zack a look only to find him staring at her and not Rachel.

"Zack?" Amos Beiler drew Zack's attention away from her and Rachel. Lizzie sighed with relief. She watched recognition dawn in Amos Beiler's expression followed by delight as he and Zack shook hands. She stood as the two men exchanged pleasantries.

"Lizzie," Rachel whispered, drawing her aside. "He is beautiful! He looks like…" She didn't say Abraham's name but gave Lizzie's hand a squeeze. "Only he's better looking."

"Rachel!" Lizzie gasped, feeling her face heat.

Esther came up from behind Zack to join Lizzie and Rachel. She'd been standing quietly, studying the church members chatting outside. Lizzie gave her friend a warning look and managed to compose herself before turning to her sister-in-law.

"Esther," Lizzie said with warmth, "this is Rachel Zook. She and I have known each other since we were children."

"It's *goot* to meet you, Rachel," Zachariah's sister said.

Her expression brightening, Rachel smiled. "It's nice to finally meet some of Abraham's family." Her smile faded. "I'm sorry for your loss," she said.

Esther nodded, her eyes glistening. "My *brooder* was a *goot* man."

"Ja," Lizzie whispered, suddenly feeling the loss keenly. She blinked back tears. "He was."

Rachel put her hand on Lizzie's shoulder. "Things will work out, Lizzie."

Lizzie forced a smile as she turned to Esther. "I miss him," she said.

Esther's features softened. "You must have made

my *brooder* a happy man," she said, surprising Lizzie. "You're a hard worker and you love the children."

"Danki," she murmured, wondering what Esther would think if she knew the truth.

"Lizzie! Rachel!" Marybeth Stoltzfus exited the house. She widened her eyes when she recognized Esther. "Esther? *Esther Fisher?"*

Esther smiled. *"Ja*, Marybeth. 'Tis nice to see *ya* again."

"Come in. Come in," the woman invited.

"I've known Marybeth since I was a girl," Esther whispered to Lizzie. "But she was a Yoder then."

The women set their dishes in the kitchen and then proceeded to the room where church services would be held. It was a large family gathering room. Benches had been placed in rows on three sides of the room, with the fourth side-area set aside for the preacher and church elders.

As she slid onto a bench next to her daughters, Lizzie recognized her sons seated next to their uncle on the other side of the room. She glanced toward Zack only to find his bright obsidian eyes studying her. She felt an infusion of heat and quickly looked away.

Preacher David Hostetler stepped into the spotlight and began the service. Everyone stood and began to sing from the *Ausbund*, the Amish book of hymns. They always sang a cappella, their songs sounding like chants. Aware of her daughters' voices beside her, Lizzie joined in to sing praise to the Lord.

A slight movement to the right of her caught the corner of her eye, and Lizzie turned to see who it was. Little Anne slipped past her older sisters toward her, apparently wanting to sit next to her. Lizzie smiled and laid a hand on the child's shoulder, pleased that this daughter, at least, loved her unconditionally. Mary Ruth shifted over to allow her little sister more room and then smiled at Lizzie, above Anne's head, as if she understood. Sensing his regard, Lizzie realized that Zack had witnessed the exchange. She had no idea what he was thinking as he glanced toward Anne then her again, before he returned his attention to the preacher.

Lizzie's heart started to beat hard as she focused on the service. Did she really want to know Zack's thoughts?

Preacher David gave a wonderfully stirring sermon, which caught and held her attention. Inspired, she raised her voice as she sang when the time came for the *Loblied*, the second hymn. When there was a break in the sermon, she prayed silently.

Soon, church service was finished, and Lizzie rose and followed her daughters out of the room and into the kitchen. The men and boys stayed behind and began to rearrange the church benches and set up tables for the shared midday meal.

When she entered the kitchen to help with the food, Lizzie was suddenly surrounded and the center of attention as the churchwomen asked about Zack and Esther and Lizzie's family until Esther walked into the room. The women's excitement rose as they recognized her. Several of the church ladies offered their condolences to Esther on her brother's death. Others questioned her about other matters, curious to know where the family had been living and what they'd been doing during all these years.

The setup of the dining area was complete. The food was unwrapped and ready to serve. The women grabbed the dishes they'd brought and carried them over to the men. Later, when the men had eaten, the women sat with their children and enjoyed their meal. The men escaped into the yard to talk about the weather, their farms, the upcoming fall harvest and other topics that the men liked to discuss.

Lizzie picked up two plates from the food table and carried them back toward the kitchen. As she approached, she overheard two women talking about the Fisher siblings and the farm. She listened, unable to help herself. When she heard someone mention her name, she froze.

"I was surprised to see Zachariah and Esther. But then, I suppose that I shouldn't be. Young Zack is the rightful heir to his father's farm." The first woman's voice came clear and strong, and Lizzie recognized her immediately as Joanna, Wilmer Miller's wife.

"What about young Lizzie? She's been a fine *mudder* to Abraham's children. What will happen to her if Zack decides to stay on the farm?" Lizzie knew the identity of the second woman as Martha Yoder.

"Zack will see that she is cared for. He was always a *goot* boy—I doubt that has changed about him," Joanna pointed out.

"But the children—

"Zack and Esther are more than capable of taking care of their nieces and nephews."

"But Lizzie is their *brooder*'s widow!" Martha exclaimed.

"*Ja*, but Lizzie has a hindrance. Do you think she can do everything that's necessary to keep the farm going *and* take *goot* care of seven children?"

"That kind of thinking is not the Lord's way."

"*Ja*, I know," Joanna admitted, "but too often things are as they are anyway."

The women's voices faded as they moved out of Lizzie's hearing. Their words still hurt her as Lizzie turned away from the kitchen, the leftover food platters in her hands forgotten, and nearly collided with someone.

"Lizzie." Lydia King stood before her, startling her.

"*Mam!*" Lizzie gasped, nearly dropping the plates in her hands.

Chapter Five

"What are you doing here?" Lizzie asked. "I didn't see you at church service."

Her mother rubbed her forehead with her fingers. "We just arrived. Went to service at the John Millers'. Then I thought I'd come see my daughter since she doesn't visit me often enough."

Lizzie stifled a growing feeling of irritation. She had lost her husband and she was dealing with the farm, the children and the house. Her family lived in another church district but close enough to come to her if they wanted, as they apparently had today. Before Abraham had died, she'd seen them often. Didn't her mother realize how much she had to cope with?

Lizzie managed a genuine smile. She loved her mother, although *Mam* had been less affectionate with her than with her brothers and sisters during her childhood. "'Tis *goot* to see you, *Mam*." She glanced behind her mother, looking for her family. "Did *Dat* come? And William and the others?" She referred to her siblings who still lived at home.

"*Ja*, the boys are here. Katie stayed at the Yoders' after service. She's interested in young Mark."

Lizzie was glad for her sister, pleased that Katie had chosen to find her own happiness.

"Lizzie, you cannot continue as you have been." Her mother regarded her with concern. "You need to find a husband, someone to help you with the farm and the children."

Lizzie disagreed. "My husband passed recently. I'm managing on my own. Did you forget that you were the one who warned me that if I didn't accept Abraham's marriage proposal, then I'd never marry?"

Lydia waved her daughter's concerns aside. "You've shown yourself to be a *goot* wife and *mudder*. Any man would be lucky to have you."

Stunned, Lizzie could only stare at her. Who was this person and where was her real *mam*, the *mam* who'd hurt her, perhaps unintentionally, with words that made Lizzie realize that her disability bothered her mother? She'd never felt as if *Mam* accepted her. *My limp embarrasses* Mam. It was obvious to Lizzie that her mother found it easy to love William, Luke, Katie and her eldest married daughter, Susie. *But not me—her crippled daughter.* Lizzie hadn't known her mother's affection during childhood, and she was afraid to hope for it now.

It wasn't that her *mam* wasn't a kind person, a godly woman who lived by the *Ordnung*—the rules and religious teachings of the Old Order Amish community. But whether *Mam* realized it or not, Lizzie felt as though she'd never quite fit in. If not for her brother William, who loved to tease her like he did all of their other siblings, she would have felt completely alone and detached from the family. When her mother had urged her to accept Abraham's offer of marriage, it had been William who had encouraged her to think about it hard and long and decide for herself what she wanted to do.

"You've lost weight," her mother said.

"I'm eating well. I've been busy."

"Are the children helping out?" *Mam* asked as she watched Lizzie's younger children playing in the yard through the window glass.

Lizzie nodded. "They are *goot kinner.*"

"I can come by to help—"

"I'm fine, *Mam*, not to worry." She smiled to take the sting out of the rejection. "We are finding our way together. We just need time."

"It's been two months," her mother pointed out.

"Not long since their *vadder*'s death," Lizzie insisted. She was glad to see her mother but wished that things would get easier between them. "You said that William was outside?"

"*Ja*, he's talking with *Dat* and your *brooder* Luke."

"I need to take these to the kitchen," Lizzie said, referring to the dishes she held. The memory of Joanna and Martha's conversation still stung. She hesitated, wondering if the two gossiping women were still inside.

"I'll take them," her mother offered surprisingly. "Go. Visit with your father and *brooders.*"

After considering her mother's smiling expression, Lizzie gratefully gave her the plates. "I won't be long."

Esther came in from outside. "Lizzie, I've brought the rest of your pie—" She stopped abruptly when she saw the woman at Lizzie's side.

Lizzie felt sure that *Mam* and Esther hadn't met. Did Esther sense tension in the air between her and her mother?

Lizzie smiled, but she could tell that her mother was curious; and she didn't want her *mam* asking questions. As Zack approached, Lizzie felt her stomach tighten when she saw her mother take a good long look at him.

"Who's this?" her mother asked, studying the young man. She frowned. "He looks like—"

"*Mam*, this is Zack Fisher, my late husband's *brooder*."

A gleam of interest entered her mother's hazel eyes. "You look like him," she told Zack.

Zack nodded. "You are Lizzie's *mudder*." He eyed Lizzie and turned back to smile at her *mam*.

Mam nodded. "Lydia King," she introduced herself.

Afraid of what her mother might say, Lizzie flashed Esther a pleading look.

"Lizzie, Ezekiel is tired and wants to go home. Perhaps we should leave." Esther gave Lydia an apologetic smile.

"*Ja*, we should go home," Zack agreed. "We should tell the children to wait in the buggy." But still he didn't leave.

Lydia's eyes widened. "You're living at the *haus*?"

"They're staying in the *dawdi haus*," Lizzie said, embarrassed by her mother's question.

"I see." The look in her mother's eyes gave cause for Lizzie's concern.

"We should go," Esther said, and Lizzie sent her a grateful look. "It's been a long day, and the little ones are tired."

Her mother's expression softened. "They are growing like weeds."

Lizzie smiled. *"Ja."* Ezekiel entered the house, rubbing his eyes. "Time to leave, Zeke. Where is Jonas?" The little boy gestured outside. "Tell him and Matt and your sisters that we'll be leaving in a few minutes." She turned toward her mother. "I'm glad you came," she said softly. "It is nice to see you." She regretted that she wouldn't have time to catch up with her father and brothers, but she needed to go.

Her *mudder* nodded. "You'll come for a visit soon?"

"We'll try." She hesitated. "But I can't promise."

Mam seemed satisfied with her answer.

Lizzie was conscious of Zack waiting patiently beside her. "I'm coming."

He nodded, hesitated. "I'll wait for you near the buggy."

Lizzie watched as he stopped to chat briefly with the gathering of men near the barn before he continued toward their buggy.

She was startled when a hand settled on her shoulder. She turned and encountered her mother's gaze. There was concern, caring and something she'd never seen in her expression. *Affection.*

"I will see you soon," *Mam* said softly.

Lizzie nodded and then retrieved her empty dishes, before she said goodbye to her parents and siblings. Then she and the children joined Esther and Zack for the journey home.

As he drove home from church services, Zack noted Lizzie's silence despite the fact that the children loudly chattered about the friends they'd seen, with Esther interjecting the occasional question or comment. He shot his late brother's widow a glance. She stared out the side window, unaware of his interest. She looked vulnerable, pensive...alone.

As he turned his attention to the drive, he could still recall every little detail about her. Dressed in royal blue with white cape and apron and white head covering, she was a young, pretty thing. *Beautiful,* he thought, *not just pretty.* He immediately thought of her problem hip. Did it pain her often? She never complained if it did, and he respected her for it. He flashed her another look, but he couldn't gauge her expression.

Turning his gaze back to the road, he recalled watching his little niece Anne as she'd switched places because she wanted to sit closer to Lizzie during church.

Things were complicated. He didn't know why he'd thought he'd be able to return home, walk onto the property and easily assume control. He frowned, unhappy with his own arrogance. He'd taken a lot for granted when he should have known that the Lord often had other plans.

Since his brother's death, Lizzie alone had cared for the farm and his children. He was beginning to realize that he couldn't ask her to leave. It wouldn't be fair or right since she was his brother's widow. He would stay to help her, see how well she managed in Abraham's absence. Lizzie needed help with the harvest. And while the community would come to assist her, there was still much to be done beforehand.

And what about the farm animals? How could she, a young crippled woman, handle the farm, the animals *and* his nieces and nephews? She was only one person, a young, vulnerable woman. He wanted to stay in Honeysuckle, but he had to make sure that the situation was fair to all of them. Zack smiled as he thought of his nieces and nephews. They were lively and smart, and they belonged on the property.

Would Lizzie be happy if he kept the children? Maybe she would be happier without the work and responsibility that had been thrust upon her.

Nay, Lizzie wasn't Ruth. Despite her disability, Lizzie wasn't weak. She'd never willingly give up the children or the farm. And he was beginning to wonder if he wanted her to.

Zack steered the horse-drawn buggy onto the road toward the house. It was late afternoon, but with the shortening of daylight hours, it seemed as if it were early evening. Sunlight had faded to dusk. The air was filled with the rich scent of autumn, the chrysanthemums planted near the house, the fallen leaves from the tree in the side yard. As he pulled the buggy into the yard and parked near the barn, he was conscious of Lizzie sitting quietly beside him. Something stirred within him, telling him that he was beginning to feel more for her than he should. He firmed his lips. *More than a brother-in-law should feel for his late brother's widow.*

He climbed out, extended a hand to help Esther out of the vehicle and then started around the buggy to help Lizzie. But Lizzie refused to wait. She scrambled out of the buggy. He sensed when she tripped, heard her cry out with pain and then watched as she quickly stumbled to her feet. He rushed to her side, but she seemed composed when he reached her. He might have thought he'd imagined her fall, if not for his niece Anne, who had witnessed it from the backseat.

"*Mam*, are you all right?" the child cried worriedly.

"Lizzie." Zack's first instinct was to ensure that she was all right. His sudden urge to protect and care for her was disturbing. He allowed his gaze to make a thorough examination of her. "Are you sure you're not hurt?"

Chapter Six

"I'm fine." Lizzie managed to smile at her daughter without meeting Zack's gaze. She was embarrassed. The fall had jarred her ankle and hip, which continued to throb incessantly while she struggled to hide the pain. She didn't want to admit to Zack that she'd hurt herself. She didn't want anyone's help, least of all Zack's. Abraham had accepted that she could manage on her own. Why couldn't his brother do the same?

Trying not to let on that she was stiff and sore, Lizzie reached down to pick up the empty pie dish and turned toward the house. She lurched and would have fallen again if Zack hadn't reached out to steady her.

"You have hurt yourself!" he exclaimed, examining her with dark eyes full of concern.

"Nay," she assured him, but she could tell that he didn't believe her. She was startled by his touch. His fingers on her arm made her feel things for him that she shouldn't. She didn't want to think of Zack as anything but her brother-in-law, but she couldn't seem to help herself. "I should go," she said, relieved when he released her. She quickly gathered her composure. "I

need to fix supper," she murmured as she turned and started toward the house. She stopped suddenly and faced him. "Will you and Esther join us?"

After a quick glance toward his sister, who was entering the *dawdi haus*, Zack shook his head. "We appreciate the offer, but we'll snack later at the cottage." He offered her a crooked grin. "Seems like we've been eating all day."

Lizzie chuckled, relaxing, no longer embarrassed about her fall. "I know what you mean." She had enjoyed a helping of most items on the food table. She shifted uncomfortably when Zack continued to stare at her. "I'll see you in the morning."

She didn't wait for his answer but continued on, looking back only once briefly to see that the children were following her toward the house. Her arm tingled where Zack's fingers had been. Her face flamed as she regretted her clumsiness in front of Zack. So much for attempting to prove that she was capable!

Once inside the house, Lizzie worked to prepare a light supper for the children, relieved that Zack and Esther had decided to eat at home. She had to process her attraction to Zack. She'd never felt this way about Abraham—theirs had been a marriage that had begun in necessity and ended in a calm and quiet love. Her feelings for Zack mortified and embarrassed her—why did she react so strongly to him whenever he was near?

Lizzie froze in the act of slicing bread for sandwiches. Did he suspect that she found him handsome, that she felt drawn to him like a moth to a flame? Closing her eyes, she groaned. She hoped not. It was wrong to feel this way. She was his brother's widow, and her husband had been dead less than three months.

"*Mam*, can we have potato chips with supper?"

Lizzie pushed thoughts of Zack aside and forced a smile for her four-year-old son. "*Ja*, Jonas, you may have potato chips," she said. "But it's important that you eat your vegetables and meat, too."

"But, *Mam*, I had lots of meat and vegetables today."

"True," she admitted with a smile. "But eat something other than just chips, *ja*?"

Jonas agreed with a grin. "*Ja.*"

Esther wandered into the kitchen and went to the pantry. She felt shaken. When Zack had asked her to accompany him to Honeysuckle, she'd been curious enough to come. Memories had assailed her when she'd first stepped into the farmhouse…of her father and mother smiling at one another, of the laughter, love and family values that had been evident within the house when her father had been alive. She still felt the loss of her father deeply although it'd been thirteen years since he passed. Mam *was devastated when* Dat *died*. Esther had worried that her mother would never recover, but moving to Ohio to live near their sister Miriam had helped *Mam* to get through.

She was glad she and Zack were staying in the *dawdi haus*. There were memories here in the cottage, too, but they were of her *grosseldre*, fond recollections of her *grossmama* baking and filling the kitchen with the wonderful scents of her cakes and pies and muffins and biscuits. *Grossmama* had kept an immaculate house, sweeping the floors and polishing the furniture daily. Lizzie kept the *dawdi haus* neat and tidy. It seemed the same but yet different. *It's the lemon oil*, she thought.

Esther caught herself staring at but not seeing the

pantry's contents. She shook herself from the past. She grabbed from the shelf the wrapped cookies that Lizzie had made earlier for them. There was also a colorful array of pint jars filled with jelly, jam and apple butter, along with quart jars of vegetables, peaches and sweet-and-sour chow-chow. And Lizzie had stocked the chest freezer with loaves of bread, meat and ice cream. She smiled. She liked her late brother's widow. Lizzie was younger than she'd expected, but it was obvious that she loved the children and the life she'd created for herself here on the farm.

Esther chose a jar of strawberry jam and set it on the kitchen table. Then she reached toward the counter for the rest of the bread that she and Zack had enjoyed previously. Next she took out two plates, a cutting board and a knife from a cabinet drawer. As she slathered jam onto two pieces of bread with the knife, she tried not to think too much about today's church service. But she couldn't get it out of her mind.

David Hostetler is a preacher. Had she ever felt more shocked to learn that the boy she'd once known was now a preacher? Never in her wildest imagination had it occurred to her the boy she'd loved when she was fourteen would grow up to become a church elder.

Her fingers shook as she transferred the bread onto a plate for Zack.

She had watched David as he'd preached the sermon and felt the heat rise to her face. He was still handsome, she thought, but now he had a beard like the other married men within the Amish community.

Who was his wife? David hadn't stayed for the post-service midday meal, so she didn't get to see or meet her. The preacher and his family apparently had to be elsewhere, which was probably a good thing. She'd been so startled to see him after all this time; she would have felt awkward in his presence.

Moving to Ohio after her *dat* died had been one of the hardest things she'd ever experienced, leaving her friends…leaving David. Her *mam* had wanted to move, so there was no question that she'd stay behind. If she'd been given a choice, she would have chosen to stay.

"That wouldn't be fair to Abraham and Ruth now, would it?" *Mam* had said. "It wouldn't be right to intrude on newlyweds starting their life together."

At the time, Esther had reasoned that if she'd stayed in Honeysuckle, she could have helped Ruth with the chores. But her mother had disagreed.

In hindsight, she knew that *Mam* had been right. It wouldn't have been fair to her brother and his new wife if she'd stayed and moved in with them.

If life had gone differently, she might have married David, instead of becoming a twenty-seven-year-old spinster. She released a shuddering breath. She'd have to see David sometime, speak cordially with him and his wife. Was he happy? If so, then she would be happy for him. She closed her eyes, seeing the teenager he'd been—smart, hardworking, handsome. *He is still handsome.* And she had no doubt that he was still smart and hardworking. It was an honor to be elected preacher. His would be a lifelong commitment.

Whom did he marry?

Zack walked into the kitchen, drawing her attention away from her thoughts. "What have you got there?"

Esther smiled. "Just bread and strawberry jam. We had plenty to eat earlier, don't you think?"

Zack grinned as he reached for the plate she'd prepared for him. "I agree." He picked up a slice of bread, took a bite and grinned. "This is *goot* jam."

"Lizzie made it," she said, watching his expression.

"She did a fine job." His face gave away none of his thoughts.

"*Ja*, she did." Esther paused and then asked, "What are you going to do about her?"

He stopped eating, his bread suspended inches from his mouth. "I don't know." He set the partially eaten slice onto his plate. "Is there iced tea in the refrigerator?"

Esther nodded, then retrieved the iced-tea pitcher and poured two glassfuls. She handed one to her brother. "Zack—"

Zack sighed. "I don't know, Esther. I know she's a nice girl. I was surprised to learn that she was our *brooder*'s wife. I didn't expect him to marry again." He took a sip from his iced tea.

"Life is never as we expect it." She studied her brother with affection. "You came here because you found out that there is a strange woman in residence. And while she also happens to be our *brooder*'s widow, you thought you could come in and take away the farm and the children."

"*Nay.*" Zack sighed. "*Ja.*"

"But now you're having second thoughts because Lizzie and the children are doing well."

Zack frowned. "You think Lizzie is managing on her own."

Esther narrowed her gaze on her younger brother thoughtfully. "She may or may not be. I'm not the one to judge. You're the one who knows how to run a farm. You worked here as a boy before we moved, and since then, you've done enough chores on Miriam and Joshua's farm to understand what needs to be done." She took a seat at the kitchen table. "Lizzie is certainly challenged with that hip of hers," she said softly. She wondered how much the young woman had been suffering in silence.

"She is determined, I'll admit. I don't know that she'd tell us if she's hurting or if the work proves too much for her."

"And if she told you, then what would you do? Tell her that she'll lose her family, her home and the life she's built for herself because she's not worthy?"

"Who said she's not worthy of this life?" Zack said with a look that made Esther wonder just what he was thinking. "I didn't. And she loves the children. She's a *goot* mother to them. They love her, especially those little ones—Anne and Jonas and Zeke."

Esther controlled the urge to smile. Her brother's defense of Lizzie was telling. "What do you think we should do?"

Zack looked thoughtful. Esther looked at him as Lizzie might see him—young but older than she, handsome, capable, too attractive for a girl's peace of mind. "We'll continue as we are for now. I'll make sure that she can manage on her own, and then it will be up to *Gott* to decide about the future of Lizzie, the children and the farm...and us."

A good plan, Esther thought as she rose to put her dirty glass in the dish basin. She could feel something happening whenever Zack and Lizzie were together, and she could anticipate the struggle that would no doubt ensue once they identified their feelings.

* * *

Zack stared at his sister with dismay. He didn't like discussing Lizzie with her. This sudden and new attraction that he felt for her was upsetting. She was his brother's widow. He shouldn't be feeling this way.

What am I going to do? He wanted to stay, but he'd be hurting Lizzie if he took back the farm. And the last thing he wanted to do was hurt her.

He was at a loss about what to do with the farm and the family.

During the days that followed, Lizzie adjusted to having Zack and Esther in frequent company. The Fisher siblings were here, and although she had no idea for how long, she decided to make the best of the situation.

It no longer startled her to see Zack tending to the horses, repairing a length of fence that needed fixing or doing some other chore. While there were times when Zack looked at her long and hard, which made her uncomfortable, for the most part, theirs was an easy farm-working relationship.

Wednesday morning before dawn, Lizzie was feeding the chickens when Zack exited the cottage, sipping on a cup of coffee. He waved when he saw her and approached.

"You're up bright and early," he said as he reached her.

She smiled. "I'm hoping to get a lot accomplished this morning. I plan to pick and put up the last of the garden vegetables." She could freeze them or make chow-chow with the leftover green beans, corn, onions and red beans. Then she needed to get the baking done. She planned to make extra loaves of bread for him and Esther.

"I thought I'd take Rosebud to get her right-front hoof checked. I think it may need shoeing."

Lizzie nodded. She had noticed the sorrel mare's slightly uneven gait lately. It was so minor that someone else might not have seen, but apparently Zack knew horses well enough to note the difference.

Lizzie mentally calculated the cost of a new set of horseshoes. Fortunately, she had enough money. Ellen Beachey had stopped by the house only yesterday to give her the money she'd earned from selling another quilt. She'd sold some smaller crafts, as well—a patchwork apron, two hand-stitched purses and a couple of baby quilts—which had made her over five hundred dollars in sales. During Ellen's visit, Lizzie had learned that Ellen had a new sweetheart—or rather, an old one, according to Ellen—Neziah Shetler, who once had courted Ellen when she was nineteen before they'd gone their separate ways because they'd thought their differences were too great to allow for a future together. Neziah, who had gone on to marry someone else, was now a widower with young sons. He'd proclaimed his love for Ellen, telling her—and proving to her—that the differences they'd had in the past no longer existed. He was courting Ellen with the intention of marriage. That Ellen was happy was evident in her bright smile and glistening blue eyes. Ellen's happiness had been infectious, and Lizzie couldn't be more pleased for her friend.

Lizzie realized that while she'd been reminiscing, Zack had begun to stare at her strangely. Embarrassed at her woolgathering, she hurried to answer him.

"I've got money inside," she told him. "Let me know when you're ready to take the mare."

Zack appeared as if he would object, but then he must have thought better of it. "Her other hooves look fine. It's just the one."

He gazed at her for a moment longer until Lizzie shifted awkwardly under his regard. "I've got chickens to feed and the milking to do," she said.

"I'll take care of the horses and then check the fence line on the east boundary," Zack called out to her as she started to walk away. "I think some deer might have broken through. I saw hoofprints near your vegetable garden."

Lizzie halted and glanced toward the garden in the side yard. It was hard to tell from this distance if deer had disturbed her plants. There were still bell peppers, pumpkins, spinach and turnips growing. She didn't want her late crop ruined. It was bad enough the beautiful animals sometimes got into their cornfields. *Better the corn than my garden vegetables*, she thought. "It doesn't look disturbed."

"Not yet," he said, "but it will be if they continue to get inside the fence."

Lizzie knew that Zack was an early riser who enjoyed a cup of coffee at the start of his day. After finishing his early-morning chores, he would be ready for a hearty breakfast, usually about the same time that the children and his sister were up and ready to eat. They studied the garden in silence, Zack with his cup of coffee and she holding a pail of chicken feed. Lizzie was overly aware of him beside her. She'd come to appreciate his help around the farm, but given her attraction toward him, she wasn't entirely comfortable with the silence between them.

"I should get back to work," she said. She could feel her face heat when he captured her glance. To hide her reaction to him, she quickly turned to scatter some chicken feed on the ground.

"Is there anything you need in town?" he asked.

Lizzie gave the matter some thought. "Some groceries and fabric. An Englisher came into the craft shop and asked if I'd make a wedding quilt for her daughter. Ellen asked me if I was interested before she took a deposit. She told me to take my time to think about it."

Zack smiled. "You make beautiful quilts." When she raised questioning eyebrows, he explained, "The covering on Esther's bed. Matt told me you made it."

"*Ja*, an easy design, but the quilt serves its purpose." Lizzie wanted to escape before she said something she'd regret.

"Will you come to breakfast?" she asked.

He shook his head. "I ate breakfast earlier."

She was surprised to feel disappointment. "I'll see you later in the day, then."

He nodded and acted as if he, too, was eager to get away. "Let me know if you need anything. We can talk about going to town later."

"*Onkel* Zack!" Matt ran toward them from the farmhouse. "Can I come and help?"

"You want to do chores?" He exchanged amused glances with her over the boy's head.

Lizzie smiled. "You're up and ready to go early," she told her son.

Matt nodded. "I meant to get up earlier in case *Onkel*

needed me before *schule*." The boy stared at Lizzie. "It's all right if I help, *ja*?"

"With the farmwork?" she teased, and Matt grinned at her. "*Ja*, help your uncle," she encouraged. "I'm sure he'd appreciate it. But don't forget about *schule*."

"I won't," Matthew replied with a grin.

Then it occurred to her that Zack might not want his nephew underfoot. She looked at Zack in question. "Unless you'd rather he didn't go?"

A strange look entered his expression as they locked gazes. "Of course he may come." He then addressed his nephew. "But, Matt, I must warn you—there's a lot of work to do." He stared at her. "Lizzie." She watched him turn and walk toward the fields with Matt.

"Zack."

Zack paused and turned as Matt waited for his uncle. "You know where to find me if you need anything," he said. "I'll send Matthew home in time to clean up for *schule*."

"*Danki*," she murmured as he left. Feeling unsettled, Lizzie fed the chickens, put away the feed bucket, then went into the barn to do the milking. As she stepped into the dark interior, she was assailed by memories of her husband lying at the base of the ladder to the loft on the left, blood pooling near his head on the concrete floor. Swallowing hard, Lizzie looked away and hurried toward the cow stalls. As she took care of the animals, she was able to put the memory at rest, at least, for the time being. She finished the chore and went back to the farmhouse. The children were awake and in the kitchen as she entered it through the back door.

"Breakfast?" she asked.

"*Ja!*" Jonas cried, and Anne and Zeke echoed him.

Lizzie decided the vegetable-garden work could wait until after breakfast and her household chores. Esther joined them for the meal and insisted on staying to help with the housework. Lizzie worked inside, pleased to have Esther's and the girls' help.

Mary Ruth, Hannah and Rebecca worked quickly and efficiently at their assigned chores, and Lizzie found herself able to get to her garden much earlier than expected. Anne and Jonas decided to help her pick vegetables. The older girls and Ezekiel had gone with Esther to the *dawdi haus*, despite Esther's insistence that there was nothing to do except bake cookies. Little Zeke had perked up at the mention of cookies. When he asked if he could watch the cookie baking, Esther had smiled and held out her hand toward him.

Lizzie sighed with pleasure as she raked the garden. She hadn't felt this lighthearted in a long time. She was grateful to have the whole afternoon ahead of her to do her work. If her day continued as well as it had thus far, she'd have time in the evening to relax and read a book or finish the baby quilt for her unborn child.

Now that she knew she was pregnant, she had to consult the midwife. She felt amazingly good for being in her first trimester. Her pregnancy nausea was similar to the nausea frequently brought on by her hip-dysplasia pain.

Would the weight of her baby aggravate her hip? It wouldn't matter if it did. The only thing that mattered was her baby. She cradled her belly, hoping, praying that everything went well with her pregnancy.

"Mam." A young voice broke into her thoughts.

"Ja, Jonas?"

"Look how many I got." He showed her the large

stainless-steel bowl, which he'd filled to the rim with turnips and bell peppers.

"You've been a busy boy!" she exclaimed with pleasure. He'd been working at the opposite end of the garden.

He grinned back at her. "I'll put these in the house and come back to pick more."

Lizzie agreed and then eyed him fondly as he ran as if he couldn't wait to return to help her.

Could a woman ask for better children? she wondered, overwhelmed with love. Since Zack's arrival, the older children frequently helped her without her having to ask. She had mixed feelings about her situation. If life continued as it had been going, then she wouldn't mind her husband's siblings living on the farm indefinitely, although things might change if they decided to move from the *dawdi haus* to the big house.

When are you going to talk with Zack about his intentions toward the farm? her inner voice taunted.

"Tomorrow," she declared. She'd talk with him tomorrow and put her mind at ease. She closed her eyes and swallowed hard. At least, she hoped her talk with Zack would calm her fears.

Chapter Seven

On Thursday morning, Lizzie was in the yard feeding the chickens. It was still dark; the sun had yet to make an appearance, although there was a tiniest hint of orange in a cloudless early-morning sky filled with stars. She loved this time of day when the world was silent, and she felt a part of God's nature. There was no one around to notice her limp or judge her. No one to condemn her for the choices she'd made.

"Lizzie."

She gasped, startled. "Zack!"

He had approached silently. She hadn't expected to see him this early.

He stood within two feet of her. She could see his gleaming eyes and the crooked smile on his masculine lips. "I'm sorry I scared you."

She had placed a hand over her thundering heart. "'Tis all right." She managed to smile. "I'll live."

His smile turned into a grin. "I wanted to ask you if you'd like to run into town today. We could go to Miller's General Store or McCann's Grocery. If you wish, we can stop at Beachey's Craft Shop. Then we can eat at Margaret's and return home afterward."

It sounded like a wonderful outing. Margaret's was the local Mennonite restaurant on the main street in Honeysuckle. For some reason, the thought of spending a couple of hours with Zack brightened her day.

"I'd like to go, but what about the children?"

"The older ones will be in school, and Esther will be here to mind Zeke and Jonas."

Lizzie grinned. "And we'll be back before the others get home."

"Then it's settled?" he asked. "Shall we leave at nine?"

Lizzie thought of all she had to do and decided that she'd have plenty of time to get her morning chores done. The rest of her work could wait.

"*Ja.* That sounds fine," she said. "I'll be ready at nine o'clock."

Five hours later, cleaned up after doing chores and wearing a freshly laundered dress, Lizzie exited the house to find Zack had brought around the family's market wagon. It had been some time since she'd taken a ride in the vehicle. The climb up onto the seat was high and was hard on her hip.

She smiled at Zack as she approached while worrying that she'd make a fool of herself when she tried to get in. She skirted the buggy to the front passenger side and to her surprise Zack joined her there. Her heart started to pound hard as she met his gaze. Overwhelmed by how handsome he looked in his burgundy shirt and triblend blue denim pants with black leather suspenders, she tried not to stare. Zack reached into the back of the wagon for a plastic crate, which he set on the ground for her to step on. He then extended his hand to assist her.

His thoughtfulness pleased her. She placed her fingers within his grasp as she put her foot onto the crate and allowed Zachariah to help her into the wagon. "Careful now," he warned as he firmed his hold when she started to stumble. She blushed at the heat of his fingers.

"Danki," she murmured as he released her hand when she was seated. The memory of his touch made her nape tingle and warmth run up her arm.

He was silent as he skirted the wagon and climbed into the vehicle's driver's side. He picked up the leathers, then turned toward her. "Where should we go first?"

She thought for a moment. Her face warmed as he gazed at her. "Beachey's Craft Shop? It's the closest."

He nodded, and then with a click of his tongue and a flick of the reins, he steered Rosebud toward the main road.

"Mam! Mam!" a young voice called out as Zack drove the buggy down the dirt drive.

Lizzie glanced back. Little Zeke raced after them, waving his arms. "Zack, please stop. It's Zeke," she explained.

He immediately drew the horse to a halt. Lizzie wanted to get down and run to her son, but she knew that if she tried to climb down without help, she'd hurt herself.

Zack got out and met Zeke as the child ran toward the buggy. He scooped the three-year-old into his arms and brought him to her.

Ezekiel's eyes glistened with tears as Zack lifted

him to a height where he was eye to eye with Lizzie. "What's wrong, Zeke?" she asked softly.

The child sniffed. "I wanted to say goodbye. I never got to say goodbye."

She reached out to tenderly caress his cheek. "You don't have to worry," she said. "We'll be back this afternoon."

"You will?" he asked, blinking rapidly as he gazed at her.

"*Ja*, of course—"

Zack hefted the child onto the front seat. "I'll tell Esther that he'll be coming with us."

"Would you like to come?" she asked Zeke.

Ezekiel nodded vigorously, his eyes suddenly bright with excitement. "Can I?"

"May I?" she corrected. She met Zack's gaze. "You don't mind?" she asked.

"*Nay.*" He grinned as he reached up to tap on the brim of the boy's straw hat. "I'll be right back."

As she watched Zack walk toward the *dawdi haus*, Lizzie sensed something shift within her heart. His tenderness, consideration and patience with Zeke stirred feelings within her that frightened her. He was the brother of her late husband, and while her marriage to Abe hadn't been initiated by love, Abraham had still been her husband and she his wife. She had no right to feel this way.

Zack was her brother-in-law. She couldn't—*mustn't*—harbor feelings for him other than friendship between one relative to another.

"*Mam*, you all right?" Zeke asked. Her son placed his hand on her arm.

She turned to him with a reassuring smile. "*Ja*, Zeke. Are you ready to go to town?"

The little boy grinned. "*Ja!* We're going to town," he chanted. "We're going to town!"

Zack returned from the *dawdi haus* and climbed into the driver's seat. He flashed Zeke a grin. "All ready for your adventure?"

"*Ja!*" Zeke cried, clearly excited at the prospect.

Beachey's Craft Shop stood on the public road. The Beachey family lived in the house down from the store on the crest of a hill. She saw Zack study the store as they approached. He and Zeke followed her inside and waited patiently while she spoke with Ellen, the Beacheys' daughter, who now ran the business for her aging parents.

Ellen smiled as Lizzie approached the counter. "Did you decide if you'll be making the wedding quilt for Mrs. Emory's daughter?"

"Did Mrs. Emory say how soon she needed it?" Lizzie asked. "It may take me a while to finish one of this size." Mrs. Emory wanted to give her daughter a quilt large enough for a king-size bed. Lizzie thought she might use the wedding-ring pattern with calico prints in soft pastels, colors that would look good in any room.

"Dana Emory's wedding is over a year and a half from now," Ellen told her. "You should have plenty of time. I have an idea what Mrs. Emory likes. She loved the last quilt you brought. I'll get it." She left the room, leaving Lizzie to wait patiently for her return.

English weddings were often large and took months of preparation, Lizzie realized. Many of the little details, such as flowers, the church and the reception, were important to them. *If the man I loved wanted to wed me,* Lizzie thought, *I wouldn't worry about such worldly things.* She'd simply be eager to become his wife.

She and Abraham didn't have a usual wedding. Their marriage had been about the children, not her and the groom.

While she waited for Ellen's return, Lizzie watched Zack and Zeke as they wandered about the store. She saw Zack bend to whisper something in her little boy's ear and saw Zeke's face light up with a big smile.

Ellen returned with the quilt that had drawn Barbara Emory's attention. "She liked these colors," she told Lizzie. "I told her that you wouldn't be able to use the same fabrics but that you could find printed material in similar colors." The colors in the quilt were blue, yellow and spring green.

Lizzie nodded. "*Ja.* I can do that."

"You'll take on the work?" Ellen named a figure that made Lizzie gasp and unable to decline.

"How can I say no?" Lizzie said with a chuckle.

"I told her that you'd need a deposit to pay for the fabrics and some of your time." Ellen smiled. "I wanted to make sure you got some money up front."

"That's wonderful." Lizzie grinned, pleased. *"Danki."* The money would come in handy. It would take months to make the quilt, but if she worked nights, she could have it finished well before the wedding. And then she'd be able to make other craft items.

She and Ellen had completed their business conversation about the Emory quilt when Zack approached with young Zeke.

"Ellen," he greeted. "It's *goot* to see you again."

Ellen stared at him a long moment. "Zachariah

Fisher?" She blinked and then grinned when he nodded. "Zack, I haven't seen you in—"

"Years," he said with a pleasant smile. "Since we were children."

"*You* were a child anyway," Ellen said with a grin. "Is there something I can do for you?"

"*Nay.*" He drew Zeke closer with a hand on his shoulder. "We're waiting for Lizzie," he said.

Compassion filled the woman's dark eyes. "I am sorry about your *brooder.*"

Zack inclined his head, clearly appreciating her sympathy.

Ellen then turned to Lizzie. "Do you think you'll be able to make a few aprons? They sell as soon as I get them in."

"Certainly," Lizzie assured her. It wouldn't take her long to stitch up a few.

The door to the shop jingled, and Neziah Shetler entered and approached the counter. Lizzie saw Ellen's eyes light up and a smile curve her lips. Lizzie shot Zack a look and saw that he, too, noticed the change in Ellen.

"We should go," Zack said. Lizzie nodded, figuring that Ellen and Neziah might want a brief moment alone. "Ellen, it was nice to see you again." Neziah approached the counter. "Neziah Shetler? Zack Fisher." He held out his hand.

Neziah smiled as they shook hands. "Zack! Welcome home. It's been a long time. You couldn't have been more than twelve when you moved away."

Zack nodded. "I was eleven."

Lizzie listened patiently and kept an eye on Zeke while the two men talked, catching up.

"It was *goot* to see you both," Zack said when it was time to leave. "I trust we'll see you again soon."

"Lizzie. It's nice to see you again," Neziah said.

"It's *goot* to see you, too," she replied with a smile. "Zeke, *koom*. We must finish our errands before your *brooder* and sisters get home from *schule*." With her son standing by her side, Lizzie turned to her friend. "Ellen, I appreciate the work. Tell Mrs. Emory that she can count on me to make her daughter's quilt. I'll purchase some fabrics for her to approve before I start."

"That's a fine idea." Ellen placed the quilt on the counter behind her. "I'll talk with her when she comes in next week."

"Can we go eat yet?" Zeke asked. "I'm hungry."

"Zeke!" Lizzie scolded gently, but Ellen and Neziah only laughed.

Zack hoisted Zeke onto his shoulders and headed toward the door. Lizzie started to follow and then stopped briefly when she saw Dinah Plank, the Beacheys' tenant who lived in the apartment above the craft shop and worked for Ellen in the store. "If you'll take Zeke, I'll follow in just a minute," she told Zack.

"Dinah," Lizzie greeted. "How is the widows' group? I'm sorry I haven't been to a meeting in a while."

"No worries," Dinah said. "We're here if you need us, but I imagine you've been busy with your company." The older woman glanced toward the door. "That is Zack Fisher, isn't it?"

Blushing, Lizzie nodded and quickly changed the subject to the upcoming widows'-club lunch. She and the woman chatted a few moments, and then after bidding everyone farewell, she joined Zack and Zeke, who were waiting for her outside.

"Miller's General Store or McCann's Grocery?" Zack asked with a smile.

McCann's Grocery was the only food store in the center of Honeysuckle, and it had other items, as well, but fabric wasn't among them. Lizzie needed to buy fabric, and the best place for material was the general store. She knew it wouldn't take long to get to the store; it was just a mile and a half past Honeysuckle village proper. "Let's go to Miller's," she said.

Zack steered the horse down the road toward Miller's General Store and then parked the wagon in the side lot. The store was a large wooden structure painted dark brown with white trim and a white roof. Glass windows ran the front length of the store, displaying a hint of what Miller's had to offer. Zack climbed out, secured the horse to the hitching post and then came back to lift Zeke down from the vehicle before assisting Lizzie. He spanned her waist with his hands and lowered her to the ground beside him. Lizzie kept her eyes downcast, aware of the way heat rose from her neck upward and the sudden thunder of her rapidly beating heart. They walked toward the store, one on each side of little Zeke, and then entered through the automatic side entrance. Walking beside Zack and her little son made it feel as though they were a family. Lizzie bit her lip and fought to banish the dangerous thought.

They walked around the store together, making a game of who could gather the most grocery items on Lizzie's list first. Lizzie won since she knew the layout of the store better than Zack or Ezekiel. Afterward, Zack and Zeke checked the candy aisle while Lizzie went to the fabric section of the store, where she chose solid material to make new dresses for the girls as well as various calico samples for Mrs. Emory's approval. During his trip down the candy aisle, Zeke asked if he could have a chocolate bar. Zack looked to Lizzie for an answer as she approached.

"*Ja*, Zeke, you may have one, but you must hold it until after we eat lunch," she told him.

"I think I'd like one, too," Zack said. "How about you?"

Lizzie grinned at the boyish, expectant look on his handsome face. "Sounds *goot*. I'll have the same as Zeke."

Soon, they were back in the buggy, heading toward Margaret's to eat.

"I've only eaten here once," Zeke said as they headed inside the restaurant. "It smells *goot*!" He studied his surroundings with wide eyes. He wasn't watching where he was going and nearly tripped. Zack quickly reached out to steady him.

"Careful now, buddy," Zack warned, but Zeke only grinned at him and headed toward an empty booth.

Lizzie smiled as she and Zack exchanged looks as they sat down. She saw the amusement in her brother-in-law's dark eyes and she widened her smile into a grin.

"I'm so hungry I could eat a horse!" Zack exclaimed. His good humor cheered her like the warmth of the sun brightened a cloudy day.

Zeke looked at his uncle. "We can't eat horses, *Onkel* Zack. We need them too much. Who would pull our buggy or our plow?"

Zack laughed as he tugged off the boy's hat and set it on the seat between them. "I wouldn't eat a horse, Zeke. Horses are big, and I'm just saying that I'm very hungry."

Understanding, Zeke grinned, and then he told them he wanted a tomato-and-grilled-cheese sandwich. Moments later, Lizzie listened with a smile as the boy gave the young waitress his food order. Zack decided on a hamburger and French fries, while she chose a bowl of ham-and-lima-bean soup.

The conversation seemed to flow easily, and Lizzie enjoyed herself as she watched Zack interact with Zeke. She felt comfortable seated in the dining booth with Zeke and Zack seated across the table from her. She couldn't help but notice the startling resemblance between uncle and nephew. The time passed so quickly that she was startled when she learned that they'd been in Margaret's for well over an hour.

"Cake?" Zack asked Lizzie when the waitress had taken away their plates.

"Chocolate?" she suggested.

He nodded. "Is there any other kind?"

"Can I have a piece?" Zeke asked.

"*Ja*, you *may*." Lizzie grinned at her son. "Or would you rather have pudding?"

Zeke appeared to give the matter some thought. "Rice pudding?"

"If you'd like."

"Can I still have my chocolate bar?" the boy asked.

Lizzie studied him a moment. "*Ja*, you may."

Zeke beamed at her. "I'd like some rice pudding, please, with a bit of cinnamon," he told the waitress when she had returned for their dessert order.

Lizzie enjoyed her cake and the company of the two handsome males with her. She was sorry to see their outing end, but it was close to one thirty, and she wanted to get back to the house before the older children came home from school.

The journey from Margaret's toward home was a ten-minute drive past McCann's Grocery and several English as well as Amish homes. Pleased with their purchases and the meal they'd shared, Lizzie relaxed and enjoyed the ride. Her ease with Zack made her realize that it was time to talk with him about his intentions for the farm as soon as she could find a moment alone with him.

They drove past the craft shop, and Lizzie waved to Neziah and Ellen, who stood outside. They must have shared lunch together before Neziah walked Ellen back to the store. Zack steered the horse-drawn wagon along the main street until they were out of Honeysuckle proper, then past the hill that led up to the John Beachey residence. Spying Ellen's father at the base of the hill, Lizzie waved. "Afternoon, John!"

"Lizzie!" The old man smiled. "Who have you got with you?"

"Zack Fisher, John," Zack said.

"Ah! *Goot* to see you back in Honeysuckle. It's been a long time, *ja*?"

"*Ja!* It's a blessing to be home," Zack agreed with a smile. After exchanging a few pleasantries with Ellen's father, he then urged Rosebud forward, steering the mare into a turn onto the dirt drive that led toward the Fisher farmhouse and cottage.

"Jonas!" Zeke called as Zack pulled into the barnyard and climbed out of the wagon to help the boy before rounding to Lizzie's side of the vehicle. The door to the *dawdi haus* opened and Esther hurried toward them.

"Zack!" she cried, her expression worried as she approached. Zack helped Lizzie down from the wagon and turned to his sister. Young Jonas, who had run out of the house, hurried to little Zeke's side.

Seeing his sister's worried expression, Zack frowned. "What's wrong?"

"'Tis *Mam*. Miriam sent word that she fell and hurt herself." Esther sent Lizzie a look that begged for understanding. "She wants us to come home."

Zack's brow furrowed with concern. *"Ja,"* he agreed. "Did you pack our things?"

Esther nodded. "And I called for a car. The driver will be here any minute."

Zack met Lizzie's gaze. "I'm sorry—"

"Go," Lizzie encouraged. She extended an arm toward Jonas, who came quickly to burrow against her side. "We'll be fine. I hope your *mudder* is all right." She bit her lip. "Will you let us know how she is?"

He nodded. He then picked up Zeke, held him at eye level. "You will be a *goot* boy, *ja*?"

Ezekiel looked as if he would cry. "I'll be a *goot* boy," he agreed.

Zack smiled and set his nephew down. He turned to the four-year-old. "Jonas?"

"I will, too," Jonas promised as he snuggled against Lizzie's side. Lizzie raised her other arm, inviting Zeke into her embrace. Her youngest son ran and hugged her about the waist, glancing back toward his uncle with a look of sadness.

"Does *Onkel* have to leave, *Mam*?" he asked.

"*Ja*, Zeke, he has to go," she said, giving him a reassuring squeeze. The day that had begun so well was ending on a painful note as Lizzie watched Zack and Esther prepare to return to their home in Ohio.

Her talk with Zack about the farm and her baby would have to wait. The only thing that was important now was praying for Zack and Esther's mother—and her mother-in-law.

"Tell Matt and the girls I will be back to see them when I can," Zack said.

"I will," Lizzie promised, blinking back tears. Today she'd enjoyed herself in the man's company. Now she wondered when and if she would ever see him again. She'd feared his arrival yet now was sad to see him leave. Her children would be upset to learn that their aunt and uncle had left without saying goodbye.

A short time later, as she watched their hired car drive away, Lizzie felt her gut wrench with sorrow. She waited until she could no longer see the vehicle before she took her two youngest into the farmhouse. "They'll be back," she assured them with more confidence than she felt. Would they return to Honeysuckle or would the seriousness of their mother's accident keep them indefinitely in Ohio?

Chapter Eight

When they returned from school, the older children burst into the kitchen, pink-cheeked and bringing fresh air and excitement with them into the house.

"*Mam*, I'm going to the *dawdi haus*," Matt said. "*Onkel* Zack said I could help him with the horses." He tossed his schoolbook onto the table and glanced down at his clothes. "I should change first."

"*Ja*, and *Endie* Esther said I could help her make apple dumplings this afternoon," Mary Ruth added, seeming pleased at the prospect. "I'm sure she's waiting for us. Did she pick apples today? There are some nice ones left to be picked."

"*Nay,*" Lizzie said quietly. "I'm sorry, but I'm afraid neither of you will be helping your *endie* and *onkel* today. They are not here." She studied them with compassion. "They've gone back to Ohio. Your *endie* Miriam called for them to come home."

Mary Ruth didn't believe her. There was a hurt look in her eyes that tore at Lizzie's heart. "*Nay.* They're in the *dawdi haus*."

"I'm sorry, *dochter*," Lizzie said gently, "but they left

earlier. Your *onkel* Zack said to tell you that he would see you again when he returns."

Mary Ruth blinked as if fighting tears. "They're gone?" She shook her head. "Truly?" She frowned. "*Nay*, they can't be."

"I'm sorry, Mary Ruth, but it's true. They left about an hour and a half ago." To her surprise, Lizzie felt the loss as keenly as the children.

"You're glad they are gone," Mary Ruth accused suddenly, her eyes darkening. "You never liked them. You didn't want them to come!"

Lizzie felt her throat tighten. Her daughter's words hurt. She had done everything she could to prepare for their visit and offered a warm welcome to Esther and Zack, despite the reservations she had about them coming to stay on the farm.

"Mary Ruth—"

"*Nay!*" Little Ezekiel sobbed. "*Mam* likes them fine. We went to town with *Onkel* Zack and had a *goot* time! *Mam* laughed and so did *Onkel* Zack!"

Her eyes filled with tears, Mary Ruth studied her youngest brother. "*Ya* did?" she said softly.

"*Ja*," Zeke said. "Tell them, *Mam*."

"Your sister—everyone—is upset because your *onkel* had to leave."

"He said he'd be back," Zeke said.

Jonas nodded. "He said that," the four-year-old agreed. "They didn't want to go, but they had to leave. *Endie* Esther said that their *mudder* hurt herself."

Mary Ruth met Lizzie's gaze, contrition in her hazel eyes. "I shouldn't have said that. I'm sorry."

Lizzie blinked and touched first one corner of her eye then the other to hide her tears. "We'll continue on as best we can as they would want us to." She managed to smile. "Maybe your *grossmama* will recover quickly, and your *onkel* Zack and *endie* Esther will return." She had an idea. "Girls, why don't you go to the *dawdi haus* and make sure everything's ready for them."

"Do you think they'll come back soon?" Rebecca asked somberly.

"If they can."

"How long do you think they'll be gone?" Matt was clearly upset to have learned that his beloved uncle had left Honeysuckle.

"That will depend on how badly your *grossmudder* hurt herself and how quickly she recovers."

"That could be a long time," Hannah said.

Lizzie nodded. "It could. But it could also be a short time. We should pray for the best and hope they come back soon."

Anne approached, placed a small hand on Lizzie's arm. "Everything will be fine, *Mam*. If it is *Gottes Wille*, *Onkel* Zack and *Endie* Esther will come back soon."

Lizzie nodded in agreement. She never expected to feel this way about Zack's leaving. She had regarded the man as a threat at first, but then he'd been so helpful and kind that she'd relaxed and accepted his help with gratitude and without reservations. As Annie had said, whether or not he returned would be determined by God's will. Until then, she would manage the house and farm while caring for the children, and she would pray that with the Lord's help she handled everything well for her family…and her unborn child.

The cramp came in the middle of the night. She gasped and sat upright, cradling her abdomen where the pain originated. Lizzie struggled to rise and barely had time to stumble across the room before she vomited into a basin.

Nay, she cried silently. *Please, Lord, not my baby.*

When she saw the blood on her nightgown, she started to cry. She knew without a doubt that she was losing her baby. And then it was quickly over. Lizzie realized that she wouldn't be having her late husband's child, the child who would have meant hope for the future. There would be no baby to show for her and Abraham's love, a love that had ended right after it had begun. While she worked at the bathroom sink to get the stain out of her nightgown, she tried to weep soundlessly so that she wouldn't wake the children. She pressed her hand over her mouth to control her sobbing gasps.

Gottes Wille, she reminded herself a short while later as she returned to bed. In the solitary silence of her room, she allowed her tears to fall freely.

She had been the only one who'd known about the baby. She'd been going to tell Zack about her pregnancy when they talked about the farm, but now the only thing she could confess was that she had lost her baby.

Lizzie placed a trembling hand over her lower abdomen and cried until she became too exhausted to continue. But sleep was a long time in coming, and the pain of her loss had settled deep in her heart as she cradled her empty womb.

The next morning Lizzie struggled not to cry or to alert the children that anything was amiss. Despite the knowledge that the pregnancy would have been difficult with her crippled hip, she had wanted the baby and been willing to endure anything to give birth to Abraham's child.

The older children were in school. Zeke and Jonas were in the yard, playing. Lizzie looked out the kitchen window and watched as the boys ran around in circles, laughing and chasing each other. The sight made her lips curve into a tender smile. She may have suffered a miscarriage, but she still had her late husband's children and she loved them. Seeing the youngest two having fun was heartwarming.

She washed the lunch dishes, then dried and put them away. Lizzie felt as if she were in a fog as she moved throughout the kitchen and the house, cleaning. The older children were due home from school in less than an hour. She half expected to look up and see them rush through the back doorway.

A sudden sharp cry broke into her thoughts, and her heart raced with fear. Lizzie ran toward the window to check on her sons. Her pulse beat harder. There was no sign of either Jonas or Ezekiel. Frantically calling them by name, Lizzie ran out of the house in her search to find them.

"Mam!" Ezekiel screamed as he flew out of the barn.

"Zeke?" She hurried toward him.

"Jonas hurt himself!" Her son's face was white, his lips quivering.

Nay! "How bad?" Lizzie asked as she ran with him into the barn. Jonas stood inside a few feet, staring down with horror at his bleeding hand. "Jonas!" she cried. "What's happened?"

Young Jonas had tears in his eyes as he met her gaze. *"Mam."* He began to sob out an explanation, but he was too upset; she couldn't understand him. Soon after talking calmly with Jonas and Zeke, she was able to discover what had happened.

"Calm down and tell me what happened. Speak slowly," she urged softly, "so that I can understand." She inhaled sharply as she saw all the blood, but she tried not to alarm the boys.

"It was one of *Dat*'s tools," Jonas admitted. "That sharp curved thing." He'd touched the sickle on the wall hook next to several other farm implements, Lizzie realized. "I didn't think it would hurt to make it swing," he cried.

Her first inclination was to scold him, but she knew that he'd learned a lesson that he might never have understood if he hadn't hurt himself.

"Let me see," Lizzie said. She gently took Jonas's hand in hers and hissed out in dismay. "Come with me." She picked up her four-year-old and hurried toward the house, checking to make sure Zeke kept up with her and Jonas, who began to cry loudly with hiccuping sobs.

Once inside, she sat Jonas in a kitchen chair, took out some clean dish towels and wrapped them around the wound. "It's all right, Jonas," she soothed. "I know it hurts, but *Mam* will help you. Hold still, Jonas. *Goot* boy!"

The other children arrived home in the midst of the madness.

"What's wrong?" Mary Ruth said with concern as she entered the kitchen. "What happened?"

Blood seeped through the towel. Lizzie flashed Mary Ruth a concerned look. "Your *brooder* cut himself. Matt?" she said. "Can you get the buggy ready? Jonas needs to see a doctor."

Looking worried and pale, the older boy nodded and

left. "Hannah, can you get me some towels from the linen chest?" Lizzie asked. "Mary Ruth, if I wrap Jonas's hand, can you hold pressure on it until Matt brings around the buggy?" Her eldest daughter nodded.

She addressed Rebecca. "Take Anne and Zeke outside. We'll be right out. Anne, don't worry—Jonas will be fine. Zeke, you're a *goot* boy for telling me what happened."

She had examined the wound thoroughly. It was a clean slice to the back of Jonas's hand, extending around to the right side. The cut would need stitching, she realized. As she hurried the children into the buggy, Lizzie decided that it would be better if they stayed with someone until she and Jonas were finished at the doctor's office. Lizzie waited while the children got into the buggy and then climbed in and took up the leathers. She gave Mary Ruth an approving nod as the girl held her injured brother on her lap.

Where could she take the children? Naomi Beiler's name instantly came to mind. Naomi was the head of the local widows' group in Honeysuckle. The woman had been the first one who had come with an offer to help after Abraham's death. She had convinced Lizzie to attend the haystack supper last month while Naomi's daughter Emma kept an eye on the younger children. The supper was a fund-raising event for Raymond, Mary Blauch's baby son who'd been born prematurely and was in the Children's Hospital of Philadelphia.

Lizzie decided to stop at the widow's house and ask if Naomi would watch the children until she could return for them later that afternoon. The children might not want to stay, but it would be less stressful for everyone if Lizzie didn't have to worry about them when her focus should be solely on Jonas.

"Where are we going?" Mary Ruth asked as Lizzie pulled into the gravel driveway alongside the widow's home.

"To see Naomi Beiler. I'm going to ask her if you can stay with her until Jonas and I are finished with the doctor."

"Nay," the girl objected staunchly.

"'Tis best for everyone," Lizzie said.

"Not me," her daughter insisted with tears in her eyes. "I want to come. I can help with Jonas. I'll hold him for you while you drive our buggy."

Lizzie drew the vehicle to a halt. "Wait here." She ran to the woman's house, explained what had happened and asked if the children could stay until after she and Mary Ruth had taken Jonas to the doctor. "I can use your help."

Naomi agreed readily. *"Ja.* I will be happy to watch them for you. They'll be fine here. Do what you need to do and don't worry."

"Danki," Lizzie said as she fought back tears.

She returned to the buggy and urged the children out of the vehicle. "Come. You'll be staying here with Naomi. Behave, *ja*? I'll be back as soon as I can to get you."

Rebecca and Hannah exchanged glances. "Is Mary Ruth staying here, too?" Hannah asked.

"Nay. Help Naomi with the children."

"We will," Rebecca promised.

"Anne, Matthew, hurry," Hannah said firmly but kindly. *"Mam* needs to go."

Lizzie was proud of her children as she watched as they stepped out of the vehicle, one by one, their gazes drifting briefly to their brother Jonas, who looked pale and lay whimpering within Mary Ruth's arms. As she drove toward the clinic, Lizzie was glad that Mary Ruth was there to hold and comfort Jonas.

"Lizzie!" Mary Ruth's cry immediately drew her attention toward her son. Blood had soaked through the double wrapping of towels.

Lizzie flicked the leathers to increase the mare's pace, and the buggy barreled down the road as fast as the horse-drawn vehicle was capable. As she spurred the horse on, the thundering of the mare's hooves on the road mirrored her wildly beating heart.

At last, the medical building came into view, and she pulled back on the reins to slow the mare before steering the buggy into the parking lot adjacent to the building.

She secured the horse and then took Jonas from Mary Ruth. They raced inside, glad to see that the waiting room wasn't crowded. Lizzie carried Jonas to the front desk and explained to the receptionist what had happened.

The woman took one look at the bloody towels, quickly picked up the phone and spoke to someone in the back of the clinic. A medical assistant appeared and escorted them immediately into an exam room. A doctor came in within minutes, and Jonas cried as the physician gave him a needle filled with numbing agent before he stitched closed the wound. When he was done, Dr. Jones told Lizzie that Jonas needed a tetanus shot.

"Farm tools carry germs," the doctor explained. "It's important that Jonas gets the injection."

It didn't take long for Lizzie to agree. The doctor bandaged Jonas's hand and gave him an injection. Jonas was given a lollipop for being a good patient, which he enjoyed as he preceded Lizzie outside. Mary Ruth, who'd left moments before, waited by their buggy, ready to help her little brother. She met Lizzie's glance, and Lizzie could only guess the girl's thoughts as she climbed into the seat next to her daughter and picked up the reins.

Lizzie was exhausted. It had been a long, tiring day after a sleepless night, and she looked forward to the hour when the children were in bed and she could crawl under the covers. But there was supper to fix first and homework to be done by her older children.

She felt responsible for Jonas's accident. If she had watched the boys more closely, they wouldn't have slipped into the barn to play.

"Mam?"

Lizzie turned, surprised to realize that it was Mary Ruth who had spoken. Until now, her daughter had never called her anything but Lizzie. *"Ja*, Mary Ruth?"

"Danki for letting me come today," she said quietly.

"I'm glad you did." She regarded her with affection. "We'll pick up the others and go home. I think we've had enough of an adventure today."

Mary Ruth smiled in agreement as she glanced at Jonas, who lay against her with his eyes closed. They stopped at Naomi's first to get the children before they continued to the farm. Jonas was tired and ready for bed early. The pain medication the doctor had given him made him sleepy.

During the remainder of the ride home, Mary Ruth had regarded her with warmth in her expression. Lizzie had returned her smile. It had been a good day for the family despite all the terrible things that had happened, beginning with her miscarriage and ending with Jonas's injury.

Chapter Nine

Saturday morning Lizzie rose after a good night's sleep. Usually, as of late, she'd suffered long nights without sleep, but yesterday's drama compounded by several sleepless nights had exhausted her to the point where she'd finally been able to sleep without dreaming. Losing her baby was emotionally difficult as well as physically hard on her. Friday night she'd been so tired that she would have drifted off if not for her concern for Jonas. She had gone to check on her son several times, worried that he'd be in pain or cry out for her, but he had slept peacefully, helped by the pain medicine that Dr. Jones had prescribed.

She headed to the kitchen to make bread, muffins and cupcakes to take to the Peter Zook farm. Tomorrow was visiting Sunday. There was a lot to do. After turning on the oven to preheat, Lizzie couldn't stop thinking about Zack and Esther. They'd left the day before yesterday. Did they get to Ohio safely? How was their *mam*?

She measured the ingredients for a double batch of corn muffins. She stirred them together in a large stainless-steel bowl until the batter was the right consistency and then filled two muffin tins until each section was two-thirds full. Next, she pulled out and mixed together the makings for chocolate cake, setting the mixture aside until the muffins were done and cooling on a wire rack. Then she'd wash and reuse the tins for baking cupcakes. She cleaned up the kitchen, and when the muffins were ready, she set each one on the cooling rack.

She had just taken the cupcakes out of the oven when she heard a firm knock on the back door. Lizzie set the tin on a hot mat and went to answer it. To her delight, her brother stood on her front porch, wearing a silly grin.

"William!" She laughed, pleased to see him. "What are you doing here?" She held the door open and he stepped inside.

"I thought I'd visit my favorite *schweschter,*" he said. William sniffed the air appreciatively. "Mmm. Something in here smells *goot.*" His familiar face had always comforted her during her childhood whenever she'd felt unhappy or alone. She watched him examine his surroundings.

"What's baking?" he asked. With dark hair, brown eyes and a mouth that was quick to smile, William was a handsome man. The young women in their Amish community were frequently seen vying for his attention. He was five years her elder, and she wondered why he'd never found someone he wanted to wed.

"I made corn muffins," she said.

He glanced toward the counter. "And chocolate cupcakes."

She chuckled at his expectant expression. "Would you like a muffin or cupcake?"

He shook his head. "Wish I could, but I've got to get

home. I needed to stop by to tell you that a call came to McCann's for you yesterday. John said he sent someone to tell you but no one was home."

Lizzie's heart skipped a beat. "Jonas hurt himself and I had to take him to the clinic." She eyed her brother eagerly. "Was it from Zack?"

"*Ja.* He left word for you that he and Esther arrived safely and that his *mudder* is well. She fell, but she's unhurt. They'll be coming back to Honeysuckle."

Lizzie put on the teakettle. "Are you sure you don't want *coffe* or tea?"

William looked longingly at the cupcakes cooling on the counter. "Can't. *Mam*'s waiting for her baking powder and flour."

"I understand," she said. "Take a muffin for the road?" She saw the gleam in his eyes and quickly wrapped up two muffins for him.

She walked outside to see him off, pretending an indifference to news from Zack. She waved to William as he left and then entered the house to finish food preparations for the next day.

Zack is on his way back to Honeysuckle. She felt nervous and excited. She'd planned to talk with Zack about the farm, but now that she'd lost her baby, she felt uneasy about the discussion.

Zack is a goot *man*, she silently reminded herself. She kept telling herself this over and over as she washed dishes and prepared to make a soup for tomorrow night's supper.

Rachel Zook paid an unexpected visit later that afternoon.

"What are you doing here?" Lizzie asked. "I didn't

expect you to come with so much to do." She blushed. "I should have come to help you."

"You have enough to worry about," Rachel said. "I just thought I'd stop by." She eyed Lizzie a long moment. "You don't look well. What's wrong?"

Lizzie swallowed against a lump. She explained about Jonas's injury and their subsequent trip to the walk-in medical clinic. After Rachel had expressed concern and checked on Jonas in the next room, Lizzie found the courage to confide in her friend. "I had a miscarriage." She explained what had happened two nights past.

"Oh, Lizzie," Rachel said as she reached to place a hand over Lizzie's on the table. "I'm so sorry. Have you seen the midwife?"

Frowning, Lizzie shook her head. "*Nay*, I didn't think—"

Rachel raised her eyebrows. "Lizzie, you must see her. You need to make sure that everything…ah…that you are well."

Lizzie understood what Rachel meant. "I'll see her Monday if I can get away," she promised.

Her friend squeezed her hand. "Why don't you go now? I can keep an eye on Jonas and the children. I'll even do some baking with your girls' help."

"You don't mind?" Lizzie was grateful for her friend's offer.

Rachel smiled. "*Nay*, I don't mind." Her expression became serious. "Lizzie, you need to see the midwife, and you need to see her today. Will you go?"

"*Ja*," Lizzie said, knowing her friend was right. "I'll go."

Lizzie was nervous as she drove to the midwife's. She felt terrible for interrupting the woman's Saturday, but Rachel insisted that it would be all right. As soon as she arrived, she realized that Rachel was right. She had no cause to worry. When Lizzie told the midwife about her miscarriage, Anne Stoltzfus was kind and sympathetic. The woman had sable-brown hair, a quick smile and a dusting of freckles across her small round nose. She was the same height as Lizzie, and the warmth in her direct gaze made Lizzie feel as if she'd done the right thing in coming. She waved away Lizzie's concerns about coming on a Saturday and praised her for listening to her friend.

When Anne was done examining Lizzie, she assured her that she was fine.

"I know this is difficult for you," Anne said. She suggested that Lizzie do something special in memory of the baby she'd lost. "It will help with your grieving."

"Like what?"

The midwife's expression grew soft. "Plant a tree? Do a craft or make a quilt? The choice is yours and only you will know or understand what it means."

Lizzie blinked back tears. "*Danki*. That's a *goot* idea."

Anne escorted her to the door and then followed her outside. "You will come to see me again? If you have pain or feel uncomfortable in any way, please come back."

Lizzie nodded. She was about to say goodbye when Anne caught sight of something that upset her. Lizzie saw what got her attention: there was a goat snacking on her garden plants.

"That old goat!" the midwife exclaimed. "Why can't Joseph Lapp mend that fence of his?" Anne stopped suddenly, looking contrite. "I apologize. My neighbor's goats are always escaping into my yard and my garden. What's so hard about keeping them penned up? All he has to do is fix his fence. I sell produce. I don't need those creatures destroying my tomatoes and pumpkins!" Shaking her head, she suddenly chuckled as if seeing humor in the situation.

"I'm glad you came, Lizzie." Anne accompanied her to her buggy. "Take care of yourself. Remember to come back for a visit if you need me for anything." She smiled. "Perhaps a checkup each year."

Smiling, Lizzie said, "I will." The woman's kindness warmed her heart and made her feel better. *"Danki."*

She left Anne's with the knowledge that her pregnancy had been terminated by nature and that there was no reason that she couldn't carry another baby to full term.

Except that my husband is dead, and I can't see myself marrying again. She had mentioned to Anne about her concerns about being pregnant with her hip dysplasia.

With a wave of her hand, Anne had brushed her concerns aside. "Advanced pregnancy with your medical condition might make things more challenging for you, but with care, I don't see why you shouldn't have a normal pregnancy and delivery. The only difference is that you may have to stay off your feet as much as possible during your last trimester, when you'd be carrying the most weight."

It was unlikely that she'd get another chance, Lizzie thought as she steered her horse-drawn buggy toward home. *Gottes Wille.* If *Gott* willed it then so shall it be. She prayed to the Lord for guidance and for strength.

During the ride home, Lizzie stopped briefly to pick

up the fabric samples from Ellen that she'd left for Mrs. Emory's approval. She was pleased to learn that the woman had approved her choice of colors and quilt design.

"Do you have anything else you'd like to sell, Lizzie?" Ellen handed the fabric to her.

"I can bring in the few items I finished the other evening. I'll stop by with them within the next couple of days." Lizzie left then continued toward home. She arrived well before lunchtime. As she steered the horse toward the barn, she noticed a car parked close to the farmhouse.

Zack? Had he returned after only two days away? Her heart started to pound. *It is Zack!* She parked the buggy, climbed out and then wandered in his direction.

Her late husband's brother was talking with the driver of the car while Esther headed toward the cottage, carrying her valise.

Lizzie rounded the vehicle and he caught sight of her. She locked gazes with him as he ended his conversation with the driver. After the man got into his car, Zack closed the distance between them.

"Lizzie," he greeted with a smile. "It's *goot* to see you again."

"*Hallo*, Zack," she said. He looked good, too good, she thought, and she was pleased to see him.

"You got my message?" he asked.

Lizzie inclined her head. "*Ja.* How is your *mudder*?"

He sighed. "Much better, thanks be to *Gott*. She fell but wasn't injured as seriously as Miriam thought. I'm glad we went home to see for ourselves that she is well."

"You must be relieved." She saw him glance briefly toward the buggy. "I ran an errand." She held up the shopping bag with fabric she'd picked up from Ellen Beachey. "Mrs. Emory approved my choice of quilt colors and pattern."

"That's *goot*." He took off his hat and ran fingers through his dark hair. "I'm sure she'll be pleased. You do fine work."

She blushed at his praise. "Rachel is here. She stopped by earlier and offered to watch the children while I was gone. I'll be making lunch soon. Will you and Esther *koom*?"

"*Ja*, if you are sure it's no trouble. I'm eager to see the children again. I'll get Esther. It was a long ride, and I know she will appreciate the meal."

Zack headed toward the cottage, and Lizzie watched him walk away. He stopped suddenly and turned. Embarrassed to be caught staring, she felt the heat rise to her face.

She had missed him, she realized as she went into the house. She felt a nervous tightening in her belly. Now that he was back, there was no reason to put off asking him about the farm. Was there?

Chapter Ten

"**O**nkel Zack!" Matt burst into the farmhouse kitchen, bringing fresh air and renewed life with him. "You're back!" The boy beamed at him before he turned to his aunt. "Endie Esther, I'm glad you're home. We were afraid you wouldn't come back."

"*Hallo*, Matthew," Esther said with a warm smile. "It's nice to see you, too."

Mary Ruth, Hannah and Rebecca with Anne entered the house minutes later. They all exclaimed, clearly pleased, that their aunt and uncle had returned.

"How is *Grossmama*?" Mary Ruth asked with concern.

"She's doing well," Esther said. "Your *endie* Miriam worries. We were glad to see them, but it was time to come back."

"Are you going to stay?" Rebecca asked softly. "We like having you here."

Lizzie listened, eager to hear the answer, as she was glad to see them, too, even though she had no idea about their plans.

"We'll stay for a while, if all goes well," Zack said vaguely, giving Lizzie cause for concern.

Why did she have the feeling that she would be involved in his decision to stay or go?

"When did you get back?" Hannah asked.

"A half hour ago." He raised his iced-tea glass to show her that he'd been relaxing and enjoying the afternoon here in the kitchen. "We enjoyed a late lunch."

"Are they staying for supper?" Rebecca asked.

"Ja," Lizzie said. "They said they would."

The girl grinned. *"Wunderbor!"*

"We missed you," Anne said as she went to her uncle. "It wasn't the same when you were gone."

Matthew agreed. "There was no one to help do chores."

Zack eyed him with affection before he met Lizzie's glance. She blushed and turned away. "Girls, Matthew, don't you have some chores to do? Maybe you should do them now before supper."

"I did mine this morning," Mary Ruth said. "Then we helped Ellen at the store," she explained to her aunt and uncle. "Ellen minded Asa and Joel for Neziah today. I straightened the shelves and put out new craft items, 'cause Dinah wasn't there to help. Matthew swept the floor, but mostly he kept the Shetler boys busy and out of trouble. Then, after she closed the shop, Ellen bought us all ice cream."

Before Lizzie could ask more about the children's day, Ezekiel and Jonas rushed into the room, drawing everyone's attention. The younger boys had been playing quietly in their room.

"Onkel Zack!" they cried in unison, *"Endie* Esther!" They ran closer, nearly colliding with Zack's chair.

Ezekiel halted in front of Zack. "Can we go to town again?"

"*Ja*, Zeke," he said with a gentle smile. "Soon."

"Can I come, too?" Jonas asked, moving closer. Lizzie spotted her son's bandaged hand and became alarmed. She'd forgotten to tell Zack about Jonas's accident during the short time he'd been back. Had Zack noticed? "I didn't get to go last time."

"Then you should come," Zack said. He spied Jonas's bandage and frowned. "Jonas, what happened to your hand?"

Lizzie felt sick to her stomach as she waited for her son's answer.

Jonas stood taller and said, "I had an accident. It's better now. *Mam* took me to the doctor, and I got quilted." He raised his bandaged hand to better show it off.

Despite his initial concern, Zack looked amused. "Quilted?"

"Stitches," Hannah said before Lizzie could explain.

Jonas tugged on the gauze. "*Nay*, Jonas," Lizzie said quickly. "You mustn't take off the wrapping. You can show your stitches to *Onkel* Zack later."

"I won't be able to play baseball until my hand gets better," the boy said. "But we can play then, *ja*?"

The creases across Zack's forehead deepened. "*Ja*, we can play then."

He met Lizzie's gaze and raised his eyebrows questioningly. Lizzie silently mouthed, "I'll explain later."

The children's prattle kept their aunt and uncle entertained for the rest of the afternoon and during supper. They ate fried chicken, mashed potatoes and the green beans that Lizzie had put up fresh that summer. They

shared apple pie and upside-down chocolate cake—
Lizzie's favorite—afterward. As the day waned and
the sky darkened, Esther and Zack stood.

"Time to head home," Zack said. "It's been a long
day. A *goot* day, but a tiring one."

"Ja," Esther agreed. "We will see *ya* tomorrow and
then we can spend more time together." The children
were clearly happy to have them back.

Lizzie walked them to the door. *"Guten nacht."*

"Guten nacht, Lizzie," Esther said as she headed toward the cottage.

Zack lingered outside the farmhouse, leaving the
two of them alone. There was a long moment of silence
while he gazed out over the yard. Finally he turned toward Lizzie and startled her when he said, "You look
pale."

Zack studied Lizzie, noting the changes in her since
he'd left. She looked tired and ill. Was she in pain? "Is
your hip bothering you?"

She jerked with surprise. "I'm fine." She stepped off
the porch and into the yard. The evening had turned
cool. The scent of autumn filled the clean crisp air,
dried leaves, the lingering aroma of baked goods, the
bread and pies that Lizzie had made earlier in the day.
As if feeling the chill, Lizzie hugged herself with her
arms.

I'm worried about her! Zack felt unsettled. This concern for Lizzie was a new feeling for him, and he didn't
know whether or not he liked it. He couldn't take his
eyes off her. His gaze caressed her lovely features, her
vivid green eyes and dark auburn hair.

"Zack—"

"Lizzie—" They had spoken simultaneously.

Lizzie chuckled. "You go first," she said.

He hesitated and then said, "I'm sorry we had to leave the way we did."

She seemed surprised by his apology. "Your *mam* hurt herself. Your *schweschter* called you home. I understood."

But Zack felt she deserved an explanation. "We've had cause to worry about her," he admitted. "Four years ago, *Mam* found a lump—it was cancer. She had chemotherapy at a medical center near Millersburg. That's why we moved from Walnut Creek. At the time, we decided the best thing for us to do was to move closer to the treatment center and the doctors who were helping her."

"I'm sorry," Lizzie said, sounding sincere. Her lovely green eyes regarded him with compassion. He studied her smooth skin, pert nose and pink lips and found that he liked her…a lot.

He acknowledged her compassion with a nod. *"Danki."* He gestured toward the porch steps in a silent request for them to sit, and they sat down, next to each other on the second step. "*Mam* has moved in with Miriam. We didn't want her to be alone while we were gone." Zack detected the light scent of soap and a fragrance that was hers alone. Lizzie seemed vulnerable and delicate beside him, but he knew—had seen it for himself—that she was stronger than she looked. He'd never known another woman with her physical limitations who could do what she did day in and day out for her children, the house and the farm without complaint. *And she's managing well*, he thought.

It was hard to picture Abraham's first wife, Ruth, as a mother to seven children. She'd been helpless, delicate, unwilling to do much without Abraham's help. He'd understood the enormity of his brother's love for his young wife—recognized everything Abraham had to do in order to keep the woman he adored happy. Had his brother cared about Lizzie in the same way?

Lizzie. He barely noticed her limp anymore. The only time he saw it was when it became more pronounced after she did too much around the farm and her hip gave her great pain. Not that she said a word. She continued on as if she hadn't done the work of three women in one day.

Zack admired her strength, her determination and the love she bore for his nieces and nephews. *And she quilts and makes crafts, too, bringing money into the household for any items the children need.* She continued to amaze him.

"Zack?" She eyed him with concern, and he realized that he'd been silent as he took his time studying her, thinking about her. "About Jonas?"

He sensed that she'd grown uncomfortable. *"Ja?"*

"I should have told you. Jonas's accident was my fault."

"Yours?" He arched an eyebrow. "How so?"

"He and Zeke got into the barn, where they didn't belong. Jonas found Abraham's old sickle. It happened so fast. One minute Jonas and Ezekiel were playing outside the kitchen window where I could see them, and in the next I heard a sharp cry." She stood and began to pace, clearly upset by what had happened. "I hurried outside to see what was wrong and I saw Zeke as he ran from inside the barn. He was crying that Jonas had hurt himself."

"And that makes the accident your fault?" he asked.

She nodded. "I let the boys out of my sight. If I'd been more vigilant—"

Zack regarded her with fond amusement. "They are boys being boys, Lizzie. When I was their age, my *mam* fretted that I was always into trouble and getting hurt. You have seven children. Do you honestly believe that you can keep track of all of them every minute of every day?"

She seemed shocked by his reaction. He became startled to see her eyes fill with tears. Had she been that worried about his reaction? She who looked vulnerable but was in actuality strong?

"You don't blame me for Jonas's injury?" she rasped in a shocked whisper.

"*Nay*, I don't blame you. Why should I? Should I blame myself because I wasn't in Honeysuckle to prevent it from happening?"

"*Nay*, but—"

"But you were on the farm," he said, anticipating her next words. "Lizzie, you are a *goot mudder* to my *brooder*'s children. Never let anyone say anything differently about you."

He was pleased to see that she was humbled by his praise.

She stared at him, clearly fighting tears until she smiled and sat down, and his day suddenly brightened. "I'm glad you're back," she admitted softly.

He returned her grin. "I'm glad you missed me," he said with a teasing twinkle. She rose to her feet, and Zack wanted to tell her to sit; he wasn't ready to leave her company, but he understood. She was a woman who had to care for children and a busy household. *I'm going to make things easier for her*, he thought.

She seemed as if she wanted to go, but she still lingered a moment longer. "Zack?"

"Ja?"

"May I ask what kind of cancer your *mam* had?" Her green eyes were kind and sympathetic.

"Breast cancer." The memory of his mother's suffering still bothered him. *Mam* had gone through so much, yet she had finished the treatments with no sign of her earlier malignancy. *Thanks be to* Gott. "She is well now. The treatments were difficult but successful."

She looked relieved. "I'm happy that your *mudder* is all right."

He caressed her with his eyes; he couldn't help himself. He scolded himself when she suddenly looked uneasy. She averted her glance. He had frightened her with his attention, he realized, and knew enough to be careful in the future if he didn't want to scare her away.

"I am, too," he admitted and smiled warmly at her. He stood, straightened a black suspender and set his hat on his head. "I'll be in the *dawdi haus* if you need me. See you tomorrow."

"Tomorrow," she murmured with a nod.

As he left to cross the yard, Zack thought about Lizzie. He'd been gone only two days, but it felt as though he had been away too long.

She is Abraham's wife. He felt as if he was betraying his brother with his growing feelings for Lizzie, but he couldn't stop himself from caring about her.

Chapter Eleven

It felt good to have Zack and Esther back. Lizzie knew that she was being foolish since there was still a chance that he wanted to take over the farm, but she liked him. How could she not? He was charming, kind and he'd understood about her son's injury. *Zack doesn't blame me for Jonas's accident.* She'd experienced tremendous relief.

Saturday during those few moments alone with him, she should have brought up the farm, but it hadn't seemed right. She had told Zack about Jonas and that had seemed like more than enough for one day. Then yesterday there had been no opportunity for discussion, as they'd spent the day at Rachel and Peter's farm. *A wonderful-goot visiting Sunday and I didn't want to ruin it.*

This morning as she worked to rid her vegetable garden of the finished plants, she glanced toward Zack, who examined the animals out in the pasture. He reached up to stroke the mare's nose then hunkered down to check her hooves. He picked up something from the ground. As he rose to his full height, he caught sight of her and waved.

A sudden warmth filling her chest, she watched him head in her direction. Zack carried his straw hat and a slight breeze tousled his dark hair, making him appear more attractive and approachable. He wore a royal blue shirt and black suspenders with his navy triblend pants. He had black work boots on his feet, and he carried a horse-feed bucket in his opposite hand.

"Hallo," he said with a smile. "Hard at work, I see." He set the bucket on the ground and the hat on his head.

Lizzie returned his smile. "I decided to clean up the garden before winter. The boys started the work, but—" she gestured toward a basket "—not everything is done. I just picked the last of the turnips." She leaned against the handle of her garden hoe, enjoying the cool breeze. "I like to work up the soil before the ground gets too hard." In the spring the weeds would cover the soil before she found the time to plant her early cool-weather crops.

Zack eyed what was left of her prized garden. "Do you need help?"

She wasn't offended, for she knew his offer was genuine and came from a good place. But she was almost done. *"Nay*, but I appreciate the thought. I'm about finished for today. I'm thinking of putting in more turnips."

"Couldn't hurt. You can pick them until late in the season."

"Ja." She hesitated and asked, "Do you like turnips?"

The smile transforming his face made her breath catch. "I've been known to take a second helping," he admitted.

"I'll plant more, then," she said. Lizzie tried not to notice how handsome he was.

They stood together for a moment in silence. She felt comfortable in the quiet, a fact that surprised her after recalling how awkward she'd felt in his presence previously.

"Rosebud is doing much better with her new shoe," she said of the mare.

"Ja," he said. "Mark Hostetler did a fine job of replacing it." A few minutes passed, yet he seemed reluctant to leave.

Lizzie was delighted. "Do you have enough bread?" she asked. "I've got some in the house and I'll be happy to make more."

Zack's dark gaze twinkled. "You provided us with enough bread in the cottage freezer to feed the entire congregation," he teased.

She blushed. "I wanted to make sure you had enough." She paused. "It's not that you're not welcome to eat with us." Jonas and Ezekiel ran out of the house and headed in their direction. "Will you take supper with us?" she asked before the boys descended upon their uncle.

"Ja." He grinned at the boys as they reached his side. "We'd like that."

"Onkel Zack?" Jonas asked. "Can I come help you today?"

"You mustn't get in your *onkel*'s way," Lizzie warned.

Zack reached out to ruffle the boy's hair. "You can help, but only if you do what I say and stay close. *Ja?*"

Jonas bobbed his head in agreement and grinned.

"Can I come, too?" Zeke asked, looking as if he was afraid he'd be forced to stay home with his *mam*.

"You can come, too," Zack assured him with a smile. He lifted his youngest nephew's hat and then set it back on his head at a different angle. "Where's your hat, Jonas?"

The boy shifted from one foot to the other as if he had energy to burn. "In my room."

Zack gestured toward the house. "You'd best get it. It's going to be a sunny day. A man needs his hat to keep the sun from his eyes."

He waited while Jonas ran into the house and returned with his straw hat moments later. "I'm going to wear my hat like a man," the boy said.

Zack nodded. He glanced toward the barn. "Time for chores," he told his nephews. "Ready?" He smiled at the boys as they bobbed their heads. He redirected his smile toward Lizzie. "I'll see you at supper."

The warmth in his expression made her tingle. "Zack!" she cried out impulsively as he and the boys headed toward the barn. *Ask him about the farm*, her inner voice prompted. *Tell him you need to talk with him later.*

Zack stopped and faced her, and she tensed inside. She knew she should ask him, but she didn't want to spoil the moment. *Tonight.* She'd ask him tonight.

"I appreciate your help around the farm," she said. "And for including the boys."

He grinned. "'Tis my pleasure, Lizzie." Then he continued toward the barn with her young sons running to keep up with his long strides.

"We'll see you for supper, *Mam*," Jonas called over his shoulder as they reached the barn.

"What about lunch?" she asked loudly. She watched as Zack leaned close to whisper to the two boys.

"We're going to eat with *Onkel* Zack in the *dawdi*

haus," Jonas said. She saw Zack lean to tell the boy something more. "That's all right, *ja*?"

She could feel the intensity of Zack's gaze across the distance. "That's fine, Jonas. Be *goot* boys and listen to your uncle."

"Ja!" her sons cried, and she caught Zack's answering grin. *That such a simple thing could make the boys and this man happy...*

Lizzie returned to work, feeling lighthearted. When Zack had first come, she'd had no idea that she'd be glad to have him on the farm. *He's* goot *for the children—and me.* The thought frightened her as much as it gave her pleasure. After supper, she would ask him about his intentions regarding the property, and everything would be fine.

Movement near the cottage caught her eye as Esther exited the house.

"*Goot* morning, Esther!" Lizzie cried.

"Lizzie!" Smiling, Esther headed in her direction. "Clearing the garden for the spring?"

"Ja." She set down her garden rake and reached for the garden hoe. "But I was thinking about putting in another planting of turnips."

"Sounds *goot*," Esther said with a grin. "We love turnips."

"You'll be coming to supper, *ja*? Zack said he thought you wouldn't mind."

"I never mind spending time with you and the children." Esther picked up a rake and began to work up a section of ground that had been previously dug up by Lizzie's children. "I'd like to contribute. How about a pie? Or some biscuits?"

Lizzie understood Esther's desire to contribute to the

meal. When she and Abraham had been asked to the neighbors' for supper, Lizzie had insisted on bringing a side dish or dessert. The two women discussed what Lizzie planned for supper, and it was decided that Esther would bake apple muffins and cook the turnips that Lizzie had picked earlier that morning.

Lizzie handed Esther the turnip basket. "I'll see you later," she said. "You're more than welcome to join me for lunch."

Esther shook her head. "I'll eat something at the cottage."

"Zack plans to feed the boys there."

"We have plenty of *goot* food, thanks to you." Esther set down the rake. "I'll see you at supper. If you need me, come get me. I'll be in the *dawdi haus*. I'll be happy to help."

Lizzie regarded the woman fondly. "You're always nice to me."

"And why wouldn't I be? We're family," Esther said.

Her throat tightened with emotion. "*Ja*, we are," she replied. As Esther left her to her work, Lizzie grinned. This was the first time she believed that her late husband's siblings regarded her as family. She felt hopeful.

Esther returned to the house and went to her room. It was good to be back in Honeysuckle. She dusted the furniture and swept the floor. When she was done, she headed toward the kitchen with a corn broom in hand. She heard a hard rap on the back door.

"*Hallo?* Is anyone home?" a deep familiar voice called out.

David? Esther froze. Why would he be visiting the cottage? She was suddenly nervous. Her dress was wrinkled from doing chores. She touched her hair, wondering if it was still neatly pinned into place.

It was still hard to realize that David had gone on with his life and wed, as if the two of them hadn't been sweethearts. She was still single, and it was embarrassing.

"Esther?"

Heart racing, her stomach fluttering, she answered the door. "David."

He smiled and her nape tingled. He was extremely handsome. "I thought I'd stop in to say hello. I thought it was you at last Sunday's service, but I couldn't stay afterward. I found out it was you after you'd gone back to Ohio." His eyes were warm as he studied her. "And now you're home again."

She nodded mutely, recalling how much she'd loved him when they were younger.

"May I come in?"

She gasped. Where were her manners? "*Ja*, of course." She opened the door and watched as he brushed by her as he entered her kitchen. She was aware of his familiar scent, and the memories came flooding back of the times they'd spent together. "Tea?" she offered.

He nodded and sat at her kitchen table. "How is your *mudder*?" he asked.

Her hands shook slightly as she put on the teakettle. She held them behind her as she faced him until she felt in control again. "*Mam* is well. Miriam sent word that she'd fallen, but she was unhurt. We all worry about her since her cancer diagnosis."

David looked concerned. "She has cancer? I didn't know."

"How could you?" she said. His kind eyes made her

relax. Suddenly it was as if they were young again and she felt at ease in his presence. He was married. She had nothing to fear. David had been an honorable boy, and she knew he wouldn't have changed. He was still honorable as a man.

The kettle whistled and she turned back to take it off the burner. She poured two cups of tea and sat down across from him. He'd moved on with his life and it bothered her that he'd found someone else to love and marry, although she had no right to be upset. He wasn't the one who'd left Honeysuckle. She wanted to ask him about his wife, but she didn't dare.

Thirteen years later and life had changed for each of them. David, at twenty-eight, had married and become a preacher. At twenty-seven, she'd spent her life taking care of her mother after her surgery and throughout her cancer treatments.

She realized that he was watching her, and she blushed. "*Mam* had breast cancer. Her chemotherapy treatments were successful. It was rough for a while, but she has been cancer-free for years now."

He looked relieved. "I'm glad to hear it. I shall keep her in my prayers."

"*Danki,*" she whispered. She took a sip of tea and set her cup into its saucer. "Would you like a cookie? I have some gingersnaps in the pantry." She started to rise.

"*Nay*, Esther. I can't stay long. I left my youngest son with Lizzie. He wanted to play with Jonas and Ezekiel, but they're out doing chores with Zack." He gave her a crooked smile. "I'm sure she's had enough of him by now."

"*Nay.* Lizzie loves children." She paused as her curiosity got the better of her. "You have a son?"

"I have two—Jacob and Jed. Jacob is five and Jed a year older."

Esther smiled, picturing the two young boys as younger versions of their father. "You've been blessed."

He nodded. David took one last swallow of tea and then rose. "It's *goot* to see you again, Esther. I'm glad you are home." The sudden intensity of his look made her face heat and her belly burn. "How long will you be staying?"

She shrugged. "I'm not sure. Zack asked me to come. He hasn't made any plans to leave just yet." She managed a smile. "We'll be here for a while anyway."

David grinned. "*Goot.* Then I shall see you again. Say *hallo* to Zack. Tell him that I was asking after him."

She followed him to the door. "I will."

"*Willkomm* home, Esther." He smiled at her and left.

She watched as he crossed the yard toward the main farmhouse. It was wonderful to see him again, but she shouldn't think anything of it. He didn't ask if she'd married. Perhaps because he knew that she was still a spinster? *Why did he come?*

David was the preacher and he simply wanted to welcome her back into the community. She stood at the door a long time, hoping for a glimpse of David's son, but gave up when there was no sign of them several minutes later. Seeing him again after all these years rattled her. He had made a new life for himself and it was time she started thinking about doing the same thing.

The weather had turned cool, but it was near harvest time, so the colder temperatures were to be expected. As she hung up the laundry to dry, Lizzie smiled at the sweet melodic chirping of birds raised in song. She realized with sudden sadness that winter would soon chase most of the birds away. *Will I have to leave, too?* There had been no time alone to talk with Zack last night. The children had kept him occupied with discussions about school and their Amish-community friends.

She pinned a pillowcase to the clothesline and then paused a moment to rub her hands together quickly to warm them. The older children were in school. Jonas and Ezekiel were with Zack in the back acreage, where he was instructing the boys about the importance of their farm crops and what it took to run a property of this size. She didn't know whether or not her sons understood Zack, but what she did know was that the boys loved spending time with their uncle.

She pinned a dress on the clothesline, then bent for another wet garment. A sudden breeze stirred the air, giving her a chill. She contemplated running inside for a heavy coat, but then the wind stopped, and the sun warmed her. Lizzie loved this time of year. The leaves on the trees splashed the landscape with color in bright and varying shades of gold, orange and red. The air was crisp and invigorating, especially during early-morning and late-evening hours before and after the sun made its appearance in the autumn sky.

Her hip tended to bother her more at this time of year, but she wasn't concerned. She was often too busy to pay much attention to the pain. This was the season for family and friends to get in their harvest before winter descended and snow carpeted the countryside. By early November, the crops would be in, the work done, and then it would be time for weddings within the community.

Until then, there was much to be done. At supper

last night Zack had let her know that he'd be starting the harvest on Wednesday of next week. When Abraham was alive, he'd worked for days bringing in the crops and ensuring that the grain and hay were properly stored for future use. Her husband had never asked for, nor would he have accepted, help from his community.

Did Zack feel the same way? Bringing in the crops seemed like too much farmwork for one man. Matthew could help, but it would take five days, probably more, for the two of them to finish the job. And that was being generous in her assumption that the two of them alone could get the job done.

She wondered about Peter and Rachel. Would they work with their neighbors to finish the harvest more quickly?

Lizzie secured her daughter's newly washed black *kapp* to the line. As soon as she was done, she would search for Zack, tell him that she had to talk with him. She could no longer put off talking about the farm, no matter the outcome of their discussion.

The low rumbling sound of tires crunching on dirt drew her attention. She moved closer for a better look as a dark automobile pulled down the driveway and parked near the farmhouse. The English driver got out of the vehicle and opened the rear door for the person in the backseat. An Amish woman stepped out.

Curious, Lizzie moved closer for a better look as the driver opened the trunk and pulled out a suitcase, which he set on the ground near the passenger. He then climbed back into his car and, with a wave, drove away.

"Mam!" Esther burst out of the *dawdi haus* and ran toward the woman in the yard, and Lizzie immediately knew the identity of their visitor.

As Esther reached her side, her mother smiled. Lizzie hung back, hesitant to intrude, anxious to meet her late husband's mother. And then she saw Zack crossing the pasture flanked by her two youngest sons.

Esther gestured toward the Fisher males and said something to her mother. The older woman nodded and waved at them.

Lizzie was unsure if she should come forward as Zack and his nephews slipped through an opening in the fence. Zack locked the gate behind them. She saw him speak briefly with the boys, who stared at their grandmother as they drew closer.

Esther spied her standing in the distance. "Lizzie," she called, "come and meet our *mudder.*"

Their *mam* spun to face her, watched Lizzie's hesitant, uneven gait as she came forward. *I have nothing to be ashamed of,* she told herself, knowing that she'd done her best to take care of the children and the farm. As she studied her late husband's mother, she thought of Abraham. *Except for one thing.*

Her late husband's mother was of average size and wore a green dress, white cape and apron and a white *kapp* on her sandy-brown hair. Were her eyes brown like Esther's? Lizzie couldn't see from this distance. The woman's appearance on the farm made her nervous. What was she doing here?

Afraid and uneasy, Lizzie froze, unable to move on. She must pleasantly welcome her mother-in-law while putting her fears and misgivings aside.

Zack and the children reached the woman first, and for a moment, Zack's mother focused her attention on Lizzie's sons. It gave Lizzie a moment to observe the woman interacting with her two youngest.

"My, but you are big boys!" their grandmother exclaimed.

Jonas puffed up and nodded. "I'm Jonas. I'm four."

She smiled. "*Ja. Hallo*, Jonas." She turned to Zeke. "You must be Ezekiel. Your *endie* told me all about you."

Zeke widened his eyes as he peeked at Zack for guidance. Zack grinned as he placed a hand on the boy's shoulder.

"Mam!" Zeke exclaimed suddenly when he saw Lizzie. Conscious of her limp, she tried to walk so it wouldn't be as noticeable. "*Grossmama*'s come for a visit!"

Lizzie regarded Zeke with affection as she reached them. "*Ja.* Isn't it nice that she's here to see us?" Zeke bobbed his head. She turned to Zack's mother. "*Hallo*, I'm—"

"Elizabeth King Fisher," the woman finished with a smile. "You're my eldest son's widow."

The smile left her face. Lizzie nodded solemnly as she was hit hard by the painful memory of Abraham's death. His mother had suffered the loss, too, and she'd learned of her son's death only recently. "He was a *goot* man," she said. "I'm sorry."

"The loss is also yours." Zack's mother's gaze warmed in shared sympathy. "I'm Sarah Fisher." She paused. "And you are my daughter."

Sarah's words touched her deeply. "It's nice to meet you," Lizzie greeted. *Her eyes are the same color as Esther's and the same shape as Zack's.* She also saw her late husband's features in his mother's face.

"Mam," Zack asked with concern, "what are you doing here?"

Lizzie felt a little better knowing that Zack hadn't asked his mother to come. She had visions of Zack declaring the farm his and them all moving into the farmhouse. Where would that leave her?

Zack's mother raised her eyebrows as she gazed at her son. "I've come to see my son and *dochter*. And I've come to meet Lizzie and my *kins kinner*."

"But we only just left. I would have stayed and accompanied you if I'd known."

Sarah shrugged. "Ted Harris brought me. When I heard he was coming through Lancaster on his way to visit his daughter in New Jersey, I was happy to ride with him."

"Ted is a neighbor," Zack explained to Lizzie. He looked relieved that his mother had come with someone they apparently knew well. He lifted his mother's suitcase. "You must be tired. I'll show you to your room so that you can unpack and rest."

"*Nay*, Zack," Sarah said as he started toward the cottage. "I'll stay in the farmhouse with Lizzie." She sought Lizzie's gaze for approval. "Do you have room for me?"

Heart racing and a little bit afraid, Lizzie nodded. "*Ja.*" She managed a smile. "We have plenty of room." She made a quick decision about where she would move the two younger girls. Rebecca could sleep with Hannah and Mary Ruth. And Anne could move into her bedroom. That would leave Sarah a double bed in a fair-sized, comfortable room.

"*Goot!*" Sarah appeared satisfied. "You and I can become acquainted, and I can get to know my *kins kinner*."

Zack seemed surprised. "*Mam*, are you sure you want to stay in the big *haus*? *Dat*—"

"Your *vadder* passed on years ago," Sarah said. "Since then, I've lived a lifetime."

Zack narrowed his eyes as if gauging his mother's reaction. He smiled, apparently pleased with what he saw. He captured Lizzie's gaze as if trying to read her reaction to his *mam*'s presence.

Seeing his concern, Lizzie smiled at him reassuringly. She could do this—be gracious and kind to her late husband's mother, the woman who had given birth to two caring sons and a wonderful daughter.

"Come inside, and we'll have tea," she invited. "Zack, I'll show you where to put your *mudder*'s suitcase."

Chapter Twelve

Zack followed Lizzie, his mother and his sister into the farmhouse. If Lizzie had reservations about her un-invited guest, she hid them well.

He had to respect the way she was handling his *mam*'s surprise visit. He himself had been stunned to see his mother. He and Esther had rushed home only days earlier, because she had suffered a terrible fall. But when they'd reached Walnut Creek, where his mother had moved in with his older sister, his only living parent had looked shockingly well, and his eldest sister, Miriam, had appeared sheepish.

Mam had been delighted to see him and Esther, although they hadn't been gone from home long. You would have thought by the way she'd acted that *Mam* hadn't seen them in years.

Later, while his mother was busy visiting with Esther, he'd pulled Miriam aside and asked the real reason why they'd been summoned home.

"*Mam* fell and got hurt," his sister had said. "She didn't seem herself. I was frightened for her. Her be-

havior right before she fell alarmed me. She was acting strangely."

Strangely? He'd frowned. "She's all right now? She
seems fine."

"*Ja.* Thanks be to *Gott.*" Miriam had looked relieved.
"It's as if she didn't fall. Do *ya* think 'tis possible that
she suffered some kind of episode?" His sister clearly
had been concerned. "She had all those terrible cancer
treatments."

Zack had studied his mother from across the room.
He had to admit that the treatments had seemed harsh,
even worse than the disease. But *Mam* had come out
of her surgery and subsequent chemotherapy surprisingly well. In fact, she'd looked better than she had in
a long time. "If she did have an episode, it's passed.
Keep a close eye on her after we go back. If it happens
again, let us know."

Something flickered in Miriam's expression. "You're
going back?"

He nodded. "Lizzie will need help with the harvest.
The children—" He smiled. "I enjoy spending time with
them. I've barely gotten to know them, and I don't want
us to be strangers."

"How does Abraham's widow feel about this?"

Zack had shrugged. "She has been kind and gracious
to Esther and me. It's obvious how much she loves the
children, although I suspect that some of them haven't
made life easy for her. She is a little thing, but she is
strong. She works hard and never complains—"

Miriam had studied him closely. Her voice became
quiet as she asked, "Do you have feelings for this girl?"

He'd felt an odd pull in his gut. "She's our late
brother's widow."

"I know that, and that's not what I asked." She'd paused. "We usually don't have a choice in matters of the heart," his sister said.

"She's only nineteen."

"And yet she married our brother, who was at least sixteen years older." She paused. "Why would she agree to marry *him*?"

"I think her mother might have had a hand in Lizzie's decision. And the children needed a mother. She has great compassion for people, and I suspect she wasn't able to deny her love and care to seven motherless children. Perhaps she agreed because of the children."

Zack stared off in the distance, not really seeing. "She has a bad leg—or hip—I'm not sure which. I only know that there are times when she must experience great pain."

"Do you know what happened to Ruth?" she asked. They didn't usually speak of the dead, but it was a question that must have been on his sibling's mind because Zack had wondered about it himself.

"You know how Ruth was," he said as if it were the only explanation.

Miriam had nodded sadly. "*Ja.* I know. And there is no doubt you are right. Ruth wasn't a strong woman physically or emotionally." She hesitated. "And what of Rosemary?"

He had stiffened. "Has she come by the house looking for me again?" Rosemary Yost was a young Amish woman who had decided that she wanted him as her husband. He'd told her that they were nothing more than friends, but she was relentless in her pursuit of him.

"*Nay*, but she asks about you whenever we meet. We

last saw her at church service and she wondered how you've been faring in Honeysuckle."

Closing his eyes, Zack sighed. "I told her that we were friends only."

"She is a stubborn one, that girl," his sister had said, and he'd agreed.

Now, days later back in Honeysuckle, Zack saw his mother comfortably seated in the farmhouse's kitchen and then looked to Lizzie for guidance. "Which room?" He held up his mother's suitcase.

"Up the stairs, turn right, first door to the left," she instructed without hesitation.

He smiled. *My old bedroom.* As he turned and headed toward the stairs, Zack heard his mother murmur to Lizzie. He thought he heard something about "boys" and "room." She was probably telling her that the room used to belong to him and Abe.

He stopped as he thought about his older brother. A wave of loss and pain hit him hard. His death had come as a shock. He remembered Abraham as a man with boundless energy, a hard worker, someone who had loved life and his wife Ruth to distraction.

Zack frowned as he climbed the stairs. Abe must have been devastated when he'd lost Ruth. His brother had loved her with a passion that went beyond anything Zack had ever seen. What would it be like to know such love?

A sudden thought occurred to him. Abraham had married again only a few weeks after Ruth's death. It must have been hard for Lizzie to marry a grief-stricken, devastated widower and take on an entire household of grieving, motherless children. The notion bothered him.

Lizzie hadn't suffered life easily, and he, his sister and mother were making things more difficult for her.

He reached the top landing, then headed down the hall to his old bedroom. When he entered, he was pleased to find that the room was plain but clearly feminine and would be much to his mother's liking. A lovely quilt in ivory, greens and blues covered the double bed. From the dresses hanging on a wall peg, he realized that two, if not all, of the girls slept here, which meant that Lizzie was making adjustments to the household in order to accommodate his mother. It was usual for women to allow for unexpected guests within the Amish community; a door was always open for family or friends to stay, but Lizzie had lost her husband recently after nearly two years of marriage.

Zack set the valise near the end of the double bed and then returned downstairs. He entered the kitchen to find Lizzie, Esther and his mother chatting and smiling over cups of tea.

A pound cake sat in the center of the table, cut into slices. Each woman had a plate with a piece and someone—most probably Lizzie—had cut a slice for him and put it before an empty chair.

He sat down and smiled at Lizzie gratefully. He saw her blush and then look away, and he was charmed. She might have been his brother's wife, but she was on his mind a lot lately. At this moment, he was enjoying himself too much to be worried.

Lizzie sat with the Fisher family in the kitchen, wondering why she felt more comfortable in their presence than she did with her own family. She loved her parents and siblings; they all meant well, even if they did treat her differently. Her mother kept herself distant from her, as if she was afraid to face the fact that she'd given birth to a daughter who was less than perfect. She knew her mother loved her, in her own way, but she felt the love *Mam* gave to her brothers and sisters more. Only William treated her like everyone else, and she adored him for it.

"More cake?" she asked when everyone had consumed a helping.

"I've had enough." Sarah smiled her thanks.

"I'll have another," Zack said with a grin. He extended his plate toward her. "It's delicious."

Lizzie smiled, amused, as she cut him a huge chunk of butter pound cake and set it carefully on his plate.

He laughed, pulled the cake closer and then dived into eating it as if it was the best thing he'd ever tasted.

She watched with a strange surge of fondness until she realized that Esther was watching her and not her brother. Lizzie caught the speculative look in Esther's soft-brown eyes and looked away. Did Esther suspect that she liked Zack but was torn over her growing feelings? Did Zack's sister know something that she didn't? Something that made Esther feel sorry for her? Like Zack's plans for the farm? As her stomach burned, she swallowed against a suddenly tight throat. "More tea?" she asked her mother-in-law.

"*Ja.* It's delicious." Sarah accepted a second cup of tea. "What time do the children arrive home from *schule*?" she asked pleasantly as she set down her filled teacup.

"Soon. Usually right around two thirty," Lizzie said.

The woman glowed with pleasure. "I'm eager to see the rest of my *kins kinner.*"

"They are wonderful children," Lizzie said, warming to her. "Do you have others?"

"Miriam has nine children," Sarah said. "Her eldest son, John, is married with two *kinner*—Jane and Jacob. Her daughter Mae, Miriam's oldest, has four and is expecting a fifth. I have sixteen grandchildren and six soon-to-be seven great-grandchildren."

"You are truly blessed to have such a large family and so many *kins kinner*," Lizzie said.

"*Ja*, I feel blessed. I thank the Lord every day that I am here to enjoy each and every one of them."

Lizzie recalled Sarah's fight against cancer. "I can understand why." She felt a sharp jolt of pain as she thought of the child she had wanted desperately but lost. She blinked back tears as she stood quickly, and with head bowed, she began to gather up the dirty dishes. She went to the sink and filled a basin with water.

"Lizzie?" Zack whispered, leaning close. He had come up from behind her where she stood at the kitchen sink. "Are you well? Is your hip hurting?"

She felt the impact of his nearness. The rumble of his deep voice shivered against her skin. Shaking her head no, she reached to wipe the corner of her eye with the edge of a dish towel, then turned to smile at him reassuringly. "I'm fine, Zack."

He considered her a long moment until the heat rose in her face. He didn't move, and Lizzie was stunned to realize that she liked having him close. Shaken, she hid her trembling hands in the water as she went back to doing dishes.

"What are you two whispering about?" Sarah asked.

Lizzie knew some measure of relief when he stepped back. She sensed rather than saw Zack shrug as if they had spoken of nothing much. "I know we just enjoyed Lizzie's delicious pound cake," he said, "but when is supper?"

His mother and sister laughed. Amused, despite herself, Lizzie relaxed, her anxiety easing. "You're hungry still?" she asked him, capturing his gaze.

His expression cleared as if he were relieved to see her smile. "I like food."

"You like cake," Esther interjected with a laugh.

"I'll bake another," Lizzie suggested. "What kind?"

"Apple, chocolate." At that moment, he looked boyishly appealing, and she could see him as an eleven-year-old boy at the time of his father's death. She blinked, trying to banish the mental image. She didn't need to be thinking of Zack as anything but her late husband's brother.

"Apple chocolate?" She furrowed her brow as she thought. "I haven't heard of that recipe."

"Both," his mother explained.

Before Lizzie could question her, Esther spoke up. "He wants both apple *and* chocolate cake. He's telling you that he likes both kinds."

Lizzie examined the man next to her, enjoying the sight of his stunning good looks. "I can make both." And his handsome face brightened as his lips curved upward. She felt something akin to happiness flush her with warmth.

He leaned across the sink as he reached for a cup and placed it in the dish basin. *"Danki,"* he leaned close to whisper before he shifted back.

The warmth of his breath brushed her neck, her ear, and then was gone, leaving her reeling from feelings she had no right to experience—or want.

Chapter Thirteen

The supper table was filled with noisy laughter and conversation. Lizzie watched with pleasure the way the children interacted with their grandmother. They were clearly overjoyed to see her. Her daughter Anne grinned happily at Lizzie, obviously relieved and glad that her grossmama was so nice.

Zack sat at the other end of the table, teasing Matthew, who seemed to blossom under his uncle's attention.

"*Onkel* Zack, it's nearly harvest time, isn't it?"

"*Ja*, Matt. It is." Zack addressed her. "I spoke with Peter Zook. He is going to help bring in the harvest. Afterward, we'll go to his place and do the same."

Lizzie was pleased at the news. "Peter's wife, Rachel, is my oldest and dearest friend," she explained for Sarah's benefit. "She will be coming, too?" she asked Zack.

"*Ja*. And why would she not? She offered to bring her specialty dish. She said you would know what that is."

Lizzie laughed. "*Ja*. I know."

Zack stared at her. "And you'll not tell us?"

"*Nay*," she said. "I'll let it be her surprise."

"*Mam*, may I help with the food?" Mary Ruth asked. Lizzie, stunned by her eldest daughter calling her *Mam*, realized that she was staring. She grinned. "I wouldn't have it any other way."

"We can all help," Esther said. "We can work together here—if that is all right, Lizzie."

Lizzie inclined her head with a small smile curving her lips. "I'll enjoy that."

Suddenly, there was excitement among the Fisher females about what to cook and bake for the harvest meal and who would make which dish. The eagerness of her daughters to assist thrilled Lizzie as did Esther's and Sarah's delight in participating and being here, on the farm, for the event.

After the main meal, Zack came up to her with dishes in his hands and a soft smile on his attractive face. Lizzie looked at him in disbelief. "You're helping in the kitchen?" she said. "That's women's work. My father and brothers would never— Zack, you don't have to do that. With all the girls in this house, we have plenty of help."

"I know it's not usual for most men, but I honestly don't mind. I did chores for my *mudder* while she was ill. I just got into the habit of helping, I guess."

Lizzie took the plates from him and put them in the dishwater. "Well, it's not necessary, though it is appreciated." She picked up a bowl of mashed potatoes and tried to brush past him to get to the refrigerator to put them away. But Zack didn't move to allow her to pass. In fact, he shifted to block her exit.

Overwhelmed by intense feelings for him, she experienced alarm. "Zack—"

He placed a hand on her arm. With the weather

cooler, she had taken to wearing her long-sleeved green dress. Still, despite the cotton fabric between his fingers and her, she felt the warmth of his touch as if his hand had encircled her bare skin.

"Lizzie," he asked softly, "are you happy here on the farm?"

She shot him a startled gaze. "Happy? *Ja.* Of course I'm happy. Why would you ask?"

There was warmth in his dark, nearly black eyes. "You do so much for everyone. I've realized how much you've sacrificed to be here for the children—and my *brooder.*" His mention of his brother was said in an agonized whisper, but she didn't glimpse anything in his expression but caring and concern for her.

She thought of her hurried wedding and her and Abraham's subsequent life together afterward. It had been rough going at first, but then it had quickly become rewarding because of Annie, Jonas and little Zeke, who had needed her desperately. Annie had been three, Jonas two, while Ezekiel, the baby, had been barely a year old.

"Don't imagine me as anything more than I am. A simple, plain woman who has done her best for her husband and children," Lizzie warned him, though she was pleased by his words.

"*Ja,* but they weren't your children."

She gasped and felt the blood leave her face. "They are my children—the children of my heart. I love them and you can't say otherwise."

Zack furrowed his brow. "Lizzie—"

Lizzie blinked back tears. "Excuse me a moment." She left the kitchen and hurried up the stairs to her bedroom. Once inside her room, she shut the door and leaned against it. *I was wrong. He doesn't regard me as family. He doesn't understand how I feel about the children.*

She breathed deeply, trying to calm herself. Closing her eyes, she replayed in her mind her conversation with Zack. She straightened and moved toward the bed, where she sat down. The mattress gave under her weight and she bent over, cradling her head in her hands.

Zack didn't mean to hurt me, she thought. He had been so nice to her at times that she'd believed she'd weep happy tears, having never experienced his level of kind concern.

She was angry with herself for caring what Zack thought, for caring about him. Given her marriage to his older brother and her current circumstances, she should be keeping herself emotionally distant from him.

She lost her battle with tears as she cried for her dead husband and for the children and the painful loss they'd suffered. She wept for the loss of her baby before the child had a chance to live. And for being afraid of losing everything—everyone—she'd ever cherished. While she may be falling in love with Zack, she knew for certain that they'd have no future together. How could they? He wanted the farm, not her. She could feel it in her heart.

A knock on her bedroom door made her spring to her feet. *"Ja?"* she asked.

"Lizzie?" It was Sarah. "Are you all right? Zack thought you weren't feeling well, and he's worried."

Lizzie wiped her eyes with both hands. "I'm fine. I'll be right down."

There was a long moment of silence, and then Zack's mother said, "If there is anything I can do, please let me know."

Her words made Lizzie smile. She went to the door, opened it. *"Danki."*

"I endured many such moments after Zack's father passed away." Sarah's answering smile was gentle.

Lizzie could only nod. If it were only the loss of her dead husband bothering her, then she would be happy to talk things through with her mother-in-law, a woman who had suffered greatly but come out the better for her losses. "I appreciate your kindness."

"Things will get better in time," Sarah said. "I never thought I'd be able to enter this *haus* again without seeing my husband, Daniel, without hurting." She placed an arm around Lizzie's shoulders and Lizzie resisted the temptation to lean into her.

"You seem to be doing well here," she said.

"Ja." Her mother-in-law looked past Lizzie into the room that she and her husband must have shared at one time. "I see him everywhere still, but it's now a *goot* feeling. I miss him, but I am happy again."

The two women made their way toward the stairs as they talked.

"You know about my cancer?" Sarah asked, meeting her glance.

Lizzie nodded. "Zack mentioned you were ill."

"Ja. It was terrible. I never expected it. I rarely get sick, and then to learn I had cancer and could die… Believe it or not, it wasn't the worst thing I'd ever lived through. That moment came when my husband died. He was gone and I was left with only the memory of his loving eyes and boyish smile. The cancer was awful, but when I was undergoing treatments, I'd lie in bed at night and think of my Daniel, and I knew he was there with me, encouraging me to fight this disease. He was

telling me that there were family who still needed me and wanted me to live." Her eyes twinkled. "We Amish are pacifists, but battling cancer isn't a fight we should avoid."

"There is nothing in the *Ordnung* about turning the other cheek to cancer," Lizzie agreed, referring to the book of their faith and rules of Amish life. There was such emotion in Sarah's voice that Lizzie felt the urge to cry again.

Sarah's eyes filled with moisture. She laughed as she blinked them away. "Enough tears, *ja*?" She reached for Lizzie's hand. "There are children downstairs who need you. And my son—he is sick over something he might have said to upset you." She seemed to be posing a question that Lizzie was unwilling to answer.

Lizzie squeezed gently, then released the woman's hand. "Then I guess we should finish the dishes so that we can enjoy dessert."

Sarah's lips twitched. "The dishes have been washed, dried and put away."

Lizzie laughed. "And the children are all waiting at the table for cake and ice cream."

"*Ja*, I'm afraid so."

Lizzie preceded Sarah through the house and into the kitchen. As Sarah had mentioned, the children—and Zack and Esther—were seated at the table, waiting for her return—and for dessert.

"Everyone ready for cake and ice cream?" she asked as she approached the table.

"*Ja!*" the children and Esther chorused together.

Zack, Lizzie saw, regarded her silently with worry in his expression. She knew then that he hadn't meant to hurt her. He probably still didn't know what he'd said wrong.

She had to pass him to get to the pantry, where she'd put the cakes—two of them—one chocolate and one apple. She grabbed both of them carefully and then reached over Zack's shoulder to set them on the table directly in front of him. She became instantly aware of his scent and his warmth as she rose hurriedly and moved to get the ice cream from the gas freezer in the back room.

She raised the lid to the chest freezer and leaned in to take hold of a tub of ice cream, one of the several she'd made earlier in the season while the little ones had napped and the older children had been in school. Abraham had been alive then, working on something out in the barn.

Lizzie spun around and nearly bumped into Zack, who had come silently into the room. She started to stumble, and he gently grabbed hold of her shoulders to steady her. "Zack!"

"Lizzie," he murmured. "I didn't mean to upset you." She saw his throat bob as he swallowed hard. "I'm sorry if I hurt you. You are a *goot* mother. I know you love the children as your own—and they *are* yours. Everyone can see it. I…" He hesitated, as if unsure how to best word what he wanted to say. "I'm only concerned with your happiness."

Lizzie looked at him in stunned amazement. "My happiness?"

He ran a hand across the back of his neck. "You work hard. You never complain. I know your leg—your hip— hurts you something awful at times, but you never let on that you're in pain." He stared at her with concerned obsidian eyes. "I'm worried about you."

"Zack, I'm well—"

"You may say so, but I think not. I worry. I can't help it. You need to take time for yourself, especially when you are hurting. Take a bath or a hot shower—"

She blushed and his eyes twinkled. "Why?" she teased. "Am I in need of washing?"

His gleaming gaze ran down the length of her, respectful but assessing and no less impactful to her state of mind. "You're in need of tender, loving care, Elizabeth King Fisher."

He took the ice cream bucket out of her hand and left the back room. Lizzie stayed behind for a moment, trying to still her rapidly beating heart and to come to grips with what he'd just said. *He cares for me.* Could it be that she was mistaken? Or was he simply a concerned brother-in-law looking out for his brother's widow? It was nice to have someone—Zack—care enough to be concerned.

Tucking a few stray strands of auburn hair beneath her prayer *kapp*, Lizzie drew herself upright, and ignoring her aching hip, she returned to the kitchen to happily join the others for dessert.

Chapter Fourteen

The week flew by despite the fact that Lizzie's world had shifted. Having another woman—her mother-in-law—in the house made her feel slightly on edge. It wasn't that Sarah Fisher wasn't kind and considerate. On the contrary, she was kindness to a fault. Lizzie realized that it was her own inadequacies that bothered her. Because of her bad hip, she was frequently afraid of falling. And she feared that she would say something unintentionally that would alert her husband's family to her responsibility in Abraham's death.

It was Friday, and this Sunday was church day. Lizzie had found out only that morning that services were being held at their farm. She had no idea why the location had changed unexpectedly. Her church community hadn't expected her to host services so soon after Abraham's death. Why had things suddenly changed? Was it because Abraham's family had moved onto the property?

"How did this happen?" she asked Zack as she met him that morning while crossing the yard toward the chicken coop. He was handsome as always in his work clothes as he was doing farm chores.

He raised a questioning eyebrow. "How did what happen?"

"Church services. I thought the Samuel Yoders were hosting this week."

Zack appeared surprised by her concern. "Their son James is ill. I thought we could fill in for them." As he looked at her, his dark eyes seemed to delve into her soul. His tone was soft as he continued, "It's been over two months since A—your husband died, Lizzie. Don't *ya* think it's time to return to the living?"

"By hosting service?" She scowled at him. "I live every day, Zack. I live for the children—and for the farm."

"When was the last time church service was held here?" he asked.

"The day before Abraham's death," she said, her eyes filling with tears. Annoyed with herself, she turned away.

"Lizzie—" he entreated, his deep voice causing a tingle to run down her spine. He sounded contrite. She paused and turned back. "I didn't know." His expression was kind and nearly her undoing.

She closed her eyes to shut out his attraction and to get herself under control. "I know you didn't." She lifted a hand to her forehead, where a sudden headache had arisen since learning that she'd be hosting services. She knew it was an honor, but on top of everything else, it seemed too much too soon.

"You're hurting," he said after a thorough examination of her face. "Hip?"

She shook her head, then promptly grimaced as the shooting pain intensified.

"Headache," he guessed, his voice—and his gaze—gentle. He approached her, and she briefly closed her eyes. This caring side of him was hard to resist and made her believe in things that couldn't be.

He shifted to stand behind her, settled his hands on her shoulders. She jerked. "Close your eyes again," he whispered. She obeyed. "Breathe deep. Don't think about what's bothering you. We are all here to help."

He began to knead her shoulders and the muscles above her shoulder blades. His touch was soothing, and she should object. It wasn't proper for him to touch her, but the pain, the worry, was slowly easing, all because of his simple touch. His fingers slipped to her neck, gently squeezed and massaged away the soreness. Then he raised his hands to her temples and began to ease away her pain with the circular movements of his fingertips.

Her headache slowly eased. She breathed deeply, liking Zack's touch. The thought that what she was allowing was wrong filtered through the enjoyment. She stiffened.

"Danki," she gasped and pulled away. "It's better."

She put a few feet between them. He didn't say anything, but she could sense that he studied her, probably wondering what she was thinking and feeling.

She drew herself up and faced him. "There is a lot to do before Sunday services."

He smiled. "That's why Rachel, *Mam* and Esther are planning to clean the *haus* and get everything ready."

She gazed at him, wishing for things she couldn't have. "Rachel's coming?"

Zack nodded.

She shifted uneasily. "I should feed the chickens," she said.

He shook his head. "Mary Ruth fed them earlier."

Lizzie gaped at him. "She did?"

"Ja." He frowned. "Has she never done so before?"

"Ja, she has," she admitted, but she didn't tell him that it wasn't without an argument. Arguing wasn't the way of the Lord, so she had stopped trying to rush her eldest daughter past her grief.

Zack seemed satisfied with her answer. *"Goot."* He glanced toward the barn. "Services in the *haus* or the barn?"

"The *haus,*" she said, resigned to the fact church services would be held on the farm on Sunday. "The barn is too drafty and there is too much to do to clear things away."

"I made a start on that," he said. "I cleaned up the clutter, and now everything is in its place." He seemed proud of his accomplishments.

She wasn't sure how she felt about his clearing the barn without telling her. She didn't want to think too closely about why he'd felt that it was his right to do so without asking.

"I'll go up to the *haus,* then," she said. He looked mildly disappointed. "Do you know when Rachel plans to come?"

The sudden clip-clop of a horse's hooves on the dirt driveway drew her gaze just after Zack, having noticed first, grinned and gestured toward the buggy that was making its way closer to the farmhouse and yard.

"It seems she's here," he said.

Lizzie was overjoyed to see her friend. She needed Rachel, who never judged, to help her sort out her feelings. But would she have time alone with Rachel? *Nay*, not likely. She would have to wait for another time to talk with her closest friend.

"Rachel!" she cried as the young woman steered the buggy into the barnyard, parked the vehicle and waved.

Rachel climbed out and went to secure the horse, but Zack was there to take care of it for her. She thanked him with a respectful nod, then approached her. "Lizzie." She smiled warmly. "I'm longing for a cup of tea. Shall we?"

Lizzie grinned. "With cake?"

"*Ja*," Rachel agreed, and the women moved toward the farmhouse. "So tell me—how are things going on the Fisher farm?"

Lizzie opened her mouth to tell her, then stifled the words she wanted to say.

Rachel slid her a sideways glance. "*Ach*, as bad as that?" Her eyes filled with concern.

"*Nay*. Everyone has been kind and wonderful."

"But—"

"I'm not accustomed to it."

Rachel laughed. "Get used to it, Lizzie. It is called family."

"*Ja*, but—"

Rachel placed a hand on Lizzie's shoulder. "For whatever reason, your family—your parents and siblings— are different, but these people are your family now."

"Do you honestly believe that?" Lizzie was afraid that things would change or that she'd wake up from dreaming—the fact of Abraham's death and the loss of her child reminded her that life offered heartache in unexpected ways.

Rachel frowned. "What's wrong?"

Lizzie shook her head and looked toward the front porch. She wanted to confide in Rachel but now was not the time. She forced a smile. "*Hallo*, Sarah. I hope you slept well. I'd like you to meet my *goot* friend Rachel Zook." She turned to Rachel. "It's my pleasure for you to meet my mother-in-law, Sarah Fisher."

She watched Rachel and Sarah exchange greetings, and they all entered the farmhouse, where Lizzie put on the teakettle and pulled from the pantry the leftover apple cake that Zack hadn't consumed the day before.

Not long afterward, Naomi Beiler, Ellen Beachey and Dinah Plank arrived to help Lizzie clean and prepare for church services. Pleased, Lizzie flashed each woman a grateful smile.

"Ellen, what about the shop? Shouldn't you be there?"

Ellen shrugged. "*Dat* wanted to work, and he brought *Mam* with him."

Lizzie understood. Ellen's mother's mind wasn't what it once was. She got lost in the past, often forgetting things. "It's wonderful to see you. I've started Mrs. Emory's quilt."

"I'm glad to hear it. Those aprons you brought already sold. I'll drop the money by on Monday."

"No need. You have enough to do. I made a few more. I'll bring what I have Monday and we can square up then."

The women went to work. Sarah, Esther, Ellen and the girls tackled the upstairs rooms while Rachel, Naomi Beiler and Dinah Plank helped Lizzie clean and prepare the first level. "I didn't expect you," Lizzie said to Naomi as they worked side by side in the gathering room.

"Dinah and I wanted to help. I know this must be difficult for you, hosting services so soon…" She trailed off, unwilling to mention Abraham's death.

"I'll get through. And I appreciate the help. You're a kind woman."

"*Nay.* I simply believe in living the Lord's way," the woman replied. She peered through the side window glass. Jonas and Zeke were playing in the yard, and no doubt Naomi could see them. "How is Jonas's hand?"

"It's healing well." Lizzie ran a dust cloth across a window in the gathering room. "It was *goot* of you to watch the children while we were at the doctor's."

Naomi paused in sweeping the floor and made light of Lizzie's thanks with a wave of a hand. "They are *goot kinner*, and they enjoyed spending time with my Aaron and Michael."

Lizzie nodded. During the ride home, she'd heard all about Naomi's children and how much Matthew, Anne and Zeke had enjoyed playing outside with them. Naomi's daughter Emma was her eldest, and she often minded her brothers. Rebecca and Hannah had talked about Emma and how much they liked her.

"Lizzie?" Dinah said. "I swept the kitchen floor. What would you like me to do next?"

"Would you mind pulling out my baking ingredients?" Lizzie asked. "I left some recipe cards on the counter."

"I'll be happy to." Dinah returned to the kitchen.

"I finished in the bathroom," Rachel said as she entered the room. She held a bucket of soapy water and a towel draped over her right shoulder. "What's next?"

Surprised, Lizzie raised her eyebrows. "I believe we've finished downstairs. I'll check with Sarah—"

"The upstairs is done," Sarah announced as she

swept into the room with Ellen, Esther and Lizzie's daughters.

"Then all that's left is the baking."

Lizzie turned to Naomi. "Tea or coffee? I'm hungry. How about lunch first?"

Naomi smiled but shook her head. "I should get home. I don't dare leave my oldest in charge for too long."

"I should get back to the store," Ellen said. "*Dat* might be ready to head home."

Dinah approached from the kitchen. "I'd like to stay if I can get a ride home."

"I'll take you home, Dinah," Rachel called from the kitchen. Dinah returned to help Rachel.

"I appreciate all the help," Lizzie told the two women who were ready to leave. "I don't know why I was so worried about getting the house ready for services. You've all been wonderful." It was the greatest thing about being Amish. The community was always ready to lend a helping hand.

"We're glad to help," Naomi said. "You know we're always here for you."

"Danki," Lizzie said. It had been Naomi and Dinah who had helped on the day of Abraham's funeral. She blinked back a tear at the memory and smiled at the women, deeply touched by their friendship. She walked outside with Ellen and Naomi to their vehicles, which were parked side by side. "I don't have much time for meetings, Naomi," she said, "but if there is any way I can help…"

The widow smiled. "You helped with the haystack supper and we loved having you. I know you are busy raising the children on your own. Take care of yourself and your family—that's the most important thing." Naomi climbed into her vehicle. "I will see you at service," she promised. Then with a wave of her hand, the woman left.

"Ellen." Lizzie regarded her friend, who'd been a godsend since her husband's passing. "You're always there for me. First selling my quilts and crafts and now this—cleaning my *haus* on a day your shop is open."

Ellen shook her head. "Having your craft items in the shop is *wunderbor* for business. As for helping you—" She smiled. "We're friends and I'm glad. I only hope I can be as *goot* a *mudder* as you if Neziah and I are blessed with a child."

"But Neziah has two sons, and they adore you," Lizzie said. "You are already a *mudder*."

She brightened. "I love Asa and Joel as my own."

"That's all you have to do," Lizzie said. "Love them and with the Lord's help all will be well. Neziah and his boys have taken to you like ducks to water."

Ellen laughed, but it was clear that she was happy with her choice of sweetheart and his two sons. "I'll see you on Sunday."

"I'll look forward to it." Despite her initial reservations and fear about hosting church, Lizzie was now eager to host church service for her community. She watched and waved as Ellen steered her horse-drawn buggy toward the main road. Then she reentered the house to find that Sarah and Esther, with Dinah's help, were preparing lunch. Rachel had gathered the children and pulled chairs from the other room to accommodate everyone.

"Where are Zack and Matt?" Lizzie asked.

"They went to see Peter at the *haus*," Rachel said. "Something about discussing the harvest."

Lizzie quickly pitched in to help and soon there was enough food on the table to feed everyone. Esther had brought bread and macaroni salad from the *dawdi haus*; she had made both the evening before in anticipation of feeding the helpers.

"This is a feast!" Dinah exclaimed as she took a seat at the kitchen table.

Lizzie laughed. "My children are healthy eaters."

Lunch was a fun affair. They ate sandwiches with Esther's bread and the roast beef that Lizzie had cooked earlier in the week. Jonas and Zeke exclaimed exuberantly over the wonderful taste of their aunt's macaroni salad, which made all the women, especially Lizzie, eye them with amused smiles playing about their lips.

When they were done, the women cleaned up quickly. "Are you sure you don't need us to stay and help?" Rachel asked after Lizzie insisted that Rachel and Dinah had enough work of their own to do at home.

"*Nay*, I have plenty of help with my daughters."

Rachel and Dinah left minutes later, heading in the direction of Dinah's apartment over Beachey's Craft Shop.

Lizzie returned inside after seeing the women off. Then with Sarah and Esther's help, she began to prepare food for the shared midday meal after Sunday church service.

Esther was excited yet nervous. It was church Sunday, and David Hostetler would be officiating services. She hadn't seen him since his visit on Monday. Dressed in Sunday best, she followed Zack across the yard to the farmhouse. Her blue dress was freshly laundered, her black apron and *kapp* newly made. This morning she had combed and rolled her brown hair with more care. She didn't want a hair out of place when she met David's wife for the first time. *Vanity is a sin*, she reminded herself. She hoped the Lord would forgive her and understand that she simply wanted to make a good impression. She entered the house to see Lizzie rushing about frantically trying to get the children ready for church.

"Esther!" she cried gratefully when she saw her. "Would you check in the gathering room, make sure all of the benches are in place?"

"*Ja*, of course, Lizzie." Esther was sure that the room was ready but she understood Lizzie's anxiety.

After lingering outside for a few moments, Zack entered behind her. He apparently heard Lizzie's concern. "Everything is ready," he said to reassure her. "We set up the benches at first light. Don't worry." Lizzie looked relieved by Zack's assurance.

Families within the community began to arrive in their buggies. Esther saw the David Hostetlers arrive, and she felt her anxiety level kick up a notch. To her surprise, she saw that he came alone, except for his children. She was puzzled yet relieved.

Where was David's wife? Esther frowned. Was she ill? She hoped not. She wasn't sure how she'd feel while meeting the woman who had won David's heart, but apparently the moment wouldn't be today.

She hung back in the kitchen, watching through the window as buggies and wagons wheeled down the dirt lane and parked in a row in the yard near the barn. Ellen Beachey arrived with her parents and Dinah Plank. In a separate vehicle, Neziah, Ellen's sweetheart, drove his father, Simeon; his younger brother, Micah; and Neziah's two sons, Asa and Joel.

"Esther!" her mother called from the other room. "It's nearly time for service."

"Coming." She felt her stomach churn as she left the kitchen for the gathering area. The room was crowded with all the benches in place, but no one seemed to mind. She approached the women-and-children's area of the room and sat on a bench near her mother. Heart beating wildly, Esther stared at the area reserved for the preacher and waited for David to appear.

She didn't have long to wait. Once everyone was seated, Preacher David Hostetler stepped into place and greeted everyone with a nod. After he gave a short but inspiring introductory sermon, the congregation opened the *Ausbund*, the Amish book of hymns, and began to sing the first of several chosen songs for today's service. They sang several stanzas but not the entire hymn, which would take too long if sung in its entirety. As it was, the chosen stanzas of the first hymn, led by Deacon John, took over a half hour to sing. Esther enjoyed singing, but she couldn't keep her eyes from David as he waited for his part of the service to continue.

Esther took note of two other church elders in the room—another preacher and Bishop Andy. She'd met the deacon at the last service she'd attended in Honeysuckle, and she'd found John Mast and his large family pleasant and likable.

The song ended, and David began to preach. He spoke of the Lord and of the teachings of the *Ordnung*. He was a wonderful, eloquent speaker, and she hung on his every word.

They sang the *Loblied* next, the hymn that was always sung second during church. Esther sang louder than she usually did, caught up in the word of the Lord, inspired by Preacher David during his sermon.

Hours went by with the deacon reading passages from the Bible interspersed with song and moments of prayer. Then church service ended. Esther stood and began to slide down the row of seats to get out so that she could assist with the food. As she headed toward the kitchen, she experienced a funny feeling in the pit of her stomach.

"Esther," her mother whispered as she made her way down the row behind her. "The preacher—isn't that David Hostetler? If I remember correctly, you used to think highly of him." She was silent and Esther could guess the next direction of her thoughts.

Esther glanced back. "*Ja*, 'tis David. He's married now."

"He was a nice boy."

Esther swallowed hard, remembering how much she'd cared for him. "I'm sure he's a nice man, as well. He is a preacher." She forced a grin.

"He's not married," Lizzie said, jumping into their conversation. "David's wife died two years ago. He is raising his two sons on his own."

Esther stopped to glance in the man's direction. David was talking with Bishop Andy. Two young boys approached him, and he smiled and placed a loving hand on each boy's shoulder. As if sensing her regard, he suddenly looked in her direction. Their gazes locked, and Esther felt her heart flutter. Embarrassed, she looked away. "We need to take out the food," she quickly said to her sister-in-law, and Lizzie agreed.

Esther didn't make eye contact with her mother, but she could feel *Mam* studying her closely.

"Mam," Mary Ruth said as she came up to Lizzie. "I'll get the drinks. Shall I ask *Onkel* Zack and Matt to set up a food table on that side of the room?" She gestured toward her selected spot.

"Ja, that looks like a *goot* place," Lizzie said.

The men, Esther saw, were moving benches to create eating areas for the church members.

Esther refused to look again in David's direction, for she knew she'd been staring. She moved toward the kitchen, eager to get out of the room before she made a fool of herself. She had nearly escaped when she heard his voice, a sound as familiar to her as her own breathing.

"Esther, it's *goot* to see you again."

She tensed, drew a deep calming breath and then faced him. The boys were no longer with him. It was David alone, looking handsome and tall. No other man had ever made her feel so small and feminine as he did. She held her hands tight to her sides to still the trembling and smiled. *"Hallo*, David."

He appeared happy to see her; she could see it reflected in his blue eyes and his masculine grin. She gazed at his handsome face and knew that she'd never stopped loving him.

Chapter Fifteen

"I didn't know if you'd stay," David said.

"I'm still here."

The preacher nodded his head, his blue eyes warm, kind. "*Goot.* I don't know if I told you, Esther, but you look lovely. You haven't changed." He studied her with an intensity that gave her goose bumps. "You're still the young girl I knew and loved."

She blushed, unsure how to answer. She remained silent, but she felt secretly pleased.

He looked around the room. "The other day I never asked if your husband was joining you in Honeysuckle."

She opened her mouth to answer. "I—"

"She isn't married," her mother said, coming from behind her. Horrified, Esther turned a darker shade of red.

David smiled, his gaze settling on *Mam.* "Sarah. 'Tis *goot* to see you. It's been many years."

"David." She greeted him with a nod. "I see you've grown up nicely."

"*Mam!*" Esther exclaimed. She flashed her mother

a beseeching glance that silently said, "Please don't embarrass me."

Mam took the hint. "I should go. Lizzie will need help in the kitchen."

David looked concerned. The mention of Lizzie, Esther realized, must have reminded him that she and *Mam* had suffered from Abraham's death, too. "I'm sorry for your loss." He hesitated, holding her mother's gaze before focusing his blue eyes on Esther. "He was a fine man and a wonderful *vadder*."

Sarah nodded, clearly appreciating his words. "*Ja*, he was a *goot* son." She addressed Esther. "I'll be in the kitchen," she said, and then she nodded toward the preacher and left.

"I should go, too," Esther began and turned as if to leave.

"We'll talk again later?" he asked.

She was startled yet secretly pleased by his question. She gave a demure nod.

"*Dat!*" An adorable young boy of about five years old rushed up to David and tugged on the bottom edge of his Sunday-best black vest.

David gave the child a tender smile. "*Ja?* What is it, Jacob?"

"Will we have time to play with Jonas and Zeke?"

Esther could see that Jacob was a miniature version of his handsome father. They wore clothing identical to that of all the men and boys within their Amish community—white shirt, black vest and pants. Like the other men, they had removed their black felt hats and hung them on wall pegs when they entered the house. She enjoyed watching father and son.

"After midday meal," David told the boy gently. "Where did your *brooder* run off to?"

"He went with Jonas to the kitchen to see if they can have a cookie."

David sighed good-naturedly and shook his head. "Tell Jed that he shouldn't be bothering the women in the kitchen. He'll have plenty of food to eat soon enough."

Despite herself, Esther watched the exchange with amusement. She knew she should leave, but she couldn't just walk away. Watching David as a father was wonderful and sweet, and she felt that little heartbreak that reminded her that she might have married him if she hadn't moved to Ohio with her mother, if she had stayed with Abraham and Ruth in Honeysuckle. Sometimes things weren't meant to be.

David shook his head with a loving look toward his son, who scampered off in search of his brother. "I apologize. That's Jacob. He's five." He frowned. "I should have introduced you."

"You have been blessed," she said with a glance over her shoulder in time to see David's son run out of the room.

The men were shifting benches. The two of them were obstacles in their path, and Esther knew it. "I'm in the way."

"You could never be in the way," he said, and her eyes widened as she looked at him. He wore the calm, contented look of a man of *Gott*. But then, David as a young man had been calm and accepting with a deep love for *Gott* and his family. And perhaps her, she thought with sadness for what she had lost.

"It was nice to see you again, David," she said, determined to leave.

"So you don't have a husband?"

She blushed. *"Nay."*

He appeared pleased. "Then you won't mind me visiting on occasion?"

"Ja." She stiffened. She liked the thought of seeing him again, but what would the community think? "I must go."

He furrowed his brow. *"Ja,* I can visit or, *ja,* you mind?" he asked.

She gazed into his eyes, wanting him to visit more than anything. She whispered, *"Ja,* you can visit."

His lips curved in a beautiful smile that stole her breath. "I will see you again soon, then, Esther." He paused. "At your *dawdi haus.*"

She didn't disagree. Her mind reeled with thoughts of him courting her. She hurried away, escaping to the kitchen and the sanctuary of the women's company with the mental image of David Hostetler on her doorstep. She gasped. *Stop*, she scolded herself. *You are being fanciful. He is an old friend who wants to talk with you. Nothing more!* As she entered the room, she saw her mother and Lizzie chatting as they worked. There were several women cramped into the room and no one seemed to mind the close proximity as they unwrapped previously prepared food and set dishes on every available space on the counter and kitchen table.

Esther went to work. She wouldn't mind seeing David at the cottage. She wouldn't mind at all. But the proper thing would be to have Zack or someone nearby to chaperone them.

"Esther?" Her mother saw her as she approached.

"Ja?" Could her mother read her thoughts?

"We have two little boys who would like a cookie." *Mam* gestured toward the corner of the room.

Esther relaxed. "Chocolate chip or gingerbread?" she asked, eyeing the eager boys with a growing smile.

"Chocolate chip," her nephew said, and his friend Jed, David's eldest son, agreed.

She pulled two cookies out of Lizzie's cookie jar and handed one to each boy. "Go and eat your cookie, but no more treats until you eat a proper meal first. *Ja?"*

"Ja!" the boys echoed each other.

Stifling a grin, Esther shooed them out of the kitchen. "You may play outside until I call you when it's your turn to eat."

"They seem in a hurry," Ellen said, coming up from behind.

"Ja, they are eager to run and play."

"I did the same thing with Neziah's two a few minutes ago. They love their cookies."

Esther smiled. "Don't we all?"

Zack sat at the table with the men of their Amish church community. His nephew Matt had chosen to sit beside him. As he ate, Zack enjoyed watching Lizzie as she moved about the room serving the churchmen. Today, he couldn't detect her limp.

She looked calm and unhurried. She had managed fine during her first church service on the farm since Abraham's death. He saw her set down a bowl of potato salad and then pour some iced tea for Preacher David.

Zack caught her eye and signaled for her to come. "May I have some potato salad?" he asked.

She smiled and gave him a helping.

A little imp inside him had him waving her over again once she got to the other side of the room.

Once again, she came, and he asked for something else, and she brought it to him.

She went back to serving at another table, and he bent and whispered in Matt's ear. Matt grinned, caught Lizzie's eye and signed for her to come.

"May I please have some iced tea?" the boy asked with a straight face as he held out his cup.

Lizzie smiled but her eyes narrowed. She poured her son's tea and then asked Zack, "Would you like some tea?"

He shook his head. "But I appreciate the thought."

He waited until she reached the other side of the room again. There were other women who were closer, but he wanted Lizzie. He again caught her attention and gestured for her to come.

She smiled, but the good humor didn't reach her green eyes. *"Ja?"*

"Sweet-and-vinegar green beans?" he asked.

She turned to get them, her stance stiff. He had irritated her, and when she turned back, he couldn't stifle a grin.

Her eyes widened. "You are a tease, Zack Fisher," she accused.

"Ja." He regarded her warmly. "I couldn't resist. You are handling everything so well today. I felt the urge to give you a hard time." He grinned. "I wanted to make your day."

He saw her visibly relax. "You had best watch yourself, Zack."

Amused, he arched an eyebrow. "Or what?" he challenged.

She narrowed her green eyes. She looked flushed, her cheeks a pretty pink from rushing to serve the men, but mostly him and Matt. A sheen of moisture glistened across her forehead and a hint of teasing retribution entered her expression as she stared at him.

She glanced toward her son. "Matthew Fisher, you had best be done with your meal."

But Matt, he saw, just raised his chin, unafraid, as he continued to play his part. "May I have some more iced tea?"

And she laughed, a tinkling sound that shivered pleasurably along Zack's spine.

"That's enough, Matthew," he warned.

The boy sighed. "But we were having fun."

Lizzie glared at both of them with mock anger. "I'll show you how to have fun doing some extra chores tomorrow, young man."

But Matt could tell that she wasn't serious, so he simply grinned at her and said, "Aw, *Mam*."

Lizzie's face brightened and her eyes filled. It was clear that Matt had never called her *mam* before, and she was more than pleased that he just had.

Lizzie woke up Monday morning, feeling good that church services had gone so well. She had thought it would be hard, seeing everyone back on the farm when Abraham was absent, but Zack, Esther, Sarah and the children had made the day easier for her. They were her family. As long as they continued to accept her, she would be content.

She recalled Zack and Matt's teasing during yesterday's postservice meal. She'd felt annoyed when Zack—and then Matt—had called her over to ask for one thing or another. She'd been on the far side of the room when they'd gestured for her to approach. At first she hadn't understood why they simply hadn't asked one of the other churchwomen serving those seated near them. Later, when she saw Zack's dark eyes full of laughter, she understood. Zack Fisher had been teasing her with Matthew's help!

She went downstairs to prepare breakfast. She put on the coffeepot and took out eggs, bacon, green peppers, onions and potatoes. She decided to make omelets with home fries. As she chopped up the onion and green pepper, she found her thoughts returning to Zack and his playful side. She liked it. That he had enlisted Matthew's help in his teasing made her chuckle. Matt's expression when she'd pretended to be stern with him made her laugh out loud. As if thinking of the man had made him materialize, Zack entered the kitchen from outside. Her amusement faded and embarrassment took its place.

"Zack," she greeted. She was surprised to see him. She thought he'd been in the barn, tending to the animals.

"You the only one awake?" he asked as he reached for the coffeepot she'd prepared on the stove.

"For the moment."

"So we're alone," he said.

Her gaze shot to his face. "*Ja*, I guess so."

His expression was sober. "There is something we should discuss."

"*Ja?*" Her heart began to beat double-time as fear gripped her hard. "Is it about the farm?" Zack nodded. "You came to Honeysuckle to claim your inheritance."

She waited several seconds while tension filled the air, making it difficult for her to breathe.

She sensed him stiffen. "Who told you?"

Fired up by the truth, she faced him defiantly. "No one. I just knew." She set down her kitchen tools and crossed her arms. "And you didn't think to tell me that you are going to take away my home?"

His dark eyes flashed. "Did I tell you that I was taking your home?"

"*Nay*, but…" She felt her anger dissipate. "But you don't deny that your father intended you to have the farm and the property."

Zack shook his head. "No, I can't deny it."

Lizzie felt as if the life had suddenly been sucked out of her. "I see." She picked up a fork and began to beat eggs.

"Do you?" he said, his voice unusually harsh.

She looked at him and received the impression that he was disappointed in her. "I—ah—I don't understand."

He softened his expression. "Exactly."

She realized that she'd made a dreadful mistake. "You didn't come to talk about the farm, did you?"

Zack shook his head. "*Nay*. I wanted to ask you about the corn wagon. One of the wheels is bad, and I wanted to get it fixed and make sure you didn't mind."

Mortified that she'd jumped to conclusions, Lizzie felt the sting of tears. "Not if you think it needs fixing."

He nodded as he set his unfinished cup of coffee on the kitchen table then left. Lizzie stared as the door closed behind Zack's retreating back. Her tears spilled over, and she swiped at them with the backs of her hands as she returned to making breakfast. She had handled that badly, but learning the truth, that Zack was indeed the heir to the farm, had hurt more because he'd never told her.

She realized that she'd had a vision in her head of how their discussion about the farm would go. She'd ask him about his intentions, and he'd tell her that she was worried about nothing. If he had wanted the farm, he would have told her, wouldn't he?

But the conversation hadn't gone that way at all. Zack had admitted that the farm was rightfully his, but he hadn't given her any insight into his thoughts or his future plans.

Then why did she feel as if she had somehow disappointed him? Because she'd been angry—a sin in the Lord's eyes—and defiant that she wasn't happy to learn the truth?

Lizzie realized that confronting Zack had only made things worse. They'd laughed and enjoyed a good working relationship. Now the farm stood between them.

Dear Lord, what am I going to do? There was only one thing she could do: pray and dry her tears before the children and Zack's mother came downstairs.

Zack stomped toward the barn, aware that he'd been remiss in discussing the farm with Lizzie. Yes, he had come to Honeysuckle to claim the farm, but after getting to know Lizzie, he'd begun to rethink the situation.

She was upset that he hadn't spoken with her about it. He had meant to, but it never seemed the right moment. They had gotten along so well that he'd decided that there was no reason to discuss his inheritance. Why should they when he'd already made up his mind that the farm was hers as long as she wanted it?

He admitted to himself that he was disappointed. She seemed to challenge him, make him feel as if he were guilty of a sin by not talking about the farm sooner. He should have told her calmly that she had nothing to fear, but he'd been too hurt to respond. Despite the right and wrong of it, he was in love with his sister-in-law. Every day he fought his feelings, but even the thought that he was betraying his brother couldn't stop his growing love.

He should go to her and explain that he wouldn't take her home away, but he didn't think she would listen. Despite their growing friendship, she had made up her mind not to trust him in this matter and there was nothing he could do.

Her behavior convinced him that she didn't share his feelings. She couldn't care for him if she didn't trust him. Was there something he could do to win her trust?

He'd done all he could, he realized. And that made him sad, not angry.

Chapter Sixteen

Lizzie went about her early-morning chores, cleaning up after yesterday's church services. She entered the kitchen and stared at the counter. Several community women had left behind food. There were muffins and a pie, cakes and cookies. She'd put the vegetables and apple salad in the refrigerator Sunday afternoon. So much food, she thought. The community women had left enough to feed a huge crowd. It was thoughtful of them and it was nice to know that they cared about her.

"Lizzie, I stripped the beds for you, and I'm going to put them in the wash," her mother-in-law said as she entered the kitchen, carrying a basket of sheets and other linens.

"You didn't have to do all that work," Lizzie said quietly. Her confrontation with Zack hadn't gone well and she hid the fact that things had gone wrong between them. "I would have done it."

"Nonsense," Sarah said with a smile. "It's my pleasure to be able to help. I'm not one to sit idle."

Lizzie saw Zack's smile on his mother's lips, and she couldn't help responding in kind, although inside she was feeling anything but happy. She hadn't seen Zack since their discussion about the farm and the wagon wheel. In a way, she was glad because she wasn't ready to face him yet, to be reminded that her life on the farm was still in jeopardy since he hadn't assured her otherwise.

"What else can I do?" the woman asked, drawing Lizzie from her thoughts. "Surely there is more I can do to help."

"*Nay*, you've done a lot—too much. 'Tis been a *goot* workday, don't you agree?" Lizzie looked about the kitchen, pleased that everything was back in order.

"*Ja*. And services went well yesterday," Sarah commented, and Lizzie, despite her initial fears about hosting services, had to agree.

As Lizzie moved about the house, checking to see that all was in place, something occurred to her that made her begin to wonder about Sarah's insistence in helping with all of the housework. *It's not that I don't appreciate her help.* Did Sarah think that because of her bad hip she couldn't handle the work? She was certainly capable of house- and farmwork. Hadn't she been doing it alone since Abraham's death?

Lizzie drew in a calming breath and silently scolded herself. Her mother-in-law was a kind woman, who only wanted to contribute. It wasn't because Sarah thought her incapable of doing chores.

She caught Sarah's unfathomable expression before the woman headed to the washing machine in the back room. The memory of it made Lizzie self-conscious. *Stop it*, she admonished. Sarah was a kind woman, and they'd gotten on well. *Stop worrying. It's nothing! She knows that I can do my chores.*

She heard the closing clink of the gas-powered washing machine lid as Sarah put on a load of laundry. In less than a minute, the woman returned to the kitchen, and Lizzie offered her breakfast.

"Are the children awake?" Sarah asked. Her appearance was as neat as a pin despite having carried laundry down from upstairs.

Lizzie nodded. "Up, had breakfast and left for school." She knew she must look a sight. She had spilled milk on her skirt when she'd poured Anne a glass of it earlier and Zeke had accidentally bumped her arm. Normally, a stained dress wouldn't have bothered her, but it did this morning.

"They're gone to *schule* already?" Sarah widened her eyes. "Did I oversleep?"

Lizzie pulled dishes from the cabinet. "*Nay.* They got up early. While I made their lunches, Mary Ruth poured each of them a bowlful of cereal."

Sarah was thoughtful as she met Lizzie's glance. "Did you eat?"

"*Nay,*" Lizzie answered. "I thought to wait for you, Esther and Zack, if he's hungry." Since their mother had arrived, Esther and Zack had been eating regularly with them at the farmhouse. Would that change after her and Zack's discussion? "Tea?" she asked Sarah as she pulled out a tin of loose tea.

"*Ja,*" her mother-in-law said. She moved toward the window, peered out. "Zack is readying the buggy. Is he going somewhere?"

Lizzie shrugged. He hadn't told her of his plans, not after the way she'd jumped to conclusions. "To the Zooks', most likely," she guessed. "He must have eaten one of the muffins from the plate I sent over yesterday."

She would miss him at breakfast. She still cared about him despite the knowledge that he could forever change her life. "Has Esther eaten?"

"I'll check." Sarah immediately headed for the door. "I won't be long."

Lizzie had gathered eggs earlier. She grabbed several from her basket and cracked them open, watching as the yolks and whites slipped into her bowl. She then whisked them with a wire whisk, added seasoning and milk, then set the bowl aside.

Her hip hurt this morning. She'd been on her feet a great deal the past two days, much more than usual. On impulse, she took a bottle each of cider vinegar and honey out of the pantry. As she put on the teakettle to heat, she added vinegar and honey to a mug. After the water boiled, she added the hot liquid to the sweet and bitter mixture. The brew was an Amish cure for pain. She took a sip of the familiar tea, grimaced and added a bit more honey. She would try this remedy first. If her pain didn't ease, she would swallow some aspirin or ibuprofen. Whenever the pain became agonizing, she had something stronger to take that the doctor had given her. She rarely used the English doctor's pills. She didn't like how they made her feel, and if she felt forced to seek one for relief, she usually took it before bedtime or during the night if the throbbing pain kept her from sleeping.

Sarah returned within minutes. "Esther will be over soon. She said that she gave Zack bread and jam, but she didn't eat yet."

"I'm glad. Eggs? Ham? Potatoes and toast?" Lizzie asked.

"Sounds *goot*." Sarah reached for a cooking apron and tied it about her waist.

Lizzie sipped from her brew and then went to work. She took potatoes from the pantry and then scrubbed and peeled them.

"Would you like me to cut them?" Sarah asked.

Lizzie smiled. "*Ja*, I'd appreciate the help."

Sarah cut up potatoes and then suggested she chop up onions to mix in. While her mother-in-law handled that, Lizzie sliced a loaf of bread and then set out some of the muffins that Katie Yoder had brought the previous day.

She had noticed her mother-in-law staring at her as Lizzie cooked the potatoes with onions while frying the eggs. Zack hadn't been to the house, so his mother wouldn't know that they had exchanged words.

She slid the cooked eggs into a stainless-steel bowl, placed a plate over top to keep them warm. "Is something wrong?" she asked, catching the speculative look on Sarah's face.

Sarah stared at her a long moment and then commented, "You're not like my son's first wife, Ruth."

Lizzie felt her happiness wither and die. "I—I suppose not." She finished cooking the potatoes, dumped them onto a plate and then excused herself to get Jonas and Zeke. She ran up the stairs, fighting tears, refusing to cry, refusing to allow Sarah's words to hurt, but as in the past when she'd been called Limping Lizzie by some of the children, words still had the power to hurt her.

"Jonas? Zeke?" She entered the boy's room to find them seated on the floor, playing Dutch Blitz, a game played with four decks of colored cards. "Breakfast is ready," she told them, forcing a smile.

"Coming," Jonas said without looking up.

Zeke caught her eye and stood. Her little one appeared concerned as he approached her and slipped his little arms around her waist. *"Mam,"* he said. *"Mam."* He patted her back as if he saw that something had upset her. And just like that, she felt better. A child's comforting touch was all she needed to pull herself together.

Her thoughts chased one after the other as she waited for the boys to precede her down the stairs. She knew she wasn't like Ruth. Abraham had mourned his first wife so deeply that she'd wondered if he'd ever get over his grief. The older children had missed their mother with a depth that was difficult to see. Ruth had been special. She was simply Lizzie, the young woman with a limp. She worked hard, loved her new family and did what she could to help ease their pain. The little ones didn't remember their mother. The memories of her youngest daughter, Anne, included those of an unhappy woman who'd had problems after the birth of Ezekiel.

She was sure that Sarah didn't mean to be hurtful. They had gotten along well, hadn't they? After a short period of adjustment during which she had come to know Sarah Fisher, she had enjoyed having Zack's mother in the house.

Lizzie followed her sons into the kitchen. Esther had arrived, and the boys greeted their aunt and their grandmother Sarah as if they hadn't seen them in weeks instead of only hours.

"Everything smells *goot*!" Jonas said with a grin.

"I'm hungry." Zeke sat in a chair and waited as the women put the food on the table.

"I wish *Onkel* Zack could have eaten with us," Jonas said.

There was a flurry of sound from the back of the house. The door opened and Zack walked in.

"*Onkel* Zack!" the boys exclaimed.

"Is it time for breakfast yet?" He grinned, and her heart started to pound as she studied him. He didn't appear to be angry with her; it was as if their earlier discussion had never happened.

"I thought you were going to the Zooks'," Esther said.

"I will, but I've time. Didn't want to miss out on breakfast with my family."

Lizzie blushed as he looked in her direction. His wink startled her. "Do I smell eggs and potatoes?"

"With onions!" Jonas told him.

"Sounds *goot*!" He pulled out a chair and sat down, and Lizzie asked if he'd like coffee. "*Ja*, and some of the delicious-smelling food."

Zack's presence made breakfast enjoyable. Something about him made her feel better now that he'd come. Had she misunderstood his intentions? Jumped to the wrong conclusions? She knew it wasn't wise to think too much about her late husband's brother, but she cared for him, was unable to get him out of her mind.

Later that afternoon, Esther sat at the kitchen table, mending one of her brother's shirts. "*Endie* Esther, do you want to play Dutch Blitz?"

She smiled at Abraham's two youngest sons. "I must finish the mending." She had a dress seam to fix and a small pile of the children's clothes. "Let me sew Uncle Zack's shirt and my dress. Then we'll see."

She had offered to watch the boys for her sister-in-law this morning. She could tell Lizzie was in pain after the busy day of church services with a meal afterward, and cleaning the house the following day. Although Lizzie never complained, Esther had seen it in her eyes.

Her mother had gone with Zack to the Zooks', and they planned to stop to visit a woman she'd known years before. Preacher David had mentioned that Alta Miller was feeling poorly, and Sarah had been concerned.

Thoughts of this past Sunday brought on her musings about David. It had been good to see and talk with him after all these years. She'd felt like a young girl again in his presence, until she reminded herself that she was not only older but still unmarried.

David is a widower, she thought. *What was his wife like? Was she comely like Rachel Zook? Or plain and big like me?*

It wasn't that she was fat. She wasn't overweight, but then, neither was she thin or small. She was a tall, big-boned woman who had never found a husband. She had given her teenage heart to David Hostetler years ago and had never gotten it back.

She plied sewing needle into cloth in neat, even stitches, mending a torn seam on Zack's shirt before fixing the hem. The image of David and how he'd looked when they'd last spoken had stayed with her long after he'd left the farm. She loved everything about him: his bright blue eyes, the warmth of his smile, the way his expression grew loving whenever he looked at his sons. She still couldn't get over the fact that he was a preacher. His sermon, eloquently given and appreciated by all, had convinced her that the congregation had chosen well in making him a church elder.

It was a warm October day, and Esther had opened the interior doors and windows to allow the fresh autumn air to filter throughout the cottage.

"Hallo!" a deep voice called from in the yard. "Anyone home?"

Esther recognized David immediately. She pushed back her chair and stood. David was at her back door with his face pressed against the screen.

"Hallo," a smaller, young voice said, and Esther saw David's son Jacob at his father's side, his face pressed against the screen and peering inside in an identical fashion.

"David, Jacob," she greeted, opening the door. With a hand gesture, she invited them into her kitchen. Esther felt herself blush and hoped David didn't notice. She stood at the door, staring out into the yard, as she took a moment to gather her composure.

"I don't see your buggy," she said calmly, although she felt anything but calm inside. The man's slow grin did odd things to her insides. Her stomach felt jittery and hot.

"Jacob and I walked over. It's a nice day for a stroll." He smiled down at his son. "Jacob was hoping to spend some time with your nephews."

"Jonas and Zeke?" she asked. Jacob bobbed his head up and down. Esther noticed that her nephews had disappeared. "They can't be far. Jonas! Zeke!" she called. "You have company."

The boys ran out from a back room. Zeke held a fistful of Dutch Blitz cards, and several of them threatened to escape from his clenched fingers.

"Jacob!" Jonas cried. *"Ya* want to play Dutch Blitz with us?"

Jacob looked up, sought his father's guidance. David's gaze was warm as he met Esther's. *"Ja*, you can play for a while," he told his son.

Stunned by her reaction to him, Esther could only stare.

"Esther?" he asked with concern.

She shook herself out of a trancelike state. "It's nice that you brought Jacob to play." She found herself fumbling nervously with her apron hem. Seeing her mess, she hurriedly picked up needle and thread and the pile of clothes, then stashed them in her mending basket.

"Would you like tea?" she asked, playing the perfect hostess. "Or *coffe*?"

David studied her, his blue eyes assessing. "Tea, please."

She sensed him watching her as she put on the teakettle, took out two cups and two plates for the cake she'd quickly decided to serve. She felt herself tremble and paused, closed her eyes and garnered control of herself again.

"I only have tea bags," she apologized as she placed one in each cup.

"I know," he said with a small smile, and she recalled that she'd made him a cup of tea during his first visit. "I use tea bags."

"I've got cinnamon *coffe* cake. I didn't bake it," she spoke quickly. "Rachel Zook did. It's very *goot*, though. 'Tis her specialty." She reached to the far edge of the counter for the cake plate. She grabbed a knife and raised it to cut, then stopped, breathed deeply and faced him. "Do you want *coffe* cake? If not, I think there are brownies left. I'll check the pantry." She moved to brush by him on her way to the cottage pantry.

David reached out, his hand encircling her arm, making the air rush out of her lungs. "Rachel's *coffe* cake is fine, Esther. Then come and sit down. Enjoy cake and tea with me."

He had captured her attention; she was reluctant to

look away. She was afraid that she was mistaken in what she thought she saw—good humor and a keen interest in her as a woman.

"David—"

"Esther, make your tea and get your cake and then sit," he urged as he released her arm.

"All right," she whispered. She blushed, and she knew her face had turned an unbecoming shade of red. She avoided his regard as she fixed two cups of tea and cut two pieces of coffee cake. After she put tea and cake before him, Esther hesitated until David raised an eyebrow. She made a move to sit on the other side of the table, but he rose and reached for her hand, stopping her.

"Here," he said with a tender smile. "I don't bite." He pulled out the chair next to his.

She saw his gentle expression and felt herself relax as they took their seats.

"Tell me more about your life since you left Honeysuckle," he encouraged. "I want to know everything." He took a tentative sip from his cup. Something flickered in his expression. "You remembered how I like my tea?"

Esther nodded. "It was just the other day," she began, but she had in fact remembered from their early days together and she suspected that he knew that.

"So you didn't remember from when we were sweethearts?" His blue gaze seemed to caress her features.

"Not exactly sweethearts," she said, not agreeing or denying it. She was stunned how he could affect her still with only a simple look. "We were just—"

"Friends," he said as he broke off a piece of cinnamon coffee cake and lifted it to his lips. "*Nay*, we were more than friends—and you know it. If you had stayed in Honeysuckle, we would have been more to each other—much more."

Esther felt a rush of tears, which she blinked back. "I should check on the boys." She stood, fleeing to hide her reaction to his words. Had he missed her as she had him? She had loved him with the passion of a young girl's heart.

"Don't go. They're fine. I can see them from here. You're not running away from me, are you?" He took a bite of cake. He watched her as he chewed with obvious enjoyment. "I told you I'd come to visit."

"I know," she whispered. She felt twisted up in knots. This was David and he was a preacher. Why was she suddenly afraid to be in the same room? *Because you still care for him*, an inner voice whispered. *And you don't want him to know or feel sorry for you*. The last thing she needed was to have David Hostetler pity her.

Chapter Seventeen

David noticed the blush rising in Esther's face and was intrigued. He had never expected to see her again, especially when she didn't return for her eldest brother's funeral.

She wasn't married. He wanted to know everything about her—what she'd done after she'd left Honeysuckle, how she'd fared over the years. He couldn't stop looking at her; it was so good to see her again. He felt the years disappear as if she'd never left Honeysuckle. He had always been comfortable in her presence, but there was something more. Being with her made him feel alive in ways he'd forgotten. Till now.

She didn't say a word as he took a second sip of the tea she'd made for him, just the way he liked it. He was still stunned that she'd remembered.

"Tell me about Ohio," he urged. He waited patiently for her answer.

She had been staring into her cup and now she met his glance. "What would *ya* like to know?"

"Where you lived. It must have been hard after you lost your *dat*."

She nodded. "*Mam* was so unhappy. She said she couldn't remain in Honeysuckle on the farm. We moved to live near my sister Miriam."

David furrowed his brow thoughtfully. "I don't remember meeting her."

"I think you did. She is much older than us. She married when I was very young. She came home once or twice to visit but not for a long time before my *vadder*—" She broke off. Cradling her teacup, she stared into the steaming brew.

"I was sorry for your loss." David studied her bent head, liking what he saw. From the first moment of their meeting, he'd appreciated her features. She had smooth skin and a pretty profile. He had never forgotten the warm brown color of her eyes or the warmth of her smile.

She was quiet for too long.

"Esther?"

She drew a deep shuddering breath. "I didn't want to leave. I wanted to stay in Honeysuckle with Abraham and Ruth. *Mam* convinced me that it wouldn't be fair to them if I did. They were newly married and needed their time alone."

Her hand shook as she lifted the teacup. Afraid that she would spill her tea and burn herself, he reached out to cradle the cup and her hand.

"And so you were a *goot dochter*," he murmured.

She shot him a look, shrugged. "I had no choice." Sorrow settled in her expression. "I didn't want to go. I didn't want to obey my *mudder*."

"But you did."

She sighed. "*Ja*, I did." He felt the impact of her warm brown gaze. "You married."

David inclined his head. He had married at age

twenty-one and had spent five years with his wife. "I did. Margaret was a fine woman. And a *goot* wife."

"Margaret?" she asked quietly.

"Margaret Yoder. She was a year older than me. We had Jed during the first year of our marriage. Jacob came twelve months later."

He saw compassion in Esther's gaze. "And you loved her?"

He looked away. "I cared for her. She was a *goot* mother for the short time she was here after the boys were born."

"I'm sorry," she breathed, warming his heart.

He rewarded her with a smile. "The Lord has plans for us that we don't always see or recognize." He watched her eat a piece of cake, continuing to study her as she finished the bite.

He wanted to spend time with her. There was something about her that made him feel at home in her presence. He longed to tell her that he needed to see her again.

"Esther—"

"*Endie* Esther!" a girl's voice called. Suddenly the back kitchen door opened and five of Abraham Fisher's children entered the room.

Mary Ruth halted when she realized that Esther had company. He saw the girl recognize him and relax. "Preacher David. I didn't expect to find you here."

Jonas and Jacob ran into the kitchen, asking for a snack. Jonas saw his sisters and brother and stopped abruptly. "I'm hungry," he told Mary Ruth as if defending his request for food.

David watched Lizzie's eldest daughter nod in understanding.

Esther rose from the table. "You all must be hungry. Sit down and I'll give you cake or brownies, whichever you prefer." She looked almost relieved as she sprang into action, getting cups and filling them with milk or lemonade and then cutting cake and brownies.

As he watched her, David realized that the time for wooing had passed…for now.

He realized that he and Jacob needed to get home. Jed would be back from school soon, and he didn't want his son returning to an empty house. As he stood and told her he had to leave, he saw a myriad of expressions cross Esther's lovely face. Relief. Disappointment. Shyness.

And he knew that they would meet and talk again, for he wanted to get to know the woman Esther had become. This time he would court and win her, for he had a feeling he was going to love her even more than the young fourteen-year-old girl he'd loved many years ago.

"So how was she?" Zack asked his mother about her ill friend. He had left her with Alta Miller and run some errands before returning to bring *Mam* home.

"She's doing well," his mother said with relief. "It was bad for a while, she told me, but she's finally recovering."

Eyes on the road, Zack steered the horse left onto a paved country road, handling the leathers with ease. "What was wrong?"

"She has been suffering from depression. She went to an English doctor. He identified the problem and treated her with medication."

Zack heard his mother sigh and he flashed her a concerned look. "Are you all right?"

"*Ja.* Just remembering how it was. If it wasn't for Dr. Rosemont, I might not be here today."

"You had a skilled doctor, and while the treatments

were—" He searched for the right words but nothing strong enough came to mind. "—hard on you, you survived," he finished. "But you would tell me if you weren't feeling well, *ja*?"

She smiled at him. "I'm not *goot* at hiding how I feel. Esther and you can tell when I have the slightest irritation."

He regarded her with loving warmth. "We love you, *Mam*. We want you with us a long time."

She sniffed. "Apparently, I'm meant to be here on this earth longer than my eldest son—"

He squeezed her arm gently. "*Gott* loves us. If He felt it was Abraham's time, then He must have had a reason."

His mother was quiet for several moments. The only sound was the clip-clip of their horse's hooves on macadam and the squeak of the buggy springs and turn of its wheels.

"I'm glad Lizzie came into Abe's life after Ruth passed on," *Mam* said.

Zack had thought the same thing more than once. Lizzie was a lovely woman with compassion and the ability to love his brother's children as if she'd given birth to them. He realized the reason their conversation about the farm had gone wrong was because he'd been taken by surprise—and was hurt that, after getting to know him, she would think him capable of forcing her from her home.

"She's stronger. Better for Abraham than Ruth was." *Mam* bit her lip as if she'd confessed something she shouldn't have. "I told her so."

Zack raised his eyebrows. "You told Lizzie that she was stronger than Ruth?"

His mother frowned. "I told her that she is different than Ruth."

"And?" he asked.

"That's all I said." Concern filled his mother's gaze. "She—" *Mam* stopped, looked horrified.

"*Mam*," he said, "how did she react?"

"I don't know. At least I didn't think anything of it, but now I recall that after I mentioned it she ran out of the room to find the children."

Zack felt an ache settle within his chest. "Lizzie married my *brooder* only three weeks after his wife's death. I'm sure it wasn't easy for her. He would have been grieving, his children devastated. Seeing their grief, she must have wondered if she'd ever win a place in their hearts and in their life."

He heard his mother groan. "Because of me, she thinks she doesn't measure up."

"Ja," Zack said worriedly. That plus the fact that he hadn't assured her that her life on the farm was safe had to be weighing heavily on Lizzie's mind.

"I'll talk with her. Lizzie is stronger. She was better for your *brooder*. Had he lived, Abraham would have found joy in having a life partner who worked by his side rather than a weak girl who needed to be coddled."

Zack silently agreed. He had come to Honeysuckle expecting one thing and found something greater, more wonderful, instead. Now the girl who had stepped in to fill a loved one's position in the house was in pain. If his mother couldn't convince her, then he would. The last thing he wanted was to see Lizzie hurt. She had brought warmth and joy into the Fisher family and she needed to be cherished, not condemned, for marrying his older brother. Could he convince her that, despite her fears, he had her best interests at heart?

Lizzie lay in bed, staring at the ceiling. She didn't remember the last time she'd been able to lie down in the afternoon. Esther had Jonas and Ezekiel over at the cottage. With the rest of the children at school and Zack and Sarah away for the day, the house was quiet, eerily so. While she appreciated the time to rest, she also felt lonely, as if she weren't needed here. It was an odd feeling since she'd been busy to the point of barely being able to take a breath since she married Abraham.

Tears filled her eyes as she thought of her dead husband. Had he felt her lacking? Sarah had. She had made it clear that she was different than the woman Abraham had first married.

Her hip still ached but it was easing as much as it could, considering her condition. She had resorted to taking two ibuprofen tablets and wondered if she should have taken four.

She sat up and had a good cry; there was no one there to hear. She wept until she was spent and could garner the strength to carry on. She would accept whatever the Lord had planned for her. She prayed for guidance and became determined to put her sorrow behind her. The children needed her, even if no one else did.

As she lay down again, she thought of Zack and enjoyed the comfort of knowing he was near. She cared for him a great deal, more than she should. *Have I ruined our friendship, Zack?*

He hadn't said anything more about the farm. He'd come for lunch at the house with Esther. His good humor warmed the room and proved infectious to his mother, sister and the children. Would he change his mind about the property? And what if he didn't? Could she fault him for wanting what was rightfully his?

The thought of leaving her home brought on a fresh onslaught of tears. She mentally berated herself. *You are a member of the Fisher family*, an inner voice said. *You married Abraham, took his name, cared for his children.*

Zack seemed to have forgiven her their argument. Perhaps their friendship would mend—it already seemed as if it had. Things would be fine as long as he didn't discover that she was the one who had urged Abraham into the barn loft from which he'd fallen to his death.

A soft knock on her bedroom door startled her. "*Ja?* Who is it?"

"Lizzie? It's Sarah. May I speak with you a minute?"

Lizzie sprang out of bed and hurriedly wiped her eyes. It was at times like this one that she understood why the English had mirrors while the Amish didn't.

She straightened her prayer *kapp* and attempted to brush the wrinkles from her dress. Knowing that there wasn't anything else she could do to hide the fact that she'd been crying, Lizzie opened the door.

Sarah stood there, looking concerned as she tentatively entered the room. She walked a few feet, stopped and turned to face Lizzie, who hoped that it wasn't too obvious that she'd cried. "Lizzie," she began, and Lizzie was surprised by the woman's look of uncertainty.

Her strength and her desire to help others kicked in, and Lizzie became concerned. "Sarah, what's wrong? Your friend—Alta—is she all right?"

Sarah nodded. "It's not Alta I'm worried about. It's you."

Surprised, Lizzie raised her eyebrows. "Me?"

"*Ja.*" Sarah studied her intently and Lizzie felt herself blush. "Lizzie," she said, "I believe you misunderstood me this morning, and I feel terrible about it."

Lizzie didn't know what to say, so she waited for Sarah to continue.

"When I told you that you were different than my son's first wife, I meant that as a compliment, not a complaint. It wasn't until Zack and I were coming home from Alta's that I realized that you may have taken my words the wrong way."

Hope rose within Lizzie and the ache in her heart started to ease.

Sarah looked about the room, her gaze settling on her rumpled bed. "You were lying down," she said and Lizzie gave a nod. "Is your hip hurting you?"

Lizzie debated whether or not to tell her. Finally, she sighed and said, "*Ja*, but it's not as bad as it was earlier. I took ibuprofen," she admitted.

"*Goot.*" Sarah lifted a hand to rub the back of her neck. Lizzie waited for her to finish what she had to say.

"You and Ruth are so different," her mother-in-law began. "We loved Ruth—we did. We knew her all of her life. When her parents decided to move from Honeysuckle, Abraham asked her to marry him, and she agreed. She loved him—I don't question that. But was she *goot* for him? He loved her, as well, but as a wife, Ruth wasn't a strong woman, while you—Lizzie—I don't doubt for one moment that you were the woman he needed. You married my son while he was grieving, took care of his children and made him a home, and coming to know you like I do, you did it with compassion and love. You are a woman that any *mudder* would be proud to have as her son's wife."

As she listened, Lizzie felt a fresh rush of tears, but

she blinked to control them. Sarah smiled as she approached and placed a hand on Lizzie's shoulder.

"Danki." Lizzie laughed and wiped her face when she saw that Sarah had become emotional and was brushing away her own tears.

Sarah gazed at her a moment and then she put her arms around a stunned Lizzie. "Never doubt that I'm pleased that you married Abraham." Sarah released her and they smiled.

"Mam!" Anne's loud voice traveled up from downstairs.

Lizzie grinned. Her mother-in-law accepted her. Perhaps Zack and Esther accepted her as family, too.

"The harvest is the day after tomorrow. The Zooks will be coming. We have food to fix." Lizzie went to the bed, smoothed the bed quilt into place. Sarah moved to the other side and helped her.

They could hear running footsteps on the stairs.

"Mam?" Anne, the first child to enter the room, saw Lizzie and her grandmother. *"Hallo, Grossmama."* Rebecca and Matthew followed her in.

"Mam, may we have a snack?" Matt said.

"Mam, Nancy wants you to look at our papers." Nancy Miller was the children's teacher. She was young, unmarried and lived near the one-room schoolhouse in Honeysuckle.

Sarah met Lizzie's gaze with laughter in her eyes. "It sounds like everyone is home and life is about to get busy again."

"Thanks be to *Gott*," Lizzie said as she urged the children from the room.

Chapter Eighteen

On Tuesday, Lizzie, Sarah and Esther worked to get ready for the harvest. Although only the Zooks would be coming to help, Lizzie felt that it was always wise to fix enough food for a large gathering.

The children were home from school. The teacher had postponed class for all students until after harvest time, as the children would be expected to help.

Zack entered the house, his hands dirty and with a streak of soil across one cheek. "Food?" he asked with a grin.

Lizzie handed him a bar of soap and a towel. "You've been digging in the dirt, Zack?" she asked, knowing that he'd been working in the barn.

He regarded her with good humor. "*Ya* want me to wash first?"

She nodded. "Where is Matt?"

He looked out the window. "He'll be here. He's cleaning up at the pump." He slipped outside again and joined his nephew, where he proceeded to wash his hands and share the soap and towel with Matthew.

"All clean," Zack pronounced as he and Matthew entered the house.

"Goot," Sarah said. "Fried chicken?"

He nodded, and Lizzie felt his eyes on her. She loved this playful side of him. She removed the frying pan from the stove and forked up pieces of fried chicken and set them to drain on paper towels layered on a plate. She took a pan of cooked corn off the burner and dumped it into a serving bowl. Sarah had made mashed potatoes, and she set a bowlful in the middle of the table.

The children were chatty as they ate their meal while the adults listened. Lizzie continually felt Zack's eyes on her, and she frequently looked his way to see if there was a problem.

"Do you need anything?" she asked him.

He smiled warmly, his eyes crinkling at the corners, lighting up his face. *"Nay,* just appreciating this *goot* food." Lizzie inhaled sharply, aware of how handsome he looked. Zack was the first man she'd ever been attracted to, and the knowledge frightened her. It was wrong to feel this way about a man with her husband gone only a little over two months—and because Zack was Abraham's younger brother. Zack was friendly and helpful, and she was grateful their friendship was still intact. He seemed to appreciate her efforts in everything she did for the farm and the family.

"What time will the Zooks be here tomorrow?" she asked, hoping that talk of the next day's harvest would help her get herself under control again.

"They'll be here before sunrise," he said, and Lizzie expected no less.

"Onkel Zack, can we help, too?" Jonas asked.

"Ja, Jonas, you and Zeke can help, but it may not be

in the fields." He took a bite of fried chicken, chewed and swallowed. "Whatever job you have, it will be no less important."

Jonas and Zeke looked pleased.

Lizzie frowned. What possible job could a four-year-old and a three-year-old do? She would talk with Zack about the matter later.

Soon, they were done with lunch, and Zack and Matthew went back to the barn. "To check on the machinery," Matthew explained before they departed.

"Matthew has enjoyed spending time with Zack," Sarah said.

Lizzie agreed. "Having his *onkel* here has been *goot* for him. Matt took his *vadder*'s death hard. All of the children did."

"And you," Sarah said softly.

"Ja," she said truthfully for different reasons. "I can't say it hasn't been difficult, but we've managed."

Her mother-in-law handed her a clean, wet dish to dry. "You have more than managed. You've done a fine job, *dochter*."

Lizzie swallowed hard. *"Danki,"* she whispered.

"Mam." Esther returned from showing her nieces what to do in the house. "Would you like your sheets washed?"

"Nay," Sarah said. "Just did them yesterday."

Esther left quickly and Lizzie heard her call up the stairs, "None of the beds, girls! Just dust and sweep and make sure all is tidy."

"Ja, Endie Esther," answered a voice that Lizzie recognized as belonging to Mary Ruth. The girls had been helpful all day and Lizzie felt pleased as Esther reentered the kitchen. The females in the house spent the

afternoon wrapping the baked goods they'd made earlier that day.

That night Lizzie fell into bed, feeling as if she'd accomplished a lot. Her hip ached as usual but not as bad as it had in the past. Having Sarah and Esther's help as well as the girls at home had made chores easier for her. It was nice to work together. Lizzie felt happy in their company, and she looked forward to seeing Rachel and Peter.

The next morning, just before dawn, Lizzie climbed out of bed, careful not to wake Anne, who slept soundly beside her. She dressed quickly and without a sound. Years of experience had her able to roll and pin her hair in the dark. She slipped socks on her bare feet and then carried her shoes out into the hall, before closing the bedroom door silently behind her.

No one stirred as Lizzie crept down the stairs to the first floor and headed for the kitchen. She lit a candle from the stove and then set it into a stand on the countertop. Then she went to work by candlelight, filling a stovetop percolator with water and then the basket with ground coffee. She placed the coffeepot on the burner to brew, then pulled out dishes and breakfast items for her family and the Zooks, who would be arriving soon.

Lizzie paused a moment to enjoy the quiet and peer out the back window. There was a beam of light moving across the yard. Zack with a flashlight, she thought with a smile. She met him at the back door, held it open until he slipped inside past her.

"*Goot* morning," he murmured, his eyes kind and his smile infectious.

She answered him in kind. "Are you ready for a busy harvest day?"

He nodded. "Busy but exciting," he said as if he anticipated the harvest. "Is that *coffe* I smell?"

"*Ja*. Want a cup?" She saw his answer in his smile and took a mug down from the cabinet. She poured him coffee, added two spoons of sugar with a splash of milk and handed it to him. He accepted the mug and took a sip.

He gazed at her warmly. "You remember how I like my *coffe*."

"It's not hard." She reached for the plate of muffins and extended it to him. "To hold you over until we can serve you a proper breakfast."

Sarah came downstairs, followed by the children. They were all dressed and ready for the day's work.

"*Onkel* Zack, we're going to help," Jonas said.

"Would you like to be our water boys?" he said. "We get awful thirsty in the fields. If you can bring us water whenever we come back for a drink, that would be helpful. It's hard work but I think you both are up for the task."

Lizzie smiled approvingly at Zack over the boys' heads. Jonas and Zeke seemed eager to help. He had chosen the perfect job for them.

There was just a hint of light in the morning sky when a buggy pulled into the barnyard. "The Zooks are here," Lizzie said.

Suddenly, four vehicles followed the Zooks' buggy. Several more arrived and parked in a row in the barnyard. She recognized the Shetler brothers with Neziah's two sons. She waved to Bishop Andy and his family and several other members of their close-knit Amish community. Anne Stoltzfus arrived with fresh pumpkin pie and a smile. Lizzie raised a hand in greeting.

Surprised by the number of helpers, Lizzie followed Zack into the yard and caught sight of her friend Rachel, a basket in one hand and a plate in the other.

"What's all this?" Lizzie asked her friend, gesturing toward all the folks who had arrived behind the Zooks. "I didn't expect everyone." She was touched that the community had taken time from their own harvests to assist them.

"This is called help, and you'll have a lot of it today," Rachel said. She held up the basket. "I brought biscuits and pancakes. Both are still warm."

Lizzie widened her eyes. "How early did you get up to cook these?"

Rachel shrugged as if it were nothing.

"No earlier than all the other women here." Women and children had come with the men, each bringing their share of food. Ellen had driven over with Dinah Plank, ready to help Lizzie feed the workers.

"Lizzie?"

Lizzie turned, surprised to see her mother, father and two brothers.

"Mam! Dat!" She was glad that they had come.

William and Luke waved as they joined Zack, Neziah, Micah and Rachel's husband, Peter, along with a man she didn't immediately recognize in the dark. Lizzie saw that he was Joseph Lapp when he stepped into the house and set down a pail of goat's milk. Joseph made his living as a dairy goat farmer.

"Danki, Joseph," she said. "It's kind of you to bring this." She saw his face turn red as he nodded, then went outside. It was rare to see the man out and about. He came to church, then went home immediately afterward. But he never ignored someone in need. She wondered

how Anne Stoltzfus was faring with the man's goats always venturing into her vegetable garden.

Lizzie's mother brought fresh eggs and bacon that was already cooked.

"*Mam*, it's so nice that you came all this way to help."

"You're my *dochter*" was all her mother said.

"How did you know we were harvesting today?" she asked, pleased that her family had come.

"I told her," Sarah admitted, coming up from behind. "Your *mudder* and I stopped to chat in McCann's Grocery the other day."

Lizzie widened her eyes. "You know my *mam*?"

"*Ja*," her mother-in-law said, "but it's been a long time."

Lizzie watched as her mother grinned at Sarah. She hadn't known the two knew each other, although she should have guessed. *Mam* had been the one to encourage her to accept Abe's offer of marriage, an offer that most likely had been her mother's idea from the start. *She knew that Abraham was a widower in need of a wife.*

The men had gone into the fields and begun work. Some of the workers used corn binders while others cut corn by hand. Zack had replaced the broken wheel on the corn wagon, and she watched as he hitched up their black Belgian and steered the horse toward the closest cornfield.

Beyond the corn crop, workers began to cut and roll hay into large round rolls, which they left in various locations in the hayfield. The weather was good for harvesting, sunny and cool with barely a breeze to stir up the corn and hay dust.

The women set out food for breakfast and served the

workers who came in from the fields to eat. They didn't
stay long, as they were eager to get the job done. Lizzie
watched with delighted affection as Jonas and Zeke ran
to Zack and the other men with a pitcher of cold water
and plastic cups. Zack pushed back his hat when he saw
their eager approach. He grinned widely as he accepted
their drink offering, and then he took a sip before tap-
ping the brim of each boy's straw hat playfully.

The boys love Zack, Lizzie thought. He was better with them than their father had been. After Ruth's
death, Abraham had grieved too deeply to pay much
attention to his children. *And now all the children call
me Mam.* She had a feeling that Zack, Esther and now
Sarah's presence on the farm had something to do with
the older ones' change of heart.

Zack. She loved him. She stiffened, startled by the
realization that her feelings for him were more than
friendship, stronger than anything she'd ever felt or
known. She knew that she was attracted to him, but
this was more. She was afraid to hope, to long for something that she might never experience…a relationship
with a man who loved her as much as she loved him.
She loved him, which meant that she trusted him. He
wasn't going to take over the farm, not without considering her wish to stay.

The men were back at work. The harvest was coming along nicely. The morning flew by and suddenly it
was time for the midday meal.

The women set out the food on tables in the yard,
and the men came in to eat in shifts. Lizzie served the
men while keeping an eye on her children, especially
her youngest three. Jonas, along with Asa and Joel Shetler, ran to bring water and cold drinks to the workers

whenever they needed them. Lizzie smiled as she kept a fond eye on them until she realized that someone was missing— Ezekiel. She searched for her three-year-old, but she didn't see him anywhere. Her heart started to pound hard in fear as she recalled the last time one of her children had slipped from her sight. Jonas's injury had been serious enough for a trip to the medical clinic.

"Have you seen your *brooder* Zeke?" she asked Rebecca.

"Last time I saw him he was over there." Her daughter gestured toward the end of the yard where several children played running games.

Lizzie hurried in their direction, but she didn't see Ezekiel in the group. And then she heard his young voice.

"Hallo!" he called, drawing her attention to the barnloft window. Terror-struck, she ran into the barn, her stomach churning with fear.

"Zeke!" she cried at the base of the ladder to the loft. "Come away from the window." Images of Abraham's body on the concrete floor near the ladder haunted her as she began the climb up the ladder rungs toward the hayloft and her three-year-old son.

"Zeke, stay where you are. I'm coming!" Lizzie placed one foot on the next rung followed by the other. Each step higher hurt her hip, but she thought only of Zeke and getting him safely down without incident. "Stay away from the window. Not too close to the edge," she warned. "How did you get up there?" She spoke calmly, but inside she felt a mess of fear.

Her foot took a sudden misstep and Lizzie slid down the ladder, scraping and slamming her fingers on the rungs as she slipped. She jarred her legs and her bad hip painfully as she fell and hit the concrete. She cried out and lay there, gasping, her hands and hip hurting. She tried to get up, but the pain in her hip was too severe.

"Mam!" Zeke cried. *"Mam!"*

Lizzie looked up to see Zeke moving toward the ladder as if he planned to climb down. *"Nay,* Ezekiel. Stay!" she managed to gasp out. "Don't move!"

"Jonas!" Zeke screamed, and Lizzie looked over to see her four-year-old son enter the barn. He caught sight of her lying near the base of the ladder and hurried to her side.

"Mam!" He looked frightened.

Lizzie attempted a smile to reassure him, but she must have failed miserably because Jonas wasn't to be consoled.

"Jonas, run for help. Find *Onkel* Zack," she urged. "That's a *goot* boy," she whispered as he ran out of the barn, calling loudly for help.

After what seemed like long minutes but must have been only seconds, Zack entered the barn and ran to her.

"Zack, Ezekiel's in the loft." She pointed toward the hayloft. "Please get him down." Her gaze begged him to take care of her son first. She was relieved when he understood.

Zack climbed up the ladder as Neziah and Micah Shetler came to stand near the barn entrance, ready to lend a hand. "Zeke, come here," he urged. The boy obeyed and Zack grabbed hold of him with one arm and then climbed down to set Zeke safely on the ground. Lizzie sighed with relief and closed her eyes.

"Mam," Zeke sobbed, running toward her.

"I'll take care of her, Ezekiel," Zack promised. "You and Jonas, go outside with Neziah and Micah." Jonas and Ezekiel obeyed, and Neziah placed a hand on each boy's shoulder as he and Micah led them out of the barn.

Zack hunkered down beside her. "Lizzie," he whispered, "you're hurt." She felt his hand brush along her cheek, her forehead. "Let me help you."

He lifted her easily and carried her out of the barn, across the yard and into the house. Lizzie felt embarrassed as she caught Bishop Andy's disapproving look. She turned away, deciding that she didn't care. Being carried by Zack was a new and thrilling experience for her, and so she focused on the joy of his rescue. Surely, the elders couldn't find fault in a man assisting his injured sister-in-law.

She met Zack's gaze, saw concern in his dark eyes. She blushed, aware that she looked disheveled. She felt her breath quicken as she closed her eyes. Why did she have to go and fall in love with him?

"You all right?" he asked softly.

"Ja." She bit her lip. She should tell him to put her down so she could walk on her own, but the pain in her hip reminded her that if he set her down she wouldn't be able to stand. So she accepted his help, hoping that by doing so she hadn't ruined her reputation and his.

His breath stirred the tendrils at her forehead that had escaped from her head covering. She swallowed hard and wondered what she was going to do about her growing love for him. Zack entered the house through the back door, then walked through the kitchen to the gathering room, where he placed her gently onto a chair.

"Lizzie—" he began, his expression earnest. Whatever he had to say was lost when her mother hurried to her side after learning of her mishap.

"Lizzie!" her mother exclaimed. "Are you all right?"

"I'm fine, *Mam*."

Her mother shot Zack a grateful look. "Zack, *danki*!" She began to fuss over Lizzie as she asked Zack to get someone to bring her a bag of ice.

Zack left and brought back a bag of ice a minute later. Her mother, who always seemed unflappable, began to cry as she accepted the ice from him. "You could have been seriously hurt or killed," *Mam* sobbed, "and it's my fault!"

Lizzie stared at her mother in startled silence. She exchanged confused glances with Zack, who seemed to realize that mother and daughter needed to be alone. Lizzie heard him as he urged the curious newcomers who suddenly appeared in the doorway to leave the room. He then gave her a look that said he'd be near if she needed him, and he left her alone with her mother.

"I'm sorry," her mother cried.

"*Mam*, I'm fine. It's all right. I'm not seriously hurt."

"*But you could have been,*" Lydia sobbed, "and 'tis my fault!"

"*Mam*, how could it be your fault? I'm the one who climbed the ladder."

To her shock, her mother began to sob in earnest, and Lizzie could only stare at her in shock and discomfort. Finally, she reached out to touch her mother's shoulder. "*Mam*, sit down. Let's get you some water. Or would you like something else? I'll just ask Rachel to—"

"*Nay!*" her mother said, clearly still upset, although her tears had stopped. "I'm fine," she said more calmly.

"Sit, *Mam*," she urged softly, with compassion. Her mother's tears had surprised and moved her.

Mam pulled a chair closer and sat down. She reached for Lizzie's hand. "Lizzie, I know you think that I didn't love you like your *brooders* and sisters. But it's not true. There is something I should have told you years ago." Her voice was calm and even, but her eyes said differently.

Lizzie frowned. *"Mam?"*

"You don't have congenital hip dysplasia," her mother confessed. "You were injured in an accident when you were a toddler. It's my fault that you have that limp."

Chapter Nineteen

Lizzie stared at her mother as the truth began to dawn on her. Is Mam responsible for my limp? "What happened?" she asked gently.

Her *mam* sat straighter in the chair and Lizzie saw that she fought tears. "You and your *brooders* were playing in the yard. I was on the front porch keeping an eye on you while I did some mending. You were two. William was seven, Luke six. Susan wasn't home. The boys were playing ball, and you were toddling about the grass." She suddenly smiled. "You loved to pick wildflowers."

Mam drew a sharp breath. "I snipped myself with my sewing scissors. Foolishly, I got up and ran inside to grab a dish towel. I was gone less than a minute. When I ran back to the porch, you were gone and I couldn't find you. I asked the boys where you were, but they didn't know. They'd been too busy playing. And then suddenly I heard you crying, and it was an awful, frightening sound. You had climbed onto the other end of the porch and fallen off the edge. You landed awkwardly, and I knew by your cries that you were hurt. I ran and picked you up, and you screamed louder. Your leg hung at an odd angle, and I knew you were seriously injured, and it was my fault."

"*Mam*, it wasn't your fault."

"*Ja*, it was. I never should have gone into the house, not even for a few seconds." Her mother lost the battle with tears. "I took you to the doctor. He said that you'd sprained your leg and that you would heal. But you didn't. You started to limp but I gave it some time. I took you back to the doctor, but he said there was nothing he could do. You had damaged your hip. He said that we could take you to a specialist in Philadelphia, but he said it wouldn't matter, because he didn't believe that there was anything that could be done."

Her mother got out of her chair, knelt before her and took hold of her hands. "I watched you struggle for years. And I was the one responsible. I had hurt you and there was nothing I could do. I knew life would be tougher for you than my other children and so I became determined to make you strong."

Tears filled her eyes in sympathy for her mother. Lizzie understood about feeling responsible. Hadn't she felt responsible for Jonas's injured hand? What if his hand had been hurt so badly that he'd never have the full function of his fingers? She knew exactly how her mother must have felt. She'd been in her shoes but had come out on the better end. *That's why* Mam *treated me differently.*

"*Mam*." Lizzie studied her mother with compassion. "You're not responsible for what happened. It was *Gottes Wille*. I've managed to live a *goot* life, haven't I? And I *am* stronger because of my limp."

Her mother stood. "I urged you to marry Abraham."

"*Ja*, and because of you, I have a home of my own and a family. I love the children and I enjoy living on the farm. No regrets," she murmured.

Lydia looked at her. *"Nay?"*

Lizzie smiled. *"Nay.* I am happy here."

Mam's sigh was released with a shudder. "I love you, Lizzie. I always have. When I heard that you'd fallen, I panicked and thought the worst. I'm sorry I didn't tell you long ago." She examined Lizzie with a concerned eye. "You're in pain. Can I get you anything? More ice? Something to drink? Something to ease the hurt?"

Lizzie managed a smile for her mother. "Upstairs in my bedroom is a bottle of aspirin. Would you send one of the children for it? Ask Anne. She knows where I keep it."

"Lizzie," her *mam* said as she turned away.

Lizzie clasped her hand. "'Tis all right, *Mam*, honestly."

For the first time, she understood her mother and the knowledge gave her peace. Despite what Lydia had told her, she didn't hold her mother responsible.

However, she *was* responsible for what had happened to Abraham. She never should have urged him to go up into the barn loft. *Abraham's family doesn't know.* What would they say when she finally confessed the truth?

Esther was surprised when David Hostetler arrived to help with the harvest. He'd come with his two young sons earlier that morning.

"Esther," he'd greeted.

"Can we stay and play with Jonas and Ezekiel?" Jed asked.

Esther couldn't help smiling at both boys; they were small replicas of their father.

"*Ja*, you can play with my nephews." She looked at David. "I didn't expect to see you today," she admitted.

"Are you glad or sad to see me?" he asked, his bright blue eyes studying her intently. He was dressed for field work in a dark blue shirt and triblend denim pants. His straw hat was pushed back slightly, allowing her a good view of his features.

"David—"

"Glad or sad?"

She blushed. "Glad," she whispered.

He grinned. "*Goot*, because you will be seeing a lot of me in the coming weeks."

"I will?"

He patted his boys' backs, urging them to find Jonas and Zeke, before he returned his attention to her. "*Ja*, Esther Fisher, because I intend to win your affection."

Her heart skipped a beat. "*Ya* do?"

He nodded, his features softening as he studied her with a smile. "It's been years since you've been in Honeysuckle. I intend to convince you to remain here… with me."

She inhaled sharply. "You are sure of yourself," she challenged, upset by his confidence.

"*Nay*." His large hand settled on her shoulder, making the skin beneath her dress tingle and feel warm. "I trust in the Lord. I've learned to follow whatever He tells me."

Her insides melted. "And you think He wants you and me to spend time together?"

"*Nay*, I believe that He wants you and me to live a lifetime together."

"Why do you say that?" she'd whispered, feeling a little thrill.

"Because I've been praying to see you again since you left Honeysuckle when you were fourteen." He left her with that startling claim as he joined the group of workers in the barnyard.

Lizzie and her mother had had more than enough time to talk alone, Zack thought as he stood at the kitchen window and gazed out into the busy yard. The workers had gone back to work. The children were running about the yard, laughing and chasing each other. Zeke and Jonas, he was glad to see, had suffered no lasting effects from their mother's fall. He was eager to see her again, to see for himself that she was all right.

The knowledge that Zeke had climbed the ladder to the loft turned his insides cold. Abraham had fallen from the loft. Seeing Zeke up there must have terrified Lizzie.

"Lizzie," he murmured beneath his breath. A sweet woman who must have captured his brother's heart easily if Abraham had felt anything close to what he himself felt.

Emotion slammed into him hard, and he swallowed against a lump. She was his sister-in-law—his older brother's widow, and he liked her. Too much. It was wrong.

He knew that he should keep his distance. It was the right thing to do—but how could he? He was drawn to her. Seeing her, spending time with her, made him happy. *I love her.* He moved away from the window as Lizzie's mother entered the room. "Is she well?" he asked her.

Lydia King nodded, her eyes shimmering. "She is a *goot dochter*," she said. "Always has been."

"Is she alone?" he asked. Lydia nodded. "I'm going to speak with her." He hurried toward the gathering room.

Seeing her in the same chair he'd placed her in, he went to her side. Lizzie had her injured leg propped up by a wooden footstool with a fresh ice pack on top of her apron in the area of her hip.

He approached and saw her through the eyes of a man who realized that he was in love and that, wrong or not, he wanted her in his life.

"Zack." She met his gaze, stark joy evident in her green eyes. Tendrils of dark auburn hair had escaped from beneath her prayer *kapp*, and he felt the strongest urge to tuck those red strands gently back beneath her head covering and around her ear.

He examined her face for any sign of pain. She seemed relaxed and happy. He felt a tremor of relief. "Are you all right?"

"*Ja.* I'm fine...thanks to you."

He frowned. "Me?" And she inclined her head. He had carried her inside, but that didn't make him a hero. He shifted uncomfortably. "Did your *mudder* and you have a nice talk?" he asked.

"*Ja,*" she murmured as she gestured for him to take a seat in the next chair. "She told me something I never knew."

When he raised an eyebrow in question, she said, "I wasn't born with congenital hip dysplasia. I fell off our front porch when I was two and hurt my hip." She blinked as if fighting tears of emotion. "*Mam* felt responsible. I always thought she treated me differently because she was ashamed, but it wasn't that at all. It wasn't because she loved me less than my *brooders* and sisters that she held herself back from me. Knowing what I'd have to face as I grew older, she wanted to make me strong."

"You thought she didn't love you because you were less than perfect in her eyes," he said, understanding. He hurt for the little girl she'd been and the pain she suffered as a young woman.

Lizzie looked down as she fingered the edge of her apron. She suddenly seemed too shy to meet his gaze. *"Ja,"* she whispered.

"Lizzie." He studied her with a surge of overwhelming tenderness. "You are an amazing woman."

He saw her surprise as she locked gazes with him. "I'm just a woman," she said. She appeared uncomfortable with his praise.

"Nay. You're a loving young woman who cared for a grief-stricken man and his motherless children. I look around this house and see all the changes you made here since you came—wonderful changes." He recognized doubt in her eyes and sought to reassure her. "You wonder why I'm amazed? Because you made life better for my *brooder* and the children and because, had she lived, Ruth wouldn't have been as *goot* a mother and wife as you."

He saw pain cross her expression. He immediately rose. "What can I get you? Do you need me to carry you upstairs? Would you like to lie down?" She quickly shook her head. "More ice?" he asked as he watched her shift the bag of ice as if seeking more relief from the cold.

"I am fine, Zack," she said softly. She moved as if to rise, but then grimaced and sat down again.

He hunkered down beside her, captured her hand and looked up into her eyes. *"Danki,"* he said.

"What for? It is I who am thankful. If you hadn't come to help Zeke…" She bit her lip, an action he'd seen her do whenever she felt uncomfortable. Did he make her uncomfortable? he wondered as he rose to his feet. He hoped not.

"Zeke and Jonas?" she asked. "Are they all right?"

"Ja. They're outside playing. I had a talk with both of them. Neither one will be climbing into the loft without adult supervision."

Her brow cleared and she seemed relieved.

"Lizzie?" Her brother entered the room. He barely gave Zack a glance as he hurried to his sister.

Lizzie beamed at her brother. "William."

"William," Zack murmured with a nod. *"Mam*, Esther and I will keep an eye on the children while you talk with your *brooder.*"

"Danki, Zack," she said, turning her attention to her brother. Zack left quietly, not wanting to intrude on them. But he would return to check on her later. He wouldn't be able to stay away.

Chapter Twenty

Lizzie met her brother's questioning gaze and arched an eyebrow. "What?"

"You care for him," William said.

She paled. "I—" She didn't like the topic of conversation. "I don't feel well." Her feelings for Zack Fisher were her own and she had no intention of sharing them with anyone, not even with her brother.

William was immediately concerned. "Shall I carry you upstairs?"

"*Ja*, I'd like to lie down for a little while." Zack had offered to take her to her room, but she knew that if he did, she might end up making her feelings for him known.

William swung her easily into his arms, then carried her toward the steps. "Do you need more ice?"

She shook her head, and he continued up the stairs to her bedroom. Being carried by her brother was a different experience than being carried by Zack. William set her on the bed, and she smiled at him. "Close the door on your way out, please," she said. "I'll be down again soon."

"Not without someone's help," her brother insisted.

She conceded his point. "Would you send Matt up in a half hour or so?"

He agreed. After he'd closed the door, Lizzie lay on her bed and stared up at the ceiling. She recalled the strength and warmth of Zack's arms as he'd carried her into the farmhouse. She'd liked the feeling. She liked everything about Zack, from the top of his dark-haired head to the soles of his black work shoes.

She closed her eyes and envisioned how it might have been if she and Zack had met under other circumstances and her childhood accident had never happened. Would he have paid her any notice if circumstances had been different and he'd stayed in Honeysuckle after his father's death? Would he have shown enough interest to talk with her, spend time with her?

Her thoughts followed that direction as her hip pain eased and she slowly drifted off to sleep.

Lizzie woke up abruptly when someone knocked on the door and she recalled why she was in her room.

"Come in," she called out as she struggled to rise.

The door opened as she swung her legs off the side of the bed and tried to push to her feet.

"Lizzie, sit down," a familiar voice scolded, and she realized that Zack had come to help her, not Matthew.

"I— What are you doing here?" she asked nervously. He shouldn't be in her bedroom. Naomi Beiler and Bishop Andy would certainly disapprove.

He approached with a small smile hovering about his lips while his dark gaze held concern for her.

"I can carry you more easily than Matt can."

She blushed with embarrassment. "How long have I been asleep?"

"Two hours."

She widened her eyes. "The harvest," she wailed.

"Done. Everyone has gone home, including your *brooders*. You'll have to accept me as your helpmate."

She was relieved that no one but the family knew that Zack was here to help. "No need. I can walk on my own." She pushed herself off the bed. As her feet touched the floor, she couldn't control a grimace.

Zack made a *tsk* sound. Then he picked her up and carried her downstairs. "Lizzie, you can be stubborn," he said softly.

She closed her eyes, leaned her head against his shoulder, unwilling for him to see how much she liked being in his arms. He carried her easily down the hallway and stairs. She could hear the thrumming of his heartbeat in her ear, smell his clean scent, feel the soft feathering of his breath against the top of her head. He took her into the kitchen, and she lifted her head away from his chest. She didn't want anyone to guess how she was feeling.

Zack's mother stood at the stove, cooking dinner. Someone had set the table, most probably the girls. Esther came out from the back room and was the first to see them.

"*Goot!* You're up. Zack, put her in this chair." Sarah didn't seem concerned that Zack had gone upstairs alone to get her.

Lizzie waved her arm. "I should help with dinner."

Sarah turned as Zack placed her in a chair. "*Nay, dochter*, you shouldn't. You fell and hurt yourself." She eyed her with concern. "How are you feeling?"

"Better." Her hip pain had eased, but her fingers ached. She flexed her hand and realized that Zack was watching her.

"You hurt your fingers," he said, as if becoming aware of it for the first time.

She avoided his glance. "I'm fine."

"Lizzie," he said strongly. She looked up, saw the look in his eyes and felt herself tremble. There was caring and concern, and something else she couldn't identify. "Let me see."

She reluctantly held out her hands. "See? I'm fine. No bruises. Just a bit sore from when I slipped."

"Let me see you move them."

She wiggled her fingers. He seemed satisfied with what he saw—or didn't see. *"Goot."*

Sarah called her grandchildren in for supper. Soon the room filled with Lizzie's seven children. Each one came in, their gaze immediately settling on Lizzie. She smiled reassuringly. "I'm fine," she said.

Mary Ruth and her sisters grinned. Matthew looked more cautious and sought guidance from his uncle, who nodded. Her eldest son looked relieved.

Jonas and Zeke weren't as easy to convince. Zeke looked as if he would cry, and Jonas eyed her with a worried expression.

"Come here," she urged with a smile.

They obeyed silently, and she grabbed each of their hands. "I'm fine. Don't worry. Zeke, next time, don't climb up into the loft, *ja*?"

He nodded. *"Ja, Mam."*

"Jonas?" The boy looked at her. *"Danki* for getting help." She managed to smile at everyone except Zack, whom she was afraid to look at, for she feared her heart would be on display for him.

"Let's see. Your *grossmama* and *Endie* Esther made

a nice meal for us, and I'm hungry. I slept through the midday meal."

Everyone sat down, and Lizzie was pleased to watch as her family relaxed, ate and laughed as they talked about the harvest and seeing their community friends.

Lizzie's gaze went from one child to another and from Sarah to Esther…and then to Zack. Zack locked gazes with her, and she managed a smile that she wasn't sure was convincing. Something about his expression promised that he planned to have a word with her in the near future. She turned away, wondering what he'd hoped to say and fearing her reply. His behavior today both pleased and worried her. He was her brother-in-law. If only she could forget that.

In the days that followed, Lizzie and Zack worked side by side on the farm in easy camaraderie. Now that the harvest was in, Zack helped her with the animals. In the afternoons, he concentrated on making any needed repairs before winter set in.

"Lizzie, do *ya* have a hammer?" he asked one morning.

Lizzie looked at him. "A hammer?" She shrugged. "In the barn?" she guessed.

He suddenly grinned at her. *"Ja."*

She stared at him. "If you know where one is, why did you ask?"

Zack chuckled. "To see if you knew."

She laughed. He was irresistible when he teased her, which he seemed to do more often of late. It was as if the topic of the farm had never been discussed between them. Not discussed, she thought. She had done the talking; he hadn't given her an answer as to his intentions.

Her smile vanished. "Where are Jonas and Zeke?" she asked.

"Safe. They are with Esther in the *dawdi haus*."

She released a heartfelt sigh. Zack placed a hand on her arm. "Lizzie, they are fine. They both know to stay out of the barn."

His touch burned through her dress sleeve. "You talked with them." She casually pulled away.

"*Ja*. They understand."

She blinked back tears. "*Nay*. They weren't there the day their father fell out of the barn loft."

He reached for her hand, laced his fingers through hers. "That's a *goot* thing. It must have been hard for you to find him."

"*Ja*." She blushed when she realized that she was squeezing his hand. "I'm sorry." She attempted to withdraw, but he held on. She was dismayed how much she liked the warmth of his hand against hers.

"I guess I should get back to work," she said.

"Me, too." He gave her hand a gentle squeeze and then released it.

"Will you be back for lunch?" She still felt the warmth of his fingers as she self-consciously straightened her *kapp*.

He nodded. Lizzie stood a moment as she watched him walk away. The friendly familiarity between them, their teasing banter, she could handle. But as soon as she felt in need of his comfort, she was afraid. She had no right to rely on Abraham's brother, no right to love him as anything more than a brother-in-law. Yet she loved him still. He was kind and funny toward her, and she knew that no matter what happened between them in the future, he would always hold a special place in her heart.

* * *

The following Monday, Lizzie noticed that Sarah had become quiet. "Is something wrong?" she asked.

Sarah regarded her with affection. "I miss my other daughters—Miriam and Sadie."

Lizzie had not met Sarah's other children. "You want to go home," she said quietly.

Sarah nodded. "I've enjoyed being here, but it's time for me to leave."

"You will come back and visit?" Lizzie had become fond of Sarah and hated the thought of her going.

"*Ja*, and perhaps Miriam and Sadie will come with me. I think you would enjoy meeting Miriam most particularly."

"Your eldest daughter?"

Sarah nodded. "We are close, but it was not always so. At first, my relationship with her was the way yours was with Mary Ruth."

Lizzie was confused. "Why didn't you get along?"

"My husband was a widower when I married him. Miriam was ten. He and his first wife had no other children. Miriam was my child in my heart, and I had to wait patiently for her to understand. Fortunately, she realized how much I loved her before Sadie was born."

"You moved to be near Miriam after your husband's passing," Lizzie said, realizing how much Sarah's situation had been similar to hers.

"*Ja*."

"And you are as close as any *mudder* and *dochter* even though you are her stepmother."

"More so because of what we've been through together."

"Do you think Mary Ruth will come to accept me in the same way?"

Sarah tied an apron around her waist. "She already has."

"But if you leave—"

"That won't change, Lizzie. Mary Ruth finally understands that you are there for her no matter what and that you will love her always."

"I'm glad you came." Lizzie took out flour, sugar, eggs and milk in preparation for baking.

"I am, too. You are nothing like I thought you would be. You are more than I ever could have wished for my son."

Lizzie had never told Sarah about her role in Abraham's accident. Should she tell her? What if Sarah didn't understand? What if Zack found out and resented her for it? She couldn't tell, at least not yet.

Tuesday afternoon Zack sought out her company. "Lizzie."

"*Hallo*, Zack." Lizzie examined his grim expression and experienced a sudden chill. "What's wrong?"

He shook his head. "There is nothing wrong, but my *mudder* wants to go home. And I'll be going with her."

Lizzie was surprised. "*Ja*, she said she was ready to leave," she said. But would he come back or stay in Ohio?

"The harvest is in, and the repairs have been made for the winter."

"*Danki*," she whispered. She wouldn't look at him; she wouldn't cry. "When will you go?"

"The day after tomorrow," he said. "I already called for a car."

She nodded but didn't meet his gaze; she didn't want to look foolish. She had no right to ask for anything else from him. He had come, she had thought, to take over the farm, but he'd stayed instead to help her with all the things that Abraham would have done if he'd been alive.

"And Esther?" Lizzie dared to ask. "Is she going, too?"

"*Nay*, she has decided to stay."

"I see." Lizzie had noticed the way Preacher David followed her sister-in-law with his eyes. Was there a relationship brewing there? She was pleased that Esther would remain. "It has been nice having you here," she admitted.

Something flashed briefly in his dark eyes. "You, Lizzie Fisher, were a nice surprise. My *brooder* was lucky to have married you. You are *goot* for the children."

Lizzie felt warmth curl in her belly. She couldn't quite process the fact that he was leaving. She had to step away now or else break down in front of him.

"I should get back to work," she said.

"I have a few more things to fix before I go." Zack's gaze seemed to focus beyond the barn.

"Will you be in for lunch?" They were talking pleasantries when they should be talking about Zack's future plans for the farm.

He nodded. "I will see you at lunch, then."

As he walked away, she could no longer hold back the tears. The wetness ran down her cheeks, and she wiped the tears away with trembling fingers.

Back to work, she thought, pulling herself together. She must go on as she had before she'd ever met Zack Fisher. It wouldn't be easy, but she would do it.

Chapter Twenty-One

"Did you tell her?" Esther asked her brother as Zack entered the kitchen.

"*Ja.* I'll take *Mam* home, and it will give me time to think about what I want to do."

Esther cut him a slice of apple pie and pushed it in his direction. "But you will return."

"I have to." Zack gratefully accepted it and forked up a taste.

"Because you love her."

His shocked look confirmed her suspicion. "It's that obvious?"

She shook her head. "Only to me. I know you too well not to see how you feel about her." She paused. "You should have talked with her about the farm."

Zack was silent for a long moment. "She brought it up. I was hurt that she didn't trust me enough, so I didn't tell her that the farm was hers for as long as she wanted it."

"You should have told her," Esther insisted. How could a man as intelligent as her brother be so dotty headed with the woman he loved?

* * *

Lizzie approached the *dawdi haus*. She had come to see Zack and Esther. She'd wanted to ask a favor of Zack and to invite Esther to move from the *dawdi haus* into the farmhouse after Zack and Sarah left.

Zack was coming out of the cottage as she neared the door. His appearance startled her and she tripped and fell.

"Lizzie!" Zack crouched beside her and helped her to her feet. "Are you all right?" His fingers remained firm but gentle after he'd set her on her feet.

She nodded. He stared at her a long moment. "Did you need something?"

"I thought to ask if you'd allow Matthew to help you finish the repairs before you leave."

Zack's dark eyes filled with warmth. "*Ja.* He is learning fast and will someday make a fine farmer."

"*Goot, goot,*" she murmured. "I should get back to the *haus.*" She started to leave and felt his hand on her arm stopping her.

"What's wrong?" he asked. There was concern, kindness and warmth in his expression.

Lizzie blinked rapidly against tears. "You're leaving and we never finished our discussion."

"About the farm." His expression became unreadable.

"*Ja.*"

"I don't have time to discuss this right now."

"Will you ever have time to talk about this?" she asked stiffly. "*Nay.*" She held up her hand when he opened his mouth to reply. She could see the answer in his beautiful dark eyes, and it stung. "I will see you later." Then she hurried off, not once looking back to gauge Zack's reaction as she limped quickly away.

Lizzie stood on the covered front porch of the farmhouse, watched as a large black car drew into the yard and Zack, with Esther, exited the *dawdi haus*.

"I loved staying here with you," Sarah said from behind her.

Lizzie smiled at her with warmth. "I'm so glad you came. I appreciated your help, and the children loved getting to know you." She saw that Sarah had carried her valise out onto the porch. "Here," she said, reaching for the bag, "let me help you."

Sarah shook her head. "Zack can get it."

Lizzie smiled weakly and turned back to watch as Zack put his suitcase into the trunk of the vehicle. "I'm sorry you have to go."

Esther spoke with her brother then approached the farmhouse. "*Mam*, you're ready."

"*Ja.*" Sarah smiled warmly at her daughter. "You're staying here." Esther inclined her head. "Does it have something to do with the preacher?"

Her daughter's blush gave her answer. "I like it here in Honeysuckle."

"You didn't want to move when you were younger," her mother said. "I should have allowed you to stay."

"*Nay, Mam.* You were right. It wouldn't have been fair to Abraham and Ruth. I'm glad I went. It was important for me to be with you when you were sick."

"I'm well now." Sarah placed a hand on Esther's arm. "Stay and live your life."

Esther grinned. She turned toward Lizzie. "You don't mind if I stay?"

"I'm pleased that you are," Lizzie said. In fact, she'd been overjoyed when she learned that Esther would remain in Honeysuckle. "You've all given so much to me and the children." Her heart fluttered as she looked past Esther to watch Zack's approach.

"Zack—" Esther began.

"I'm here," he said from behind his sister. "It's time," he said to his mother. Sarah handed him her valise.

"You will let us know that you arrived safely?" Lizzie asked.

Zack held her gaze as he agreed. He addressed his mother. "All set?"

"I'll be right there," his mother said. As Zack headed toward the car, Sarah turned to Lizzie. "You're a fine young woman, Lizzie Fisher."

Lizzie blinked back moisture. *"Danki,"* she whispered, trying not to cry. "I hope that we will see each other again."

"We will," Sarah promised and then she asked her daughter, "You will write?" Esther nodded.

Sarah joined Zack near the vehicle. Esther trailed her mother but Lizzie remained on the porch. There was a huge lump in her throat, and she didn't want them to see her tears. She didn't want Zack to go, but at the same time she was afraid what would happen if he stayed. She didn't understand. Why was he unwilling to discuss the farm?

Zack assisted his mother into the car. While his sister talked with Sarah through the open window, he returned to the porch. Lizzie held her breath as he drew closer.

"You've done well here," he said with a look that melted her heart. She managed to return his smile. "I'll be back," he promised, giving her hope for the first time. He continued to study her with intense dark eyes. "And then we will have that discussion."

"We will?" she whispered.

He cupped her face, and she blinked up at him, aware of his touch. "I have to go, but when I return…" His voice trailed off. "We'll talk about the future."

Heart racing, Lizzie stepped away. "Have a safe trip, Zack." Whose future was he talking about—his or hers?

"Take care, Lizzie." Zack left her where she stood and climbed into the front passenger seat of the vehicle.

Lizzie waved from the porch as the car drove away with Zack and his mother.

Esther climbed the porch steps, her gaze compassionate. "You will miss him," she said.

Lizzie nodded; she couldn't deny it.

"He will be back."

"But will I be able to stay?" Lizzie murmured beneath her breath. Esther looked at her with concern until Lizzie smiled at her reassuringly. "Would you like to move into the farm *haus*? We would love to have you live with us."

"*Nay.* I'm happy in the *dawdi haus*. I'll stay where I am, if you have no objection."

Lizzie assured her that she didn't. "I'm glad you're here."

A buggy entered their dirt lane and pulled into the yard, drawing their attention. Lizzie recognized Preacher David Hostetler. Her quick glance toward Esther noted the revealing pink in the woman's cheeks.

"I have work to do," Lizzie said, excusing herself. "I'll leave you to visit with David."

Esther flashed her a look of surprise, and Lizzie grinned at her knowingly before she opened the door to enter the house. She couldn't keep her lips from curving upward as she overheard David greet Esther warmly and her sister-in-law's shy, telling reply. Once inside, Lizzie moved to the window to watch Esther and David as they walked together toward the cottage with David's youngest son, Jacob, running ahead of them.

She loved Zack. She had prayed to the Lord about her feelings, and she had the sudden thought that He approved. She loved her first husband, Abraham—it was a quiet love that had blossomed from friendship and the shared task of raising the children and working the farm. But her love for Zack was different. It was warmth and racing hearts and the wild excitement she felt just being in his presence. She loved Zack as a woman loved a man. She'd loved Abraham as a young girl cared for her mentor.

Lizzie felt a burning in her belly. She wasn't betraying Abraham with her love for Zack. But Zack might feel differently. She sensed that he cared for her, was attracted to her, but could he get past the fact that she was his brother's widow?

Chapter Twenty-Two

"I thought you'd left," David said as he walked with her toward the *dawdi haus*.

"*Nay*, I decided to stay." Esther was pleasantly aware of every little thing about him—the way he moved, the warmth in his smile, the tenderness in his azure eyes. "I like it here in Honeysuckle."

"Goot." His pleased voice made her look at him. "I'd like you to stay," he said softly. "I'd like to court you."

Esther felt her face redden. "You would?" she whispered.

He grinned, and she caught her breath. Age had made him even more handsome than when he was a teenager. "*Ja*. You're the woman for me. I felt it when we were young, and I believe that God brought you back to me for a second chance."

She didn't know how to respond. Joy filled her heart but she was afraid to trust it. "I—"

"I want to marry you, Esther Fisher, and I'm not patient enough to wait too long." His blue eyes regarded her with love.

Her heart tripped for joy. He wanted to marry her—

November was the month for weddings and that was only a short week away. She lifted her hand to touch her *kapp* self-consciously. "David—"

"*Ja*, Esther?" He stopped near her door and faced her, and she felt the impact of his regard all the way down to her toes.

"Why?" she asked breathlessly. "Why do you want to marry me?" No one had shown an interest in her since she was younger.

He furrowed his brow as he studied her. "Why wouldn't I want to marry you? You're a kind and compassionate woman. You were lovely as a girl and you're even more so now. I look into your eyes and see the truth of you. I love you. Never doubt my affection for you. We were made to be man and wife."

Joy flushed her with warmth. "I—I love you, too."

Her words made him grin and his blue eyes darkened to navy blue.

"The boys?" she asked. "Will they object? They must miss their *mam*."

"*Nay*, they barely remember her. They've spent time with you and your nephews." His expression softened as he glanced toward his youngest son, who had stopped ahead to watch a squirrel run across the lawn and climb a tree. "I can tell that they already love you." He faced her. "My sons need a *mudder*. They need *you*. Are you ready to be their *mam*?"

Esther thought of his young sons. They were adorable and sweet, and while she didn't expect them to behave always, she knew that she wanted to be their mother. "Your sons are precious," she said with a smile. "I'd like nothing better than being their *mudder*."

"Nothing?" he teased with a gleam in his eyes.

Face turning red, Esther laughed. "Except to have you as my husband." David grinned, and Esther knew that she would marry this man this moment if given the chance.

His voice dropped. "As I wish you to be my bride."

Tears filled her eyes as she gazed up at him. "After we left Honeysuckle, I never thought I'd have you again in my life."

"If you'd stayed, I would have asked to court you once we were older, and we would have married. But then you were gone, and so years later I married Margaret. We had a *goot* life together and when she died…" He trailed off, and she could feel the pain he must have suffered after the death of his wife. "I never forgot about you. *Never*. But I can't say that I didn't love Margaret, because I did."

Esther remained silent. He had loved another woman, but why shouldn't he have? Neither one of them knew that she'd return to Honeysuckle, and they'd been so young. Loving Margaret, being a good husband to her, was so like David. She would have been disappointed to know that he'd married without love. His successful marriage to Margaret boded a happy future for her and David.

David stood watching his son Jacob, who had gone on to discover Lizzie's freshly tilled vegetable garden. The boy glanced toward his father.

"*Dat*, can we have a garden someday?"

He blinked and smiled at his son. "It takes hard work to have a *goot* garden." He met Esther's gaze. "I admit I've been buying produce from Anne Stoltzfus, the local midwife. She's an avid gardener with the best vegetables for purchase in the area."

Esther could tell that he was concerned with her lack of response. "You said that you never forgot me," she said, bringing the subject back to the past. "I never forgot you, either." She blinked back happy tears. "Years ago, when *Mam* moved us to Walnut Creek, I wanted to stay in Honeysuckle to be near you." She sniffed and then tried to laugh but failed. "I wasn't allowed."

David tenderly wiped away her tears. "Your *mam* needed you," he said with understanding.

"*Ja.* Although I didn't realize it back then. I believe *Gott* has a plan for each of us. I realized after my *mudder* became ill that He wanted me with her to help."

He nodded. "And now He brought you back to me."

She beamed at him. "*Ja*, so it would seem."

David reached for her hand, clasped it within his warm fingers. "I want to be your husband."

The heat of his touch made her feel alive. "And I want to be your wife," she admitted huskily.

David appeared overjoyed. "Let's have a cup of tea and talk about our life together." He kept hold of her hand as they continued toward the cottage. "We can ask Jacob how he feels about having you come to live with us."

"All right."

They followed young Jacob into the house and sat, enjoying tea, while Jacob drank milk and ate cookies. His father addressed him. "Jacob, how would you feel about Esther coming to live on the farm?" He paused and Esther waited expectantly. "As my wife and your new *mudder.*"

"Can Jonas and Zeke come sometimes to spend the night?"

Esther chuckled. How like children to look at life

so differently than adults. With a glance, she sought David's approval and then said, "*Ja*, they're my nephews and I love them. They can come visit and spend the night."

Jacob bobbed his head as if satisfied. "I like Esther and I think she should marry us."

Esther and David exchanged happy looks. "Sounds like a *goot* idea to me," his father said.

"You're quiet," Zack's mother said as their hired driver drove his car away from the farm and turned onto the paved main road.

Zack looked at her, managed a small smile. "Just thinking."

Mam regarded him with understanding. "You didn't want to leave."

He released a sharp breath. *"Nay."*

"But you'll go back."

He certainly hoped so. He nodded.

"You needed time to think," his mother said, surprising him as she often did.

"Ja."

"You love her—Lizzie," *Mam* said, shocking him with her knowledge of his feelings and thoughts.

"She was my *brooder*'s wife." Despite his feelings for Lizzie, he still struggled with the thought that his love for Lizzie was a betrayal to Abraham.

"She is your *brooder*'s widow," his mother pointed out gently. "He is no longer with us." She paused, placed a hand on his arm. "He is with his beloved Ruth now. Why shouldn't you be with the woman you love?"

Zack felt his throat tighten with emotion. "You don't think me wrong for feeling the way I do?"

"I told Lizzie and I'm going to tell you. She is a woman I'd be happy to have as my son's wife." She smiled. "You are my son, *ja?*"

Despite himself, he chuckled. "*Ja.* There is no doubt about that. *Dat* always said that I take after you in stubbornness and determination."

"That you do, Zack." Her smile widened. "Since we are so alike, I suggest you think about what I would do if I were you." She squeezed his arm gently before releasing it. "If I were a man who loved a woman as much as you obviously love Lizzie, I'd take my mother home and head back as quickly as possible to Pennsylvania. Then I'd do everything I could to win her heart so that she'll marry me and spend the rest of her life with me... but that's only what I'd do if I were you."

A gust of wind blew through the open car window, and his mother reached up to hold her head covering in place. Their driver apologized and rolled up the glass.

"That sounds like you," he said with a grin.

"And you," she pointed out. "There is something else you need to think about," she continued. "If Lizzie hadn't married your *brooder*, then you and she never would have met. What if Lizzie was meant to marry Abraham because the Lord's plan was for her to be with you?"

"I never thought of it that way." Zack leaned in to kiss her cheek. He felt a lightening in spirit; he was pleased that his mother saw things differently. "I love you, *Mam*," he said softly. "You are a smart woman."

Sarah lifted her chin as she straightened her *kapp*. "*Mudder* always knows best, son. Never forget that."

"Abraham!" Lizzie screamed as she jerked awake. As she sat up in bed, she realized that she'd been trapped in

her recurring nightmare. It had been weeks since she'd
had the dream, but apparently it was back to haunt her
sleep and her waking hours. In the nightmare, she re-
lived the day of her husband's death, when she'd gone
into the barn and found Abraham's broken and bleeding
body lying on the hard concrete floor. He had taken a
tumble from the loft after climbing up to remove a nest
of kittens. Lizzie had asked him to bring them down
because she'd feared the children would be unable to
resist the climb to visit with them and then fall.

I'm responsible, she thought. If only she'd blocked
off the base of the ladder instead of asking him to take
down the kittens.

Her heart beat rapidly as she sat up in bed, shuddering, hugging herself with her arms. It was afternoon.
The older children were still in school, the younger
ones with Esther at the *dawdi haus*. She had decided
to try to nap because sleep had eluded her since Zack's
departure. *And now I'm dreaming of Abraham's death
while napping.* Would she ever be free of the nightmare?

Tears rolled down her cheeks as she pressed a hand
over her thundering heart. "I'm sorry, Abraham," she
sobbed softly. "You were a *goot* man and husband."

She longed for Zack. She missed having him near.
He said that they would talk when he came back, but
would he return or would he change his mind?

And if he doesn't come back, what then? Lizzie
gasped a sob of pain. She brushed her tears away but
she couldn't stop crying.

I love him.

But does he have feelings for me?

She climbed off the bed and moved to the adjoining
sewing room, the place where she'd slept alone dur-

ing the first year of her marriage. She took up a needle and worked on Mrs. Emory's daughter's wedding quilt, which was coming along nicely. She concentrated on the task of making neat, even stitches in her attempt to block out the horrible images in her nightmare.

Quilting and other crafts continued to be her solace when she couldn't sleep. The work was also her joy during the happy occasions in her life. Quilting was the Lord's gift to her, and she was grateful for the talent He gave her.

As she fingered the quilt's edge, Lizzie closed her eyes and prayed. *Please, Lord, help me to accept whatever happens. Give me the strength to endure and the knowledge of Your will.*

Lizzie sighed as she left the sewing room. She needed to bathe. Her body ached all over, especially her hip. The hot water would help ease the soreness, and then afterward she'd fix herself a vinegar-and-honey tea.

She filled up the tub after carrying clean clothes into the bathroom. She felt her eyes tear as she turned the tap and adjusted the water temperature. "Come back, Zack," she whispered. She prayed for him to return. No matter what they might discuss during their talk, she knew one thing.

She loved him with all her heart.

Chapter Twenty-Three

Lizzie kneaded fresh bread dough at the kitchen worktable. She planned to make several loaves today for her, the children and for Esther to keep in the cottage freezer. She smiled as she thought of her sister-in-law. She and the good preacher were spending a lot of time together. Late yesterday afternoon, Esther had confided in Lizzie about David's marriage proposal. Lizzie had been happy and excited for her.

"Am I foolish for agreeing to wed him?" she'd asked. "I'm not a young girl."

"He loves you. You love him." They'd been sharing a pot of tea, and Lizzie had set her teacup back onto its saucer. "You'll be foolish if you don't marry him."

Esther had eyed her curiously. "It wasn't the same for you when you married my *brooder*," she said as if she'd just realized it.

"*Nay*, but I don't regret my choice. Your *brooder* had lost his beloved wife. I came into the household when he and the children were grieving. It was difficult at first, but things got better between him, the children and me."

"But you were not the *mudder* they'd lost." Esther reached for Lizzie's hand.

Lizzie had managed a smile, although remembering that time in her marriage was difficult for her. "*Nay*, I'll admit that life here wasn't easy at first. The older children resented me, but Anne, Jonas and Zeke accepted my love and loved me in return. That was all that I needed to keep me going."

Esther gave her fingers a squeeze and then withdrew. "I hope someday that you're as happy as I am."

"That's a lovely hope, Esther." But without Zack's love, she knew such happiness would be elusive.

Esther had hugged her, and Lizzie had returned the embrace with tears in her eyes.

Thinking back to their conversation, Lizzie felt glad for Esther. She would do everything she could to make sure that Esther and David's marriage ceremony would be a celebration to remember.

Zack will come, she thought with a tingle of anticipation. He wouldn't stay away from his sister's wedding. She had thought that Zack would have returned by now. He had promised to come back, but other than a call to Beachey's Craft Shop to say that he and Sarah had arrived in Walnut Creek safely, there had been no word or sign of him.

Lizzie froze while working the bread dough. She wiped her brow with the back of her hand. Closing her eyes a moment, she sought to regain her balance, and then she went back to working the bread. Lizzie focused all of her attention on the work so that she wouldn't think, wouldn't worry that her feelings for him were unreciprocated.

She pounded the dough with her fist, rolled it and

then kneaded and pressed it. Lizzie was so involved in the work that she barely heard the door opening behind her. It was as the door shut with a click that she realized she was no longer alone.

"Mary Ruth?" Since it was late afternoon, she figured the children had returned from school. Her eldest daughter was usually the first to arrive, with the other children coming a few minutes afterward. She was deeply touched that all seven of them had continued to treat her with respect and love. Every time one of them called her *Mam*, her heart melted.

Mary Ruth hadn't said a word, so Lizzie said, "Not a *goot* day?"

"It's an extremely *goot* day," a deep masculine voice answered.

She gasped and faced him. "Zack," she breathed.

He looked wonderful. She studied his handsome face, noting the red in his cheeks from the cooling temperatures, the warm gleam in his dark eyes and the heart-stopping smile that curved up the corners of his attractive mouth.

"Lizzie," he said as he approached. She couldn't move as she stared at him. The last thing she'd expected was to see him again—so soon after his departure.

And while joy filled her at the sight of him, a niggle of fear filtered through the gladness, dimming the happiness as she wondered about the talk they were going to have.

"You—you're back. Did Sarah come with you?"

He shook his head. "*Nay, Mam* wanted to stay."

Her hands were covered with flour and she knew there were streaks of flour dust on her face. "I wondered if you'd changed your mind." The intensity of his gaze made her look away.

"Lizzie." His voice was soft, almost tender.

She was surprised to see a look in his eyes that she'd never expected to see. Affection. *Love.* She drew herself to her full five-foot height. *Nay*, he didn't love her. She was a fool for even entertaining the thought.

Zack studied her closely. A myriad of emotions passed through his expression. "Walk outside with me," he urged.

"I'm making bread," she hedged. What if she were wrong about the warmth in his dark eyes?

"The bread can wait." His presence frightened her, not because she was afraid of him, but because her love for him was so strong.

"Do I need a coat?" She covered the dough with a clean tea towel, then went to the sink to wash her hands. She tried brushing off her face to remove any flour dust and then gave up because he'd already seen her.

"*Ja.* It's chilly," he warned. Lizzie retrieved her winter coat from a wall hook and was startled when he took it from her hand and held it while she slipped her arms into its long sleeves. She felt the weight of his hands settle briefly on her shoulders before he released her and stepped back.

Lizzie couldn't contain a shiver as she stepped into the chilly outside air. She didn't feel the cold; she was too aware of Zack beside her. It was only as she began to fear their discussion, what he had to say about the farm, that she experienced a chill.

They walked past the barn and into an open field until they were out of view of the farmhouse and cottage. Zack stopped suddenly, placed his hands on her shoulders and turned her to face him.

"There is something I need to tell you."

Aware that he didn't remove his hands, Lizzie trembled, expecting the worst. *"Ja?"* She stared at him. "Is it time for our discussion?"

He furrowed his brow. "Discussion?"

"About the farm."

He nodded. "About the farm...and something else." He focused his dark eyes on her.

She closed her eyes. "Something else?" she echoed.

"Lizzie, look at me."

She reluctantly opened her eyes.

"I had time to think about the farm—and you—while I was away."

"You're going to move into the farm *haus*," she said. She hugged herself with her arms as she met his gaze. "Zack, I know the farm is rightfully yours. Abraham was only managing the farm until you were old enough."

"I admit that it was my first thought when I learned that you had married my *brooder*," he said, and Lizzie felt a shaft of pain. He reached for her hand, pressed it against his chest. "I didn't know you. How could I leave the farm to a woman I didn't know? How could I leave his children with a stranger?"

"I understand." He must have been shocked to learn that Abraham had remarried, especially given the knowledge that his brother had been deeply in love with his first wife.

"And then I met you. You were nothing like I expected." He gave her a crooked smile. "You were a slip of a girl, and I didn't know if or how you would manage. So I convinced Esther to move into the *dawdi haus* with me." He smiled and the warmth of it made her breath catch. "It didn't take long before I saw that you managed," he said, "well beyond my expectations."

"And you were torn," she offered, understanding how he must have felt. "You wanted the farm, but I was living in the farmhouse with the children."

He gave her a nod. "But then I saw how hard you worked and how much you loved the children. I saw your kindness and compassion and the way you gave of yourself to everyone and everything, and I—" Lizzie blinked up at him "—started to care for you."

She felt her heart leap in hope. "You did?" she said, unable to believe it was true.

Zack nodded. He lifted a hand to touch her cheek. The warmth of his fingers sent away the cold. He caught her other hand, placed it next to the one against his coat front. "I love you, Lizzie. I want to spend the rest of my life with you."

Lizzie stared at him in shock. *"You...love...me?"* She was afraid to hope, afraid to believe. She didn't know what to think. He couldn't possibly love her—it was all too good to be true. "You can have the farm," she said. "Just please let me keep the children. I don't know where we'll go, but we won't stay and be in your way."

He frowned. *"Nay*, you'll not be going anywhere. The farm is yours. I don't want it if you're not living here with me as my bride. I'm not asking to marry you so that I can have the farm. I want to wed you because I love you and want you to be my wife. The farm will always be your home, and if you don't love me as I do you, then I will leave and return to Ohio."

"You love me," she gasped, blinking against tears of joy. "You really love me as much as I love you?"

"You love me?" he said, his dark eyes brightening with joy. "Thanks be to *Gott*," he breathed. "Then it's set. We'll marry next month—"

Zack had yet to learn the truth of Abraham's death and her role in it. She retreated several steps back, her spirits plummeting. *"Nay,"* she said. "I can't. You won't want to, once you find out what I did."

Zack tried to pull her into his arms, but she resisted. "Tell me what's so terrible that I won't want to marry you."

"I'm responsible for your *brooder*'s death."

"*Nay*, I don't believe it."

"It's true." She hid her trembling hands in the folds of her skirt. Lizzie released a sob. "That day…there were kittens in the hayloft. I was afraid that the children would try to climb up to see them. I didn't want them to fall and get hurt, and so I asked—*begged*—your *brooder* to go up and bring them down."

She hugged herself, lost in the awful memory of that terrible day. "I still don't know exactly how it happened, but when he didn't come back to the house, I went to check on him. I—I found him lying in a pool of blood on the cement floor. He had fallen from the loft and landed hard."

She realized she was crying openly and swiped a hand across her wet cheeks. "I could tell by the angle of his head that he had broken his neck and died instantly." The tears splashed onto her hand that held the collar of her coat closed. "The blood was from where he hit his head." She dashed a hand across her face.

He stared at her in silence. She spun as if to escape. "Lizzie—" His soft, even voice stopped her.

"I'm sorry," she whispered brokenly. "Your *brooder* was a *goot* man. He didn't deserve to die."

Zack pulled her into his arms, stroked her hair as she leaned into his strength. "You're not responsible for his death, Lizzie. It was his time. *Gott* called him home. It was *Gottes Wille*. You were thinking of the children's safety and that's a *goot* thing. Do you know how many times Abraham climbed into that loft?" he asked.

She shook her head as she met his gaze.

"Hundreds of times." He regarded her with tenderness. "You are *not* responsible for his death."

"I'm not?" Dare she believe him?

Zack shook his head. *"Nay."*

She began to tremble. She felt a burning in her gut that spread to her throat and her eyes. "I'm sorry," she gasped, turning to escape.

He caught her arm, drew her back into his embrace. "You've carried the weight of this on your shoulders," he said gently. His gaze filled with compassion and understanding. "You should have told me sooner. I would have comforted you if I'd known."

"You would have?" she ventured, afraid to hope. He didn't blame her for his brother's death. His concern was only for her. She recognized his love for her in his eyes. Lizzie caught her breath with joy.

Zack settled his head on hers. "Marry me."

"I'm a cripple," she gasped. "Why would you want to marry me?"

"You are not a cripple." He caressed her cheek, her shoulder. "You face life with spirit and everything you have to offer." He cradled her cheek and stroked her with his gaze. "I love you. Let me court you starting now, right from this moment. We can post the banns and marry next month."

Lizzie saw the further proof of his love in his smile. *He loves me!*

"I don't know if I can have children with this hip," she said sadly. She would tell him about her miscarriage later. That belonged to her marriage with Abraham, and her life with Zack was a fresh start, a new beginning.

"We have seven children. Why should we need more? The choice is the Lord's and not ours to make." He smiled as he touched her cheek. "You alone make me happy."

She ran trembling fingers along his jaw. "Then I will marry you, Zack Fisher. And I will love you forever and until the end of time."

Zack shook his head. "And I'll love you for as long as I live and beyond."

With a cry of happiness she hugged him, loving the feel of his strong arms around her. They held each other quietly for a time. Lizzie loved the rhythm of his steady heartbeat beneath her ear and his soft breaths against her neck and head.

"Mam?" she heard Mary Ruth call.

"The children!" Lizzie gasped. Would they be happy about their plans to marry?

"They love you as I do," Zack said, sensing her concern. "They'll be happy to share our lives as a family."

"Then we should tell them the news." He released her reluctantly, and Lizzie clasped his hand as they started back toward the farmhouse. Lizzie recalled the forgotten bread dough and understood why Mary Ruth sounded concerned.

The children were in the yard as they strolled hand in hand toward the farmhouse. Mary Ruth was the first to catch sight of their approach.

Mary Ruth grinned as she glanced down at their clasped hands. "Welcome back, *Onkel* Zack. *Mam*, I can tell you're glad to have him back." Her eyes twinkled. "So when are you getting married?"

Lizzie released a pent-up breath. Her daughter's simple words were enough to reassure her and Zack that all would be well in the Fisher household. *Thanks be to* Gott.

Epilogue

Lizzie and Zack decided to marry on the third Thursday of November. Esther and David decided to wed, as well, and share their special day. Their banns had been published in church right after the brides-to-be had accepted their sweethearts' wedding proposals. The November morning of their wedding day was chilly, but Lizzie and Esther were too excited to care about the cold weather. They had talked until late the previous evening before retiring to their rooms for a good night's sleep. Their only thoughts were of love and their spouses.

It was not yet dawn, and the farmhouse overflowed with family and friends. Fifteen married couples had come the previous day to prepare the wedding feast and set up the house for the bridal party and guests. Lizzie was in her upstairs bedroom donning her wedding gown with Mary Ruth's help. The plain dress of light green, according to her daughter, brightened her eyes and made her beautiful. Lizzie's mother and sisters were also in the room. They had come to help the bride and wish Lizzie happiness.

After Mary Ruth was called downstairs, *Mam* pinned

Lizzie's dress closed and fixed her hair. Lizzie knew it gave her mother pleasure to see her happy and in love, so she regarded *Mam* with a tender smile as *Mam* stepped back and studied her with affection.

"Are you ready?" her sister Katherine had asked.

Lizzie smiled with pure joy. "*Ja*, Katie. I've never been more so."

It had been months since she'd seen either one of her sisters. Katherine had been too busy at home to visit, walking about with Mark Troyer, while her married sister, Susan, had been living in Indiana with Amos Mast, her husband of six years. All of her siblings had come for her wedding, and Lizzie was pleased and grateful to have them share in the day. Her relationship with her mother had improved since her mother had confessed that she felt responsible for Lizzie's limp. Lizzie finally felt her mother's love.

"You look…lovely," *Mam* said.

"*Danki,*" Lizzie whispered. She reached to capture her mother's hand and then turned toward her sisters with her other hand extended. "*Mam*, Katie, Susan— I'm so happy you're here."

The females in the King family blinked rapidly against tears of emotion. They formed a circle and briefly held hands. "We should head downstairs," her mother said briskly. "There's still much to do."

"Go. Zack and I will be leaving as soon as Esther and David are ready." Lizzie peered out her bedroom window toward the *dawdi haus* across the yard. Dawn was but a promise in a star-studded sky when the cottage door opened and Esther appeared, followed by her mother and her sisters, Miriam and Sadie. Sarah King held a lantern to light the way. As if drawn by sense, Esther glanced toward Lizzie's bedroom window. Lizzie, lit up by the burning oil lamp behind her, waved. With a huge grin, Zack's soon-to-be-married sister waved back. God chose that moment to make the sun rise. Lizzie felt as if the dawn brightening the dark sky was the Lord's silent message of His approval of her marriage to Zack.

William brought around the buggy that would take Lizzie and Zack with Esther and David to the wedding services at the Peter Zook farm. Zack waited downstairs as Lizzie descended the steps and saw him. He looked up, and their gazes locked with silent messages of love.

Zack held out his hand as Lizzie came abreast of him in the hall near the bottom landing. "Are you ready?" She nodded as she locked fingers with his. "Nervous?" he asked.

She smiled as she shook her head. *"Nay."*

He grinned, and his dark eyes brightened. "Then let's be on our way, shall we?"

Esther and David stood by the buggy. Lizzie gave them a grin, and then she and Zack waited while the preacher and Esther climbed into the backseat. Zack and Lizzie then climbed in to sit in the second row.

Lizzie's brother Luke sat beside her brother William as William drove from the Fisher farm toward the Zook property less than a mile down the road. Rachel and Peter were happy to host the wedding nuptials. With the opening of a pocket door between two rooms in their house, there was extra space for the large congregation of wedding guests who would arrive later that morning at nine o'clock.

Zack bent and whispered in her ear, "So, how do you feel about becoming Mrs. Fisher?"

Lizzie chuckled. "I'm already Mrs. Fisher."

He caressed her with his gaze. "Mrs. *Zachariah* Fisher."

Lizzie caught her breath. She was aware of his scent, his warmth, his closeness, and she had thanked the Lord over and over throughout the night that He'd given her this special man to marry.

"I'll love it," she murmured huskily, "as I love you."

He gently squeezed her hand. The vehicle shifted as William steered the horse onto the Zooks' dirt driveway. "We're here," her *brooder* announced.

"We're here," Lizzie called back to Esther. Esther and David were quiet. Lizzie glanced over her shoulder and saw that they were too busy gazing lovingly into each other's eyes to hear or notice anything going on around them.

Lizzie laughed and tapped David's knee. "Preacher?"

He seemed to realize that he'd been addressed. *"Ja?"*

"It's time," Zack said with a grin.

David laughed self-consciously while Esther beamed at her bridegroom and then transferred her glowing gaze to her brother and Lizzie.

Rachel and Peter were in the bridal party. Normally, each couple would have two couples standing with them, but since they were family and sharing their wedding day, they decided that they would share the same wedding party, as well.

"Are Susan and Amos here yet?" Lizzie asked. Her married sister and her brother-in-law would be the second bridal-party couple.

"They're in the buggy behind us."

Lizzie sighed. *"Goot."* She stifled the strongest urge to touch the face of her husband-to-be.

Zack's gaze flared, and she knew he understood what she was feeling.

When the weddings guests arrived, each bride and groom with their attendants were seated in the front row of church benches. After the house was full, the ministers went into the next room followed by the brides with their grooms while the congregation sang hymns from the *Ausbund*. The elders gave a brief instruction about the couples' marital duties before the couples returned to the main room for the sermon and wedding ceremony. The sermon was long but meaningful. When he was finished, Bishop Andy invited both couples to come forward. He placed a hand over the clasped hands of each couple. He gave them each a blessing; then the couples said their vows.

Bishop Andy spoke. "So then, may I say that the God of Abraham, Isaac and Jacob be with you and help you fulfill His blessing abundantly upon you, through Jesus Christ. Amen."

The bishop then pronounced Esther and David as well as Lizzie and Zack newly married. The newlyweds climbed into separate buggies and headed home for the wedding feast with William acting as hostler, or driver, for Zack and Lizzie while Lizzie's brother Luke drove David and Esther.

Zack turned to Lizzie as William drove them toward their destination. "*Hallo*, my wife," he whispered in her ear. He leaned in to kiss her, and she closed her eyes to the sensations that sent her spirit soaring. Zack sat back against the seat, smiling at her, as she opened her eyes.

"*Hallo*, husband." Lizzie gave in to the temptation to caress his jaw. His chin was warm and smooth—but not for long. Now that he was married, he would grow a beard along his jaw like those worn by other married men. Their life together would be a busy joy-filled journey. She realized that there would be bad times with the good, but she knew that with Zack by her side, they'd find happiness.

The buggy stopped, and William got out and opened the door for them. Zack and Lizzie stepped out of the vehicle and were greeted by their seven children and various other friends and relatives. Esther and David's vehicle pulled up behind them, and the preacher and his new wife alighted.

It was the children who had garnered Lizzie's attention. She was pleased to see all seven of them grinning at her and Zack.

"I'm hungry," Zeke stated suddenly, and Zack laughed, scooped him up into his strong arms and reached for Lizzie's hand. Then together he, Lizzie and the children entered the farmhouse to enjoy the festivities of their wedding celebration.

* * * * *

Love Inspired®

Save $1.00

on the purchase of any Love Inspired®, Love Inspired® Suspense or Love Inspired® Historical book.

Available wherever books are sold, including most bookstores, supermarkets, drugstores and discount stores.

Save $1.00

on the purchase of any Love Inspired®, Love Inspired® Suspense or Love Inspired® Historical book.

Coupon valid until March 15, 2016. Redeemable at participating retail outlets in the U.S. and Canada only. Limit one coupon per customer.

5 2 6 1 3 3 5 3

5 65373 00076 2   (8100)0 12127

LIINCICOUP

*As a young woman seeks a better life for herself
and her son in Amish country, will she find happiness
and love with an Amish carpenter?*

*Read on for a sneak preview of
A HUSBAND FOR MARI,
the second book in the new series
THE AMISH MATCHMAKER.*

"That's James," Sara the matchmaker explained in English. "He's the one charging me an outrageous amount for the addition to my house."

"You want craftsmanship, you have to pay for it," James answered confidently. He strode into the kitchen, opened a cupboard, removed a coffee mug and poured himself a cup. "We're the best, and you wouldn't be satisfied with anyone else."

He glanced at Mari. "This must be your new houseguest. Mari, is it?"

"*Ya*, this is my friend Mari." Sara introduced her. "She and her son, Zachary, will be here with me for a while, so I expect you to make her feel welcome."

"Pleased to meet you, Mari," James said. The foreman's voice was pleasant, his penetrating eyes strikingly memorable. Mari felt a strange ripple of exhilaration as James's strong face softened into a genuine smile, and he held her gaze for just a fraction of a second longer than was appropriate.

Warmth suffused her throat as Mari offered a stiff nod and a hasty "Good morning," before turning her attention to her unfinished breakfast. Mari didn't want anyone to get the idea that she'd come to Seven Poplars so Sara could find her a husband. That was the last thing on her mind.

"Going to be working for Gideon and Addy, I hear," James remarked as he added milk to his coffee from a small pitcher on the table.

Mari slowly lifted her gaze. James had nice hands. She raised her eyes higher to find that he was still watching her intently, but it wasn't a predatory gaze. James seemed genuinely friendly rather than coming on to her, as if he was interested in what she had to say. "I hope so." She suddenly felt shy, and she had no idea why. "I don't know a thing about butcher shops."

"You'll pick it up quick." James took a sip of his coffee. "And Gideon is a great guy. He'll make it fun. Don't you think so, Sara?"

Sara looked from James to Mari and then back at James. "I agree." She smiled and took a sip of her coffee. "I think Mari's a fine candidate for all sorts of things."

Don't miss
A HUSBAND FOR MARI
by Emma Miller,
available February 2016 wherever
Love Inspired® books and ebooks are sold.